AFTER THE SMOKE CLEARS

Also by Kylie Kaden
The Day the Lies Began
Missing You
Losing Kate
One of Us

AFTER THE SMOKE CLEARS

KYLIE KADEN

PANTERA PRESS

PANTERA PRESS

This is a work of fiction. Names, characters, organisations, dialogue and incidents are either products of the author's imagination or are used fictitiously. Any resemblance to actual people, living or dead, organisations, events or locales is coincidental.

First published in 2023 by Pantera Press Pty Limited
www.PanteraPress.com

Text copyright © Kylie Kaden, 2023
Kylie Kaden has asserted her moral rights to be identified as the author of this work.

Design and typography copyright © Pantera Press Pty Limited, 2023
® Pantera Press, three-slashes colophon device, and *sparking imagination, conversation and change* are registered trademarks of Pantera Press Pty Limited. Lost the Plot is a trademark of Pantera Press Pty Limited.

This work is copyright, and all rights are reserved. Apart from any use permitted under copyright legislation, no part may be reproduced or transmitted in any form or by any means, nor may any other exclusive right be exercised, without the publisher's prior permission in writing. We welcome your support of the author's rights, so please only buy authorised editions.

Please send all permission queries to:
Pantera Press, P.O. Box 1989, Neutral Bay, NSW, Australia 2089 or info@PanteraPress.com

A Cataloguing-in-Publication entry for this work is available from the
National Library of Australia.

ISBN: 978-0-6454985-9-2 (Paperback)
ISBN: 978-0-6454984-8-6 (eBook)

Cover Design: Elysia Clapin
Cover Image: Arun Clarke/Unsplash
Publisher: Kate Cuthbert
Editor: Lauren Finger
Proofreader: Lucia Nguyen
Typesetting: Kirby Jones
Author Photo: Anna Gilbert Photography
Printed and bound in Australia by McPherson's Printing Group

The paper this book is printed on is certified against the Forest Stewardship Council® Standards. McPherson's Printing Group holds FSC® chain of custody certification SA-COC-005379. FSC® promotes environmentally responsible, socially beneficial and economically viable management of the world's forests.

To Dad
For setting the bar high

Chapter 1

LOTTI, 2009

You have reached your destination.

I craned my neck, scanned the nothingness on all sides. 'And where the hell would that be, exactly?'

Pulling over, loose gravel chinked beneath my tyres. I lowered the window. A stifling warmth wafted inside, as if I'd opened an oven door. There were no cows, no horses, but the air was thick with the smell of both. Further afield a wrought-iron gate was wedged permanently open to reveal a long crusher-dust driveway cutting a line through the bush and leading to a cluster of tiny houses squatting in a circle. I half-expected a cult of breatharians to appear between the trees, the vibe was so weird. What is this place? My car smelled like feet and was littered with evidence of carb-drenched meals-on-the-go. I'd driven all day with a talking fart machine in the back to rush *here*?

The first clue about where we were was an old, rust-bitten sign. Peeking through overgrown lantana, it was so bleached of colour I could barely make out the details. *Brightside.* The letters bled into a scene of a mother with a manic grin serving rosy-cheeked children; its wholesome goodness reminding me of a retro Vegemite commercial.

It had been thirty-six hours since August left. Left, in the dead of night without any explanation. And the bastard still hadn't even called to say he was okay, or to check on his son.

August being cagey about his past wasn't unexpected — besides the fact that I was inexplicably drawn to the man, all I knew for sure about August Silverfell was that he had a son, he was a mechanic and he liked to swear a lot. He never talked about himself, but it felt uncharted when August had said he couldn't take his son, Otto, with him — 'not for this' — and asked if I could have him 'for a bit'.

Otto was my favourite six-year-old ever. I met the kid when he walked himself into my classroom on the first day of school. He was a puzzle — always curious and engaged, polite and clean (even if his uniform was crumpled and two sizes too big), but he had a wildness to him. His naturally fair skin was a sun-kissed brown as if he spent his days mustering cattle, not smothered in sunscreen and rashies like most kids. He had a dark bob that reminded me of Mowgli from *The Jungle Book*, and his eyes, I would come to learn, were the same deep chestnut as his father's.

August looked a little like an extra from Underbelly. Tall, muscular, and rough around the edges. He wore black ruggers with a black shirt and got away with it, probably because it fit with his no-fucks-given attitude, scruffy hair and goatee. His fingers were callused, he had stubble by morning tea, and anger was the only emotion he knew what to do with. My father would have described him as the type you'd be wise to run a background check on before getting involved with.

The man had something against owning stuff, about putting down roots — even his home was on wheels. But early on, there was an edge to him that woke something in me. Besides, we kissed the same. Surely, that was some biological marker for assessing our genetic compatibility? Either way, that fact made me happy enough to wait around and find out. But this turn of events had me in a flurry, a flurry of doubt, with dirty clothes and a bad case of indigestion. I really didn't do impulsive decision-making well.

Deflated, I checked my iPhone. When August hadn't called, hadn't texted to let me or Otto know where he was or when he'd return, I had to resort to the only breadcrumb trail I had – destination tracking recorded in the location settings of his iPhone. He'd have no idea it was linked to my account, being my old phone. Neither did I until he left, and I was fumbling for evidence of why.

I was in the right place. This was it. The place August ran to.

I shook my head. 'Why here, Augie?'

Our impromptu road trip started with a text two nights earlier. I could tell by the way August's face fell in the millisecond after he received it, that it wasn't good. I had been at August's place all weekend, and I was just about to drag myself home to shower and fall asleep on a pile of class 2B's spelling tests when the text arrived, and the unravelling began.

'Is that your other life calling?' By life, I meant *wife*. He'd never provided the synopsis of his son's mother or his relationship with her, just withdrew a little when I'd asked, said that he'd loved her, and she was gone. Gone, except for the photo perched on the windowsill near Otto's bunk in her memory. I'd wondered what she knew that I didn't. Why she left.

'No other life. Just Brookes – my old mate.'

Mate. That didn't denote male or femaleness.

He had paced around after the message like a kid with attachment issues, waiting for a tardy parent. Scraping his stubbly chin with his hand, he thumped the door open and skipped down the front two stairs with his phone.

Skulking outside was the only option you had for privacy at his place. August and Otto lived in a bus, a giant converted school bus that was permanently parked near a shallow stream, and I was a sucker for shallow streams with ducks at your doorstep, along with the other quirks of tiny living. The stream was so close you could hear it burble if you kept the window open. A field of green surrounded his patch, which August kept short with a ride-on mower he'd built from parts, and a thicket of ferns separated the bus from the iron sheds and spare parts rusting on gravel at the industrial estate where Augie worked, so you could pretend you were in another world. But I was still getting used to some aspects, like the lack of hot water. The boys had no problem showering at August's garage. Said shower had a *Baywatch* poster on the door, and a window that was not nearly as frosted as it should have been given the clientele that smoked outside it.

The security light cast a dim shadow over Augie's features as he made a call. I peeked at him through the window, phone to his ear, eyes to the ground, trying to make out what the expression on that rugged face of his revealed. After a few minutes, he lowered the phone from his ear, squared his jaw as he looked at the mobile in his palm as if he was getting ready to fling it into the creek. He turned away to the creekbank, steadied himself with his hands on his knees before turning back and returning inside.

We'd only been dating a few months. We'd never navigated a personal emergency together. 'Is everything okay?'

He frowned, parted his lips, then hesitated, as if sizing up how much to say.

Even though Augie was two feet away, the distance between us felt wider now.

'There's, um, there's just a bit of a shitstorm, back home … We have this thing, me and Brookes. If we're in trouble, we show up for each other,' he muttered, distracted. More imprecise notions. August's eyes flittered around as he found an old bag and shoved in socks, jocks and a wad of black shirts. I felt useless, standing off to the side like an extra as he rummaged around dealing with this personal emergency of an undisclosed nature.

'Sorry to just piss off, but it's a bit of a hike back home so I kinda gotta get my arse into gear.' He didn't look at me while he said it.

'As in, *right now*?'

He packed his toothbrush, stopped to think. 'Brookes's in trouble … it's like a Camira with the "check engine" light on—'

My face pinched the way it did when he went on about internal combustion engines.

'—an accident waiting to happen. You're best to deal with it before it kills you.' His thick brow furrowed, and he answered as if it was an afterthought to whatever worries were flooding through his mind. He placed his bag down, put in more socks, took pairs out, swore. I could feel his confusion, his pain, and I was surprised at how much it hurt to see this competent, unflappable man crumble from the inside. I fired questions – why the rush? Could I help? Should he start a long drive this late?

'I'll keep the windows down, play some Accadacca.'

I could see Otto's sleepy face squashed into his pillow from the kitchen (which was also the living room). Was he just going to wrench the kid from his bed without explanation? It was Otto's turn to read a chapter of *The Twits* to the class the next day. He'd been counting the days.

'What about school tomorrow?'

The lump of a man stared out the tiny porthole as if the answer was written in the stars, then decisively dumped his bag on the lino and looked at me, the earlier haste seemingly forgotten. 'I've kinda been meaning to show you something – it's not finished, but …you might need it while I'm gone.' August's eyes met mine in the direct way that never failed to set off the flutter in my chest.

'What happened to the emergency crisis?'

He hooked one finger through mine. 'It'll just take a minute,' he said, then mumbled, 'Just in case …'

'In case of what?' *Your secret wife takes you back?* August had never said it out loud, but given the sadness that overtook him whenever Otto's mum was mentioned it was clear she'd died, but Augie was thirty-five – plenty of time to stash another one somewhere by now.

Our bodies slipped sideways through the narrow folding door. He towed me along the row of ferns towards a thicket of trees and a pile of fresh dirt I hadn't noticed before. A pathway of cobblestones led to a bamboo hut hidden in the ferns. Flicking open the latch that secured the door, he led me inside. A string of naked bulbs illuminated an outdoor shower, complete with a slatted wooden floor, a side table and shelf.

'This better fucking work,' August said, fumbling to connect something overhead. August used pliers to turn the tap. 'That's temporary.'

An unsettling gurgle, a rush of water and a moment later the cubicle was clouded with steam and a waft of teatree. All it needed was towels shaped like elephants and it'd pass as a

Balinese spa. The moonlight cutting through branches, the string lights, the mist – it was enchanting.

'You ... built me a shower?' Except for the odd mangled clay pot or macaroni necklace, no one had ever made me anything. I loved it. My mum taught me that you had to know what you wanted in life – *how else could you ask the universe to give it to you?* – and I was the kind of girl who wanted a deep claw-footed bath, complete with bamboo bookrest, heated towel rack and Sheraton bath sheets. Was that wrong?

'Easier than hearing you bitch about the workshop one,' he said gruffly. I'd noticed the kinder the sentiment, the throatier his voice became. 'Come here,' he ordered in his gravel voice, stepping under the spray. We were still dressed. He dragged me under anyway.

I inhaled a mouthful of spray, hands waving, hair dripping, then squealed, claws out like a kitten in a rainstorm.

'You're such a princess.' He smiled, spitting water on the wall, flicking wet hair from his eyes.

I swept water from my face and punched him on the arm. Perhaps I was a little pretentious. Maybe my father's advice that his only daughter deserved nothing but five-star suites (August was more of a backpackers' dorm) was misguided. Maybe that's what was wrong with my life-compass, as it had only gotten me lost, until now.

He kissed my forehead with his wet lips. He smelled like an intoxicating mix of soap and spice. That heady feeling, that complete contentment I felt standing under the stream of water with his arms around me, our clothes soaked, his skin glistening beneath the moonlit sky; I'd never been more terrified. Drenched, on a floodplain behind a shop full of rusted wrecks, I felt as if I'd navigated towards something right.

Our clothes clinging, he yanked off his sodden shirt, then guided my dress over my head, discarding it at the side of the hut. I tensed as I heard it slosh in a muddy puddle. 'My dress ...' I said, not realising how pathetic it sounded until the words were outside my head.

His face pinched. 'It's just stuff.'

'I know, it's just ... dry-clean-only stuff.' I was making it worse.

'Stop speaking.' Pulling me hard against him in a heady kiss, we rocked as one dripping mass, the water spraying our shoulders. When I came up for air, I trailed my fingers down the rivers flowing over his pecs, gazed up and said, 'I thought you were in a hurry.'

He shrugged, his eyes on me as if I were the only thing that mattered, as if he was savouring the very look of me. I still didn't know why – why he'd rushed to show me this, why he'd gotten so intense.

'I made it for you, so you don't have to leave.'

A lump lodged in my throat. I wanted to sink into this feeling of wanting and being wanted, but something stopped me. He was expert at pulling out the tricks just when things were getting weird. Tricks that made it impossible not to fall for him.

'Is this thing, whatever it is, really that urgent? I mean, no one's dying?'

The heat from the shower was dissipating.

'What?' He frowned. 'Not me, well, no more than anyone else.'

I kinked my head. 'Is your *mother* dying?'

'Jesus – you're as bad as Otto with your death talk.' His eyes fell. 'She did that already. Long ago.'

'I'm sorry.' I blinked at him through the drips. 'Your father?'

'Carked it, before her.' He was less worried by that disclosure, but I added 'orphan' to the thumbnail-sized fact sheet I had on August Silverfell. 'Look, my lot's all gone. My sister, too. Everyone's gone. Which pisses me off 'cause the people who have families take them for granted. Having people that belong to you is precious, but other than a scruffy deaf kid, there's no one left.'

'I'm sorry.' My throat tightened, thinking of his life of pain, not to mention the chaos of his past. It triggered a few alarm bells. I understood loneliness, but didn't want to equate being an only child living in boarding schools and three-storey homes with his experience.

Augie turned all sweet and serious, tucked a tendril of my dark hair behind my ear. 'Yeah, well, you're my family now.'

I ran the tip of my nose up the side of his, flattered but a little taken aback.

'Can I ask a favour?' He grazed his fingers over my damp cheek and grew serious. 'Is there any chance you could keep an eye on the boy for a bit?'

August had just packed enough clothes for a week. 'A bit?'

He squared his jaw. 'A few days? Not exactly sure. I'll call, let you know.'

I was silent. Otto and I had spent time together out of school off and on for months, I knew his reading fluency levels and numeracy gaps, but I wasn't mother material. I spent all day with a bunch of small humans, but I'd never had to keep one alive overnight.

'But I don't know how he likes his eggs, whether he has his crusts cut off, whether he sleeps with the light on....and you know I kill house plants.'

He saw my hesitance and huffed, turned to get out of the misted room. 'Forget I asked …'

'Wait – Augie, I just – you can't take him?'

We stood, the unspoken between us. *Otto*. Quirky, literal, big-hearted Otto. Not to mention the other thing about Otto.

He shook his head. 'Not for this.'

'Is it drugs, or money trouble or … ?' August did take a particular interest in True Crime documentaries.

'What? Jesus, no.' He slicked water off his arms, naked in front of me with no self-consciousness. He turned off the water and the cool night air infiltrated the warmth. 'Fuck.' He looked around. 'Forgot the fucking towels.' He opened the door and did a nudie-run to the clothesline, returning with two scratchy beach towels.

He threaded one behind my shoulders and tucked it under my arms like he was folding me up, warm and safe, but I didn't feel either, and neither would Otto in the morning when he discovered his only parent missing.

'I just know how much you ground him. You're his hero.'

His eyebrows raised. 'He already told me he likes you more than me. You're a kid magnet. I've seen you crawling with that dinosaur tail strapped to your arse, roaring after the little rug rats – you couldn't give a shit what anyone thought, or how crazy your hair flipped out of place. It was all about them. I knew you'd be like my mum – the kind that does the voices when you read bedtime stories.'

Mum? The word reverberated in my mind and hit a chord. I usually complained about August stalling on the commitment front, but now I felt the unease of things moving too quickly to process. 'So why is it you can't take him? Doesn't your other girlfriend like kids,' I mumbled.

'What? Augie's face pinched as he stifled a burst of anger. 'You really think I could be fucked dealing with two chicks' grief when I'm not exactly managing yours?'

I narrowed my eyes, pulled the towel tighter. 'I'm causing *you* grief?'

'That's not what I said.' He went cagey again.

I milked the water from the hair hanging loose over my shoulders that was already beginning to wave the way I hated. 'I'm getting cold.' I opened the bamboo door, which made a satisfying thud as it hit the wall.

A huge muddy puddle had formed outside the stall, a perfect pond for toads. My nose screwed up before I could hide it. I didn't *do* mud.

'How do expect me to get back to the van?'

'I told you. It's not a fucking van. It's a bus. And, for the record, drainage was next on the list. Wait fucking here.' He stomped into the bus that wasn't a van. I reached out and grabbed my sodden dress from the side of the hut without moving my feet, and he was already on his way back with a pair of glorious rainbow gumboots he'd had stashed in a side storage panel.

I checked the bottom as if it mattered. 'You know my size?'

He shrugged, gave me a look that said he knew every part of me, and the anger dissolved from his face. 'And I know you're an entitled upper-class princess who doesn't like to have creek mud *squelch* between your pretty little toes.'

'Don't say that grotesque word.' I balanced my hand on his broad shoulders as he slipped each boot on my wet feet. I looked at the mud again. 'But they're cute. I don't want to get them dirty. And what if there's toads?'

'Fucking women.' He picked me up, my colourful gumboots kicking as he carried me like a bride to his front door.

My arms around his neck, I admired his strong brow, his dark eyes. Was this first flush of lust going to fade? I'd expected it to, after months, but it showed no signs of waning. It was a hunger, a primal need for my skin to be touching his. 'You're a sweet, infuriating man, you know that?'

He lowered me down and guided me inside, the rubber squeaking in the rhythm of our steps. We found dry clothes scattered around the van and a strange silence crept between us. The shower reveal ticked off his list, August regressed to panic mode and my mind followed. The reality of him leaving me with a kid hit me.

'What do I do with Otto when I'm at work?'

He frowned. 'You're his teacher.'

'There are rules. It's weird.'

Otto was still asleep in his curtained-off bunk above the driver's cavity. I knew Otto couldn't hear us – we'd made enough noise behind the folding screen shutting off August's room to know that for sure, but I still wasn't comfortable arguing around a little kid, deaf or not.

He looked bemused. 'Weird how? You need an excursion form signed?'

I glared. 'I don't think the school's keen on staff babysitting students after hours.'

He glared back, the annoyance flickering again. 'Babysitting? Is that what we're doing? Shit, I must owe you some real coin by now.' He turned away, dried his hair off and pulled on shoes. He began to fill a thermos with coffee as black as the night sky.

I gathered my things, then paused. I'd barely known him a few months. Did he expect me to move in here, with his kid, indefinitely? 'What are we doing, Augie?'

Augie's eyes narrowed and I regretted broaching the issue, now, when he obviously had priorities other than me. 'Huh? I thought we were good now. I mean, I know it was a rocky start, but—'

'We're *good*?' I'd done it now. We were finally talking. I was going to make it worth the angst that came with it. 'You don't talk about your past, your family, your childhood. If you were serious about me, you'd tell me all the messy bits, give me a chance to accept all the parts of you.'

'You … accept mess? You can't even leave your bed without making it.'

'You could try me.'

He squared his jaw, considered it. 'You have no idea what a cluster-fuck I'm talking about. It's not worth it.'

I'm not worth trusting? Perhaps this man was chronically unknowable. I swallowed. 'Am I temporary? I just need to know because that's not how I feel and I'm a real pain in the arse when I get hurt.'

'Yeah, well some bastard musta really done a number on you already,' he said.

'Screw you!' I blurted. I'd been aiming for assertive, but it came out all angsty and winey.

His face fell. 'I'm sorry.' He went to touch my shoulder, but I retreated, arms folded.

He exhaled, flopped on the thin bed, and grew still. 'I'm not good with all the thoughts, explaining all the feelings, but I reckon you're the first person to see me, to see who I am and stick around, so I'm trying my best here.' He huffed out another long breath as if stringing together the words was physically exhausting. 'That, and you're … I mean, I'm still pretty crap with all the talking stuff but I was always told actions speak louder than words. I joke that you're a princess, but the way you devote yourself to those kids – the way you push them to be their best, push me to be better – you're like a warrior.' The sentiment was kind, but his delivery was laced with anger. 'You're smart. Do I have to say it? Can't you tell I fucking love you?'

His eyes locked with mine, and I was back to smitten. I should have guessed the first time he said the word there'd be a 'fuck' before it. *Damn it, Augie.*

But he wasn't getting away again without an explanation. 'You disappear all the time,' I said.

'What do you mean?' he asked. 'I'm right here.'

'I mean from me. From us. You make me fall for you then you run from me. You're running right now, away to help this friend.' I used my hand to stage inverted commas over the word 'friend' even though it made me cringe. I hated myself like this. Insecure. Indecisive. Gesturing speech marks.

'It's not me freaking out this time – I have no choice. We have this thing, Brookesy and I – if either of us are up the creek we text SOS and turn up for each other … I can't *not* turn up. That's who I am.'

'SOS? Like, like a pact?' This thing just got weirder. Was it some sort of cult?

'Look, if I don't sort this out now, the next time I see Otto he'll be shaving.' August blinked fast as if he had said too much.

I looked up at the boy in the bunk and my heart lurched. 'Is this a custody thing? Does his mother want him back? Do you still love her? Why won't you trust me enough to just tell me the truth?'

'Don't pin that on me – you're the one getting calls from some tosser you've never mentioned. What kind of name is Grayson, anyway? Sounds like a fucking tool.'

Changing the subject was an expert move that my father would be impressed by, but it left me rattled.

He scribbled something on an old envelope, then placed it under Otto's pillow and turned back to me. August's lips hovered over my forehead before he kissed it, turned to go, then hesitated. For one optimistic moment I felt the relief that maybe he'd changed his mind, that this mysterious SOS call could wait. But he puffed up his chest and said, 'Maybe this break will be good for us. Maybe you need to take these few days to think about who you want to be, who you want to be *with*. See if I'm even close.' He left with his bag and an abrupt swing of the van door.

It clicked closed, robbing any right of reply. His truck skidded off, the ute's taillights two specks against the black-forever sky.

SOS. Those three letters are what started it all.

Otto's questions began the morning after August abandoned us, continued on the way to school, around playground duty and all the first night. *'Don't you usually sneak out when it gets light? How come you had a sleepover? Is it because of the shower that you didn't go away? When's Daddy coming back? Do I still have to go to school? Does that mean if Daddy dies you turn into my mum?'* The second night, we had brownies for dinner, tuckshop for lunch and he'd watched *Cars* on repeat that many times he really didn't need the subtitles. I was faking this parenting thing rather convincingly thus far and if it wasn't for the loud farts, the kid was okay company.

The disbelief that Miss Hill (I had a reputation for being mean as I 'always gave homework') would sanction a day off school caught him unawares. All I'd said was that we were going on a road trip to find Daddy; the trusting little goofball just smiled, grabbed his toothbrush, and proceeded to ambush me with more questions.

'A road trip? Like Lightning McQueen and Sally? Can we take Route 66? Can we visit Radiator Springs?'

'That's up to Daddy – we're going to find him wherever he is.'

'Like hide and seek?' Otto had asked, wide-eyed.

'Kind of,' I'd said, a little guiltily. Otto and I were willing participants in the game, but August didn't know he was playing.

August was suspicious of technology. He liked uncomplicated. He drove an old sixties Ford Falcon (which I'm sure had bullet-holes in the boot). He preferred engines he could fix with a wrench and spray of CRC. He boiled water for his tar-thick coffee in the microwave instead of the kettle (it was quicker and required one less appliance) and swore like a sailor despite mistrusting the sea. He'd have no clue his phone was transmitting his location, miles away. He only had a phone at all because my father got a box of them for his office and gave me a new one every few months and I gave Aug my old one.

Why would Augie have stopped here? The utopian grins on that sign – for whatever it was, or had been – felt creepy. Abandoned for a reason. I drove along the tree-lined avenue and entered the complex between two filagree gates left permanently open. By whom? And why?

'You awake, Stink Bug?' I whispered, forgetting again that Otto couldn't hear me anyway. All his tools – lip-reading, signing, facial-expression decoding weren't accessible when I was in the front seat, and he in the back. I'd even brought a white board to communicate when my Auslan fingerspelling was left wanting.

I touched his cheek, astonished part of me wanted him to stir – I'd been praying for a moment of peace the whole way to silence the kid's dark tales of serial killers. He'd started to obsess over another wildly inappropriate library book he'd borrowed, reciting deathly facts as we drove, but now the little monster was asleep, I missed the animation in his face, the wonder in his eyes. I never did do alone well.

Otto stirred, shuffled his feet in a sleepy kick. Dribble glossed his chin as he gave a wispy little-kid snore. His dark hair fell over his eyes and hadn't been stuck down with a mother's wet thumb in a while. Was that my job now? I'd always found the practice, often seen at the classroom door, kind of gross. It was one of the many reasons I didn't plan on having my own.

Otto stretched out, gave a loud yawn.

'Sleeping beauty awakes,' I said, and he screwed up his nose.

'I'm hungry. Can we go to Maccas?'

'None around here, kiddo. Roadkill, okay?' I half expected a tumbleweed to roll across my field of vision.

'Where are we?' Otto said as I drove down the driveway towards the buildings and stopped the car only a hundred metres from the Brightside sign and thought of The Killers song that I loved but Augie hated. I turned my head so Otto could see my lips and told him his guess was as good as mine. Temporary fencing circled acres of land, but with gaping holes between panels it was clear no one obeyed the signs zip-tied to the wire saying 'Construction site. Do not enter'. Other ugly signs warned of open mineshafts in the area. Excavation equipment sat dormant in the distance, waiting for instructions.

I craned my neck to get a better look at the cluster of buildings, then got out. There was no indication anyone was around, not even a parked car. My kitten heels crunched gravel. A row of graffitied weatherboard cabins flanked the valley. They all had broken windows, missing doors and rotten stumps, the sun-bleached paddocks surrounding them now bare but for ants' nests and thistles. A cricket pitch was now just fragments of cement held together by straw-like grass grown in clumps waist-high. Further afield, a steeple towered above a stone church with rows of pews visible through the arch-shaped entry, the door stolen long ago. A shiver, something ominous, coursed through me, something I couldn't name but felt with every inch of me.

There was a gap in the rooflines, a cleared area with what was left of a large building – a grid of blackened concrete stumps with their heads exposed as if the buildings had been picked up like the house in *The Wizard of Oz* and set down in a better place.

'Why would Daddy stop here? It's not very nice,' Otto asked.

Perhaps it was once a holiday camp like Kellerman's from *Dirty Dancing* that went bust in the seventies? A cloud of something hovered in this valley like a scene from a *60 Minutes* promo – with replays of girls escaping some evil cult. 'Maybe he just got sleepy driving or had to change a tyre?'

A blue-eyed raven swooped towards me, settled on the brim of the rusty basketball hoop. The feathers on its hackles extended as it rasped loudly and dived towards our car, the only shiny new thing of interest in this forsaken place.

Otto unclicked his buckle and was out of the car a moment later, exploring.

I followed, hoping to find answers. All I discovered was a broken bottle of Bundy Rum, a dozen kinked cans of XXXX, and the stink of old wee reminiscent of the senior boys' toilets.

August and his school mate had camped here, I was sure.

Otto scampered ahead, and I extended my arm to stop him. 'Glass, Otto – get your shoes.'

He kept walking, exploring, couldn't 'hear' me in the dark.

I took his hand, veering wide to avoid the glass and a waft of earthy mustiness filled my nose. Muddy footprints led to the back of the cabin, and I followed them. A pile of freshly dug dirt, an abandoned shovel and a six-foot-deep open trench.

We stumbled back from the pit, and both of us bum-planted into a soft mound of soil. The kid's long fringe had fallen over his eyes and was speckled with black. He spat out dirt.

'You okay?' I said, brushing off his fringe.

The kid nodded. 'This is awesome!'

I gazed into the trench. There was nothing but black. Nothing but a shallow hole the size and shape of an open grave.

Chapter 2

AUGIE, 2009

Two beams guided the Ford along the dark desert highway, with nothing but a few long-haul lorries and suicidal roos for company. The landscape changed from drought-stricken farms and scattered struggling towns, to stretches of fuck all. Nothing but road trains, bloated wallabies, potholes and time to think. I wasn't a big fan of that, as a rule. And if I had to, I shoulda been thinking about the pinhead forcing me down memory lane and the shitstorm waiting at the end of this road, not what *coulda been* with a highly strung daddy's girl. All I wanted was for her to be there, without question, but all she had were questions. Who, what, how, why? And, yet, she reckons *I'm* the one pussyfooting around this idea of having a proper grown-up thing.

Lotti buffed all the chips from my paintwork, made everything in my life run smoother, especially my kid. But she was what Billy Joel would call an Uptown Girl. I shoulda known better than to even try with a woman like Charlotte Hill. I knew that the first time I saw those big beautiful eyes of hers – she reminded me of that kooky, gorgeous chick out of *That 70s Show*. Telling Lotti about Brookes would have been like pouring four-stroke oil in a two-stroke engine – mixing worlds that didn't go together. Besides, spilling the 'mess', as she called it, about Brookes would mean nothing without the context, and giving that would have meant coming clean about Becca, about Freya, about the woman who raised me. About what we all did.

But now that she had a whiff of who I really was, there was relief in it, knowing I was right about her being too good for me. Where would I even start trying to put it into words without the whole story erupting like an engine towed in gear?

Both sides of my AC/DC tape spooled through, and I was 600 k's west of the big smoke in under six hours. Even with the windows down, I kept having to sweep the side of my hand across my brow to stop the sweat dripping down my face, and it wasn't from the stifling heat.

SOS.

Three dots, three dashes, three more dots. That's all the message was, and all the message I needed to suck me down a wormhole to 1988. It ripped me back into reality, where I couldn't go on pretending Eldham was just the set of some old telemovie. That Brookes, his sister and Margo were actors, not real people I'd abandoned. Now, the distance between me and the living, breathing versions of that lot was shrinking with every minute. My guts felt as broken and wrong as after an all-night bender, with just the idea of what I'd find waiting at the end of this highway.

The 'check engine' light on the situation with Brookes back home had flickered a year or so back. I knew in my gut that it was a mistake, leaving him to his own devices now his sister had gotten her own life. I still remember the stabbing feeling when Brookes said his sister was 'up the duff'. Becca. She was something, a real-life version of Tamara from *The Henderson Kids* – even down to the Stackhat and roller skates. She got all the smarts and the looks, while Brookes got the guts. They'd both got the auburn hair – the colour of fire, she used to say – but even that looked better on her. Becca having a rug rat (with that short-arsed bald bastard she was too good for) somehow felt more permanent than getting hitched to the putz. I was happy for her, knew she'd be good at it despite having a toxic old lady to learn from.

Brookes had SOS'd before. First time was as a scrawny twelve-year-old, sent from his van park on his walkie talkie when his mum was so plastered, she'd passed out (he couldn't lift her on his own, but together we kept her safe 'til the next bottle). But since we'd grown up, it was only twice. Once, at twenty-three, when his god-bothering wife left him. And once more, in the aftermath of his divorce, when he couldn't see any point in sticking it out any longer. This was the third strike.

The difference between then and now was those reasons weren't about me.

About an hour from where I had to meet Brookes, the denial I'd tried on faded. Even as I'd skulked outside after his text to call him properly, to get the details, I'd told myself it was just his ex-missus having another crack at getting full custody, not about what I feared. Hearing the panic in his voice made my legs go to jelly. Before I had a chance to even process what he'd said, I was chundering on the grass.

Lotti had distracted me for a while, but now the gravity of what I might face was on top of me. My breath felt like shattered glass in my lungs, and told me the not-too-shabby life was no longer guaranteed. Jesus, I had to get a grip. *Stay calm, stay clever.* That's what Lotti whispered to Otto when he started to melt down. I told myself I couldn't solve this shitstorm with my brain doing cartwheels. Cranking the window low, I stretched my forearm into the cool night air, extending my fingers in the breeze and relaxing at the distraction until the steel-blue 'B' tattooed on my forearm from long ago, caught my eye. Stupid teenaged fool – I'd now lived enough to know you didn't need to inject ink beneath your skin for someone to be part of you. They just were.

I'd left them all eighteen years ago. Becca hadn't escaped like me. Now I had no choice but to be pulled back too, but I couldn't take my boy, and Becca was one of the few that knew why. I missed that about her when I asked Lotti to take Otto. I saw the look on Lotti's face – it said 'disappointment', confirming I was a shit dad as well as a shit boyfriend. Then I dug myself in further like a fool, spitting out the L word. That got the gears in that pretty head of hers going, the doubts about the loser she'd shacked up with festering, and I could see things between us were about to stall.

And she didn't know the half of it. Not yet. She said I made her feel temporary. That was the part that got me in the guts, that I made her feel like she was just a quick fix to survive through to the next service, not a quality repair to last a lifetime. Maybe her instincts were right. Girls like her don't end up with guys like me.

Didn't change the fact that I fucking loved her.

Growing up barefoot in the dusty six-street town of Eldham, when people called Brookes my 'special friend', I thought they were being nice. Even when the two of us lined up outside that wobbly demountable on the first day of grade one, me in those shiny shoes I tried my best to scuff, him in that too-big, faded uniform, I knew he was different. In a town full of fuckwits and arseholes, his straightforward honesty and glass-half-full attitude was easy to be around. So was his fire-haired sister, keeping him out of child services down the track, despite being younger.

He couldn't read much, took everything at face value, and had a head like it'd been screwed on the wrong body, but Brookes was one of the few completely honest people I'd ever known — loyal, brave and, yeah, a little slow on the uptake. I don't know how many times I tried to teach the stupid bastard to wait for his change at the shop, make sure it was enough, but Brookes would offer up all his cash, and skip away with a goofy grin, without a care. There was a kind of beauty, being that innocent and carefree, that I was envious of.

My best mate's heart of gold wasn't enough to make me be a good person and stick around. But here I was, back in town, for my sins. The red-ringed signs slowed the speed limits, and there it was, the wonky electricity poles, the old smelters and abandoned mines, the outskirts of my hometown. *Welcome to Eldham, population 3145.* I knew the stories of all the lives that played out in those chamferboard shacks through the snippets I'd see through the front windows riding past. The Delaquas with the grandpa that wandered, the whore house with the twin sisters with hair so bleached it went green, the Schmitz with the angry arsehole who beat his wife every Friday night but was Mr Charm all the other days. Where were they all now?

My heart clawed its way into my throat as I approached the main drag. I braked for the corner that still had Stephen Mahoney's faded runners hanging from the powerlines. I could repaint the scene blindfolded: the IGA with the terracotta tiles specked with bird shit, the heritage-listed pub with its grand old verandah, Timmo's Bakery with my graffiti still on display — the messy apostrophe handpainted in the crowded letters above cartoon pies on the shop front. Every faded zebra crossing, every rusted streetlamp unlocked another story, most of which involved Brookes. We'd built ourselves around each other, us two.

One heat-hazed night, the local lads (including Brookes and Becca's fuckwit cousins) had convinced the gullible fool that they were gonna all be mates now, took him under their wing, doubled him on their ten-speeds down the lake, shared their Sunny Boys and Redskins, even bought him potato scallops from the good shop, all the while plotting his humiliation.

After finding Brookes an hour later tied to a stop sign, starkers, those bullish Harris brothers pissing on his shoes, I promised Becca that I'd always be at his side and I was, for a while. Until I wasn't. I could still hear the Harris brothers cackle, laughing at their handiwork as Brookes blubbered, hunched over himself in a miserable attempt to hide his wanger from the scrum of Harris bastards. They circled in on him, perched on their shiny-rimmed bikes like the vultures they were. *'The funny thing is, Pinhead, the bike chain's not even locked, ya fuckin' retard!'*

They say it's not who you share blood with but who you'd shed it for. I was outnumbered four to one in that fight in '86, the one that took place beneath the powerlines dangling Stephen Mahoney's shoes, twenty seconds after I found Brookes, looking even scrawnier naked, cowering and in tears. The only reason I got out alive was thanks to the crowbar, still in my backpack after I discovered it with my metal detector that morning. All I can say about that was I felt no remorse about Joel Harris's scar.

Except for teeth a darker shade of nicotine-stain, Brookes looked exactly the same, sitting on the bonnet of his Hilux, smoking a durry, tapping his foot impatiently like he was warming his engine. He'd always had that malnourished, unwashed look about him even before things got ballsed up. Marrying a nice Christian girl just out of school didn't end well. Employing substances as his coping mechanism didn't improve things. Nor did it help the custody battle for his daughter that he lost in a blaze of restraining orders he didn't understand. Only this man could get me back through the 'Brightside' gates of hell.

There was good reason we called this place Hotel California and, like the song, it had something to do with never getting to leave, but of course, we never said that out loud. A certain look between us had always confirmed we both knew.

'Still haven't fixed the bloody muffler, mate,' I said by way of greeting after I found his car at the end of that long drive and pulled up beside him.

He gave me the double forks, like his brain had been stunted for growth since 1982. 'Still haven't got a car from this century,' he shot back.

'That the best shit you could think to shovel on me in the two years since I've seen you?' I asked.

His chin trembled a bit, which had me worried. He slid down the bonnet and threw his arms around me and held them there for a long time. His mullet smelled like stale cigars. It felt good and bad at the same time. Good to see him, bad 'cause of the reason. He didn't let go.

'Mate, hope you're not pledging undying love 'cause I'm still into tacos, not hot dogs, if you know what I mean.'

'Calm your farm, bro.' Brookes pulled away, flicked me in the centre of my forehead just to lighten the mood. Bring us back to the fools we were.

I looked over the old place – it never had mirrors on the ceiling but, like us, it had seen better days. Hotel California, that's for fucking sure. I'd never left.

'Are you into self-harm now or is there some other reason you chose to meet here?'

He didn't answer.

Here I was again at Brightside; the backdrop of adolescence for this shitty town's fuck-ups, and just a sweat-soaking BMX ride over from Main Street. The place still gave me the heebies. You wouldn't know it. I'd spun a burnout over the cracked cricket pitch when I arrived back, driven over the fallen down fence palings of the horse paddock just because I could, but every memory fizzed in my throat. Other than this eyesore property, this side of the lake was for the normal folk, the farmers with money (that was before the drought), the boarding school kids with two parents and shiny shoes that fit and bikes they didn't get from the dump.

Brookes shook his head, exhaled smoke into the night air. 'Forgot how fucking chilly it gets out here at night. Freezing my balls off.' He flicked a cigarette stub into the gravel, ground it in with the heel of his worn old sneakers. It reminded me when we'd do the same thing when we lived here, except with white Dunlop Volleys snuffing out stolen Winfield Reds. 'Wasn't sure making a fire was the best idea. Figured I'd wait, leave it to the expert.'

I exhaled through my nose. 'Still an arsehole.' But he was right. With the day's heat all but gone, we'd feel the pain if we stood around too much longer. I started gathering sticks, shards of memories hitting me like random sparks flying in the breeze, not all of them bad. The campfires. The dirt bikes. The horseriding. That's if we didn't get caught breaking pointless rules and lost our privileges, got thistle picking to 'atone our sins'. I hated those goddamned thistles – spikey evil fuckers with their milky white juice that stung like fire. They used to make us 'garden' till our fingers bled. The irony was that those bastard thorns, there to protect the damn thistle, blossomed somethin' beautiful. I was still waiting for that part to happen for me.

I lit the fire, and the roar of the flame, the intense heat stilled something within me, like it always had – stuffed if I know why. Flames got me into nothing but trouble, but we sat in silence, and even before the tinnies hit my bloodstream, I felt more relaxed than I had in months.

'Still got that flava-sava,' Brookes said, gesturing to my goatee. 'Ain't them things kind of a nineties trend, bro? At least you've got more hair on your head than your back.'

He crapped on, more small talk, like it wasn't me and him. It had been a long time but there was something about the people you shovelled shit with when you were growing up that made the gap shrink to nothin'. But he was as jittery as he was when we had to dry him out that year we don't speak of.

Hotel California in the flesh. Here we were, living it up.

'Your old lady's been naggin' me about ya,' Brookes said. 'I dunno what her problem is but she's been a bit off lately, but still good value – always up for a hot feed or a bed for the night when I's need it. Top Sheila. Would it fuck'n kill ya to pick up the phone, see how she's getting on?'

'Not my business,' I said, sculling another beer. I turned away. I'd had ten missed calls in the last week from the lady in question. All that was ancient history.

'She stood by you when you were in trouble, bro.'

'Oh, yeah? So, how'd I end up here, then.' I gestured to the dive surrounding us, or what was left of it. The church sat stout on the hill, the walls a little crumblier, the steeple a little worse for wear. I laughed. 'Remember stealing the Sunday-school moneybox?' I asked Brookes, his gaunt face across from me, the fire roaring between us.

He spat beer over his flanno, dripped froth on the dusty ground as the laughter came. 'Fuck yeah. I felt so sick from them Snickers – but, God, the first few were ace before the pigs ruined it on us.'

I smiled. 'Never been so grateful for the congregation's generosity,' I said. It felt good to hear him snort-laugh at the memory. Stealing the collection money and escaping this place was our 'best day ever'. We'd called a Yellow Cab from the teacher's quarters, got two towns over and when the driver stopped at the Shell for petrol, we stuffed our backpack full of all the junk food we'd missed and spent the rest of the trip scoffing what we could in the back before the cabbie got suss – two scruffy fourteen-year-olds with a bag of money – and called the cops. The slack bastards hadn't even realised we'd escaped till the cops rang, asked if they'd lost anyone. 'Never got such a hero's welcome as when we got chauffeured back to Brightside in the good ol' blue-and-white-checked XD Falcon.' I glanced over to the stump remains of the amenities hall, and could hear the hoots and cheers from the motley crew of the lads, roar in my ears.

While downing the sixpack that followed, we summarised the last two years. Brookes filled me in about working on a cattle farm, and the fruit-picking Scandi girls he went through like socks. They seemed to like his goofy grin and adoring ways.

I wasn't confident enough to mention Lotti at first – that could all be past tense anyway by the way it got left, but before we stuck into the Bundy rum, her name snuck out my lips. Lotti. Lotti. Lotti. Was I ever gonna be with her again? Why was I surprised? Everyone that mattered, left. I was a fucking fool to expect her to be any different. Brookes carried on like a pork chop about me being in a 'relationship' like it was a big fucking joke. Maybe it was. He nagged me for intimate details about the shape of her tits as if we were still twelve, and I kept my mouth shut like I was ever a gentleman.

'So, your bird, she knows?' he asked.

'Shit, no,' I said. 'That's not what we agreed, right?'

'Nah, I don't mean about that. Just about, you know, Otto and all that.'

'No. Not that either.' I sniffed.

'Fuck me.' Brookes laughed his goofy laugh.

'I will fucking tell her. About Otto.'

'So, you haven't like, *had a chance*?' Brookes shook his head and grinned at my idiocy, did some rank gesture with his crotch as if I was busy doing something else. 'You've been banging her for months. She's stuck with the young fella now and she thinks—'

'Yeah, I get it, mate, Jesus.'

'You're an old fart now.' *Since when was thirty-five old?* 'If she's the real deal you gotta let her *in* man.'

'Dude, I'm not taking advice from a guy who thought the salami circles on meatlovers pizza are called "lovers", all right? So, go fuck yourself.' Half of Brookes' appeal was his lack of taking things seriously, and I wanted that version back. 'And you're forgetting I'll probably be dead before I hit forty with the way things are in my family.'

'Yeah, righto, arsehole – you still buying that? Sounds like a bullshit excuse for not livin' the life youse got.'

I shrugged. 'Speaking of lives unlived,' I asked, 'how's that younger sister of yours?' I still couldn't say her name without heat bristling my collar.

'Becca's good,' Brookes said, lighting another fag. 'She's still keeping our fuck-knuckle uncle outta jail by ironing them books.'

'You mean laundering?' Breaking the law didn't sound like the nice Catholic girl I knew, but saving face for her family did.

'Yeah, that. I dunno. How else did she get such a big yuppie pad? But, mate, I'm an uncle! I told you she's got a rug rat now with that putz.'

He was right about that part. Becca's husband Peter was a putz – a salesman that pitched himself to her so well it took years for her to realise it was mostly spin. But at least she'd freed herself from the pattern of her mother's life. Pete was as benign as a beige Magna and looked after her from what I'd gathered. Part of me just wondered what it was like to have what he had. Becca and I were gonna name our kids Scott and Charlene. I hope she grew outta that, for the kids' sake.

The whole time Brookes and I caught up, I was distracted, wondering when he'd get to the point. To the reason we both knew he needed me. Nervous energy radiated off him. His foot tapped nervously.

'I guess you're wondering why I made you come back.'

'That'd be a good start.' I turned to make out the shadow to my right. Two long-handled shovels sloped against the splintery weatherboards of End Cabin that I hadn't noticed before. 'What's with the spades, mate?' I asked. 'Too late to bury our secrets.'

He nodded to himself, winding up to say what we both knew he was trying to spit out.

There was a silence, and then he began.

Chapter 3

LOTTI

Before I laid eyes on him, my impression of August Silverfell was 'absent parent, bordering on neglectful'. He was just a name in the next-of-kin field for Otto Silverfell. For a while, I thought he was a mythical creature. Unlike the helicopter parents hovering in the halls for feedback regarding their beloved princes, dropping in an umbrella as if children were gremlins that couldn't get wet, August was elusive, expecting his six-year-old to be self-sufficient.

When I first came to the school, I barely bothered photocopying Otto's homework sheet as he rarely attended on Mondays. When he did he arrived late, had leftover pizza for lunch and walked home unaccompanied in his too-small shoes and Ampol-branded cap. He was the kid I'd started teaching for, not these ones with private tutors and personalised totes. I liked Otto as a human, not just because I was paid to. It was because of the way he always shared, never pushed and seemed to be innately aware of others' feelings even though he couldn't hear their words. He was less immersed socially on account of not hearing half of what he needed to, but he still got it better than most.

The pressure to teach inclusively kept me awake at night, and I enrolled in an online Auslan course to make sure he didn't fall through the cracks. I'd asked the Year 6 teacher, Pia (the owner of the biggest smile in the staffroom, who I befriended my first day despite noticing her disturbing addiction to green tea), about Otto's story. 'Why hasn't he got an IEP? He could be getting teacher's aid support, extra funding.' Not that he was struggling. Otto was as sharp as Pia's eyebrows and reading lips was one of his superpowers.

'The loser dad,' she said. 'Never got him assessed. He refuses to do anything that makes him different.'

What's he got against different? I'll see about that. 'What about the mum?' I turned my mug to avoid the chip in it.

'Not in the picture.'

Absent dads were common. Absent mums were gossip-worthy. But it didn't matter which; if a kid had one person in their corner, they had a chance.

'What sort of parent doesn't jump at support their kid is entitled to?'

Pia's eyebrows arched high, precise like her severe bob but somehow the angles suited her sharp wit. 'Don't say that to his face. I'd hate to see yours messed up.'

I didn't know her well back then, and laughed despite her straight face, but then fear crept in. 'Is that likely?'

Pia delighted in the topic. 'He works at the mechanic's, right, and – get this – when one of his customers drove off without paying for his windscreen, he followed him, and when the bloke denied ever having the repair done, let alone agreed to pay for it, Otto's dad smashed it again. Total thug.'

The story seemed at odds with the kind of family I thought the kid I knew was raised in.

Curiosity got the better of me that afternoon when I spotted Otto's skinny legs in too-long shorts skipping over puddles in the park. I stopped my car despite the rain and hurried after him on foot through the wet grass. His backpack was larger than him, jolting from side to side as his scrawny legs ran ahead. I called out to him, angry that he wasn't slowing for me, then remembered he couldn't hear, which forced me further across the rain-soaked field.

'You made me jog,' I signed, too puffed to talk once I caught up to the kid, speckles of rain like a rash all over my ankle boots.

'Did not,' Otto said. 'Your legs did.'

'You're not meant to get suede wet, you see.'

'I can seeeeeeee.' He pointed to his eyes and then his ears. 'I just can't hearrrrrr.'

I couldn't decipher much either over the pelting rain, and for a moment understood how he might feel all the time — excluded from conversations.

'And what's the point of shoes you can't get wet? Isn't that, like, their job?'

Little brat had a point.

I laughed. 'Are you always this cheeky outside class?' At least I think that's what I said. He told me months later that I sucked at signing, he just read my lips and pretended I was okay at it so as to not hurt my feelings. I could have said he was a chalk salesperson for all I knew.

A sheet of rain blew across the open space, spraying our faces, and he sprinted away again.

Otto called, 'Come on, Miss Hill.' Then ran towards the gravelly industrial area made up mostly of panel beaters and storage sheds.

I groaned, obliged to follow to find cover.

From behind a clump of shrubs I saw it.

'You do live in a van!' He'd told me as much when I saw him drawing a bus one day, but I'd thought it was nonsense.

I laughed in disbelief as I took in the sight – a giant converted school bus nestled in the clearing. The walls were mostly bare aluminium, patched and soldered together in places with different coloured panels at the top as if it had been raised. Solar panels lined the roof. Pipes ran the length of the undercarriage. Blue and red curtains with racing-car motifs were gathered along a curtain rod blocking off a view of the inside through the windscreen. It reminded me of the cubbies I made as a girl but with less frill. 'When you told me you lived in a bus, I thought you were telling fibs.'

He frowned, the way he did when he was frustrated in recorder practice, then he asked me what I meant. I was touched he felt comfortable enough to ask, to admit he wasn't sure and wanted me to help – it was the best thing a teacher could ask for.

'You mean what is a fib? It's like saying I live on the sun – a lie.'

'You mean horseshit?' Otto was so casual with the word.

My laughter erupted before I could scold him. Otto had already retrieved the key from the wheel arch, finessed the door at a well-worn patch with the heel of his hand and kicked the base, which made the slender door fling open. I tripped up the double step as Otto towed me inside. The rain pelted harder, leaving no time to doubt my decision to stalk a kid along a creek and follow him inside a secluded van. The long carriage had pine roof panels and white VJ walls, and the dashboard behind the driver's station had been converted to a couch. Fresh produce hung from net bags, a quilt with a volcano print covered a cosy high bunk. A ceramic butlers sink not unlike where we cleaned paintbrushes at school was built into a bench that, along with a hob and bar fridge, made up their entire kitchen. Other than a partial view of a cordoned-off bedroom (semi-private behind concertina doors that reminded me of my uncle's accordion) there weren't many nooks for a grown-up to have privacy.

'Where's your dad?'

'Work.'

I frowned. I was more expressive around Otto – I wasn't sure if that was subconscious, knowing he relied on it to interpret his surrounds, or if something about him made me *feel* more. He left a sweat mark on the vinyl seat when he raced to place a saucepan beneath a dribble of water that leaked through a roof panel, and the drips pattered in a regular beat. The boy then pulled out premade cordial from the miniature fridge in a miniature jug, as well two miniature cups – his was apple-green and mine, pink. Everything was space conscious, only essentials making the cut.

I slid my legs beneath the small booth with a sparkly red laminate top and an aluminium strip on the side that reminded me of jam scones and my grandmother's kitchen. We were soaked but it was cosy, the windows misting over as we drank. Raindrops chipped against the oversized windows that opened out to the field behind the lot, which had a carpet of vivid green grass puddling with the downpour. Shaded by a thicket of trees, the view made you feel as if you were in the English countryside, not out the back of an industrial area.

My long dark hair lay limp against my neck and wet the collar of my wheat-coloured T-shirt which clung to my chest.

'You walk home every day on your own?' It was a safe neighbourhood, but he was six. And deaf.

He shrugged, seeing nothing remarkable about this. 'You can't stay for tea, but. I get put in trouble.'

'What sort of trouble?'

'Dad makes me go straight to his work instead of home if I break rules, which is stinky and hot and boring.'

'So he works over there? In those sheds?'

He nodded. 'You won't tell him, will you? That I let you visit?'

A robotic hamster squeaked. 'That's Ralphy, my Zhu pet.' It scampered along the floor of the tiny van and hit the skirting. As Otto showed me his things (he could only keep five toys, he explained, and not exceed the space of the tidy tray kept in his bed nook above the driver's cabin). 'Sticks don't count but.' He moved to the corner. 'My collection,' he said, pointing to a stash of twigs of different lengths. 'Me and Ma made a Christmas tree out of them, but I lost it, so Dad said we'd collect sticks and make a new one.' His face pinched a little, his eyes squinting.

And where exactly is said Mum, now? Hopefully not in the trunk.

'I've got to wee,' Otto said, walking to the back of the bus and closing a teeny door that looked more like a cupboard. While I considered the weirdness of peeing that close to your kitchen, I did my teacher due diligence and snooped.

I spied a box up high that had a 'don't touch' sign on it, and started with that, pulling it down on my lap. Inside was a random collection of retro toys: a game, some cards, a Barbie, a Care Bear with its signature velvet heart and, then, rustling further, I found a single well-thumbed Polaroid of four teens – a tough guy sat next to a weedy kid smiling at a blonde with the cheekbones of a supermodel, but he only had eyes for the redhead laughing beside them. Were either of these couples Otto's parents? I rummaged through papers and found an old dictionary with an inscription from the Eldham Council Library thanking Judith Nash for twenty years' service. Water pumped from the cupboard-sized bathroom and I hastily returned the box before the kid caught me snooping.

'Do you have a sister?' I asked as he washed his hands.

'Ew. Nup.'

Otto scampered about the bus with ease and familiarity, dropping crumbs, dragging a heavy book from his toy tray titled *World's Worst Disasters and Epic Tragedies* that looked like middle-grade fiction not suitable for a second grader.

'Mrs Jeffreys let you borrow from the senior library?' The corners were dogeared.

'No, der. That's why I nicked it. I'll bring it back.'

'What is it about death that you like reading about?'

He shrugged. 'One day we'll all be dead.'

'But not today,' I said, trying to keep it breezy. The rain had eased to a rumbling misty cloud, and I thought I should trek back to my car – realising I'd probably left it unlocked – and dry my Milano boots before they watermarked, but I felt weird leaving such a young child unsupervised around a gas hob. He assured me his dad's work was across the park and he'd go there soon. I'd have to talk to Pia, see if it was something I had a duty of care to report or if I'd just cause trouble the kid didn't need. 'Want me to walk you over to your dad's work?'

His face scrunched even though he didn't take his eyes off the page. 'He wouldn't like that. He doesn't like people.'

I frowned. Trying to gather evidence without looking suss, I poked my head behind a pantry cupboard: Band-Aids with *Cars* characters, Omega-3 gummies for kids, and string beans drying on a tea towel – all incongruent with the neglect theory I'd fixated on. Satisfied he wasn't in any imminent danger, I figured I'd bolt before the antisocial father returned and asked questions.

'Time for Miss Hill to hit the frog and toad, Mister Otto.'

His big brown eyes looked up from his book. 'But you'll miss the Black Death page – it's about the plagooooeey.' Otto mispronounced words he'd learned from books, not speech, but that was a challenge for another day.

'Tomorrow, okay? And don't let anyone in, like your dad says – and no cooking or using the kettle or—'

He rolled his eyes, and I was pleased he'd heard these things before and waved as I left.

My boots squelched, the insoles unglued and crept up my heel as I sloshed back to the car. Flowers speckled the bonnet and leaves rested on wiper blades from the brief summer storm – they always landed at pickup time just to punish the breeders. I got in, thankful my father chose the heated-seat range, turned the ignition – nothing.

'Poo, bum, wee.' I groaned, considered walking. It wasn't far but I'd still have the transport problem tomorrow. I called the number on the sticker, explained my situation and gave the name of the closest side street. A serviceperson would be with me in under ninety minutes. Stifling a growl, I settled into the driver's seat, found my purple pen and began marking spelling tests, leaning against my steering wheel. Galahs weighed down bottlebrushes and an orange hue swept the sky with no hint of the earlier storm. I'd worked through the entire class's pages, when an oversized red-and-beige ute rolled into the street and parked as if trying its best to hem me in. This wasn't your usual service vehicle – more like an eighties Texan cowboy's wheels, and I wasn't sure if I should get out or find a tyre wrench first.

Steelcap boots hit the wet bitumen as the driver got out, and the rest of him arrived all at once; thick thighs, broad shoulders and eyes as dark as the scruff of hair that fell every which way over his face. The unkempt, black-haired version of Ryan Reynolds turned to retrieve something from the cabin, and I hoped it wasn't a gun. Grease-stained ruggers pointed my way as he reached inside and pulled out a set of red cables. The mechanic's strong brow was furrowed, his mouth matching the mood with a thin scowl, while the bloke's goatee concealed much of what could have been a handsome face beneath all that attitude.

I lowered the window as he approached. 'Hello, busy time?' *Code for 'What took you so long?'*

He smelled like my boots the time I accidently splashed petrol on them. 'Let me guess, left the lights on?' His tone was smug, like his smile.

The one I returned was just as hollow. 'Not sure. Just won't start.'

'The starter motor click in?'

Inwardly, I winced at the question, but it must have spilled out my face.

'Your old man never showed you basic car maintenance?'

'My old man has a driver.' And a fortnightly manicurist appointment. And a publicist. We didn't exactly sleep on wads of cash but we probably could have, not that I saw any of that now. There was a definite eye-roll. I thought of when my best friend, Jess, and I were carjacked in Rome. I hadn't seen that coming either. 'How do I know you're from Volvo Roadside Service?'

'What, you think I do this for kicks?'

I huffed. Where was the usual RACQ man sporting clean overalls and dad jokes? I had questions: Where was he from? Did he have ID? Would he have to tow me? And isn't it usually a banana-yellow truck?

He scratched his goatee as he pulled equipment from his tray. 'You always ask so many damn questions?' Gruff, bordering on rude. This guy had a classic-underdog chip on his broad shoulders. 'And, no, I'm not from Volvo. They contract out to the local garage. And, yes, we do have a banana-yellow RACQ ute, but Davo's got that over on the freeway helping some other bird who can't change a fucking tyre so unless you wanna wait another hour on the side of the road you're stuck with me, Mr Charisma, here. Take it or leave it.'

I thought the question was rhetorical, but the mechanic stopped as if I had a choice to engage his services. I looked around the empty lot and darkening sky. Clearly, I had no choice.

'Do you use that word with all your customers, or just the women?' I asked Mr Underbelly.

'What, *fucking*? It's a firm favourite.' He seemed proud of the fact. 'Right up there with horseshit. You got a problem with that?' He swaggered towards me as if he were a thug in a pub trying to pick a fight. I imagined if he did have ID, it would be more like a mug shot. 'If not, can you pull the bonnet release. Please.'

My face gave away the fact that I wasn't entirely sure where that was, and his eyes narrowed. I huffed to hide my ignorance. 'Do you get off on treating women like they're beneath you or something?' Without my permission, my mind pictured lying beneath him and my neck burned.

The tall man opened the driver's side and leaned close, his arm framing the door. I flinched. The way my wet T-shirt clung left nothing to the imagination. I fumbled for the right position for my crossed arms to hide the most curves, but it only seemed to draw attention to them.

His eyes darted away when he noticed my situation. 'Sorry, but we kinda gotta access the battery …' He stifled a smile, and his face lost the attitude it previously held but simultaneously made me feel more exposed.

'The bonnet release is that little lever with …' He gestured under the dash.

Attending to that meant moving my arms. We both realised this.

'May I?' he asked, softer now and close enough for me to see whiskers on his sideburns. He stared at me for a beat, at my eyes now without wandering lower, as if he'd just realised I was an actual person with feelings, not a chore to get over with.

I nodded. I pressed my back into the seat to make room. He smelled more earthy now than oil spill as his shoulders filled the cramped space between me and the windscreen. Tentatively, he extended his arm between the legs of my black cropped cigar pants. His tattooed arm pulled a hidden lever under the dash. Something popped. The mechanic gazed up and stilled as our eyes locked at close range for a moment too long. His were hazel with specks of gold. Mine were a little startled.

I bit my lip as his bulk retreated from my personal space. I breathed out. He bent to pick up the red leads coiled on the wet bitumen to the left of his blokey steelcapped boots. I smiled, thinking of Otto and how he'd like this man with the serious boots you could stomp through puddles in, unlike the soggy pair in my footwell. The mechanic connected the clips to a box in the back of his truck, did the same to my car's battery. He paused.

'Does she have a name?'

Was he referring to me as *she*? 'You should have my name.'

'I meant the car. You have to ask her nicely before you start her up.'

'I'm not in the habit of naming things that don't breathe.'

He seemed to grow more suspicious of me and my values. He looked the type to forget his mother's birthday, tats up his arm, grease under his fingernails, and yet he was a strong believer in respecting inanimate objects.

'What, she's a 2008 XC60? Let's call her Frida. Mighta paid to go with a car that has a battery shut-off instead of heated seats since we, ah, don't live in Sweden. But that's Volvo for ya.'

'Excuse me?' I got out, folded my arms dramatically, the road's surface sharp on my bare feet but I wouldn't let it show. 'Now you're bagging my car? Statistically, it's the safest car on the road.'

'Probably right. But Volvos don't exactly make your brain feel alive, I'm guessing.'

I was annoyed to realise I liked what he said. It gave him a depth I never imagined he had. I blurted out, 'I've always wanted a duck-egg blue Beetle, but when I researched it, air-cooled cars were unreliable.' My best friend, Jess, always rolled her eyes at me when I justified decisions based on numbers, telling me decisions should be made by feel. I still preferred the black-and-white of numeric facts.

His eyebrows hitched. 'And yet, here we are,' he mumbled, gesturing to the safest car in the world in a way that made me plummet from feeling alive to stupid and boring again.

'If you must know, my father bought it.'

He rolled his eyes. 'Of course he did.' His words were back to patronising, but his body language was still relaxed, like this was a game. He then disappeared beneath the bonnet before mumbling, 'You still go to bed by ten with a glass of milk, too?'

How did he know that? 'Perhaps I should mention this to your supervisor.' I'd managed to match his tone, caustic with a side of whimsical, but I'd stepped down from the high horse I'd been on earlier.

His brow furrowed. 'This?'

'You, being a judgemental ...' I wavered, before ending with, '... arsehole.'

Now it was a real smile, and stifling it was futile. 'Ooh, was that your first swear?'

My face pinched. 'Judgemental much?'

'Like you haven't been judging me as some sort of dumb-arse grease monkey. Start her up, madam.' He bent his head to the side. 'If it's not too much trouble.'

I shot back in my seat, turned the ignition, my platinum engraved keyring dangling under the genuine walnut dash, and the newly named Frida sung like a nightingale. At least this grease monkey was useful. The penny clicked. Pia. Today. The thug mechanic. 'Oh, God,' I thought, then realised I'd said it out loud, eyes closing in embarrassment.

'You praying, now?'

'Um, no. Just curious, legend has it a local mechanic smashed a client's car when they didn't pay up. Know anything about that guy?'

He smirked. 'Didn't know I was the stuff of legends. What of it?'

'No, nothing. Sounds like a reasonable reaction,' I said, tongue in cheek. Otto. *That adorable little boy spawned from this guy?*

'Fucking oath. I'm guessing you didn't grow up running a small business.'

School parent or not, I was going to defend myself. 'No.' My father made his first million in technology before he was twenty-one. 'But a business owner would know that manners cost nothing.'

He leered through the open door, his mouth opened like a goldfish, then hesitated before finally speaking. 'Let Frida run for a bit. No stopping off for manicures, okay? Don't stall it on the way home or you're fucked.'

'It's an auto,' I said in my best six-year-old voice and slammed the driver's side door.

He nodded. 'Of course it is.' Even his tone said *arsehole*.

I wanted to reverse over his steelcap boots. See how robust they were. As I steered out of his way, he waved childishly. I was going to offer a sarcastic note of thanks but decided he already had an unhealthy dose of arrogance, best not make it terminal.

Chapter 4

AUGIE, 2009

Brookes was a human TARDIS, sending me back to 1988. The way he spoke, the immature terms, the smell of him – a mix of Lynx, bitter coffee and old socks. His uncanny blue eyes, trusting yet naïve, his perpetually oily hair. He spoke with a cigarette bobbing between his lips like a fishing rod as we sprawled over the patchy grass, our beers balanced between our knees.

I lifted my hand in front of my face. It was thicker now, more callused. But when I closed one eye and pointed to the big country sky above us, the waxy moon was still obscured by the nail of my thumb. Some things never change.

But some had. We'd parked clear of the cabins, down the back near the old sports ovals. Tops of gumtrees were swallowed by night. I let my eyes adjust to the darkness, scanned the fields. There were surveyor pegs and portaloos, which meant one thing: excavation. And as much as I wanted this place bulldozed to the ground, these were not good signs. I clued what this meant for us, what vagaries he'd mentioned on the phone, and turned back to Brookes, his face a little warped with the reflection of the flames dancing on his face. Or maybe it was something else. 'What's with the dozers? Who'd develop this place?'

The firelight danced along a bare patch on his temple, a scar I could claim responsibility for that involved a deadly combination of a pre-teen temper and a hoe.

'I thought them mines were like, fucked for life, you know. Unsafe 'causa all the explosives 'n shit.' He gestured to the dark-forever sky, the absence of anything before us. 'But the fellas at happy hour reckon the mine's tenure had run out, that they'd assessed it as safe. They're doing it.'

'Who?'

'Who do ya reckon? My fat Uncle. Thought I'd come have a gander – spied on 'em sizing up the place, pegging in markers… thought you should know, yeah?'

'That's your emergency?' I said, a little relieved. This was not ideal, but the risk of us getting pinned for anything they uncovered now was unlikely. Brookes had the heart of Makybe Diva but his basket case mum'd pickled his brain with gin before he was born, and he was a little low on good judgement because of it. A little panicky for no good reason.

His brow furrowed. 'You forgetting what's down that mine shaft, you nuff nuff?'

My eyes flicked to our surrounds on instinct. After twenty years we were back to this. A conversation in the dark of night, taking the lead with this numpty as my only backup. He wasn't the best wingman. The can of XXXX crushed beneath his fist and he threw it in the long grass beside the last block of cabins, then got up and started pacing the carpark.

I whispered just in case. 'Think about it, mate. If diggers turn up anything weird, after twenty-odd years, there's no evidence of us doing it. They didn't even officially pin the whole thing on us, let alone what happened after.'

Brookes' face fell and he sniffed in the way he used to when he'd snorted too much crack. Was he back on the blow? His face morphed from sheepish reluctance, to twisted, agonised fear. 'I fucked up, man.'

And there it was. The fire roared, sucking the oxygen from the air.

My eyes narrowed and I put down my beer in case I needed to throttle him. 'What did you do?'

His nostrils flared like Brother Malcolm's when he found us spray-painting a cock-and-balls on his car. 'It's your fucking fault for not being around – you know I'm a dumb-arse. I was trying to help.'

'Brookes?' I stretched my neck, casually at first, nodded like this wasn't a disaster. Like we weren't fucked. He was always the weak link. If anything was going to happen it would be because Brookes blabbed – not intentionally, just through stupidity or getting high. *Snitches get stitches.* But he was overreacting. I knew from back when I was applying to build the garage on that commercial-lot land it took months for council bureaucrats to just tick a box.

'I was just looking out for you, mate.' He scuffed his shoe on the dirt. 'Once I heard them pricks were digging up the place, I hung around, tried to get the inside story – keep a step ahead like Jessica Fletcher on *Murder She Wrote.*'

'What did you do?'

'Nothing, right, but I s'pose I was around a lot, scratching my head and folding my arms and, you know, getting a bit sweaty about it. One of them guys in the high-vis even joked about why I gave a shit about the old mine. Said, "Mate, anyone'd think you stuffed your mother-in-law down there." And His Mugs and his mates laughed till their bellies shook. Thought I'd stay away for a bit then, not make 'em too suss, you know? But, fuck me, the next day them cops are on my case, following me ute.'

'What the fuck for?'

'They found bones.'

I swallowed. Weirdly, I'd dreaded this day my whole life. Now it was here I was calm. What could they really do to me that I hadn't already faced? Like that game Margo'd play with me to calm me down when I'd hyperventilate myself into a stammer. When I was expelled from Year 10, just before everything turned to shit, she'd asked, 'What's the worst that could happen if you don't finish school?' and I'd replied, 'I'll never get a job. Starve to death.' And she'd said, 'Not my amazing Augie. He'll always find his feet – and there's always a roof and a hot meal at my place. You know that.'

The problem was, I'd believed her.

'Pyro?' Brookes's agitated voice brought me back. Back to that name after ten blissful years of denying that part of myself. We'd checked out of Brightside, but we'd never left.

I shut my eyes to think better. They had come a long way with DNA since those bones were weighed down and shoved in that mine. 'Do they know *whose* bones?'

His voice rose in a burst of confidence. 'Nope, them pigs don't know shit. Only got wind of me 'cause the high-vis blokes on the site gave 'em a heads up that I might've known the body was down there, help 'em figure that part out.'

'How do you know that?'

''Cause I camped up in the bush, Gus, got my binoculars too, so I'd be less in their face, I went in all careful like, yeah?' He tapped his forehead and gazed at me for recognition of his wisdom. 'Heard 'em bag me out saying the "village idiot" was "sniffing around".'

I shook my head at the stupid prick, but it wasn't Brookes I was mad at. This was my doing. He didn't know any better, but I did. I should have got him out of town when I left. I should have protected him. Brookes and I were a popular duo when we were young fellas. Our connection did not go unnoticed. I would be next on their radar, which is why I should have stayed clear, not raced towards the epicentre. At least Otto was left out of this mess. I didn't want him anywhere near the Gus I used to be.

'What did you say to them?' I asked.

'Nothing, mate! I swear on me daughter's life. Snitches get stitches, right? I told them pricks I just needed a job, was just sussing the site out for work.'

I nodded. His explanation was sound, but Brookes was as gifted an actor as Pamela Anderson. And something about the way his eyes avoided mine told me there was more to this story.

'Some crazy shit, hey? I think we should tell Margo. About what happened that night. I stayed with her after them pigs came for me, and she knew something was up like she always does. She's suss,' said Brookes.

I felt the surge of heat flush my neck, move up to my face. I'd spent twenty years hiding these details from her, and he wasn't going to blow it all up. 'Nah, mate. Let's keep her out of it, like we said.' Aunt Margo was once my favourite thing, and Mum's only sibling left, with her easy laugh and endless jam drops. She had a heart of gold but was also big on her goddamned principles – like forgiveness and taking responsibility for your actions – and citing them to justify hers.

My eyes were drawn to Cottage Nine and my jaw tightened.

Ward of the state, which everyone knew was official talk for the pound for humans. That's what she made me into. Aunty Margo, world's biggest traitor. I could see her standing tall on the verandah in her posh Sunday clothes, sucking up to the staff when she dumped me here like a stray mutt, jabbering on about how a stint in Brightside would be character building, how the teachings of Jesus were 'never easy on the ego but good for the soul'.

'Keep telling yourself that,' I'd spat back at her, hurling a golly on the pathway to the cabin, arms stiffly folded across my scrawny chest. The head brother had given Aunty Margo a look as if to say, 'That's the sort of attitude we'll guide out of him, here.' As baby-faced Brookes had stumbled over to welcome me through the gates of hell, my aunt had exhaled in relief. 'And look! Your best friend is here to help you settle in!' The twist in my gut did loosen a little at the sight of his goofy grin. Being able to have his back, make sure he was okay, was the only reason I hadn't run far from this town and Margo's good intentions.

It's not as if I hadn't thought about the possibility of what we did being discovered, the potential unravelling of a knot we twisted into place when we were sixteen, and pulled tight on ever since. And was there any point wiggling the frayed edge, twenty years later? Things like alibis and fingerprints didn't really come into play decades on, but new threats like DNA just might.

'I've put together a list,' Brookes said.

'Jesus, Brookes ...' I turned to him with a frown more severe than usual.

'In my head, not written down, don't worry. So, like, the only people that know are like you and me, right? And we don't have any of our stuff, right?'

I thought about it, that night, what we did. He was probably spot on about that. I had nothing from back then. Not the clothes, not the bike, not that FM104 Rock in Stereo bag with the broken zip.

'Only other clues been lost long ago,' Brookes said.

'My bag reeked, so I dumped it in the bins outside the shops,' I recalled. What else could potentially turn up in their dozer scoop? 'You had that baby-turd-brown kit bag ...' Brookes used to think it looked like an army duffle bag. Like he was an SAS deployed to save the world.

He looked confused, then nodded. 'Yeah, got rid of that. Chucked it in the lake the next day, I reckon it was.' It probably had his name and address written in Nico pen on the flap, so I hoped the rot had destroyed it by now. Besides, that bag meant nothing on its own.

'Okay, so what now? Why am I here? Just so you can warn me about this all coming up? Okay, I hear you. Thanks for the heads up.' My voice was nonchalant, but my body felt as if worms filled my veins, swimming, endlessly swimming.

There was nothing to be done other than sticking to the plan and going about our normal lives. I was a little relieved. I wanted to get back to Otto and Lotti and my garage. I had a box of carbies and two mufflers arriving the next day and figured if I stopped drinking now, I could sober up and make it home by dawn. But the dark truth of exhaustion had me worried.

'No, August, I haven't told you the reason I called. There's something else, remember? Come here ...'

I pulled myself up from the splintery log and followed Brookes past the remnants of the rec room and the barn, and around the back of the amenities block that still held dark scars from that night. My face flushed like that time when I was eleven and Margo spent hours pressing washers on my burning forehead till the fever broke. The Heat. It got to me, crawled up my throat. It was as if I was battling something every cell was fighting off but still couldn't manage.

'Mate, it was good to see you, but I really could do without the trip down memory lane,' I said.

He paused at the old pole the plaque used to be fixed to, looking over a flat section of sunken, faded pavers. Flashes of 1988 splintered in my mind; bright terracotta bricks in a herringbone pattern bordered by maroon-and-yellow pansies. A dozen scruffy-looking boys standing around with their arms crossed, kicking gravel with their worn shoes, and some shiny politician talking about the Bicentennial as they lowered the time capsule into the damp clay, not to be opened for thirty years. It was meant to be a cache of historically significant artefacts to share with our future selves, a way to communicate with the next generation about life, about preserving how we lived in 1988. It was a cornerstone of the new recreation shed, but all that got destroyed, so it would now be commemorating something that was already gone.

'I never told you, but I read what youse all put in there. When I went round all the dorms to collect everyone's letters the night before Brother Daniel welded it shut. Remember?'

I didn't. All I remembered was not wanting to preserve anything from that chapter of my life. It could all go to hell. But that was the funny thing about Brookes. His processer was a laggy old Pentium, but he had the RAM to remember everything – yet this time he must have had it all wrong. I looked at the pavers, sunken but undisturbed.

'Mate, that capsule was sunk well before that night. How could there be anything incriminating down there?' It was all crap – a video cassette of the fat kid breakdancing, a jar full of Simon Barker's chewing gum, a broken Rubik's Cube Frogger had pulled apart trying to solve and ruined in the process, and a few old *Neighbours* cards with Scott and Charlene's headshots defaced. How was any of that junk relevant to all this now?

'The letters we put inside. We all had to write something, or we didn't get supper, remember?'

I flexed my shoulders, feeling uncomfortable and stiff but I didn't know why.

'I read yours,' Brookes said, a little sheepishly. 'I knows what you wrote.'

Chapter 5

LOTTI

With white knuckles and dirt under my broken fingernails, I steered to escape that place and whatever happened there. *'What was that big deep hole for? Was that a grave where zombies sleep? Why are you pulling my arm? Are the walking dead going to eat our brains? Where are we going? Why can't we camp too, like Daddy did? I need to wee. Did you know all the bodies that went overboard on the* Titanic *are still in the ocean with the fishes?'*

It was probably just Otto's obsession with all things tragic that had me yank his arm, drag him back to the car and engage central locking. But now all these questions were only deepening my concerns about what that ditch was about. I wasn't going to loiter around to find out. One thing I knew for sure – there was nothing in it, no dead body or coffin or anything sinister. But the disturbing thing is, there was *absolutely* nothing – not even a few broken pipes the developers might have damaged with the equipment. Or soil-test markers. Or any explanation for digging a human-shaped hole in the centre of a circle of old cabins in the middle of nowhere. Whatever Augie and his 'friend' Brookes had unearthed – it was long gone, and so were they.

What now? How did that eerie place form part of the history of the man I'd shared a bed with? I couldn't reconcile it. *Stay calm, stay clever.* I told myself this Brightside was just a rest stop, and that grave just some drunken challenge they dared each other to do after a few drinks. Who could dig the quickest? Who could chug three beers the fastest? That's the sort of bravado guys like Augie got up to with their mates. The only person who could explain this was Augie, and the faster he did, the quicker my life would go back to its normal, predictable pattern.

I didn't need to refer to my phone to know where Augie had headed next – I'd cyber-stalked him on playground duty every day since he'd left. The next stop was a tiny township not far from here, an old mining settlement built on the banks of a lake – this whole area had goldfields and opal mines from bygone days. Augie had tripped around (maybe catching up with family?) but then his phone had lost signal yesterday. Perhaps he was camping remotely or had no power to charge it. Was he off-grid, fishing? Drinking? Burying the cash he'd unearthed from a coffin hidden in that ditch in a new secret location? This was all becoming ludicrous. This was Augie!

My hands-free unit answered a call I would have ignored from anyone but her.

'Hey, stranger,' Jess said. It sounded as if her twin two-year-old boys were screaming directly into her phone. I secretly liked to feel a little smug when my procreating friends provided evidence of the mayhem that was family life. 'I'm hiding in the laundry so they can't find me. I've only got minutes but I haven't spoken to a grown-up in days, please come over with wine.'

Part of the reason I took the outer suburban Brisbane teaching post over another was Jessica Adams. She was an hour away from my flat, up in the hills of the Sunshine Coast, which still felt too far when we'd survived boarding school together.

I didn't even resent her life turning out perfectly and mine still being under construction. 'I'd love to, J-Girl, but I'm chasing a ghost in the middle of Fuck Knows Where.' August's gutter talk had begun to infiltrate my vernacular.

'You went after Wrench Boy? What did I tell you about making the blokes chase you?'

'Isn't that sexist?' I asked. With all the focus on droughts and the GFC, no one talked about sexism anymore.

Jess paused. 'I'm not surprised though, after what you told me ...' Her voice lowered conspiratorially. 'You know, the bit about how he finished you off with one finger in under a minute ...'

I was aghast, heat flushing my neck, relieved Otto could not hear such filth over the speakerphone. 'I never said that!' Didn't mean it wasn't true. A shiver ran through me at the thought.

'Drunk in the beer garden outside your dad's awards do – remember?' Her voice went all serious. 'You also said you loved him.'

'Now that's a *total* lie.' I hadn't even told *him* that, or myself for that matter. Wasn't that half the point of this trip – figuring it out?

'Honey, I just spent an hour scrubbing skid marks off kids' shorts – I live vicariously through you. I remember everything. You also cried ugly tears on the phone the other night because he hadn't called you back in days. It's not even school holidays and you're tripping around the country? It doesn't sound like you're thinking with your head right now.'

'I have no idea what I am doing,' I half-cried into the phone, staring at the white line disappearing beneath my wheels. I gave my oldest friend a synopsis of my predicament, how August had basically told me he loved me, and to figure out if it was reciprocated. She always had my back, was kind to her core, but also the only one who'd tell me straight when I was being precious or paranoid.

'Charlotte. I know you're indecisive but this is not a question you can work out with paper-scissors-rock.' A highly effective decision-making process in boarding school. 'There's a little person involved.'

There was that.

'So, you have no idea why he left?' Jess asked.

'I told you – his old friend from school.'

'Well, that's BS if ever I heard it. Did you check his phone?'

'I may have glanced at it. It definitely was a text from "Brookesy"'

'Which could be a Brooke with boobs, or someone he listed in his phone under that name.'

'Or it could just be a male friend that needed a mate?' I threw in, headlights from a truck harsh in my eyes. A string of missed calls from 'Margo' also stood out on Augie's recent-calls list. I'd seen the name flash up another time when August was reading with Otto and his eyebrows pulled together as he said, 'Not important.' But something told me not to tell Jess this, nor the fact that I'd been suspicious enough to save the number in my phone contacts for potential future reference. I knew what she'd say. I didn't want to hear it. 'I know I sound like one of those naïve chicks who write to prisoners but August just isn't like that.' He was closed off emotionally, our sex life was complicated, but we were working through all that. 'He's never given me reason not to trust him.'

'He's run away, left his kid, turned his phone off, hasn't called you …'

'I did tell him to screw himself.'

'Abandoning his son without so much as a call?'

'He's deaf.'

'A text?'

Ignoring me was one thing, but Otto? It had made me feel like hired help, not his partner. If I'd trusted August, why had I ditched work and chased after him?

'Look, I know how you like your research, on account of how uncomfortable you get with uncertainty, so let's try that. What school did he go to?' Jess asked. 'I'll see if I can check online.'

'He never told me.' *He never told me anything.* That word, unknowable, wafted into my mind again, but I wanted to know him. I'd find a way in.

'He said he lived in the moment, not in the past.' I inwardly cringed as the words left my mouth.

Jess paused. 'Wait – hear that? It's an alarm bell.'

I huffed, craned my neck in the driver's seat. I was comforted by the fact Otto couldn't hear this. He couldn't even read lips from the angle of his seat. 'I've only known the guy a few months, and he had a couple of mysterious absences but only a few days. But, Jess, the thing with Augie and I – it doesn't feel new. It feels safe and familiar, like we had an instant connection.' I knew it sounded bad. But it was the truth.

'Said every scam victim ever. And he knows your dad's loaded? Not to mention your other biggest fan …'

'Now you're being ridiculous, Jess. I've never mentioned Grayson, or my dad much. Besides, you've never even met August.'

'I've seen *Homicide*, hon, this is how they trap you. Next comes the white van and the ransom note. Use your head. Haven't you seen the stats on gender-based violence – you're safer on a tram at midnight than at home with your partner.'

'That can't be true.' Well, not for me. Not for us.

Back through the wormhole into Jess's world, a muffled scream choked the airwaves. 'God, my time's up, hon.' I felt relieved. I'd had enough reality check. 'Think about turning back. Whatever he's got himself embroiled in, he doesn't want you or the child involved or he'd call. Come home, hey, girl? And, maybe change your locks? Call me tomorrow so I know you're not in that ditch, okay? Ciao, Bella.'

August and I had never discussed money, but I got the vague impression he came from humble beginnings. Wealth wasn't important to either of us, or was that just the impression of him he wanted me to have? Maybe that grave was intended for him, and his arch enemy or debt collector had him dig it before he escaped his fate?

I shook my head to rattle away the conspiracy theories I was back to, thanks to well-meaning, straight-talking Jess. She didn't know him. She didn't know he built me a shower with rainbow boots for squelch protection. Or that he arranged the pastry chef from the food van that parked at his garage to deliver an almond croissant at school every morning with 'Miss Hill' scribbled on the box because he understood I never had time for breakfast or to queue at the tuckshop like an overgrown student. I trusted Augie. He was helping a friend. A very male friend called Brookes. That was the Augie I knew. Steadfast. Dependable. Shower-building.

Private.

My thoughts roamed before my driver's seat almost ejected me, followed by another bash, then a rhythmic general vibration from the back seat. I'd forgotten about the kid. I wasn't used to having them for homework.

'What's for tea?'

Without a school bell to remind me, I also forgot he demanded watering and feeding every few hours. I was hoping he was like Pavlov's dogs and only got hungry when the bell rang.

'Maccas?' Otto begged from the back seat for the eighth time, despite there not being one for miles.

'Roadhouse nuggets?' I bargained, seeing a sign for a petrol station with wooden picnic tables advertised for the next exit.

We pulled over not long after and entered the diner that sold everything from battered fish (despite no coastline within half a day's drive) to fence posts. Every wall, every inch of counter space was cluttered with stock. I could barely see the cash register, but I could smell the grease wafting through the small window that allowed a view through to the deep fryers in the kitchen. I ordered Otto's requests. 'Do you have anything green?'

The man at the register raised an eyebrow. 'Karen sometimes puts garnish on the side of the burgers – that do?'

I gave a thumbs up to hide the fact I died a little inside at the thought of more grease. The man spoke while chewing gum, which I found just as impressive as his 'Kevin-07' visor but chose not to mention who my father was. I didn't have a spare hour to talk about the GFC or how we could better support agriculture or how much politicians got paid.

Otto was sitting at a ghastly brown booth, still kicking his heels against the seat so loudly it distracted from the country twang blaring through the tinny speakers in the store.

'You out from the city council?' the man asked.

'Council? No, just seeing a friend. What makes you say that?'

'The dust. Your mags – they're still silver.' He sniffed. 'Everyone else who looks like you's here about the red tape with the Brightside development. Reckon the old school's heritage listed or somethin' – all bulldust. The only thing that went on in that place of any cultural significance was how many birds got their cherries popped with all the parties the kids had there in the last twenty years. The developers have gone apeshit over the fuck around. Scuse my French.' He could even smile while chewing gum.

I nodded and he spat his chewy in the bin and went out back to start our meals and the teacher in me had to restrain a need to remind him to wash his hands.

I spent the next minute or two hoping he'd washed his hands.

Otto had started playing a game of Twister for one on the black-and-white chequered tiles of the diner that was empty but for us.

After Jess's negativity, I needed an antidote to reality, and rang my mum, hoping she was having a good day, hoping she'd provide a virtual warm hug. Her answer was spritely, and I was relieved.

'Hey, Mum. You okay?' There was a fifty-fifty chance of lucid.

'Why wouldn't I be, love? How are you? Your father there yet?'

'Why would he be here? I'm not at home.' She probably thought it was 1999. 'I've gone away for a few days.'

'Oh, your father didn't ring? He's up your way for the campaign – was looking forward to dinner with you.'

It was likely I was his (unknowing) alibi for dinner with an entirely different woman. Mum probably exceeded his expectations by remembering his decoy at all. Or maybe she was remembering wrong.

It was only six-thirty, but I knew she'd already be wearing that faded pink chenille dressing gown, blending moisturiser on her elegant fingers as she relaxed in the wing chair. Mum updated me on Dad's campaign trail, on the rosebush's recovery from the gardener's overzealous pruning, on their red border collies, Sherlock and Watson's, latest wayward act. It was reassuring, speaking with Mum like she was still herself and I savoured it like a rainbow. You never knew when the mirage would melt away.

'I'm out in central Queensland to see where August grew up.' It was misleading but sounded reassuring, and that's all I wanted to impart. *Everything's alright...* I wanted every second to feel like Mary Magdalene anointing Jesus like in the musical she dragged me to when I was ten that I secretly loved.

'The outback? On your own?' Mum had wandered into a Sunday matinee of *Wolf Creek* a couple of years back that fundamentally altered her perception of the world and she'd become as obsessed as Otto about all things sadistic.

'I'll be with Augie soon, Mum.' And as the man of mystery said, he was built like a brick shithouse. No harm would come to me with him around, unless, the thought inserted itself, it was him doing the harm.

Dad had insisted on meeting the new man in my life a few months ago when he'd travelled up from Canberra for work and met us for dinner, but the cornerstone memory of that night was August not having the right shoes, telling the host how fucked the rule was because his steelcapped boots were both leather and enclosed, and Dad's chauffer (by a stroke of luck was size 11, too) lending Augie some. But Mum wasn't there that night. For the past few years, Mum was rarely there. But they had spoken on the phone by accident.

'Augie with the gravelly voice?' she asked in her version of gravelly, and warmth spread across my cheeks and down my neck, grateful at being present for part of her precious good day.

'That's the one.'

'You know they do talking books now – not just for the blind – you get them on tapes. He'd do a lovely grumpy old detective in one of those cosy mysteries.'

I baulked a little. She was right. His voice had that low sexy timbre that could do voiceover commentaries. David Attenborough with f-bombs.

'Did you see your father made the news this morning? Front page! Just below the news about Michael Jackson dying – so sad.'

I rolled my eyes. 'What's Dad done now? Visited a chook farm? Eaten a sausage at a by-election?'

Otto started shaking the gum machine, checking for loose change, making funny loud noises that he couldn't realise he was making.

'You're still at school at this hour?'

'No, Ma, that's just Otto – August's little boy.'

'Oh, yes. The photo on the Facebook. Have those chubby cheeks changed your mind on kids yet?'

'No, Ma. Kids are so' – I glanced at Otto, determined to get that gum – 'relentless. Think I'm happy to hand them back at bell time.' As the words left my mouth, I realised they felt like a lie. Mum was always my litmus test for the truth.

Her voice was barely more than a whisper, her way of trying to not sound pushy. 'The scans didn't rule it out, love, so you shouldn't either …'

I was twenty-nine. Was I meant to know that yet? Maybe I just hadn't wanted kids with Grayson. I shrugged. 'I don't know, Ma.'

'Well, baby girl, if you don't know what you want, how can you ask the world to give it to you?'

I rolled my eyes. 'Yes, Ma.'

'But you like this mechanic and his boy, yeah?'

Otto found a twenty-cent piece in the last gum machine and screamed in delight, bringing it over to show me and bask in his success. I smiled, stroked his chubby cheek. 'Yes, Ma.'

'Good.'

Was it good? It might be easier if I didn't.

'Oh, that's the housekeeper leaving, better go, love you.' Mum faded off.

I didn't want her to. Every turn in my life created questions needing her input, her knowledge of the essence of me that no one else knew, that would keep demanding answers with or without her.

'Love you, Mum.' My lips puckered to make a smacking sound and she was gone. I held my phone, warm in my hand and wondered when she'd be back. I missed her already.

Otto frolicked like a deer in the playground near the diner as we waited for our food. He'd been staring at something on the grass, obscured from view the whole time I was on the phone. I waited, watching, amazed at his stillness. He stood motionless for a minute before a crow swooped to his feet, pecking at the ground with gusto. Otto's high-pitched hysterics pierced the low hum of the highway noise. I quickstepped over to him. An evil-eyed crow matched his antics, squawking, wing-flapping, biting and tearing at something with its beak. Otto stomped on the grass near the crow, chasing it, arms flailing, face determined and fearful. I flinched at the scene: the carcass of a dead possum nested in long grass, ants crawling through its orifices, its rotten flesh pecked and raw.

'Leave it alone!' Otto cried.

I shooshed the vulture away, then pressed Otto's shoulders firmly with my palms to calm him. I considered shuffling him along, but I didn't need to shelter this kid from death – he'd experienced it firsthand. Death was part of life.

'It was hurting the possum!' he blubbered, eyes shiny with tears.

'I know. Poor possum. It seems awful, doesn't it? But one good thing about death is you can't feel anything. No pain. No grief.' I hoped I wasn't overselling it.

His barely-there eyebrows threaded together. 'How do you know, have you been dead?'

'Nope, but does the TV work when we unplug it? Without our heart pumping blood around, the pain signals don't get through to our brain to tell us to feel hurt.'

His mind ticked over. 'The iPad works when I unplug it – maybe the possum can still feel the crow pecking his eyes!' His eyes fixated on the roadkill, wide-eyed, panicked that he might be right. Had I converted him to vegetarianism? 'Do ants eat people flesh, too?'

'My sweet O-man, come here.' I gave him a big hug. 'People can rest in peace because they're protected in coffins.'

'In a grave, like we saw?'

'We don't know that was a grave …'

'Mummy's coffin was the same shape. A rectangle!' His eyes looked to mine for endorsement and I hope I gave it even half as much as I felt it.

'You've always been good with shapes, dude.' *And death.* Whenever I mentioned an explorer, he'd ask if they were dead and if I knew how they died. I diverted him back to the possum and we talked about what it was best to do about it. I promised I'd find a number we could call for someone to collect it, let Mr Possum sleep in peace like he deserved.

'Do you remember your mother, Otto?'

'Ma's in heaven.'

So that confirmed what I'd assumed when August said Otto's mother was 'gone'. Dead gone. Proper, forever gone. My throat tightened and I signed how sorry I was, to which Otto said in a soft voice, so soft I could barely hear him, 'I know. The whole world cried when her coffin got carried out.'

'The whole world?' I gestured, squatting to his height.

Otto nodded. 'Her coffin. There were tears splashing all over it, pouring down from the sky.'

My throat caught, picturing his sausage hands reaching for his mother's coffin in a rain shower, surrounded by suits. I'd forgotten the words I needed to sign, so I went with an exaggerated frowny face and gave a thumbs down, which made the kid smile.

'That's all I remember. Oh, and the free bickies that no one even told me to stop eating. I threw up on the grass.'

'You once told me how you built a Christmas tree from sticks together. Sounds like she was creative.'

He nodded.

'And you've lived with just your dad since?'

He nodded again, as expansive as Augie when it came to emotions.

After a quiet minute, we returned to the diner to find our meals ready, and the kid bounced back with the influx of calories. We ate in comfortable silence, then the nags for an ice block began. Otto spent forever choosing between a frozen Milo cup and Bubble O Bill from the board above the freezer, which was right next to a newspaper stand. And there he was. My dad, with his thick silver hair and Bill Clinton smile, gracing the front page, shaking hands with the prime minister. I pulled the paper from the wire rack before another story caught my eye. *'Brightside finds new light'* along with a picture of the creepy place we'd just left and some positive quotes from Eldham locals.

Otto pushed my thigh and handed me his ice block to help him open the wrapper.

'Ever been to Eldham, O-man? That's where we're heading next.'

He jumped on the spot. 'To see Margo with the dogs?' Missed-Call-Margo.

I pulled out his Bubble O Bill. 'You've met Margo?' Whoever the hell she was.

He looked confused. 'Dad showed me photos.'

'Is she young and pretty?' I asked, feeling the shame of stooping that low to gather info.

'Nah, that's Becca,' Otto said before he ran outside to the picnic area, now cast in a warm glow from the streetlight. He sat on the swing holding the cone in two hands in front of his lips like a microphone. When that got eaten and the swings got old, we played a few rounds of hide and seek behind the trees buffering the diner from the road, and I tried not to think about the young, pretty Becca.

I'd saved Margo's number from Augie's phone as Missed Caller before he'd disappeared. My finger hovered above my screen. The prefix was the same as the one plastered over the diner. She was local, and likely connected to him being here. She may even be with him now. An urgent need to know if she was came over me. I rang, unsure of what I'd say until the moment the woman's voice answered on the second ring.

'Margo?' I asked.

'That you Becca, love?' *Who the heck was this Becca?* Her voice was rougher than expected, perhaps from tobacco, perhaps from life. Either way it put a question mark over the 'bit on the side' theory and now confronting her about why she'd been calling my boyfriend incessantly felt a little dramatic.

'You don't know me, but my name's Charlotte Hill. It's about August.'

A humourless cackle. 'You journos've got no respect for privacy. Was that you outside church?' There was something in the way her voice strained, as if stretched to a place she didn't want to go. 'I got nothing to say about August Nash,' she spat, before dial tone replaced her voice.

Dread clawed at my throat.

He'd told me his name was August Silverfell.

Chapter 6

AUGIE, 2009

Brookes had given the giant missile-shaped capsule about forty strokes with an axe, right where the bastards had welded it shut. All it'd done was create a few teasing sparks and a few ugly dents. That weld would have survived an apocalypse, not just the fifty years the Brightside Motherfuckers had hoped. I was too old for these sorts of shenanigans and wished I was back at the bus with my kid and my peace of mind. I had neither now. All I had was a stiff shoulder and what felt like a drill bit tunnelling through my temple. The ute's spotties were the only light source, shooting two glowing arcs high into the surrounding blue gums that were so much thicker than I remembered. Brightside did what it did best, lurking in the shadows behind us as we fumbled in the dark.

He bent forward in exhaustion with the axe as a prop. I was less drunk than him, so had another crack myself, but it was futile.

'Jesus, Brookes, if this was your caper, you didn't think to ask me to bring something to open this up?' I asked the numpty.

'Like what?' He was confused. 'Explosives or somethin'?'

'A grinder with a decent cutting wheel?' I said. 'TNT'd probably work but it might draw attention, don't you reckon, mate?' It was like talking to Otto sometimes.

He nodded. 'You got one?'

'I'm a mechanic.'

His eyes scrunched in that way they got when he still had no clue. I'd forgotten how literal he was.

'Yes, mate.'

The grin lit up his face. 'Well, what are we waiting for?' Brookes never was good at problem solving. Not without me or Becca prompting each step.

'It's back at the shop, mate, and this pisser is not opening without it.' As sealed as their lips about the truth. 'I'm gonna have to cart it home to my place, grind it open, burn all the shit and chuck what's left of the shell out at the wreckers.'

Brookes, long and lean, a face as innocent and naïve as any kid's, scratched his slightly balding head. 'Yeah, right, that makes sense. Good thinkin', 99.' He tapped his temple and sat, relieved to have reached a solution to our immediate problem. If he was Maxwell Smart then Agent 99 was a lot hairier and mud-mouthed than I remembered.

It took drunk courage from both of us to lift the bullet, weighed down with the sentimentality of some troubled kids' childhood bullshit, into the back of my truck and replace the cover over the tray. I'd have to use the hoist to get the bastard out when I got it to the workshop – it wasn't exactly the usual cargo the boys would help me unload. The less questions back home, the better.

Home. I shoulda called to say I was here but it was so late. I checked the screen and it had run outta juice. I was still hoping to get back soon enough that the boy would barely have noticed I left. He'd already had enough people leave.

'You better be right about what you think is in this fucker. Hate to have this thing scratch up my tray just to open it up and find a lot of junk. Wouldn't they have vetted all the things we put in it back then?'

'I snuck into the barn, slipped our stuff in when it was getting sealed up all good – got the truth saved away to tell our futures selves.' He looked proud, not considering the plan had backfired royally. 'So, that was good of me, huh, thinking about the evidence – calling you and stuff,' Brookes asked, his tone the same as Otto's when he'd show me a Lego creation.

'That was good, mate. Glad you were thinkin' of me.' I would have preferred he stay the hell away from all of it, but it was too late for that option. Classic Brookes.

I secured the last hook on the leather tray cover and leaned on the side of my truck. We talked as though no time had passed. Something had shifted, though, and I think it had to do with me having something to lose this time. Two things, in fact, unless I'd already fucked things with Lotti.

Brookes crushed the last can of XXXX Bitter in dirt-caked fingers and opened his mouth that way he always did when he had something to say but the processor hadn't worked out 'what' yet. I hoped it wasn't a confession that he'd told three chicks at the pub what we did that summer night, long ago. But something in my bones told me I didn't need to worry. His allegiance was never in doubt.

He sniffed, then came out with it. 'I was thinking the other night, Gus. About how we were born the same day and, like, what kinda cool person we woulda made if, instead of being two kids, we were, like, one person with your brains and my looks.'

I shook my head. 'Jesus, you on the weed again, mate?' I couldn't help but smile. 'But, yeah, your way with women and my head for engines would have been a good all-rounder bloke.'

'Yeah, man! That guy – he woulda scored big time! Like Warney or some shit.' His laugh reminded me of Goofy, big, dopey and benign.

His lips spread into a foolish grin that made me forget all the stupid crap he'd got us into. Like crashing Margo's Festiva and blowing up that wreck we thought no one would miss. That was the start of all this.

'No other bits of stray incriminating evidence you think we need to blow up before I leave town?' I asked. I was not coming back here for a while. I realised I wouldn't see Becca even after coming all this way, and wasn't sure if that was a good thing or a bad. Probably safest.

'Think we're good,' Brookes said.

'Nothing left at your parents'?'

'Shit no, they chucked everything neither of them thought was worth fighting for in the divorce.' Brookes and Becca grew up in a caravan. It was a six-wheeler, but no room for mementos. He hated living in a van park, but we had the best sleepovers there, blow-up mattresses outside in the annex, the night breeze flowing through the gaps in the canvas.

I'd often escape to Brookes' place when the bed bugs and the bullshit got to me, but when his olds were at each other, his place was bad for a whole swag of reasons. His dad used to smoke cigars, sitting in his crackled vinyl chair, highlighting the shows he planned to record on his VHS from the TV guide, and if you interrupted him programming it, he'd throttle you, and his wife for letting you in the house. So, me and Brookes built a safe harbour … up a tree.

It wasn't intentional. We built a raft out of an old crate, carted it between us all the way to the dam one Christmas holiday with the idea we'd float it somewhere no one would find us. We tried tying on a drum, but when that failed we used the wood to build a platform up a gum tree. It was high enough and remote enough that you couldn't really see it unless you went looking. And no one ever looked.

'Remember the treehouse?' I asked.

His eyes came alive with the memory.

'Built out of crap even my mum would throw out,' I joked, and it was nice to be open about her with someone. It had been a long time. I hadn't realised how long until a laugh rose in my throat.

'Not funny, man.' Brookes had always had a thing for my mum as she'd given him the affection he'd craved from his. The only thing he got from old Rhonda were the sloppy bear hugs she'd give when he'd pull her from the bar at closing time. 'It's still there, Gus.'

I smiled. We didn't need our walkie talkie to know where we'd head next.

The first part of the walk to the treehouse was easy as they'd cleared the first few hundred metres where the bones were found. Police tape looped along a wide circle of star pickets flapped in the breeze, and I figured that was where the mine shaft had once stood. There were hundreds of them abandoned all over Queensland – mostly opal and sapphires out here, copper further west at Mount Isa. The distinct smell of menthol hit me as we trekked deep into the bush, a dense litter of foliage underfoot that reminded me of conditions when I was a volunteer firefighter in my late twenties. It still lit something in me, that smell, that association with fire, but it didn't control me the way it once had.

We made it over to 'No Man's Island' in less than an hour with nothing but moonlight and memories guiding our way, instinctively heavy-footed to scare away the snakes like we always did. There was no dam, no island, just a basin of lower-lying cracked clay so dry it crunched beneath my boots for as far as I could see to the east. He slowed as he approached a blue gum. It was less grand than it had been in my memories.

'This is it,' said Brookes.

I circled the wide trunk and, as I looked up, there it was, the splintery old crate we'd slowly built up each holiday, high in the branches. Brookes scaled the tree, relying on muscle memory to propel him from the nest of hard brown fruit and leaves blanketing the ground. Once he reached the platform, he dropped a rope and I followed. The view was familiar and comforting, the earlier drama forgotten as we breathed the sweet smell of eucalypt, listened to the hypnotic wash of crickets and the clicking call of birds drawing us into the stillness.

'Don't get so much of that in the big smoke,' I said, my voice carrying through the night air. 'Still good.' In the quiet, I could make out the soft, repetitive grunting of a tawny frogmouth, along with the rustle of leaves, the flapping of wings.

Below a couple of ripped boob mags, I saw the Arnott's biscuit tin, the faded parrot on the lid now rusted like its feathers were speckled with disease. Dirty water dribbled down my jeans as I yanked it open and smelled mildew. A pile of yellowing Polaroids, folded foolscap notes, cinema tickets and a cigarette lighter scattered from the tin across the treehouse floor. 'Jesus, Brookesy,' I said, flicking through the artefacts. 'This takes me back.'

A wad of negatives nestled behind a stash of random photos. Some of Brightside. Some outside the school hall at a senior disco – Steph's up-herself smile, Brookes in his Michael Jackson gloves, Becca in her Cindy Lauper try-hard phase. The fringes. The colour. The ballsiness of the eighties was obvious even in the black of night.

'We should get rid of this shit, mate – they'll probably clear it – run huge drains through where the dam once was, who fucking knows what else is in this pile.' My thumb rested on a note from Becca. She was the only person I'd ever written to.

Was I any less a fool since the last time I paced the rickety floor of this treehouse, sweaty palmed and seventeen, waiting for a green-eyed redhead to turn up? I'd had my licence, my truck left from my good-for-nothing dad. I had it sorted, had whispered the plan into Becca's hair the last day of Year 12: *Meet me at the treehouse at midnight, you and me, girl.* She'd beamed her wide smile, kissed me hard on the lips and skipped home to pack. I could still taste the adrenalin at the back of my throat, the ache of it, knowing everything pivoted on her – if she'd run away with me like she'd promised, save herself and rescue me while she was at it.

Everything unclenched that night, when I heard rustling in the leaves, saw a flash of yellow between branches as she approached our meeting place. 'I'll help you up,' I'd said, beaming like a fool, my life set.

'No, it's okay,' Becca said, her arms folded across her chest. She wore the yellow sundress that she'd made in home ec. It was the only new thing she had.

'You're freezing – have this.' I'd worn the leather jacket that'd been left in Dad's closet and finally fit. I shimmied down the rope, jumped to the ground and stripped it off. It was still warm when I threaded her arms through its too-long sleeves. Then I showed her my surprise, the still-tender tattoo I'd persuaded the travelling ink artist to do for a bottle of booze I'd stolen from Becca and Brookes' caravan, thinking their mum was flammable enough. 'See what I got?'

She grazed the swirl of the 'B' with her fingers. 'For Brookes?' she asked.

'For you, ya dork.'

She swallowed, her eyes flicking to the stars above.

'Did you leave your bags at the truck?' I asked, my throat tight.

Panic rose in her eyes. 'Let's just say the B's for Brookes, okay?'

I saw her tears and I knew. There were no bags. She'd only turned up to say she wasn't coming. I squared my jaw, heat clawing my neck. I started loading rebuttal phrases in readiness for a fight, but then she hit me with a simple, 'I can't leave him.' All my talk of how great life in the big smoke would be, how she'd go to TAFE to study bookkeeping while I did my apprenticeship, how we'd never set foot in this dive again – poof. Counted for sweet F.A. Trumped by my best friend, the needy little weed. And instead of admiring her selflessness in sticking around for Brookes (who we both knew would end up on crack or in the clink without one of us around to keep him straight) I did what I did best. My always-ready anger rose as if it had been waiting for a reason, swearing she'd regret it, how her big stupid brother would just shack up with the first chick to flash her knockers and wouldn't even realise the life his sister was giving up babysitting him.

'You're too good for this place, Becca.'

She stood beneath the treehouse, fragile and tiny in that big coat, choking back tears, and said, 'I'm not, Gus. This is where I belong.' There was nothing more to say.

I left town without a backwards glance. I'd left them both here to rot. Thinking back to the grief I dished out that night, thick with disappointment, I reckon I made that decision easy for her.

Now, the adrenalin had worn off, and the silence slowed my breaths to a yawn. It had been a long day driving, digging and walking, and I was beat. I rested my eyes, tried my trick of separating the bird calls like guitars in a band. The treehouse creaked and the floor sank a little.

When we woke, birds were singing. It was a rookie error. Foolish.

We took the tin, the mouldy smut mag and our memories, scaled down the old gum for what was likely the last time, and headed back through the dry, menthol-smelling bush, humming and singing like we were twelve years old again, out for a Sunday hike like they'd make us do, back to Brightside. And it felt good – until we saw the lights.

Flashing blue and red, roadblocks, the whole damn circus.

'What the …?' Why the fuck did I let Brookes lead me back to the scene a week after they found bones here? It was impulsive. It was brainless. It was everything I used to be but thought I'd outrun. This wasn't the eighties. They had a media to placate now. A World Wide Web to look noble for. We were roos in the headlights, mesmerised, just waiting to be run down. The tin was still tucked under Brookes' arm with all the fodder the cops needed to haul us down to the station – not to mention the time capsule ticking in my ute tray in the lot just behind them.

'Well, looky here, would ya fellas?' old mate Troy Harris said to his copper pals. 'If it isn't Dumb and fucking Dumber.'

Chapter 7

LOTTI

The sun lit its last match of the day, and the birds made their presence known, scattering along the verge near the old diner. Otto twirled the chain tighter before releasing, his overlong hair covering his face as he spun around and around with a grin. I wondered how his mother died, if he'd witnessed it, and if that related to his interest in the afterlife.

I glared at my phone, feeling stupid and somehow offended after this Margo person hung up on me. I could have dealt with the rejection, and the fact she knew my boyfriend by a different name (maybe Otto took the name Silverfell after his mother, and Augie changed his in a sign of unity?), but mistaking me for the media told me something was very wrong.

Diner Man had pretended not to notice my phone call, but I could tell he was listening as he wiped down our booth with a green-and-white Chux. 'How is the old bird?' he said, still wobbling a cigarette between his chapped lips.

'You know Margo?' I asked, half an eye on Otto in the playground as the light faded outside.

'Everyone knows Margo. She's like the unofficial mayor of Eldham – except she actually helps and doesn't get a brass razoo for it.'

I smiled and nodded. 'That's our Margo.'

'She's the friend you're in town to catch up with?'

I nodded. It felt easier than lying out loud. 'She still at the same place, right?'

'Surely is. She's had that eyesore since before I was born – nice view of the dam from Thomson Road, but. They'll have to take her out on a gurney – she'd never leave those mutts – we'd need to get an actual animal shelter if she did.'

'She loves those dogs,' I said agreeably.

'Almost as much as them kids. You stayin' with her tonight?'

'Not sure. Is there anywhere in town?'

'Just the pub.'

I noticed the name *Henry* sewed in cursive on Diner Man's navy shirt. He was approaching his senior years. 'You know Augie, then?'

'Surely do. His sister used to teach our Tessa guitar in fact, way back. She was a sweet thing. Haven't seen those Nash kids for donkey's years.'

Nash. August Nash. Why the need for an alias? My throat tightened.

'How's he doing? Heard he was in the clink or somethin'?'

'Jail?' The word caught on my lips. August had alluded to a chequered past, but not a criminal one. That would explain the name change.

'Years ago, now. Me uncle did time and he's the best bloke you'll ever meet. Maybe I heard wrong. Gus was an alright kid, though. Used to sell papers for me old man at the truck-stop, never stole or nothin', pretty good rugby player. I don't reckon he did what them folks said. You know him?'

Do I know him? I couldn't answer. But that was the status of my life: decision pending.

The hotel room at the back of the pub had a bedspread the colour of vomit, but I flopped on it with delight, exhausted. I stared at the still life on the wall to distract myself from the ruminating thoughts about what greasy Henry had said about absent Augie, or Gus, or whoever he was today. At once I felt desperate to have the lump of a man in my arms, and yet fiercely betrayed by the false impression he gave me of himself. This state of limbo on how to feel was doing my head in.

Jess was right about me. I'd never been a decisive person. I'd flip-flopped on career choice until my late twenties before sloping over the line for a teaching degree on the back of an almost-completed stats degree. I hated people with no backbone. I had strong values, it was just finding the best way to apply them that I struggled with.

Otto was occupied jumping on the bed, which slid further and further along the brown tiles towards the fake-wood laminate walls (even browner). Was I meant to stop him? It looked too much fun to make him stop, and besides, it would wear him out. I needed air, but again had forgotten I had a child with me. You couldn't just leave human kids alone like houseplants and do whatever you liked, which was a definite disadvantage. I skulked out to the verandah and sat among the depressing row of wrought iron outdoor chairs, nodding politely at a smoker slumped outside their room looking as desperate as I felt. Ironically, the further away I drove from the polluted city the more people sucked smoke in their lungs on purpose.

The voice inside told me who I had to call next. I cringed, then charged on anyway with my newfound determination.

I would not be like the still life on the wall. I was an active protagonist, carving out my own life.

It took eleven rings before Grayson Wright picked up, and even that annoyed me. He was playing it cool, even now, a year since I'd ended things with him. It grazed my pride to be the one to contact him after months of asking him to stop calling, but this was the new me with a strength of character and a firm sense of purpose and resolve.

'Hey, it's me,' I said sheepishly.

'Who's this?' His voice, so preppy and formal, the plumb sounding more pronounced after the country drawl I'd heard all weekend.

Regret unfurled instantly. 'Don't make out you don't have my name in your contacts, Gray.'

'You're right. I'm playing with you. But one day, Charlotte Hill, I'll get over you and delete you from my phone.' *I can only dream.* 'Let me guess, you're drunk and have run out of money and need a lift home?' My girlfriends insisted on giving me grief about 'finding Mr Right' when I started going out with Grayson Wright, but from my perspective, it was more a case of him always having to be right. He usually was, except when it came to me. 'Need a reference letter to get into a university course even though you'll never actually attend the course?' he said, so smug, so loving this chance to one-up me.

I rolled my eyes, then returned to glance at Otto inside, watching TV on the bed with his socks on his hands like puppets. 'No, none of those, in fact.' I could see him, probably still at work despite it being after 7, tilting on his executive leather chair in his chrome and glass-walled office overlooking Lake Burley Griffin.

'You've finally put down roots and want custody of Howard?'

The sound of our dog's name sucked me back to a time when we were one entity and I was hit by memories of our golden retriever's big brown eyes, the way he would grab the closest smelliest thing to bring me every time I entered a room. When the dog did it, it was endearing. The problem was, Grayson had been the same – always out to impress me, but with objects I didn't want or need. He'd named my (ex) dog after his favourite prime minister, which, having had distance from him, now seemed way too nerdy for my liking.

'I do miss Howard, but I still only have a flat.' And I barely slept in that.

'Okay, then the only reason left for you to initiate contact is to ask for a divorce.'

Inwardly cringing, I swore under my breath. I knew this would come up and yet decisive me rang anyway. 'Well, I'd like one if you're offering, but that requires money I don't have.' Not since I'd told my dad I didn't want his financial support, which in hindsight was rather impulsive and put me off making grown-up decisions even more.

'Why would I offer something I don't want?' Grayson asked.

Why stay married to someone who doesn't want you? I ploughed on, regardless. 'I'm calling for a favour, Gray.'

I could hear him smile, satisfied with my need to grovel. 'What's wrong, Lott?'

I was happy to be called Lotti – Charlotte sounded way too upper middle-class for my liking – but I realised I hated him calling me Lott. It was as if Grayson thought the more intimate your relationship, the shorter the nickname. Sometimes in bed he'd just called me 'L', which I found weirdly distracting. It was as if he were mid-sneeze, and I was waiting for the rest to follow.

'It's about a parent at school. I was hoping your research team could give me a heads up for any red flags, if you know what I mean?'

He rattled off all the reasons why that sort of snooping was illegal, how difficult it could be for him, and that processes needed to be followed, like he usually did, then moved on to more direct insults along the lines of why he should put himself out when I didn't even return his calls and didn't I get the message we weren't together anymore, but then ended with a reluctant, 'What's his name?'

'August Silverfell.' Somehow even saying his name to Grayson felt like betrayal.

Grayson asked what else I knew about the 'suspect' and I told him, which was rather little. Tapping on his keyboard, he must have been contacting one of the police officers who owed him one.

'Nothing. Not even an unpaid parking fine.'

'What about August Nash?'

More tapping, humming in that way I hated; the way he used to hum to signal he was in the loo. 'Yeah, this guy's got form. Says here, charged with arson in the eighties. Some other smaller stuff.'

Arson? I inhaled sharply and covered it with a yawn as if I had been growing impatient. 'Are you sure? That doesn't fit.' Those who destroyed public property on purpose, not to mention risking lives, were down there with fraudsters and bank robbers.

'Does he have all his fingers?' Grayson asked. 'Pyros – they're fucking nutters. Get off on the smell of lighter fluid and matches. Don't tell me he burned a kid, did he?'

I cringed at the thought. 'Nothing like that.'

'I've got another one with a few assault priors – but wait, that guy's sixty-five.'

Grayson seemed desperate to continue the conversation, but I was just as keen to end it.

'I don't think that's our man either, but thank you.' Ending the call before he wanted to rehash our relationship for the fiftieth time, I should have felt proud at my new decisive self, but my soul felt dirty. I still had no pivotal info that made any sense and had called in a favour I didn't really want to reciprocate.

Frustration ached in my shoulders. I sat with my iPhone in my palm, indecisive. A moment later, the handset buzzed into a wave of vibrations, and I almost peed myself. *Dad* flashed on the screen. 'Did bloody Grayson call you?'

'Hello to you, too, Charlotte. No, why would he? Do you have good news for me about a reconciliation?'

I screwed my nose up at the thought. 'Is Mum okay?'

'Yep, yep. I know it's late, sorry, just asking a favour and I've got back-to-backs tomorrow. It's *The Age*, they want to arrange a photoshoot. You've seen the latest Morgan gallup? They're after a family shot and interview this week. We can arrange it after class if that's a drama. Maybe Thursday?'

'I'm away, actually, Dad.' I should have left it at that. A firm no. That's what someone with 'balls' did. Someone with *agency*. But then I added, 'But I'll try to get home by then if it's important.' For the millionth time I wished I'd had a sibling to share the burden of expectation.

'That's my princess. You up the coast seeing Jessie?'

'Out west, actually – seeing August's family.'

'Thought he was an orphan? Or was that just spin so we didn't have to meet them.'

'Extended family.' That's all he needed to know. I'm a grown woman. He's not my keeper. But then the sense of obligation kicked in, the need to do what was asked of me. 'Yep – Eldham, Central Queensland.'

Otto had stopped jumping on the bed and was looking a little sleepy. I knew how he felt. My brain needed recharging, too.

'Why does that town sound familiar?'

'Not sure, Dad, just a little old mining town.'

'Wait – is that where there was some protest about the safety of developing over disused mines?'

'Ah, yeah. I did hear about that.' Did he have a finger in every pie in the country? He was thousands of kilometres from this dust bowl. 'Dad – doesn't Sandra organise your publicity? How come you're ringing me yourself?'

'Do I have to explain that?' he asked.

'Guess not.' Sandra was Dad's PA. Sandra was also sleeping with him, and I may have mentioned that a little rudely last time she called to arrange something. That was the beginning of another attempt to bring out decisive, assertive Lotti. 'And Mum's okay?' The subject change was entirely intentional, reminding me that passive aggressive was my natural style.

'Same. I've looked at a few homes, kid. Just planning …'

I huffed. 'Mum would rather die.'

'Just planning. And with you impulsively moving interstate, I don't have too many options.' His subject change was entirely intentional, too.

I wanted to say, 'Quit your stupid job and look after her, spend a couple of years doing what she did for us for decades.' But the conditioning kicked in and I held that thought, swallowed it down, leaving an awkward silence for a beat.

'You don't seem yourself, shortbread. And why would Gray be calling me?'

'No reason, I just called him for something.'

'You called him?' His voice went all singsong, and it reminded me of the fun dad he once was, pre-politics. 'Have you woken up next to a dead guy or something you need me to make disappear?'

'Not today, Dad.'

'Well, goes without saying, Charlotte – but the election's called so you know the drill. I'd prefer not to see photos of you snorting coke at a nightclub or sucking shots off some footballer's abs – nothing but good vibes for the next six weeks, okay, Char?'

I rolled my eyes. *Does the same go for you, Dad?* 'No drunken orgies. Check.'

'Use your head. Sunday-best behaviour and we might just have this one in the bag.'

He told me he loved me and hung up to finesse his next constituent.

I spent the next while lazing on the awful bedspread, gazing up, trying not to think too hard about the stains on the ceiling tiles and how they came to be. I wondered what name to give this untethered loneliness and settled on 'lost'.

Otto had succumbed to sleep on top of the covers, fully clothed. I took off his shoes, placed them together in their pair by the door with mine like we did outside the bus at home, but there were no steel cap boots in the line-up. A lump formed in my throat that wouldn't budge.

Perching on the bed, I stroked the edge of my phone, willing it to comply. Augie was still offline with no new location data added, no hint of where to go next. Of course, I called him anyway, just to hear his gruff voice message. Just to remind myself who he was. I listened twice, wanting to grasp the thread connecting me with the man who somehow made me love him when others had tried and failed. The familiarity of his husky, perpetually frustrated tone made my eyes mist.

I pulled the bedspread off the twin bed beside the one Otto was sleeping in, draped it over him. The springs argued as I slid the nearly naked bed closer to Otto's, pulled the plasticky sheet over my tired limbs, and sunk into oblivion.

When I woke, the world was shaking. Startled, fearing earthquake tremors, I sat up. 'What the?' As the bed sank and rose in a rhythm, I realised a bright yellow glow framed the windows, despite it only feeling like a second ago that I drifted off last night.

'Good morning, Miss Hill.' Otto said, swinging his arms up and down with each jump, his long hair lagging a second behind the bounce of the two tiny feet, pummelling my mattress.

'Why the jumping, dude?' I sank my cheek back onto the scratchy pillow. Extending my sleep-in was futile. Without sitting up, I grabbed my phone from beside the bed, desperate for a message to have landed overnight. My heart sank when the screen was blank. My thumb hovered over Augie's number to call him again, as pathetic as that felt. *No one would know.* I pressed redial, expecting it to cut again to the message, to hear that voice again. Then my heart skipped. It rang. *Oh, thank God.* I bolted up in bed. My relief was short-lived as the familiar message bank cut in. 'Ahhh!' I let out an animal cry, the phone dropping to my lap.

Otto didn't flinch.

It hit me – switched on meant locatable. I checked my app – a pulsing red beacon on the corner of Spring and Main in the middle of Eldham not ten kilometres from our brown hotel room.

'Gotcha.'

But my breath caught when I saw where he was.

Augie was deep inside Eldham Police Station.

Chapter 8

AUGIE, 1989 – Brightside

It was about a half hour's ride to the swimming hole, even less if you were used to hard yakka pedalling in the heat, like we were. The Ruffles packet crinkled inside my FM104 backpack with the broken zip the whole ride, and I was glad it and the Orchy bottle didn't fall out on the way there. My blotchy face had a thin sheen of sweat by the time Brookes and I pulled our BMXs under the patchy shade of the gums.

The lake wasn't exactly tourist-worthy. It was the colour of dirty dishwater, except when the algae got going and it took on a pink hue. Unless we'd had heaps of rain, the beach was more mud than sand, but it was fun to swing from ropes into the depths, and float on rafts made of old crates and off-cuts we nicked from abandoned building sites around town. It was wet, and had a certain charm in the moonlight – if you squinted at the water, it could pass for blue.

There were a few permanent vans of local fishermen who puttered dinghies around the inlets sometimes, a few bushwalkers who fossicked for rare orchids and birdlife in the wet season. Other than those blow-ins, no one bothered with the lake. And even we didn't go near the east bank – they reckoned the old mine shafts still had enough explosives to blow you to a zillion bits.

We stripped off, floated, enjoyed the silence beneath the waterline. No coppers on our case, no teachers nagging for homework, no Margo asking me to mow the lawn. It was bliss. Me and Brookes spent the afternoon climbing trees and bomb diving from the branches until our legs were jelly and our feet were raw.

There was movement on the shore near the cottages squatting on the dodgy side. I squinted to the distance. 'Is that the girls?' I asked when Brookes came up for air. We were sixteen, our sisters almost fifteen. I still reckoned they'd piked on us. Too fucking hot, and by the time you rode home you were a stinky sweaty mess and needed another swim.

Brightside had shut down a few months back at the end of '88 and no one had set foot there since. No one except broke bored teens looking to hang out without their olds breathing down their necks. Margo didn't say why it closed, exactly. She had her finger in every pie in Eldham but waved her hands and said it was 'politics'. I figured it was 'cause the do-gooders ran outta money. Suited me in any case.

Brookes and I splashed about in wet ruggers. Mine were hand-me-downs from the church, with coloured hems and the elastic so loose I had to pull them up every five seconds to avoid flashing bum crack. I was midair, swinging from a rope with a driftwood footrest tied to the base when I heard a wolf-whistle before I landed in the depths of the lake.

Two girls approached the bank. Neither were my sister. We got out, feeling their eyes, hearing their giggles as we milked wet hair with our fingers, slimy strings of weed stuck to our bare chests. I smiled when her face came into view. Becca had Cindy Lauper plaits, that hot pink mesh singlet she loved from the Op Shop, and tiny white shorts. She stood all shy behind her loudmouth friend – the 'spare'. Brookes and I joined them on the bank.

'No Frey?'

Becca screwed up her nose. We both knew the answer, and the reason. 'Said she'd peopled enough today.' Becca smiled, tightened a fluro scrunchie. My sister rarely made it to the dam. Too many questions about why she wasn't swimming, taunts of how she should just strip off, get in, which horrified her to her padded bones.

So, instead, we had Stephanie Lawley. Stuck-up Steph had her arms permanently folded, that same neon pouf dress with shoulder pads and a wide belt like something out of Dynasty. She was some kinda exchange student from California, reckoned she had been in a real movie. Up herself, anyway. I was less excited about a day that had her in it. I didn't get Steph – calling Brookes the village idiot one minute, then flirting with him the next. Besides, Becca was always quieter when Steph was there as if it wasn't worth competing with.

Becca perched on a boulder and dipped her toes in for cool relief. Suddenly tongue tied, and self-conscious, it took me a few seconds to realise Steph was talking – carrying on about the Blue Light disco last week and how they didn't even play any George Michael. 'Where were you, Gus?' Steph asked, poking me with her elbow. 'Like to see you breakdance.'

I hadn't gone to the disco, not after how the one before had ended, but Steph wasn't around then. 'Didn't want to miss "Red Faces",' I smiled. Plucka Duck on *Hey Hey It's Saturday* made me smile, which was something.

'And get this,' Steph went on, turning to Becca, 'I caught your loser cousin behind the PCYC dunnies, sucking face with Kirsten Bush – beard rash all over her chin from the creepy Harris.'

'Which Harris?' Becca asked. 'They're all creeps.'

'Does it matter?' I added. 'All dipshits.' There were four of the louts – Joel, Troy, Brad and Sean, all equally loutish. The

Harris family owned the pub and half the town so you couldn't say a bad word about 'em or you'd find yourself without a watering hole or a roof over your head. The four teens were pretty boys, captains of the footy teams and got away with shoplifting, drink driving, you name it. No one with half a brain said anything to their faces. The older one had gotten into local politics, which had only tightened the family's grip on the town, not to mention their drug trade.

We spent a good hour swimming, and getting hot again, lazing on our towels as the sun crept below the hills, talking shit. The shade from the gums stretched across the lake's surface, patching the edges like a picture frame, and the cicadas chirped to signal night was falling.

A flash of something over on the bank. I wasn't sure if I was seeing things.

Steph stopped talking. 'What was that?'

Everyone's head turned, curious.

'I've heard this place is haunted,' said Steph.

'Bullshit,' Brookes said, but he looked like he wasn't sure of that.

'One of my friends reckons it is,' Steph said. 'Some priest guy drowned here but his spirit won't leave, sees his ghost kayaking on the lake.'

Brookes was all ears. 'You mean one of the brothers?'

Steph shrugged. 'Some dude that looked after some school for delinquents?'

'You mean Jock-itch? He camped out at Brightside when it first closed but he's long gone now,' I said.

'Jock-itch?' Steph asked. 'Is that his name?'

Brookes explained with a smile. 'We put itching powder in his jocks, and he couldn't walk for days.' He grabbed a smoke from his hessian bag and lit it up, along with a whole lot of memories.

'Wait – you guys used to go there?' Steph asked. 'Like, for reals?'

'It was just a boarding school. No biggie,' Becca added.

'His real name's Brother John,' Brookes said.

'Yeah, that's the guy!' Steph said. 'He's, like, camping out, haunting the place.'

I rolled my eyes and smiled at Becca. As for me, ghosts were in the same category as God. Even though I'd tried, I couldn't find it in me to believe they existed.

'Don't you have to be dead to haunt stuff?' Becca asked with a furrowed brow. ''Cause I heard someone pray for him at Mass. Mrs Mac said he piddled all over the floor of her fish and chip shop not long ago, all grubby like he's a hobo.'

'Maybe, what did you call him – Scratchy-shorts? Maybe he's just a vagrant now, drinking himself to death where he last had purpose.' Steph delivered the words the way a newsreader shared a headline.

Brookes' eyes danced. 'Yeah, that sounds about right – he thought he was king shit there. That guy's got no conscious.'

'Conscience,' I said. I didn't make a habit of correcting him, but sometimes I couldn't help it. I blamed having a librarian for a mum.

'Huh?'

'Nothin'.' I shrugged, not sure why I said anything when Brookes was already antsy. Maybe I was, too.

'Always was a drunk, stupid prick. I'd fucking take him if I saw him in the street, you know.' Brookes talked tough but he was a bunny rabbit, crying himself to sleep half the time over some of the bad shit that went down at Brightside. I'd never asked for details, but he was there longer than me. Friday-night biff-ups – where we'd get bashed by the older boys until the director waved his hand to stop – were a rite of passage in that joint. A bit like the showers with no doors that were 'getting installed soon'. We were so naïve, thinking the cottage mums – who were nicer than the brothers – would tell someone who cared, but nothing ever changed. And if we did jack up, at best we'd lose our 'privilege' smokes, at worst we'd get chased with the cow prodder. Any attempts to bitch about how rough they got just strengthened the wall of silence growing around the place.

'Let's go, find the fucker,' Brookes said, standing knee deep in the shallows and splashing me in the face. 'Smash up his shit and piss on his pillow. C'mon, it'll be fun.' The way he said 'fun' didn't sound like he meant it. He was trying to hide the fact that he was worked up.

'Nah,' I said. 'It's probably all locked up and he'll be long gone by now.'

Brookes ignored my protests, grabbed his knapsack and was egging on the girls.

'C'mon, ya pussies, let's go check it out!' His voice was jittery, his feet fast and lacking coordination, like his cerebellum had failed to engage.

'Brookes – this is dumb, Mum'll crack it if you get in any more trouble – let's just get some chips,' Becca said, her jaw tight.

'Nah, c'mon! Let's wreck him!' He flicked me between the eyes, which always made them sting and I always pretended it didn't. Before I could build on all the reasons why it was a bad idea, he set off down the path to the west bank in a rush of shivering bushes and catcalls.

'Becks, let's get this party started!' Steph said, gathering her stuff.

'We don't have to,' Becca said to me, knowing I hated the place.

'C'mon, it'll be fun!' Steph elbowed Becca. 'We can, like, make a fire, and drink this!' Steph grinned and retrieved a bottle of bourbon from her crescent-shaped leather bag. It was clear Steph and Brookes wanted the story of sneaking into the old place. 'You guys are always so boring. I've only got another few weeks here, you know, before I go back to the States. We can have a bonfire like we do back home,' Steph said, pulling her friend up off the rock and grabbing her bag.

Becca and I watched the other two skipping and skylarking through the scrub, giggling along the path like besties.

'I thought those two hated each other,' I said.

Becca shrugged. 'You know we can't leave the kids without supervision.' She smiled, and her eyes went all crinkly in that way that blocked every synapse in my brain. I grabbed my towel, which had been flapping from a tree branch above the shallows. Becca and I took one bike each, and followed the numpties to Brightside. My brain felt like it had never left the place, so what would it matter? It was just weatherboards and corrugated iron. It couldn't hurt me.

Turned out it did.

Going back – that was our first mistake.

Chapter 9

LOTTI

With the phone beside me, sliding along the passenger seat with every turn, I kept glancing at the screen to make sure the location marker didn't move as we approached. It didn't. Wherever August was, he was staying put. I couldn't say the same for his son, who was dragged into town before he'd even had breakfast, having been bribed with chocolate to comply with my impromptu plan. Strangely, he thought I was awesome. I was starting to get this parenting thing.

My unease grew as I approached the location and set eyes on a tidy, red-brick building with white window frames, a chain-wire fence and a glowing blue light. It was the only building for a hundred metres, so there was no mistake. August must be inside. My stomach flipped. I hoped he was just in the drunk tank overnight, and we could put all this mystery behind us and go home. Or perhaps Brookes had gotten himself into legal trouble. Was that why he'd called August? To bail him out?

'Are we lost?' Otto asked from the back. 'Mummy always said to go to the police if I was lost.'

I smiled in a way I hoped was convincing while scanning the street for August's truck. 'That's a really good tip. We just need to go in and ask for directions to the place with the best pancakes – we won't be long.'

I parked and got out, and Otto unclicked his seatbelt and followed. He held my hand as I pushed open the heavy front door and approached the policewoman with a pixie cut and lots of keys on her belt, gazing at a boxy old computer screen.

'Can I help you, honey?'

'Hello, I'm looking for August Nash. Is he here?'

One of her eyebrows rose. 'One sec.'

Otto began balancing along an invisible tightrope, toe to heel, across the floorboards of the old building. I hoped this would entertain him for as long as it took to work out what was going on.

A cop that looked more like a cowboy approached, introduced himself as Detective Troy Harris and asked who we were.

'I'm Charlotte Hill. I'm a friend of August Nash.' The name hurt to say but something inside made me keep the one I knew him by all to myself for now. 'Is August okay? Has something happened?' My voice failed to hide my concern and I was glad Otto couldn't detect my tone.

The detective looked sideways at the desk clerk, who now raised both eyebrows – clearly, they weren't fans of my boyfriend – then took another look at Otto.

'He's fine, Ms Hill. Mr Nash is just helping us with our enquiries.'

'Enquiries? Regarding what? Is Brookes in trouble?'

Detective Harris smiled as if this were amusing. 'You know Brookes?'

'No. But that's why August's in town.'

'Is that right?' The cowboy cop looked at the keyed-up receptionist with another smile, but it lacked warmth and made me feel as if I'd provided a missing part of a jigsaw they'd been scouring the house for. 'This your first time in Eldham, Miss?'

I frowned, feeling small. 'How is that relevant?'

They gestured for us to wait and moments later the receptionist directed us through to a poorly lit side room with an old brown table, two plastic chairs and a box of tatty toys in the corner. Otto immediately gravitated towards a one-legged Spiderman figurine and crept him up the wall while making loud zipping noises.

Detective Harris returned with a notebook. 'Cute kid.' He then suggested Otto and his Spiderman play outside in the entrance area. 'Sharon will keep an eye on you there while I speak to Mummy for a sec.'

'That's not Mummy. That's Miss Hill,' he said, having read his lips to perfection. The policeman would have no idea he was deaf.

I was a little unsure, but decided having a police officer as a babysitter was probably safe.

The detective sat at the desk across from me before digging in deeper about the nature of my relationship with Augie, when I saw him last, what the nature of his business in Eldham was. 'And the reason you're here, Charlotte?'

'It's been three days and he hasn't called.'

The long stare he returned told me he thought I was an insecure stage-five cling-on and this concern was not a police matter. 'And that's unusual?'

I wanted to say no, but lying to a cop didn't seem wise. 'He wouldn't leave his son without making contact.'

'And he placed Otto in your care to visit Brookes?'

'Yes.' It didn't take long to share the broad strokes of what I knew.

'And you usually look for lost boyfriends at police stations?'

I thought about the phone tracking data. About the shallow grave. About his secrecy regarding his past and chose not to answer why I knew he was here. The good citizen that I'd always been, the responsible daughter, the people pleaser who had no reason to lie to a police officer was another version of Lotti. A paper-thin version. The new Lotti followed her gut and looked out for herself. 'Aren't police meant to help with missing persons? And you've said he is here. Can we just see him?'

'Believe me, we all want to resolve this. We're not used to this kinda thing around here. But your friend was kept overnight and is still helping us with our enquiries, Miss Hill.'

'He's been here all night? Surely I have a right to know what this is about. How long do you expect to be questioning him?'

'That depends on him.'

I shook my head. 'I can't even speak to him for, like, a second?'

He didn't speak.

'Is Brookes under arrest? I mean, do I need to get a lawyer or something?' I laughed as I said it, but he didn't, which cemented the nerves.

A flutter in my chest. 'Augie?' I called down the hall.

Detective Harris was not pleased, and guided me to the door. 'I'll just call you at Margo's, hey? Assume you'll stay there until he gets home.'

How far did I push this? I was caught between quiet compliance and a fierce loyalty I hadn't expected, towards a man I barely knew. I had no clue if making a fuss would help or hinder Augie's predicament, so I backed down, and nodded as if I knew that, to August, Margo was home.

'Did the police lady tell you where to go next?' Otto asked as I strapped him in the back of the car.

'Yeah, kiddo, she kinda did.'

Margo. Whatever situation was unfolding, she was the only link I had to the August I knew. And weren't all answers found in the past? Now that I had proof that there was something going on more sinister than a bloke's night out that had taken a day to shake off, I had to make use of the tufts of info greasy Henry had spilled at the diner.

Thomson Road, Henry had said. I found it easily enough but it was hard to decipher which 'eyesore' belonged to the elusive Margo. Self-doubts crept in – I didn't have the energy to canvas every house on the street. I wouldn't even know her if I saw her.

Driving the length of the road, the blocks widened in size, and peeking through the gap between the brick-box dwellings I could see the dry salty hollow of the dam. Was this empty brown basin the lake Henry had mentioned? The last house in the dead end was a paint-flaking old Queenslander on stumps, with nods to a lost elegance; a grand stairway, sweeping verandah and rust-red corrugated iron roof. The front yard was a circle of bare lawn and had a 42-gallon-drum makeshift bonfire as its centrepiece, and was flanked by dug-up gardens and a chocolate-brown dog lazing on a half-chewed recliner. Chunks of foam upholstery scattered the yard like snow. Hadn't the guy mentioned stray dogs?

'Is Daddy here?' Otto asked, his sweet face hopeful. 'He is the only one that puts chocolate chips in pancakes.'

I turned to the back seat. 'Have you been here before?' I asked.

He shrugged, his brown fringe falling over his eyes.

An open window upstairs. A car in the drive.

I signed to stay in the car, adding a grumpy face for effect, and powered down the windows so he could get fresh air. Walking along the cracked path to the door, a curtain billowed, then sharply pulled closed, a chorus of barking began, and a figure moved across the pink and green toned textured-glass window next to the entry.

'Hello?'

A muffled call from inside the large old house. 'I have nothing to say, bloody vultures!' It was the same weathered voice from the phone.

'Margo? I'm not from the media.' I was about to say I was Augie's girlfriend but had a fleeting concern that there may be more than one of those. 'My name is Lotti. I was just down the police station this morning. I don't want any trouble. I'm just a bit … lost.'

The curtain pulled across again and a slight, older woman with curly salt-and-pepper hair peered out. Her eyes focused on the street, to my Volvo, which was dusty now but still out of place in this breadline suburb of utes and old bombs. 'Yeah, that's just the kind of thing the media would say.'

I hadn't been sure what to expect, but her paranoia assured me she knew something.

A soggy tennis ball hit the weatherboards with a splat before rolling directly to the sleepy dog in the yard. Otto had escaped the car and was playing fetch with the fat old greying lab in the sunshine, grinning like they were old mates. I signalled for him to go back to the car with a grimace and firm pointing gesture, but he looked away on purpose.

The door opened. I took in the rest of Margo. She was older than I first estimated, the colourful overalls she wore you'd expect on a middle-aged hipster artist in Byron Bay, not a sixty-something woman in a remote town. She was stick-thin and her hands seemed to be covered in a thin coat of dried clay residue. Her eyes met mine, before I was upstaged by the kid.

'Otto?' Her gaze fixed on the scruffy six-year-old running up the stairs behind me, and her eyes brightened. Her mouth softened and relaxed into a smile. 'Otto-man!' Margo's arms extended wide as she bent a little to assume six-year-old height. 'You remember me, love?'

He looked unsure, but was taken in by her warmth and a long bear hug ensued.

'Look at you, it's been too long, petal.' There were tears of relief in her eyes, a sudden contrast to her demeanour. Margo's hand reached her mouth, concerned as she scanned the street. 'Is Gussy with you?' Her gaze reminded me of the headmistress at school. Deadly. 'I don't know who you are, but you shouldn't have brought him here.' Her lips were tight.

Why, is there a warrant out for his arrest, too? I heard cowboy music in my ears, pictured Augie and Otto holding up a saloon with Nerf guns. But I was slowly realising this was no joke.

She waved Otto across the threshold like a lollypop lady. The smelly dog ran inside and Otto followed before I could stop him. 'Just him,' she said behind the door. 'Not you. Not yet.' The deadbolt clicked into place with a terrifying jerk.

I shook the knob. I banged the door. I was about to run down the stairs in search of another entry when I heard them moving around inside and my throat tightened. I could hear her singsong voice, and was that a biscuit tin being raided? Was he asking for pancakes?

'What are you doing!?' I was crying. 'Otto!' Was this why August left Otto with me and didn't want him here? *What have I done?*

Another glare through the window, but less cutting this time. The door unlatched and her face appeared at the opening.

I considered pushing through to rescue Otto, but I could see him playing happily behind her.

'Who the bloody hell are you and why do you have our boy?' Margo was small, I could have almost picked her up and carried her like a surfboard in the crook of my arm, but she was fierce. I had no doubt she could gouge out my eyes with those twig-thin arms if she felt the need.

'Who the hell are *you*? You just kidnapped my student!'

'Student?'

'My name is Charlotte Hill and I'm his primary school teacher,' I said, palms up as though appeasing a senior at school with an army knife and an anger management issue 'August left him with me to look after.'

'Why? Where is he?' Her chin wobbled. 'Is Gus dead?'

'No, nothing like that.'

Her nose turned up, and she shot her hand up to hide the morning glare from her eyes, gave me the once-over. 'Why should I believe a word you say?'

I pulled my phone from my jeans pocket, flicked to the camera; there were only a few images of Augie and I – we'd only recently got to the stage of taking candid photos together without it feeling weird. But it was proof enough.

Her hand to her mouth again, her face fell. 'He never returned my calls. He changed his name. I thought he was dead.' When she'd gathered her composure, she opened the door wide and let me in. I raced through the house, panicked, scanning each room flanking each side of a long hallway for the kid before hearing his giggle outside. I watched him out the kitchen window. He skipped through patchy grass, reached to turn a leaning Hills Hoist and several more large, goofy dogs that flocked to sniff him.

I raced down the few back steps, checked him over, hugged him close, his face squashing into mine.

'Too hard!' he complained.

'We need to go,' I signed, wanting to drag him back to the car, keep him safe. For all I knew, this old bat had a child-trafficking syndicate operating from her garage.

He shook his head, pulling free, then skipped back to the dogs.

Margo watched us from the top steps. She screwed one eye shut and exhaled. 'Enough with the hysterics, he's fine. C'mon, Charlotte Hill, let's have a cuppa, clear the air.'

I shook my head. She was my only pathway to answers. I followed her back inside, leaving Otto in my eyeline.

She hesitated, leaned on the rustic kitchen counter. 'Sorry for the drama. Just have to be careful – should be fine as long as people don't put two and two together with the boy and get four, you know?'

I pretended I knew what that meant with a nod. 'Do you know why August's being questioned?'

'He's in town?'

I nodded and her brows furrowed. She filled the kettle and flicked it on.

'Well, it could be one of many things with that man. Don't tell me. Did Harris get him?'

'Detective Harris, yes.'

'Bastards, all four of 'em. If I had a dollar for every black eye Augie got from one of those toads.' Margo made tea, glancing sideways to subtly size me up. The original kitchen was grand and clean, with a long farmhouse table in the centre, framed by walls of cupboards and benchtops.

I couldn't take my eyes off Otto, scurrying around outside, half expecting him to be stolen before my eyes. But he was comfortable here. Was this his maternal grandmother's house? I needed to stay to find out.

I pulled out an upholstered orange chair from an eclectic mix of choices and sat tucked beneath a long timber dining table. She was obviously no stranger to welcoming visitors to her kitchen. Or dogs to her yard. One of those square, steel electric frypans sat on the orange laminate bench, stacked with egg rings as if waiting for a mob to feed. There was a whiteboard, too, with errands and appointment times listed. Every spare surface, from the fridge to the faded wallpaper, was covered with a cluster of mismatched photos featuring at least a dozen different children of various ages and stages, some I recognised as faded Polaroid snaps from back when that was the only way to make a selfie you didn't have to wait a week to see.

We did not speak until she'd sat in the chair directly in front of me and had taken her first sip. She seemed a kind woman who evidently held Otto close to her heart. 'You're the boy's teacher? Or are you with my Gus? Which is it?'

'Well, both. Augie … Gus and I are … in a relationship. Otto's just how we met.' I left out the detail that I had been stalking him for evidence of child neglect.

Over Delta Creams we did a dance, both unwilling to show our hand, but keen to stay in the round. I'd started with general facts. That I was from Brisbane. That I was looking for August Silverfell. That the cops had told me he was being questioned and that it somehow related to Brookes.

This woman was a contradiction. Thin and fragile in physique, with a weathered face, tanned leathery limbs and thinning bob, she also had a self-assurance in the way she spoke, in the way she unselfconsciously asked the questions, sugared the tea, stirred it in, that I respected. There were times she repeated questions she'd already asked, which were either senior moments or a tactic to check if my answers were consistent each time. In either case, this was a lady who knew her values and was loyal to them. A lot like Augie Silverfell.

'On the phone, you said August Nash. That's not the name I know him by,' I said.

The woman was hard to read. Her manner was warm, yet she had a caginess about her that made me wonder what she was guarding. She had a small tremor in her left hand. Was I making her nervous? Was Augie held up in a room somewhere, on the run?

'Not surprising, with everything.' Her mouth bent to one side as she opened a packet of Arnott's mixed creams and placed them gently into a biscuit tin. 'He needed a new one to get lost. He hated the lack of anonymity here. Small town, you know?'

I didn't, but I smiled anyway, a streak of unease in my stomach at why he felt the need to. Although hadn't that been why I moved to Brisbane? Was this all due to a romance that had gone wrong for him? I could hardly blame him for not disclosing that, given I hadn't.

'As for what's going on with August – you'd know more than I. Haven't seen him for two years. He never so much as sent a Christmas card to tell me he was still kicking. Now I know he is, the bugger's in even more trouble. Is he still pissed at me?' she asked in jest, but failed to hide the weight of the words. The importance of the answer. She kept glancing out at Otto under the floodlit back, now playing fetch with the dogs who were lapping up the attention like the fresh water from the bowls scattered all over the property.

'He never spoke about his past.'

'Sounds like Gus.' She smiled as she took a sip of black tea, her earrings – handmade ceramic swirls of black and white – spun a little with the movement. 'Why use three words when one will do.'

I smiled in recognition of the trait. 'I copied your number from his missed calls list before he disappeared.'

Her eyebrow rose almost undetectably. 'Trusting, aren't you?'

'No offence, but didn't you just lock a kid up in your house?' I said.

She laughed. 'Fair call, honey. Well, when you've fostered as many as me, you get finely tuned protective instincts. I'm still working out if they were off with you.'

I tried to smile. 'You don't know Brookes, then?'

'Cooked him a fry-up just the other day, love.'

I stared. 'He didn't mention August? That he was in trouble?'

'Brookes would never betray Gus, never says a word about him. As I said, I thought he was dead.'

'All I know is August said Brookes asked him to come back, and now I've discovered he's being held for questioning by the police.'

She nodded into her tea, guarded but still with a kindness in her silence as if she were placing pieces of a scene together in her mind. 'August was always looking out for poor old Brookesy – not the full quid, you know? But he's got a heart of gold, that one. Hope he's not back on the smack. He was a bit flighty the other morning, come to think of it.'

'Drugs? You think that's all it is?'

'All? Drugs are the devil's work, honey.'

August had never taken drugs with me. Never given a hint that he used anything other than beer. I was missing something. I rose to look closer at the faces in the old pictures, hoping they would provide answers. At first glance I thought it was Otto, stretched, but looking closer the boy had Augie's bushy eyebrows and strong forehead. A black T-shirt-clad adolescent Augie had a slightly younger girl's neck in a loose armlock, her long plait flicking out as she grinned at the camera. He had a wry smile and a glimmer in his eye, and I fought off the idea that the Augie Silverfell I knew was a mirage and this was the man I had to catch up to.

'Why did you think I was media?' I asked.

'They're the only people that ask about Gus. Everyone else around here knows.'

'Knows?'

She shook her head as if regretting saying anything. 'I'd like to help, truly, but Gus made it very clear that he didn't want me getting involved in his life.' It was like she was conflicted about letting me in – one minute interested in getting to know me, the next wary of saying too much.

'Can I just be honest here, Margo? I don't know everything about Augie, but I know enough to be sure that I care about what happens to him and Otto, and so do you. So maybe we can work together on this. I problem-solve a bunch of catastrophes every day for my Year 2 kids, and I've gotten pretty good at it.'

She waited, listened, without impatience or interruption, like an expert interrogator.

My eyes misted up, trying to articulate the ambiguity pooling in my brain these last few days, contemplating if, or how, I should get involved. 'He's been gone longer than he said, without calling, and I've tried to be calm about it, but the truth is I'm freaking out and don't even know where to start. And now the police …' I exhaled, relieved to blurt the truth after so much second-guessing.

'He doesn't know you've brought Otto here, does he?' Margo asked, although it didn't seem like a question requiring an answer. 'And he hasn't told you why he left his family?'

'His family? Is that you?' I sat back down. 'He told me he had no family.' *He told me I was his family now.*

Her reaction was instant, her face crumbling. She pressed her fingers, dotted with age spots, against her lips to hide the quiver rippling on her chin. I took her other hand in mine and squeezed. He'd told me his mother and father were dead but I wondered now if they were just 'dead' to him.

'You're his mother?'

'Gus and his sister lived with me for many years, but no, I'm not.' The loose skin of her neck wrinkled as she swallowed. 'I'm his aunt.' Otto's great aunt gazed outside at Otto playing in the gravelly backyard below – he was still as enthralled with the dogs as they seemed to be with him, running up and down a crumbly besser-brick retaining wall after a faded tennis ball. There was no boundary fence. The dogs were likely strays, just here of their own volition, free to roam and return for a feed from this kind soul. I wondered if she had the same relationship with the kids on the fridge. Was Brookes among them? Nieces and nephews? Foster children? Margo beamed with joy as she watched Otto, giggling as he scampered about. What happened to their mother that led to them living with this colourful, protective aunt? Is that why drugs were the devil's work?

'Can I see that camera again?' she asked.

'It's a phone, actually,' I said.

She baulked at the idea. She still had her guard up about me. I wanted to find out why and I wanted to connect, so I opened the pictures that had earned her trust and showed her how to flip between them. Her head tilted to the side as she savoured each image, as if the details I was revealing were satiating a thirst she'd ached to quench, just like the waterways in this town. It occurred to me for the first time that me being here, stirring the pot, may not be in August's best interest. Doubt crept in once more.

I let her study each one, adding context now and then. We chatted and sipped our tea, teaspoons tinkled on saucers as she commented on each picture. I scanned the remaining photos on the fridge – a patchwork of memories, a horde of kids, scraggly, all elbows and knees and pimply chins, but happy, and often with a dog sprawled by their side. Two, at least, were unmistakably Augie and, by the looks of it, the pictures were taken in this very house. I'd seen that expression before –when his brow formed a ledge in mock anger, but his eyes twinkled, and he couldn't stop the smile about to stretch over his lips. Those beautiful soft lips I'd spent hours grazing with my finger in the darkness, trying not to move suddenly so the vibrations didn't wake Otto in his bunk. An aching need rose inside that I didn't trust.

Now Margo made no attempt to sniffle back tears – they poured out in a torrent. 'It's so good just to see my precious Otto again. I haven't seen him since the funeral, not for the lack of trying.'

'Funeral?'

'For my darling Freya.'

'Oh, right – Otto's mum, of course.' I'd seen photos of Freya on the ceiling atop Otto's bunk in a cluster of glowing star stickers, and Otto had since told me she was looking down on him from heaven. She had a beautiful face, intelligent eyes that gazed adoringly at the bundle cradled in her arms. Margo looked up at her photo wall and pointed to the same beautiful young woman with deep-brown eyes that seemed eerily familiar.

'I've got a whole family album hidden away in here.' Margo walked over to a slatted hall cupboard and attempted to grab a box from a high shelf. I could tell no amount of stretching would allow her to reach it and went to help. 'Always wanted to be tall,' Margo said as I effortlessly retrieved a box of photo albums. 'The one I want is stuffed behind it – in that mango box.'

I brought that down too and returned to the table. Margo began flicking through an old spiral photo album with a waterfall on the front. The pages were yellowing, the film folded over and unstuck in places and they seemed to bring on a wave of nostalgia for Margo, her voice thick with emotion as she described who everyone was.

'August and his mum – my sister, Judith. Although she liked it better when people called her Jude, like the Beatles' song. She never believed me when I told her it was written about a little boy called Julian Lennon. Gus would have been about seven then. I remember Jude making him that shirt from a Butterick pattern I found at the church rummage sale.'

Messages such as 'my daughter's first tooth' or 'first bike' had been written beside the pictures with care. 'Things blew up in the end with all of us – August loved his mum fiercely, but they fought all the time (as teenagers were programmed to do), especially before she died. Made it even harder on him.'

A lump formed in my throat, thinking of him dealing with that grief, and how Otto had also suffered the same one.

'And who's the little girl?' I asked. 'She's so much like Otto in the eyes. Is that your daughter?' A sharp realisation – it was the same girl in the high-school shots, with a teenaged Augie grabbing her in a playful head lock, both wearing the same uniform. Were they childhood sweethearts?

'That's Freya. I never had my own kids.'

I frowned. Freya as in Otto's mum? Freya had Otto in her twenties, by the look of the photos, so if that were true, August and Freya's relationship must have spanned a decade. I often overheard him telling Otto things to keep his mum's memory alive – her talent on the guitar, how she won every trivia night and saw light in everyone. But he remained tight lipped whenever I asked about her. 'They look so close, her death must have been hard on him.'

Margo nodded. 'It was as if he'd let out a breath the day she died and never filled his lungs the same way again.'

'I didn't realise they knew each other so long ...'

Margo frowned. 'What? Gus knew Freya since the day she was born – as brothers do.' The woman's face changed. She slapped the old photo album closed. 'Which is information you would know if you'd met August for more than five minutes.'

'Brother?' A swirl of nausea lifted into my throat and my feet refused to move.

The woman stood, unsure of what to do about me, this stranger in her kitchen. 'Who are you really and why do you have Otto? Did that Harris toad send you? Is he in on this? You seem too switched on to be his type, but that has fooled me before.' She paced to her kitchen window and called to the yard. Her switch in mood was sudden and severe. 'Otto, love?'

Of course, he couldn't hear her.

'Freya – Otto's mother – is Augie's sister?' I choked on the words. 'But ... that's not possible, surely. Not if August is Otto's dad.'

Margo turned, a frown etched on her weathered face. 'Is that what he told you?'

Chapter 10

AUGIE, 2009

I guess it's pretty lame for your little sis to be your best mate, but I'm man enough to admit that Freya was mine. She was the only person who listened, who wasn't just waiting till you finished to blurt her two bob's worth like most people. She was the only person who didn't question me about things I did. When you came from a family like ours – shit-for-brains dad who left when things got hard, and a mum known as whack job to some, it was hard to find friends who could see past the kinks.

My sister was twenty-five– older than a lot of girls around here get up the duff – when she told me through a grin that she was pregnant. But I had my doubts it was a good thing. Freya was strong and wise and caring, but she was also fragile, like a quirky VW that was forever overheating. She had days when her self-loathing could eat away at her to the point she couldn't get out of bed. Other days, I was sure she could change the world with her smile. Was it fair to throw a baby into the mix of that? But, like every other bloody thing, she grabbed the chance by the horns and didn't let go. I could still picture her getting so upset at my doubt, bawling her eyes out, quilt tucked under her chin, spouting, 'You don't get it, Gussy, look at me!

Big girls don't always get to be mums. This is it. My *chance*, and I'm going to take it.'

Big girl. It was the only way I'd let her describe herself, physically. I still didn't like it – why was her size used like a car's make or model? But she couldn't separate who she was from her shape. We'd all tried to make her see that it didn't matter, but she always found a way to feel bad about herself. 'At least if I'm preggers I have a good reason to be fat,' she'd laughed, but the smile didn't hide the shame.

I just wished she'd picked a better dad for her kid – instead of the worst human on earth. The best thing he could do was stay out of all our lives, and the only way that could happen was by never telling him the kid existed. It was the one thing we all agreed on. Even Margo was pragmatic enough to see Freya raising the baby alone was the only way it had a chance.

Freya had never looked so beautiful, so alive as when she first held that squirming red bundle in her arms. The boy had her eyes, full of intelligence. Even before he was born, the seed of hope he gave sparked a sense of purpose in her – to leave town to escape the fuckknuckle father, and finally dive into the uni course she'd never had the confidence to try before.

Before she started to show, I moved her and her hippie stuff in my ute up the range to a granny flat in Toowoomba that was walking distance to the campus, bought a bed and a cot and some basics from the Salvos, got her settled in. The brainiac won a scholarship, tutored at night, and got her shit in a sock without Otto's dad pissing all over her life. I visited all I could, but it was hard with the garage starting up and no one I trusted to run it in my place.

Funny how the dramas you worry about never come true – it's always stuff you never would have predicted. Like the fact that she made herself irreplaceable to the little tyke, then left this world before his fourth birthday.

She'd just run into traffic, the witnesses said.

Three different accounts. All the same story. The cops had closed the case as a tragic accident, no foul play. Just like when Mum died, some locals put it down to suicide. That Freya was lonely since leaving her comfort zone in Eldham. Toowoomba wasn't big, but it was big enough to get lost in, and cliquey in a private-school kind of way. But I never bought it. She was happy there. She managed amazingly until Otto got sick. Hospital stays. Tests. It was a viral thing he never seemed to kick. Trying to study and look after a three-year-old whose hearing was slowly declining was a struggle, but I thought they'd found their stride.

It made no sense when the police called. It didn't make any more, now.

Her wake was the first day I'd been to Eldham since she'd escaped the place. I'd distanced myself from town ever since that day I left Becca at the treehouse. Margo and I had lost contact and with my sister up at uni, and Becca and Brookes both married off, there was no reason to visit Eldham. But there was something about funerals that made the small stuff harder to sweat.

The whole church lost it, seeing Otto clinging to his mother's coffin. I was a total fucking write-off, barely able to walk and talk at the same time. All the bullshit consolations – how she was 'an angel with God now' – made it hard to bear. Even the weather was a savage prick that day, the coffin slipping from our hands in the pissing-down rain. Two years on, there were days when Freya's death was as raw as a fresh gash, when the slightest breeze brushing my skin set off an ache I couldn't stem.

Alone with Margo, after the guests and the façade of coping was long gone, I was dreading what would happen next. Something had broken between us the day she left me at Brightside when I was fourteen, something I didn't know how to fix. I'd always been too cowardly to bring it up, but all that thinking about death had a way of brushing aside the bullshit.

Margo had cracked the Smirnoff before I'd loosened my tie, and we'd drunk half of it by nightfall – me in my boxers, her in her cheesecloth dress that billowed when the fan swung in her direction. We sprawled on that threadbare orange couch, the rough fabric forming chequered marks on my thighs, the dogs licking the sweat off my toes. We started with Frey's music, watching old VHS recordings of my little sister singing Bob Dylan tunes better than he did. By the time we'd moved on to 'American Pie', Margo was a blubbering mess, and to this day I can't hear 'the day the music died' without thinking of the agony in her eyes. No word exists to describe the depths of that pain.

After she'd let that wave of grief plough through her, Margo grew pensive. 'Do you think she'd have lived differently if she'd known she'd never make thirty-two?'

'Nup.' I stared into space, took another swig. In my mind she was ten again, flapping around in her plastic glitter shoes with a dumb Barbie doll in one hand and a popsicle in the other. She loved those cheap-arsed shoes, pleaded to get them even with only wrong sizes left. The straps made blisters that she covered with plasters. But Freya never complained, never took them off. 'She was always in the moment. Never took anything for granted.'

'Would you?' Margo had asked. 'I mean, if you knew you wouldn't live to say, fifty?'

'Fuck no. God, who'd waste breath thinking about when you run out of time? Figure at the rate Nashes have been falling off the perch before their time, I won't have to worry about sticking around long enough to get dementia.' Heat filled my head about some other unfinished business. Otto's dad. 'Glad the fuckknuckle wasn't crazy enough to set foot in that church yard. Has there been any word of the prick? Are you sure he has no clue about Otto?'

'How would he?' said Margo. 'The only people who know are you and me. She had no contact with him once she left town, as far as I know, and I certainly haven't.'

I shrugged. 'I dunno, people drive up there to drop kids at boarding schools, do a supply run – maybe someone saw her in T-Bar with a pram and joined the dots …'

Margo dismissed it. 'Even if they did, how would people even link them as a couple – it's not like they were openly courting.'

That was true. Freya regretted telling me how she scraped her leg once climbing the back fence behind the house her so-called 'boyfriend' shared – the bastard made her sneak out the back door after he'd had his way with her so his roommates never clued in. What sort of prick does that? I may have had a quiet word about that to him, down the pub, which put an end to their fling. I didn't regret it until I saw how sad losing him made her. Can't fucking win.

I scraped the stubble on my face. 'It's just too random. She wasn't drunk. She wasn't drugged, and neither was the driver. He didn't mount the footpath. It wasn't even fucking dark. How could she just step in front of a truck?' There was a shudder in my voice, unrecognisable to me. The head of the investigation called me personally to confirm there was no one with the name Harris driving the vehicle that hit her. I still had my doubts.

Margo was staring into space, probably picturing the same thing I'd imagined for days – Freya's last moments. 'You've always liked pointing fingers. But, love, sometimes there's no one to blame but the devil. You should come to Mass on Sunday – talk to Sid – he'll help you forgive—'

'No fucking chance.' I said the thing I'd been dreading but needed to get out. 'Is there a chance she did it … that she …' I swallowed hard, couldn't find the breath to say it.

'Gus, no. You saw how she was with Otto. She'd never do something that would make his life harder – not on purpose. She hated leaving him for a haircut.'

'Felt like Mum loved us too. Look how that ended.'

It *had* been twenty years. Now we were clearing the tanks on the truth, surely that was long enough to be honest about why Mum died. Margo had shut down any gossip at the time, dished out her infamous glare of steel so no one was game to even suggest her sister killed herself – back then or since.

'Wash your mouth out, young man. Don't you say that. Don't even think it.' She squeezed my hand hard in case her words weren't enough. 'Gus, your mother loved you more than anything. So did Freya.'

I held out my arms. 'Just not enough to stick around for me, huh?' *Some things are true whether you believe them or not.* 'Either way, we're fucking cursed, our lot. Every fucking one of us has died young either by their own hand or someone else's. Watch out, Margs, you'll be next – we haven't had a plane crash yet, maybe that'll be your end. Unless, of course, you quit on me too.' In a way, she'd done that already, when I was a gangly fourteen-year-old, and she signed that paper.

She grabbed my collar, her frail, bony hand pulling hard. 'It was an illness, Gussy. Your mum had no choice. She was sick.'

'Yeah, Freya wasn't …' I wish I'd protected her better from that bastard. I wished I'd moved to Toowoomba with her. I wish …

The heat in my head wouldn't let up. Being back here, seeing Brookes and Becca, who I knew I'd let down – I thought I was a bitter prick before, but this was a whole new level of pissed.

I'd lost touch with everyone, busy trying to get the garage afloat, the van liveable – I'd usually visit my sister during her exam weeks each term to give her some kid-free time to study. I thought it had been just a couple of months since I saw her and the boy, but it had stretched out to six with the Christmas break, which was a huge chunk of a kid's life when you were only three.

The first time I saw Otto at the funeral, the kid didn't recognise me. I'd wiped his arse a thousand times, knew every wrinkle on his chin, rocked him to sleep till I wore the varnish off the floorboards, and my nephew looked at me like I was some random. I guess grief does weird things to kids, too.

Freya was clear in her will that I was to have full custody of Otto. Not Margo. Not Becca. Me, a single bloke of questionable character and breeding. Maybe she wasn't as intuitive as I'd thought. She always did have an inflated view of me, saw the good in everyone, even the losers, but I guess I was the youngest family the kid had. The transition to become the primary caregiver of a ratty nearly four-year-old didn't go well, to say the least. He hated everyone. Wanted his mum.

The social worker had to supervise the 'exchange' the week after his mum died, which made me feel like a kidnapper. She said it was standard after a change of custody. I got it. In my eyes, the government didn't do enough to protect kids. Too busy protecting the trees or the ozone or the koalas – sure, they were good things to protect, but not as important as little kids.

Our chaperone, in her cheery clothes and sensible shoes, suggested our first intro take place in the park. It sounded relaxed, so I was up for it, not anticipating 'public' meant far more of an audience to Otto's absolute and utter rejection of me. Otto screamed the roof off the picnic shelter, which was kind of how I felt about the situation too, so I didn't hold that against him. I wasn't his mum and I'd never come close to being anywhere near as good as she was at this stuff. She was soft and smelled good and had wisps of biscuity blonde hair framing a round, warm face. I was a barrel-chested giant with stubble and cheap aftershave. She sang like an angel, could play anything on guitar – the only thing I could hold a tune on was a six-stroke engine.

He was almost four but made the noise of a terrible-two, carried on like a pork chop for about an hour – hid behind a tree making howling, guttural cries. That's the thing that struck me first – you'd expect deaf kids to be quiet but they're anything but. I kind of admired his complete uninhibited freedom to let loose, to be honest. I waited for him to burn some fuel before I crouched down near him under the shade of the leopard tree. His face was shiny with snot, but he still had her eyes – bright, alert, searching mine. *This kid is all that's left of that fucking legend of a human. I've gotta take care of him.*

I shrugged, unperturbed by his song and dance and, without much thought as I figured he couldn't hear me anyway, said, 'Just let it out, kid. I get it. She's gone and it's not fair. It's fucked up.'

Our chaperone flinched when I swore. That I expected, but Otto flinched too.

'He can lip-read, Mr Silverfell.'

I laughed. I'd been rattling on, assuming he couldn't hear a fucking word, which he couldn't (or only a few decibels in outer frequencies, Freya had said) but he'd outsmarted me. Gone and gotten himself a superpower. After a bad virus earlier that year, Otto started acting out, disobeyed, never listened and his learning flatlined. Frey thought it was just from missing so much kindy, or maybe he had attention issues, but the audiologist in Brisbane told us the virus caused sensorineural hearing loss. I was there when they said we could consider surgery to 'rectify' his impairment, but it would destroy any residual hearing he had left. 'Don't cochlear implants occasionally fail?' Freya had asked, eyes wet with tears. Determination marbled her voice as she'd declared there was nothing needing fixing, that Otto was perfect just the way he was.

And there he was, my kid. My kid, whether he liked it or not.

His carry on continued and I admired his commitment to the cause. 'Tenacious, aren't ya, hey?'

The normal-looking parents in the park still pretended they weren't curious about me, about my situation. About why my kid was blowing a gasket. They probably assumed I was a Sunday dad, just out of jail and reconnecting. I decided to take charge.

My car – I named her Jude – was too long for a normal car space, and I'd chosen, delinquent that I was, to rest her up the grassy patch beside the lot. Grabbing his suitcase from where the chaperone had parked it near her safety-yellow Magna, I chucked his bag in the tray of my ute. I ignored the booster seat next to it – the kid wasn't a baby.

I stood near my ute, opened the passenger door, and waited.

There was beautiful silence. The kid stilled, gazed over at Jude, and sniffed. She was the love of my life; fire-engine-red paint with a cream panel, reconditioned 460 V8 engine and a new gearbox. She even had a tape deck.

Otto flicked his fringe from his eyes, wiped his tears and approached the ute with caution. He checked out the red leather upholstery, the polished chrome wheel arches. I could tell he had good taste.

'She's a beauty, ain't she, mate? Wanna ride?' At least, that's what I thought I said. He looked at me like I was a basket case. I'd done a weekend course in Auslan at the local TAFE, but fuck knows if I understood any of it, making up stupid gestures when memory failed me.

So that's how me and Otto became an unlikely bachelor duo.

I'd have taken the boy on this trip if I'd had any choice. It took months to get him to sleep without her, longer to get him to trust I'd still be there in the morning, after she wasn't. I had never planned on leaving him, not even for a night. After losing his hearing and his mum, the last thing that kid needed was to find out his substitute dad was as shoddy as the one he never knew. But I reckoned that was what I was about to unleash.

Chapter 11

LOTTI

'If August isn't Otto's father, whose child have I just carted across the state?' Had he been taken from a Westfield? Ordered online?

Margo didn't answer. Was she going to make me work for this? My throat tightened. I glanced over at Otto, his small hands perched under his chin adorably as he watched a *Brum* repeat. 'Tell me this then – does the father know he exists?'

'I hope not.' Margo assessed me as if she were a detective. I must have passed the test as she spilled a crash course on August Nash and the life he had before changing his name to Silverfell, and about halfway through the synopsis she'd fed Otto some brunch before stepping up her drink from tea to whiskey. At 11am.

I said yes when she offered me a nip on the rocks, even though I hated the stuff about as much as I hated what she had to say. 'Is Otto's father dead?'

'I wish. Piece of work, that one. Still in town, hence my concern.' She took another sip, her hand unsteady. Had she started drinking before breakfast? Something was a little off with her. 'A bloke called Joel Harris – arguably the most toxic of the Harris brothers. I used to change his nappy, think that would have earned me some respect but that man doesn't know the meaning of the word. Never had to. His father unofficially runs the town.'

'Take it he's not the type to get involved then.'

'We didn't give the toad the chance – Freya was too switched on for that, choofed out of town before she was three months gone. That was never common knowledge so keep it to yourself, Charlotte Hill – we don't want no trouble concerning the lad, do we? And when she died, August adopted Otto like his little sister wanted – without hesitation.'

It still didn't excuse the fact he'd lied every day, in every interaction with that precious boy where I'd assumed they were father and son.

'I woulda taken the boy in second, but I was so happy he got to stay in the family, not that August has kept me in his life … He hated me for sending him to that home. Decided I'd given up on him – I hadn't. I thought it would heal him. I was wrong. I've never forgiven myself, but Gus was lost to me, after his mum died.'

'Lost to you?' August was a devout atheist and I wondered if that was part of their relationship breaking down.

'At first it was just lighting fires in the bath, but it got worse when he was fifteen. At the time I thought Brightside would find the good kid I saw inside, keep him on the straight and narrow, you know? I've seen God's light turn around so many lives.'

Brightside. The word jarred. 'He stopped there the other night before coming to town.'

'Says who?' Margo's eyes flared for a millisecond, but then looked away. 'Doesn't sound right. He hated it there. Resented everything about it – especially since I kept his sister, but chose to have him made a ward of the state. That was the kick in the guts. He felt I'd put him in the too-hard tray. I was single. I had no clue about raising an angry, grieving young man.'

A rumble of engine noise flooded the kitchen as a car stopped outside. I paced to the front windows and saw a woman about Augie's age in what looked like an all-black hospitality uniform, staring at my car in the drive with concern. The striking redhead unbuckled a toddler from a car seat and installed the child on her hip. She had a Cate Blanchett kind of elegance, and a sense of urgency as she climbed Margo's front stairs.

'Margs?' the woman called from the shaded verandah.

Margo opened the door to the woman, whose green eyes were framed under a furrowed brow, and tickled the toddler in her arms. 'Hello, Princess Ruby.' Margo melted at the sight of the little girl. 'Becca, love.'

So, this was the Becca Otto mentioned.

Margo's voice changed to one of panic. 'What's wrong?'

'My bloody brother again. He just called from the station when I was on the way to work. Troy's hauled him in for something. Had him there all day and night just to be a prick.'

'Sorry love, I just heard.' Margo said with disappointment. 'They came looking for him the other day. Drugs again?'

'Not this time,' Becca said, eyeing me off. 'Who's this?' Margo told her my name.

'Hi, sorry to hear about your brother,' I said, stepping forward.

'How do you know Brookes?'

'I don't...'

She frowned, as if waiting for further explanation on who the hell I was. When I didn't give it, she focused back on Margo. 'He said something about bones dug up at the new housing estate. Seemed shaken up about it.'

Bones? I gave up on hovering out of the way to appear polite and forced myself into their chat.

Margo's face paled. 'Nothing like that in the local rag. Probably cow skulls from the old dairy farm and they're just bullying the poor lad.'

'I dunno, Margs. Got me thinking about, you know who, how she disappeared in grade eleven all those years ago …'

Margo frowned. 'What are you saying, love? My brain's slowing down – it's the menopause. Who do you mean?'

Becca looked over at my sticky beak, hovering with interest, but continued. 'Stephanie Lawley – the exchange student? Blonde? Cheekbones?' Her eyes widened.

'Oh, course. The one with tickets on herself.' Margo frowned. 'That girl's still missing? If they thought it was her, wouldn't it be all over the news? They always do stories if the victims are pretty. Look at Schapelle Corby and that pot in the boogie board scandal,' Margo added.

'My uncle won't let this out,' Becca said. 'He doesn't want the publicity to threaten his project. I gotta go down there, see what's going on.' Becca placed her hand on Margo's shoulder, inspected her face. 'Are you feeling better now? Up to watching Rubes for a bit? You know what my brother's like. Still needs someone to sign off on the words before he spits them out.'

'Of course, love.' Margo dismissed her concern over her health, then took the toddler from the woman's hip with familiarity. I felt a wave of tension between them as Brookes' sister noticed Otto on the lounge-room floor.

'How do you know Margo?' Becca asked me. The woman was as guarded as an ATM. She just stared at me, at Otto.

Margo filled the silence, the child on her hip pulling on her swirly earrings. 'Told ya petal – this is Lotti. She's alright, love, keep your knickers on. She's the boy's teacher from the city.'

'I'm also, ah, Augie's girlfriend,' I spat out. Considering the lies he'd told me, even that statement was uncertain right about now. Anything seemed possible – for all I knew this pretty redhead might be his wife.

Her posture changed. Becca's attention turned to Otto, lounging on the shag carpet, oblivious to their conversation. 'That's not who I think it is, is it?'

Becca's hand covered her mouth in a gush of an emotion I couldn't name.

Margo's eyebrow cocked. 'I was filling Lotti here in on the situation ... I'll explain when you get back, you've got enough on your plate.'

'She brought him here?' Becca asked. 'Margs – what are you doing?'

Becca huffed, went to leave but turned back to have a final word. 'All the things she lost to keep him safe. She'd never want him here.'

Margo gave a thin-lipped smile as the little girl pulled from her arms and went and sat by Otto watching TV on the big boxy set.

Becca looked me over once more. 'Anyway, Troy's had him and Gus down at the copshop all night.'

I butted in. 'Did you say *bones*? I went down there but they wouldn't let me in.'

Another silent look exchanged between Margo and Becca.

'Troy'll fill me in,' Becca said. 'I've got too much on that prick for him not to.'

Margo rubbed Becca's arm. 'I'll look after Rubes, you keep us in the loop, hey?'

I was torn between wanting to follow, gather more evidence, and wanting to step back a moment from the unravelling. I had no clue what I'd stumbled upon.

Otto snatched the remote and started rubbing his eyes, complaining about the new girl dancing in the way of the TV. He was getting crotchety.

Margo read my mind. 'You need a place to stay, Charlotte? Or we could keep Otto?'

I frowned, the idea of leaving him here unnegotiable. 'We're at the pub.'

'The pub?' the ladies said in unison.

'That's a bad idea. Too many locals,' Becca said.

'It's not like they'd have any reason to link me to Freya, or Augie for that matter. And, believe me, I'll be laying low – I don't know anyone in town.' I gathered up the shoes Otto had kicked off across the lounge and turned to Becca. 'Maybe you could let me know how you go?' I gave her my room number and phone contact.

Becca nodded and left.

Was this fire-haired woman one of the four in that dog-eared photo I'd seen in August's van, all those months ago? She was obviously a key player in his life. My chest was tight with something I couldn't name – I wasn't sure if it was grief for the life I thought I'd had, or fear for what I was about to find out. As I grabbed my phone, checked for missed calls, I couldn't help viewing the man in the background photo in a new light.

Otto grabbed my hand as we negotiated the stairs. I'd grown attached to the kid, more than a teacher should. I may have even been stupid enough to picture making him a cake on his birthday next month. That was something parents did, not teachers. What was I thinking?

I barely knew this man. I had no business falling for him. And I definitely shouldn't be falling for his kid. It didn't stop me curling Otto's fingers in mine, and taking him home.

Otto complained the whole drive back to our crusty pub room.

'Straight inside, Stink-breath.'

He kicked his legs against my chair with the fury of a caged possum. 'You said you'd play hide and seek!'

It was early afternoon but he was exhausted. So was I. This is why my interaction with kids was best concluded by 3 pm. '*Cars* movie and chill time?'

'You said the police lady gave directions to snacks!'

'Dude, I'm sorry, I did say that but you ate at Margo's and we just got back.' He seemed to tire quicker than hearing children and I put it down to the effort required to keep up. I tried to appease him with something from the minibar.

'It's just nuts, and I hate nuts! Snacks then hide-and-seek!' A bottle shop drive-through was attached to the back of the pub and it had bright signage for specials that included Pringles. 'Chips!' Otto called.

I parked in the drive-through area to duck in. 'Stay in the car this time — count how many boxes are on that pallet while I'm in there and let me know in two minutes? Stay! Right! There!' I rushed inside, grabbed a big bag of overpriced crisps and a bottle of white to calm my nerves and lined up behind a tall, jet-black-haired man paying for a six pack. I craned my neck to check on Otto through the signage on the window, pointing at the boxes as he counted like a sweetheart. He was just like his father — prone to high emotions but easily distracted.

Then it hit me. He is not just like his father. Otto doesn't know his father.

I wasn't comfortable with any of this — surely even a rotten bloke had a right to know they'd fathered a child, and for a child to know that man at some point and determine for themselves just how rotten they were? Plenty of losers I knew turned out to be reasonable fathers later in life. How bad could he really be?

As I waited to pay, I turned it all over in my mind. Freya was Augie's dead sister. Augie was Otto's uncle. Brookes linked with old bones. None of these weird facts seemed to connect.

The customer in front was rabbiting on to the cashier. He had biceps bulging from a black Silverchair-concert singlet. I read the whole 2007 tour venues to distract my mind from churning. He was tall, dark and attractive in an obvious, John Stamos kind of way. That changed when he opened his mouth.

'Mate, I can live off a roo for a good month – bonus if you get a joey – sweet meat.'

I threw up a little in my mouth. I eased my bottle into the prime bench spot, and the joey killer turned and noticed me for the first time.

'Who have we here?' the disarming man said. 'New to town?'

'Just passing through,' I replied then turned to the shopkeeper. 'I've got cash if that's quicker ...' I slid over a twenty.

'Anyone ever said you look like Mila Kunis? You know, from *That 70s Show*?'

I said nothing. Was he going to tell me how beautiful my eyes were now, and how he'd give them a sight to see?

'Where you from, sweet cheeks?' There was something a little too direct about his gaze. Maybe I should have watched *Wolf Creek*.

'City girl.'

'Long way from home, then. If you need a place to crash, I've got a spare couch – plenty of grub.'

'No thanks,' I said, wanting to add that I was all good for murdered baby wallaby but also wanting to avoid ending up in a body bag in the dusty ute outside. I grabbed my change with a smile and shuffled out, peering through the dark tint of the back seat of my car. No Otto.

Otto? I scanned the drive-through, the road in the foreground. No Otto. I ran over to our motel room across the carpark, thinking he'd gotten bored and restarted on the hide-and-seek. Not there. 'Fuck, fuck, fuck.' I chanted under my breath.

Returning to the bottle shop, I heard a muffled scream. Banging, from the storage room. 'Oh, no, you didn't.' I ran over, pulled at the lever. The door was locked at the base. I let out a guttural cry, bashing the metal door with my fists, knowing Otto couldn't hear it, but might feel it and be reassured.

'Excuse me!' I yelled inside the grog shop. 'There's a kid locked in there.' The banging grew more desperate.

The young cashier heard me and left the counter, keys jangling as he approached and took out his keys. 'Gets stuck all the time.'

'I'm sorry. He wanted to play hide and seek …' The door shook, a loud thud as if the poor kid was trying to body slam it open with his tiny shoulder.

'It's okay, mate, we're gonna get you out real soon,' the nose-ringed cashier called.

Kicking. Screaming. My heart was in my throat.

The other customer appeared from the store, with two six packs when I was sure he'd only paid for one. He noticed the commotion and swaggered over. 'Need a hand, mate?'

The young staffer had found the right key. We both wrenched on the lever, but it wouldn't budge. 'The bugger's bent out of shape.' Otto's wail grew more desperate, and I started crying too, imagining him alone in the cold dark space, unaware help had arrived.

'Guys, leave it to me,' the roo shooter ordered, dismissing us with a shake of his head.

We stepped aside. Tendons in his neck strained and his white knuckles yanked the lever hard, and it came unstuck.

Otto lay on the floor between stacks of cartons, wide-eyed, one black jogger raised for another kick. He flinched as the door opened, the sunlight flooding in. He pulled himself up and bolted to my arms, snot dripping from his nose, his fingers cold, his face flushed from exertion. I kissed his soft brown hair, then crouched down. I didn't know the sign for 'safe', so I finger-spelled it. But I saw there was no need, he could see it, he could feel it.

'Thank you so much,' I blubbered to the two men. 'I'm so sorry to take up your time.'

Otto continued to hide in my chest, his shoulders still heaving with sobs.

'What do you say, mate?' The rescuer raised his jaw, the arrogant smile fading from his face, brushing his palms together as if his dirty work was done.

Otto wasn't looking so would have no clue he was spoken to. He pressed his head back into my stomach, his arms gripping my waist.

'What's wrong with him?' Roo Shooter sneered. 'Stuffs this man's lock, made me late, now he can't even say thank you?'

'He's upset, but I really do appreciate it. And, of course, we'll pay for the door if it is damaged,' I said.

The young staffer waved away my suggestion. 'Nah, nothing a good bash won't fix. I'm just happy the little fella's okay, huh?' He grabbed a can of lemonade from the cold room for Otto, checked there was nothing more he could do and returned inside.

We stepped across to our car, desperate to park it near our room and stay put inside when I heard Roo Shooter call,

'Nah, where do you think you're going? If he's not going to say thanks, I think you should be the one to repay me, sweet cheeks.'

I cringed at this egotistical arsehole, fought the urge to scream at him and squatted again next to Otto and asked him to say thank you.

'Thank you,' Otto said. He was usually so articulate. He'd learned so much before his hearing declined that you would never know he was deaf, but with all the emotion the words came out guttural and dense with the lisp of a younger child who hasn't quite learned how to command his tongue.

Otto gazed back at me, and I nodded with a smile, turned his face away from the man. The neon lights. The giant man. His skin, still cold to the touch. It was all too much for me, let alone a little boy. But the arsehole wouldn't let up.

'What was that kid? You one of them retards or somethin'?'

I resisted the urge to explode, tucked Otto under my arm, thankful he could not hear this man. But then I couldn't let it go. I turned back. 'He can't hear, but you know what? Most of what you have to say isn't worth listening to.'

'Hoohoo! You've got a bit of fire in ya, hey, love?' He smiled then made a disgusting display of mocking Otto's tone that said more about him than it did about anyone else. 'The names J-oe-l.' He spread out the consonants like a twerp. 'Can you say "Thank you J-oe-l"?'

Otto turned his head back to the arsehole, just as the name clicked in mine. I grabbed Otto's hand tighter than I'd ever held it before, my knuckles white. This can't be the Joel Margo had mentioned, the Joel Augie had gone to such lengths to keep Otto away from.

Stupid, stupid girl. This is why nature decided you should never be a parent.

Joel did a pretend stomp in front of us, a waft of dust flying in the air, then cackled to himself, mimicking what he thought he heard as he reverse-pedalled his long legs back to his ute, hopped in the driver's seat and skidded off.

It was strange — Otto's greatest fear was being left out, but I was happy he'd been oblivious to some of the words spoken, simply by him turning away. What you didn't hear didn't exist. What you didn't know couldn't hurt you. It had worked for Otto so far, keeping his real father an unknown.

Was that the strategy Augie had also taken with me?

Chapter 12

LOTTI

It had been three days since I'd seen Augie – I hadn't had any bursts of clarity on our situation, and adding mysterious bones, fake fatherhood and name swapping to the equation, even less made sense – but I could still feel a flush on my thigh thinking of the featherlight strokes of his fingers from the last time he touched me.

Otto was a little clingy and withdrawn after the rattling episode at the bottle-o, and had conked out sprawled diagonally across the bed with the remote in his hand and the hard-won chips unopened. A creased piece of paper that had been bent over and reduced to a tiny square lay beside him. Unfurling each fold, there it was – Augie's late-night note that he'd placed under Otto's pillow before he left the bus the other night. *Be right back, kid*. I turned the scrap paper over and read the address on the old envelope for 'Silverfell Holdings'. I added that snippet of evidence of his character to all the things I knew to be true about Augie, starting with the day he jump-started my car.

I assumed I had not impressed the straight-talking mechanic after he helped start my battery that day after the storm, and hadn't lost any sleep over the fact given his chauvinistic impression. It was only when he began picking up Otto from school that he started to occupy my thoughts. By then he'd already bought me coffee twice, sent Otto to my class with a pouch of spare fuses for my car, explaining my model was renowned for 'shoddy wiring', and found a few lame reasons to discuss Otto's homework. He seemed to have a few Ampol coveralls on rotation with grease smears up the sleeves, but he always smelled like fresh sheets.

I was never one for meaningless flings but I had been known to draw out the flirtations at bars with men. I liked the chase. A few weeks in, he hovered by the storeroom while Otto cleaned brushes in the sink. The afternoon storm had left condensation on the double-hung windows, which made everything feel snowy and fresh. I'd perched on a low student desk, folded my legs. I'd thought about him every night since we'd met, but told myself it was just out of curiosity, to understand Otto's situation better. But this feeling had no business being felt in a classroom.

August finally asked me out.

'You mean, like a date?' I'd selected a tone that sounded like the concept had never entered my mind.

'It doesn't have to be.' His prominent forehead creased as he backtracked his offer.

'I'm just surprised. You were kind of a dick, at the start. I didn't see this in our future.'

'A "no" then. That's, yeah, probably best.' He picked up Otto's schoolbag, hurried him along by returning the glitter and paint pots to the storeroom.

I followed him in. 'Did I actually answer, though?'

He looked like a bunny cornered by a fox. He stilled and focused on me, finally. That's when I noticed glitter sparkling along his cheekbone. His prominent, strong face. The way his shoulders filled out his (kind of lame) polo shirt that I guessed he got for free. He was no fuss. No horseshit, as Otto would say.

I leaned in and stroked his cheek free of glitter and he looked at me. There was something in that look that made me more than curious. 'I get the glitter rash, too.'

He took me out for fish and chips that night, and our first date began in the front cabin of a ute with a six-year-old leaning into my leg at every corner. The core components of the night had strong potential: Sandgate Pier at sunset, a fresh breeze on my skin, my secret favourite student skipping ahead, smelling the salt and the bait and the hot chips, the laughter shared by families huddled around picnic tables – these were all good things. The only problem – August had barely said a word.

I filled the awkwardness with my life history. 'So, ah, I was born in Melbourne, but we moved to the ACT for Dad's work, and I only moved up here and started teaching again a few months back after a breakup.' I tried to relax but talking to August felt a little like coaxing a chin-trembling preppie into joining in.

He listened, but didn't contribute.

I kept talking. 'I, ah, was working in politics before here – good grounding for wrangling twenty-eight six-year-olds all day.' Again, my date had nothing to add. 'So, um, you lived in Brisbane long?'

'Few years,' he mumbled.

I nodded. It felt like we were a couple of bobble-head dogs, bouncing away on a dashboard in silence. He didn't elaborate. We walked. 'I grew up on the Mornington Peninsula.' I babbled on about wineries and penguins and headlands and how much I loved Victoria and he nodded along without a word.

Otto ran between us, asked when dinner was. We grabbed battered cod and thick cut chips and spread the white paper they were wrapped in over an aluminium picnic table on the water's edge. The tide was in and the air was cool. As soon as Otto ran off, throwing chips at seagulls on the rocky foreshore, the conversation waned once more.

'Sorry, I'm kind of out of practice with this,' he said.

'I couldn't tell.'

I smiled, and he frowned then relaxed into a smile with me.

'I do have first-day-of-school icebreakers in my teacher's arsenal of "get to know you" games …'

'What's wrong with silence?'

I looked down my nose at him. 'Are they comfortable silences? I'm not sure they are. How about we try to get to know each other. What's your favourite book? Mine's *The Book Thief*. It's narrated by Death.'

One eyebrow rose. 'I can see why Otto wants to go to school every day now. You're both the same kind of weird.'

I frowned, but took it as a compliment. 'Conversations are meant to go back and forth.' Silence. 'You haven't said yours …'

He panicked for an answer. 'The dictionary. The only book that has the words in the right order. Also the only one I had for a while, read the whole thing when I was fourteen.'

I nearly choked on my chips. *And you think I'm weird?* 'Well, I have to ask – favourite word?'

'Discombobulated,' he answered in a flash. 'What's yours? Don't say "serendipity". It's so naff.'

I laughed. Two full sentences. We were getting somewhere. I thought for a second. 'Ineffable.'

He frowned. 'Nah, sounds kinda rude.'

'Coming from a man whose favourite word is "fuck".'

'Far more offensive things than that. Racism, for one. Rick Astley music …'

I smiled, took his hand, and he flinched, but I held it till he relaxed. 'How about, who'd play you in a movie?' I asked, starting to enjoy the power. 'I think you look a little bit like Joshua Jackson.'

'Who?'

'That guy from the new sci-fi show – *The Fringe*? He was Pacey on *Dawson's Creek*.'

His face pinched. 'That putz.'

'Oh, but Joshua Jackson's everything Pacey never was.' I smiled. 'Who would play me?'

His eyes narrowed. 'Mila Kunis?'

I rolled my (apparently prominent) eyes. I'd heard that before. 'Is that a nice way of saying my eyes are too big?' I'd gotten that all through primary school, along with that I looked more European than my very Caucasian parents, sparking questions about whether I was adopted. I figured there were worse things to tease someone about.

He frowned. 'Don't knock her. Can't have too much of a good thing.' His lips relaxed into a smile. 'I can also see a bit of Joey Potter, I mean, you know, Cruise's missus, but with longer hair, and better choice in men ...'

'Didn't Joey end up with Pacey?' It came out flirtier than I'd planned, and I felt something shift. Like this thing might be salvageable. At least, the palpitation in my heart said as much.

'You're asking me? Only thing I've watched for years is Otto's three DVDs on repeat.' He smiled, a glimpse of who he really was slipping out. August Silverfell was closed off, gave one word answers half the time, but he was attentive. He listened. He was polite, in an aloof way and we sank into a cosy silence.

At the end of the night, he drove me back to my car, parked near his van.

Otto hugged my leg goodbye and before the kid ran inside, August kneeled down and used his index finger to rub back and forth along his pearly whites, and Otto groaned but skipped up the pebbled steps, waving as he went in the van. My heart skipped a beat.

I smiled at August as he stood, awkwardly beside me. 'What?' he said, perplexed.

'There's something sexy about a man going down on one knee to ensure his son cleans his teeth.'

'Really? I've been nervous as hell about what to say around you and that's what gets to you? I got plenty where that came from.'

I placed one hand on each of his shoulders – strong and firm beneath his usual Shell branded polo shirt. At least he had clean ruggers, this time. 'It only works if you're wearing oil-branded fashion, though.'

'Plenty of that, too.'

Our breath mingled as I leaned in and covered his mouth with mine. His lips were full and soft and a little salty. August Silverfell kissed me back, but – in a word – I'd have called it polite. I couldn't tell if I'd felt anything much.

'It's been a while since I did this part, too. You gettin' anything?' he said, finally being natural, and what I could only guess was entirely himself.

'It was a little G-rated,' I said. 'But had potential.' The last part sounded like a report card.

'Alright. The boys at the garage, they just warned me, chicks are kind of into not wasting time, after a certain age. Want to cut to the chase.'

'How old do you think I am?'

He frowned. 'That sounds like a trap.'

'The whole biological clock thing? That it?' I asked. 'I haven't really made up my mind about kids.'

'Yeah,' he said, distracted by a noise inside. 'Me neither.'

The van was lit up like Christmas with lights strewn along the perimeter of the canvas awning, a little too girly for this alpha male. He leaned over and tapped on the window where Otto's nose was squashed up, and the kid disappeared with a giggle, leaving a sweat mark on the glass. August jumped the two steps inside and disappeared for a few minutes. I figured that was that. We'd ticked the box for the goodnight kiss. The jury was still out. Besides, it was hard to do further investigation with an audience that included a student that I had to teach come Monday.

Five more minutes. A light turned off inside the big white bus. Had he fallen asleep putting Otto to bed? Jess told me that's the sort of lame thing parents did. I started towards my car, perplexed. But then August returned, made a beeline towards me.

'You waited. Sorry, had to make sure the bugger was definitely out.' He stood a foot from me, his eyes on my shoes before slowly snaking up to my eyes. Without warning, he leaned in and ramped things up to Mature Audience level, his mouth firm on mine, finishing with a slight graze of his teeth on my lower lip that lingered like salted caramel.

I hadn't felt that kind of buzz since pashing a Spanish bartender, years ago. Before Mum had Alzheimer's. Before Dad lost the election. Before breaking Grayson in two. I tipped forward a little in my boots, righted myself, then, after a second to recover, said, 'I guess that was *okay*.' I adjusted my dress as if that would piece me back together. 'You could say it was serendipitous that my car broke down that day, if we used fickle words like that.' He smiled with his whole, scratchy face and I knew I'd never be the same.

He took my hand, guided me around to a moonlit corner at the back of the van, telling me about the trips he'd take Otto on once it was done. Then he stopped talking.

He leaned me against the metal corrugations and pressed his body on mine. As we kissed, frantic and impatient, I felt him hard against me, his fingers beneath the fabric of my dress, searching for the heat between my legs. The quiet man I'd coaxed out of his shell had transformed, now self-assured, bold. His eyes locked with mine and softened as I groaned as each stroke propelled me closer to the edge. All I could hear was the rush of blood in my ears. His breath was hot on my cheek, his rhythm perfect and I'd have rather died than stop. His grip supporting my leg was firm, but his fingers were feather light. The pressure of his body released a little, creating a gap between us. 'Don't you dare stop.' He didn't. What he did was watch my expression as I came.

Blushing, I ran the tip of my nose across his cheeks, and it felt more natural, more exposing than I expected. I smoothed down my dress, refastened and adjusted things back into place. Then this almost-stranger kissed the palm of my hand in a way that made me feel like a princess and – like in a golden, rom-com moment – he gave a whole face smile that pinched his eyes. I blushed even more. It was one of those moments you lived for. Frightening. Fearless. I went with the mood, following his bold lead, and pulled him sharply towards me by his belt buckle, turning so he was the one flush against the wall.

He covered my hands in a move to slow me down, turned his eyes to the stars, the trees, anywhere but near mine. At first, I thought he was embarrassed, or tired, or things had come to an end without me realising. But I'd felt him, ready and able. I paused. 'Are you okay? Did I …' I wasn't sure how to finish that sentence. This was uncharted. 'Is this not something you want?' *Was his wife on her way here?*

He adjusted his shirt collar, scratched his head and cleared his throat. 'No, it's just weird, with the kid just there, you know?' His voice was even deeper, lower than before.

I frowned, nodded like that was cool. 'I get it.' I didn't. Not really. It was dark. He'd made sure Otto was asleep inside. August had been fine when it was me, vulnerable, pinned against the wall. An awkward silence ballooned in the space between us yet again, and I felt an urgent need to escape. 'You're right – seeing your teacher pashing your dad is probably against school rules.' I revealed my palms, but smiled.

'He's not, ah ...' His gaze fell again.

I waited, but he'd reverted back to mute. 'I should go.'

His face twisted, but he didn't object.

I grabbed my bag from the folding chair under the van's awning. 'My car's just out on the road, so ...'

He stood there, making me feel like a stranger, this man who'd just had his fingers inside me. I shook my head.

He frowned. He looked gutted. 'I'll walk with you.'

I swallowed, without words to reply.

He did walk with me, two steps ahead, and not a word was spoken.

I clicked on the central locking, turned to say goodnight. 'It's no big deal ... whatever that was. I had fun. You don't have to be weird about it at school or ...'

His eyes were misty as he stroked his goatee, mortified and I had no clue as to why.

'Sure you're okay?'

He shook it off. 'All good, yep.' His voice was stupidly loud and chirpy. He waved as he trailed off. 'Night ...'

I cried all the way home, which only made me feel more confused as I didn't know why. I put it down to the uncertainty. Was he married? Did he pull the plug out of guilt? Had I done something to turn him off? I wasn't sure why, exactly, but decided it was the worst first date I'd ever had. But, also the best.

Weeks later, when he'd finally called, and we'd progressed past second base, I'd told Pia over the photocopier about August's habit of never letting my hands near his bat and balls. It wasn't my usual MO, telling tales about men, but in my defence it was at the beginning of things with Augie, when my loyalty was still tipped towards girlfriends.

Pia picked white threads off her mandarin and looked puzzled at my concern. 'And you don't have to so much as look at the ugly thing? I'm not seeing the problem, here,' Pia whispered as we collated photocopying in the staff room. 'You get a full service, faultlessly, by the sounds of it, then he just … rolls over?'

I frowned. She was missing the point. 'It's unusual.'

She shrugged. 'Maybe *it's* unusual. Maybe he has a tattoo of another woman on his cock. Or a swastika?' She screwed her face. 'Warts?'

I shook my head. 'Nope. I've seen it and it's beautiful.'

Pia's lips puckered like she'd sucked a lemon. 'None of them are beautiful, honey.' She grabbed my pile of school newsletter handouts.

'Hey, that was my pile!' I said. 'Print your own!'

'Ran out of credits.' She bit into a segment, chewed, then said, 'Actually, when I think about your so-called-dilemma, perhaps I wouldn't prefer women if I'd given Hot Dad a run. His wardrobe could do with a makeover, but other than that, he sounds perfect.'

Other than his inability to talk about himself, he was.

After that, I liked him being selective with words, not rattling on like my ex, who shared details about his day like an appointed spokesperson commentating on every aspect of his life as if it were riveting. But with this new turn of events, with this snapshot of his mysterious past, it was clear August's selectivity in the parts he was willing to share wasn't about me; it was about him.

The real question was why, and I was no closer to the answer.

A knock at the door made me jump. I peered through the dusty orange curtains, fearing Joel the Joey Murderer from the drive-through had found us again, before seeing Becca outside my hotel room. The look of mild annoyance about having to come to her brother's aid at Margo's this morning had escalated to one I could only describe as freaking out.

'Lotti – we need to talk,' she'd whispered, having looked over to Otto and seen him asleep.

'It's okay, he can't hear us.'

Becca shook her head. 'Of course, Freya told me. From that awful virus. Anyway …' She looked towards him with the same depth of emotion I'd noticed when she first saw him at Margo's, then ran her hand across her forehead. 'I'm not sure what they've got on Gus and my brother, but it's enough to get warrants to search Gus's vehicle.'

This all seemed like a huge misunderstanding that just needed to be explained. 'His truck? For what?'

'Whatever they dug up from Brightside the other night.'

The grave. The camp.

'But Margo said you already knew about that bit.' She said it with a side of suspicion, as if I had something to do with this, whatever this was.

'I have no clue what they found,' I said.

It seemed to appease her. 'It's not good, Lotti,' she said, as worry swam in her eyes. 'If I know Troy Harris he's probably already searched it and found something on them, and he's just making it official. They're my family. They run this town. He's out to get him.'

'Get him? For what?'

'Murder.'

Chapter 13

AUGIE, 1988

The day Freya and I were sent to live with our aunt was a stinking hot Wednesday in 1988. It was also the day everything we had burned to the ground. I was a scrawny twelve-year-old. Freya was eighteen months younger, two inches taller and ten years more mature. We had nothing but the tatty school bags on our backs but Margo, magician that she was, had warm beds, new toothbrushes and PJs folded under our pillows by the time we'd finished our tinned fruit for dessert. She played her VHS recording of *Charlie and the Chocolate Factory* on the old boxy telly. She even cued the ads for us, not realising neither of us were watching the screen.

To the world, my mother Judith died in a house fire at the age of forty-three. 'Faulty Christmas lights' was the most popular theory for what caused the blaze that burned so long they had to evacuate the neighbours. Let's just say there was a lot to burn.

I remember every detail of the day we buried Mum. It's like my brain was hypervigilant, determined to make sense of it all. The air was thick as custard at the service, and even the pastor unbuttoned his shirt at the wake. Church folk had their heels off, and people drank twice the booze Margo had catered just because it was wet.

There were more attendees than chairs gathering underneath Aunty Margo's giant fig, the legs of the plastic seats unevenly balanced between the knotted roots bulging through the grass, cool beneath our toes. That was the thing about Mum – she was loved. Still worked. Still baked her famous quiche for the neighbours when they had surgery or got sick. Still went to our school things until the last year when finding clothes and the room to iron was increasingly challenging. But, generally, she was a high-functioning basket case. We went to other people's shindigs. They were just never invited back.

All the grown-ups sat fanning themselves with the memorial service booklet, my mum's face flapping back and forth between their fingers as they banged on about what a great lady she was. What a tragedy. How she was a respected member of the Ladies' Auxiliary.

After walking past wilted curried-egg sandwiches and prawn cocktails, I grabbed a handful of Ruffles and scoffed them like a toddler but they stuck to my throat like papier mâché. Freya had already escaped inside Margo's house with a lemonade popsicle, following the arc of the oscillating fan in semicircles since the button broke to make it stop. She'd even flicked off her jelly shoes. 'I got it first,' was all she said, then I burst into tears, which she thought she'd caused and ran after me, begging me to have a go with the fan. Promising I could have it near my bed that night.

'I don't want it,' I said, turning away, the grass hot and spikey on bare feet. 'Go back inside, okay?' I didn't want to cry in front of her, so I hid out the back of Margo's yard. Margo and Mum were big on keeping private things private, and I figured this was one of those things. I hid between the mower shed and the umbrella tree, my feet propped up against the incinerator we sometimes sat around, toasting marshmallows.

'Honey?' It was Margo's husky voice. She'd found me. 'You okay?' She sighed, said something about how I may not be stuck with her forever, that maybe I'd get adopted by a millionaire like that red-haired orphan, Annie. When she started singing *Tomorrow,* and about how it was only a day away, I figured she'd had a go at some of that booze herself.

'I don't want to be adopted,' I said, tears flowing no matter how hard I pressed my cheeks.

She mistook my tears for sadness over losing my only remaining grown-up. But Mum had been slowly disappearing for years. I missed the person she used to be. She used to save every scrap of our childhoods – not just report cards and baby teeth, but everything from Freya's pigtail when I hacked it off in jealousy, to the pizza box from the takeaway we had on Freya's first day of school. Her warped relationship with 'treasures' she'd assigned ridiculous meaning to hadn't just taken over our hallways. Like Pacman, they had eaten up all the spaces in our minds.

'I know your mum was … complicated, but she loved you both so much, Gus.'

'Just not as much as her stinking treasures,' I'd said, sniffing and looking for somewhere to wipe my tears before someone came and saw. But my shirt was no use, as stiff as a board, hot, scratchy, and smelled like the starch Margo had sprayed all over it. I put the practice in the same category as wearing stockings on Sundays or Mum slicking my fringe down flat with her spit. There was no point to ties, or stockings or starch. It was just useless stuff some gumby decided we should do to make others think we were 'good people'. I had no interest in being good people. I just wanted to be me.

'Hate this shirt,' I said.

'Hate these stockings,' she echoed.

'Then why do we wear 'em?' I asked.

'Out of respect. For your mum. For God.'

'But don't they know the real us? Why do grown-ups lie about who they are?'

Margo laughed. 'I don't know. To fit in?'

I wondered if God knew about Mum's collecting. If he knew everything, how could he not? Back in those days, there was no official 'hoarder' illness, the town just saw her as a bit peculiar, or too lazy to keep things in order. That's all it seemed to be from the outside. All that was obvious from the street were a few windows covered in boxes, a carport overflowing with old furniture. Inside was an entirely different monster. There were four bedrooms, but with Freya's old room becoming chockers with piles of mouldy magazines, stuffed toys and broken appliances, Freya and I had to share. Even in our designated three-square metres of space, the walls were closing in like that rubbish-compactor scene from *Star Wars*. The verandah was the last place with space for all three of us to sit together and that too had been lost to her mounting collection of indispensable treasures. I could catalogue the most recent ones: an abandoned shoe she couldn't leave at the playground, a broken exercise bike someone had chucked on the roadside. She'd needed me to help her lift that one into the boot, and she'd hurt her back doing it herself when I'd refused on principle.

'She did this to herself, didn't she? Even if it wasn't on purpose.'

Margo's face looked like it did after our dog Peggy died – broken. Mum had been Margo's only family who wasn't dead or in the clink. 'I can see why you'd think that.' She squatted down like a pitcher, not wanting to get her dress dirty I guessed, but her stockings laddered anyway, and I took that to mean

God wasn't that big on starch or stockings or lies after all. 'I didn't realise how bad she was getting towards the end, and I should have done more when you asked for help.'

I'd told Aunty Margo when the toilet kept leaking, flooding water down the cluttered hall that stank like old flower water. She'd called a plumber for me, but he came at the wrong time and Mum refused to let the guy in to fix anything, scared they'd report her to the government.

Margo did nothing but defend Mum's memory and blame herself. 'She wasn't well, August. It wasn't her fault. And, besides, she never hurt you, kept her job at the library after your father left, made sure you and your sister went to school in clean clothes with cut lunches and full tummies.'

I shrugged. I secretly loved hanging out at the library after school with my mum, not that I'd admit it out loud. 'Not because she cared about us. Because she cared about her stuff. And if someone snitched on her they'd find out, take her things.' I was jealous of rubbish. Maybe I was the crazy one.

Margo blew her nose into a light-pink hanky and pressed it to her chin. 'Your mum read a new book to you every night of your life. That wasn't for show. That was for love.'

I still had her old dictionary – one of the few things I'd kept at school so it didn't burn. All that stuff, and that was about all I had left of her. It made me think of the afternoon she caught me underlining all the rude words in the dictionary, starting with 'sex'. She started to laugh and instead of taking it off me, pointed out the ones I'd missed, told me how to use them, and when it was dumb to say them out loud.

Margo sat down next to me proper then, in the ant nests and dirt, leaning her good black dress against the rough brick firebox. She didn't care about stuff. She cared about people. I hugged her for it, for not being like Mum that way. For having space for us. Maybe I would still have someone to share things with if I did good.

She blew out an exasperated huff. 'I should have made her get help.' Her hanky was now balled in her fist. 'Got another skip. Done something.'

'Nah.' I wasn't even thirteen, but even then I knew it wasn't that simple.

'She hated it when anyone touched her stuff, so I don't reckon you coulda.' I'd discovered that the hard way when I messed with it. After waking to the sight of a stranger's shadow, their arms reaching for me, only to realise it was one of those plastic ladies you see at Myer, I'd chucked the thing in the outside bin the next day, smothered her under food scraps as deep as I could reach. Mum found it and was in tears that I'd treated 'her mannequin friend Maddy' with such disrespect, leaving her naked headfirst like worthless trash.

I'd screamed back, 'What mum chooses a stupid doll over their own kid? The house is full, Ma, don't you get it? I have nightmares about you getting trapped, piles of books crashing down on you in your sleep and you don't even care!'

Freya had shoved her hands over my mouth then and pulled me inside. I understand now that Mum chose to hide what was too hard to admit to herself.

Margo and I heard cackles of laughter from out front beneath the fig. Margo adjusted her shoulder pads, slipped her pantyhose off completely and said she better get back to the wake, worried she'd have an unruly bunch of drunks on her hands if she didn't line their stomach with more than crackers and dip.

After the fire that killed my mum, I'd played all the theories over in my mind like a choose-your-own-adventure book, even went back to the library, hid in the carrels, and read up on things called accelerants and the likely reasons house fires occur. But when I tried to relate it to our house, there were so many fuel sources, so many hazards it was impossible to narrow down. From what the books said, most house fires started when upholstery was lit by something they called a smouldering source. A lamp? A broken chord? Who knew?

'Wait – Aunty Margo?' She was a few steps away by then.

'Yes, love,'

I sniffed up snot in my nostrils. 'Do you think she tried to get out, that there was just too much in the way?'

Margo's face changed and she gasped a little. Was she imagining it too? My mum, trapped, the flames fencing her in. That's what I saw when the nightmares came.

'I think so, hon. She wouldn't have wanted to leave you and your sister for anything. I know that for sure. She was always telling me how she was saving this and that for you, wanted to see Freya in this at her wedding, see you driving that Ford your father left for you at your graduation. She wouldn't have wanted to miss those moments. She told me to love you enough for both of us, and that's what I intend to do.'

And Margo did keep her word, for a while.

Freya got Margo's sewing room, the frilly pink bedspread and the curvy white dresser because she was the girl. She needed the bed to line up her Pooh Bear, Peaches N Cream Barbie and freaky-looking Cabbage Patch dolls. I was relegated to the hallway and only after dark. But I could walk a path straight to the toilet at Margo's. And the toilet didn't leak stinky water down the hall into piles of infested newspapers. Back then, Margo was the only thing stopping me and Frey from foster care. We could run through her house without piles of everything blocking the light. She had milk in the fridge and smelled like the spearmint gum she chewed to mask the smell of her cigarettes. I still remember the night that Mum and I were talking about Margo's stinky ashtrays. As we ate frozen pizza in a kitchen crammed to the ceiling with crap, mould and rot, Mum had called smoking a filthy habit. We were quiet for a bit, then we laughed out loud. Me, Mum, Frey. Mum was good at laughing at herself, just couldn't do anything about it.

Even though I had to collapse and store my bed in the laundry during the day, I had more room at Margo's than I'd had at home. It turned out I'd left a few things at Brookes' place too, by accident: my broken Donkey Kong, a stack of water-damaged cricket cards and a couple of invisible ink quiz books. But the rest was toast.

Seven broken kettles. Eleven toasters. Five sewing machines. The list went on. I wouldn't miss any of that crap. I hated it. But I did miss Mum and the way her eyes lit up when she saw us, peeking around from the piles like an endless game of hide and seek. Margo was a more pragmatic version of my mother. Mum wore floral dresses that looked like something off *The Sullivans*. Margo wore corduroy overalls and flowy dresses – always violet or emerald with big wooden beads and funny print tights. She worked as a teacher's aide at the high school for as long as I could remember, the unofficial guidance counsellor, foster mum, hem fixer, Band-Aid dispenser, birthday-cake maker, hairdresser and whatever else the local kids needed to feel human. And the dogs, for that matter. She had two, according to the council, but about six bowls sat at the back door of various sizes that all got licked clean every dusk. That's the thing about strays – they didn't fight, just were thankful for what they got, always looked up to see who was feeding them with gratitude in their eyes.

I had been grateful. She did her best.

But that fire, what it took from us – it lit something inside my twelve-year-old brain I couldn't seem to snuff.

Chapter 14

AUGIE, 2009

The police kept me cooped like a caged hen all the next day and delirium set in by nightfall. I wasn't sure if it was 'cause my brain had spun back to 1989, or if I'd downed too many beers on an empty stomach, or the fact that I'd spent the previous night up a fucking tree, but I felt ratshit and just wanted to ease into the oblivion of sweet, solid sleep.

The only thing keeping me alert was the flicker of the fluro at my back and the coffee the lady cop kept pouring in my chipped mug. Detective Troy Harris, I'd seen firsthand, had grown into an even bigger dickwad now his bullying tactics were sanctioned with a shiny badge. Most of what he said were old jokes he'd already dished out at the skate park long before either of us could shave, and weren't any funnier now.

The insults came in waves, like he was conducting an orchestra. First it started with mum's hoarding. *Hey, Pyro, your mum's like, smoking hot! I'd do her but she'd probably want to save the condom.* Then he added in the fire stuff. *Hey, Mum, am I a pyro? Yes, you arson.* Last, like a crescendo, he progressed to fat jokes about Freya. *What do mopeds and fat chicks have in common? Both are fun to ride till your mates find out.*

Even though he was mid thirties, I couldn't get over him in uniform – he was like a kid playing dress up.

'How is the lovely Freya?' Troy Harris asked like he didn't know she'd died two years before.

I'd managed to keep it together until then. Once he said her name out loud, a burst of adrenalin charged my limbs and I stood, flipped over the desk, spilling coffee on his crisp blue shirt. 'Your whole family know exactly how she is,' I spat, the blink of the camera in the corner the only thing stopping me from punching the bastard.

'Oh, that's right. Hit by a truck. Geez, that's rough, she was such a healthy girl, too. I'd a thought she'd be hard to miss.'

The lino screeched as the table slid on its side with a little help from my wrist. I grabbed his collar with my dirt-caked hands. 'What did you fucking say, Harris?'

His hot breath smelled like coffee as he calmly went on, even as I hurdled the upturned table to see if I could push him further across the room. I pressed him firm against the wall but with his height, his power, he wasn't fazed.

'Everyone knows you lit that fire, Gus. We've always known. Because you lit every fire in town. My colleagues let you off back then on account of your mum being a nutter and the fact no one was hurt – or so we thought. But I reckon finding bones down the hill from a burn we know you started might change that a bit, don't you?'

'I don't know what you're talking about.' I pushed him without conviction, paced the small space and turned away from the prick, unwilling to let him see my fear. Back and forth, back and forth I paced, raking the sweat and dirt and stubble on my cheeks.

'I can tell you straight,' Toby Harris went on, 'your idiot pal is spilling his guts, admitting what you firebugs did. Can you hear him? We've also catalogued what was in that tin we found on his person – may as well put your side on record, huh? There's only half a brain between you and he ain't got it.'

I wasn't fifteen anymore. I was determined not to give him the satisfaction of egging me on.

'Just tell me – who'd you throw in that mine? You kill one of the blow-ins? The backpackers from the orchards? What about Steph? Remember her? Cheekbones of a supermodel, that broad.'

Stuck-up Steph. I hadn't forgotten, but didn't show it.

'You don't forget a piece of arse like that. Yankee exchange student that apparently "left town" suddenly after the fire. Did little Stephanie not put out, mate? We know how she felt about my cousin, poor old Brookester – pretty sure he was one of her favourite targets to terrorise. You probably thought no one would miss her – turns out she was an orphan like you, the American thing all a big fat lie, or did you know that already? But someone missed her – she was declared a missing person the following week, never found. Sweet Fake-Yankee Steph.'

I hunched in the corner of the interview room, unwilling to give him the satisfaction of seeing the rise he'd given me. The four walls closed in. A halo appeared around the fluro above our heads – or was that my eyes packing up?

Troy settled into what he did best: casual intimidation. Flicking imaginary lint off his blue uniform. Straightening papers in a line along the table's edge. He wasn't quite as good at it as his brother, but he was the youngest. Give him time. 'Twenty years she's been rotting in that bushland, poor thing. Never got to have a family. Tell me now, and I'll go easy on you. Was Brookes your accomplice? Or was it an accident? Did one of his moronic pranks go wrong and you helped him hide the evidence? Or did you get her drunk and she did the rest, stumbling up the hill, forgetting you lit the fire with the distraction. Few days and we'll have dental records, mate. DNA.'

Silence. Nothing I could say would help. I knew he had nothing on me, even with the evidence in the truck and whatever Brookes had in that tin from the treehouse. I was not under arrest. I knew they'd have to release me soon. That I just had to survive his goading a little longer and I'd be home. Home with Lotti and Otto, tuning engines and keeping my head down. But I couldn't help myself. I wasn't the type to sit by when dickheads had the floor.

'I know nothing about any bones – lotta trouble over nothing if you ask me. Hell, do you even know they're human? Not some cattle gone to pasture in the fucking war?'

'Oh, they're human, mate,' Troy said.

'Okay, well, maybe an old miner blew himself up in the sixties or … or a piss-wreck stumbled into an open mine? Who fucking knows? A lot of history in those hills.'

He turned when I said it and that pause gave me a leg in, so I went on.

'Pretty sure you're still working for the family business, am I right? Your unofficial pub trading stock? If I were you, and thank Christ I'm not, I'd be keeping this to yourselves – not a good look for your dad's new project. Not exactly the ambience you want in a nice family estate, is it? Dead bodies turning up. Might be more the deeper you dig. Serial killer stuff. Might really slow down your plan – don't want the family's cashflow tied up for months while the archaeologists come out and make sure there're no sacred burial sites. How old is your dad now? Getting on? It'll be your inheritance soon, I'm guessing.'

This is why I didn't talk much. All those words. It was exhausting.

His bottom jaw slid to the side as he pondered my point of view. Who was I kidding? He wasn't deterred. Harrises never were. They had all bases covered – the publican licence, the copshop, half the commercial buildings in Main Street, and now the residential estate would be tagged to their brand like cattle. I wondered how embroiled Becca had become in her Uncle Graham's underbelly schemes.

'Let's see how murder looks next to your other records, huh?' said Troy.

I laughed. 'That's a bit of a reach – you don't even know *who* is dead, when, how or why, but you're talking charges.' Spin. It had never been a skill I aspired to have, but I was doing it better than expected.

'We'll get the DNA back soon. We'll get a witness. Don't you worry.'

'Witness. You don't even know how long they've been buried. You gonna question anyone that's been in that bushland the past fifty years?'

'Ah, Gus. C'mon, Pyro. We both know when this all began. That night. The fire you started. Does it give you a hard-on just thinking about it? All that destruction, all because of you.'

It stirred something inside, but I exhaled, in and out, let it go. 'You don't know shit.'

'How 'bout the medical records for Brookes' burns? You didn't know that, did ya? Doctor's records are a bit of a chink in your armour. Blame the meat-head's sister for that one – no surprise she's so good with her kid, she's an old hat at parenting after raising her brother half her life. How else did he get those scars all over his back?'

'Brookes is a fucking klutz. Always burning himself lighting up his farts. You got nothing.'

'All adds up to the Brightside fire. I don't need to remind you of that night, do I, Gus? That stinking hot Australia Day in '89 … Just after Queenslanders voted out Jo.'

Shame the Fitzgerald enquiry didn't end the corruption in Eldham. 'Course you don't. The whole town came out to see the place burn. Smoke stung our eyes for days. You couldn't live in Eldham back then and not know about it. It was a pile of old wood, left in the sun in the middle of summer, wires hanging from the walls, never maintained. Discarded cigarette butt. Burning off at a nearby farm. Wouldn't have taken much to light that place up.'

'And you know all about lighting places up, don't you, Gus. Like that property you destroyed just after your mother fried, over on the Thomas farm.'

'What?' I scoffed. 'A bonfire completely contained in a rusted old tractor no one had touched in forty years? You were fucking there, Troy, pissed as a fart from memory, you bloody hypocrite. I did that farm a favour — nest of rats got chargrilled instead of eating through crops. We even cleaned up the empties the next morning. That's why he dropped the charges, as you well know. But that was before Brightside burned, and I have no clue why you've assumed some old bones have anything to do with me or Brookes, and I think it's time you admit you've got nothin'.'

The detective lifted his legs onto a spare chair and thought for a second.

I exaggerated a yawn to show how unrattled I was by this bullshit. 'It's been a long fucking night — longer than the 8 hours you pricks can hold us without an arrest — or is that just due to your conversation skills?' I frowned, leaned forward on the desk he'd righted earlier. 'Have you asked your brother where he was that night?'

'Which bloody brother?' The first flare of emotion from Troy Harris.

'The arsehole. Ah, yeah, I see your problem – doesn't narrow it down. Joel Fucking Harris. Why don't you ask him where he was?'

'We fire up the barbie every Australia Day, even back then. His whole family can vouch for him. How would you know he was involved, unless you were?'

I shrugged. 'Just a hunch.'

Detective Harris was silent for a moment. 'What is it with you two? You were sling-shotting spit bombs at each other when you were six and still haven't let up.'

'Don't start me,' I said. 'Or we'll be here another ten hours.'

The lady cop came in, whispered something in Harris' ear and he smiled. 'Would you look at that? Magistrate's just signed off on a warrant to search that retro shit-box of yours and whatever it was in that tray. Let's see what's in that chunk of metal you went to a lot of trouble to unearth.'

Chapter 15

LOTTI

'Murder? Are you joking?' I blurted to Becca as we perched on the ugly bedspread of my cheap pub room. I was still processing the story around Otto not being Augie's real son, hadn't even started on losing him at the drive-through – now this?

Becca wasn't kidding. Her face wasn't just sunken, her eyes not just mum-tired. She was scared. Scared for her brother, mostly, but also for August as it sounded as though they were both in as deep as each other.

I knew anyone was capable of killing, under the right (or wrong) conditions, but my mind reached back to quiet nights in the van with August, the compassion in his eyes when I'd share my schoolyard dramas, the way he listened to Otto's needs – that man was incapable of killing. 'That's not possible,' I said.

Small crow's feet appeared as she squinted at me with a look that said I was as naïve as that comment sounded. 'Ah, need I remind you, he did lie to you about other things hon, so, you know …' Did she mean about being Otto's dad, or something more?

It scared me when I realised I had no idea how well this woman knew him. Perhaps she was his ex-wife. He was the most closed-off person I'd ever met but maybe he was different with her. Maybe it was *me* he didn't trust? And, in that case, what did she know that I didn't?

August was a contradiction – he could fly off the handle, not hesitate to get physical with deadbeats at the pub that threatened those he cared for, but also the type of man who rescued a nest of abandoned baby birds found at the P&C working bee and fed them with an eyedrop just to show Otto that every life was precious. Even the ones no one seemed to care about.

'How is he meant to have killed someone? You mean, like in a car crash, an accident?' Something like that could happen to any of us.

Becca rubbed tired eyes. 'I tried putting the heat back on my cousin to find out – I've got enough dirt on that family to put them away for a long time, but Troy wouldn't say much. Uncle Graham – his dad – bought that land around the dam they're developing, and I reckon he's trying to keep it all under wraps, so it doesn't slow them down if someone claims it's an Aboriginal burial site. No one's talking about it yet. But he said he wants to question me too, which makes this all about something from when we were kids, back when I … knew Gus. Troy wouldn't let me speak to either of them so I'm trying to piece it together.'

'Margo said something about a fire,' I said.

Becca rolled her eyes, leaned on the door frame. 'Which one?'

My brain spun. Otto was sound asleep beneath the fan. I wasn't getting any rest tonight with all these questions in my mind demanding answers. 'I think we both need a drink.' I grabbed the bottle and two chipped mugs and slid into a chair. My legs barely fit beneath the tiny table. Becca hesitated. I could tell she was keen to get back to her daughter, to get away from me; that she'd reached her limit of being everything to everyone, like so many mothers, but she sat, regardless.

The fading sun filtered through the hotel curtains, and I was now close enough to see Brookes' sister was striking, the kind of woman that was hard to forget. Instinct told me August had loved this woman. Maybe he did, still. Maybe she was at the core of all of it. A bar tussle over a girl that went too far. That, I could believe. Thoughts quickly diverted down a rabbit warren; that August had gone straight to this leggy redhead's house before he was caught by the cops, that she was the thing I needed to be worried about, not this police drama.

We sipped warm wine as she filled in gaps about young Augie. 'Brookes wouldn't have survived high school without him. I was kind of glad when they sent Gus to Brightside too – more chance my brother would make it out. But he never forgave Margo for leaving him there. She was worried sick that she'd failed her sister in looking after him. She tried, she just couldn't handle him – the pyro stuff was too much for her, still grieving Jude and she genuinely thought they'd help him – she's never quite been the same since then.'

Pyro stuff? 'Is that why he left town? Why he's not in contact with Margo?'

Becca gulped more wine. 'They were never the same after that place – it was a rough boys' school. Freya's death just divided them more. He had so much anger – it was just a freak accident up at her uni, but blaming Joel was the way Augie could live with losing her.'

I tried to make sense of it. 'Because he was the reason she left town, to hide the baby from him?'

'It was more direct than that. I got it – Freya was my best friend, I was lost too – but he was way off, blaming Joel for her death. Margo encouraged him to see reason but they had a big blow-up after the funeral – and have barely spoken since.'

'So, Joel Harris is Otto's dad, and August thinks he was involved in Freya's death?' It was as if I had to keep saying it to make it sink in. Otto was not August's son. There was definitely a family resemblance with those dark, enquiring eyes, but I guessed uncles and nephews could look alike.

Becca nodded, eyes wide. 'A real piece of work, that one. All my cousins are dipshits. My uncle owns the pub – I've been doing the books for them, just to keep on their good side, you know? Friends close, enemies closer. But Joel can be such a charmer and turned it on long enough for Freya to get sucked in a few years back. Not many choices in small towns, if you know what I mean. I don't actually wish badly on Joel – treats women like toys and I'd never want Otto to be in his life – but he did, unknowingly, give Freya a piece of happiness before she died. That baby turned a light on inside her, you know? She was complete. But, yeah, Joel has no idea Freya had his child from their brief hook-up. She made sure of that, fled town as soon as she found out and Augie was always dead keen on keeping it that way for their safety.'

Otto. Joel. Safety. I swallowed hard. 'Ah, Becca? I think I fucked up. Otto got stuck in a storage fridge over at the drive-through and a roo-shooting arse of a guy helped us get him out.'

'God. Sounds awful, poor kid.'

'Yeah, thing us, the guy who helped said his name was Joel.'

Becca's eyes widened. 'Jesus. Okay. I guess that was inevitable being in town. Did he guess who you were? Your connection with the family?'

I shook my head. 'I didn't give a name, said I was from the city, didn't mention Otto's name or August. But he'd remember us for sure.'

She nodded, concerned. 'Just don't leave Otto alone – Joel's such an egotistical prick he'd want to piss all over anything he thought was rightfully his whether he wanted a child or not.'

I didn't need to be told that Joey Killer was not father material. But were we talking *Wolf Creek* kind of bad, or just your average intolerant arsehole? Was August's changing his name all in aid of keeping Otto clear of that man? Or was there more?

'You know their mum died when their house burned down and his Aunty Margo took them in. That's when he went off the rails – got obsessed with flames, got caught lighting up a wreck – another time Brookes lost half his thumb with him setting off fireworks down the dam.'

'Yep. Margo said as much. It's … a lot,' I said, still not used to this version of the man I thought I was finally cracking open.

'And I'm guessing you've seen Gus's scars …they were from juvie.'

I didn't answer. I was too busy processing the fact that she had (and they weren't exactly on his face). I confirmed what I'd started to suspect. The 'B' on August's forearm was for Becca. My instinct should have told me to run. To leave Otto with this woman, who seemed perfectly capable of caring for him, and return to my life. August had lied, or lied by omission, about everything important. His name. His son. His family. I had been under the illusion we had something good, that he'd begun to trust me. But he'd never shared any of this and these things were the major plot points in his story – they informed who he was. How important could I really be to him?

Becca continued with intimate details of the man I thought I knew – pub brawls, expulsions from school, homelessness – and I felt as if I'd been sleeping with a stranger. A decoy. A clone of the man she described. Her voice took an upward inflection as she drank more. 'He came good, though – whether he wants to accept it or not Margo saved him from jail, most likely. He eventually found a healthy avenue for his obsession, enrolled in a welding course, found a mechanical apprenticeship.'

Young Augie. He lost everything, and carried on. He wasn't a Rhodes scholar or a billionaire, but he'd made something of himself.

'I thought I knew him,' I said to this stranger, the tears pouring out. 'I didn't even know his real name.'

'He's still Gus, Lotti. Whatever last name you tack onto him. He's still the same person – sure, maybe a damaged one, but most of that wasn't his fault. Bad luck, that lot. His mum and dad, his sister – all dying on him in separate events. His grandparents never knew him – died before he was even born. Margo's slowing down too, won't tell me why she's quit her volunteering but it'd have to be a good reason for her to stop helping people. She laughed at me when I asked if she had cancer or something, and she was adamant she didn't.'

My head hurt. 'Okay, getting back to the murder part – you're saying he might have killed someone but he had a bad life so I should be fine with it?'

'They were kids, hon.'

I let out a slow breath. I had to be smart about this. 'You're basing that on a hunch it's about some fire when you were at school? You don't know that. We don't know who or how or why those remains are linked to him. I mean, when was the last time you saw him?'

'Some people you can never un-know.'

I tried to mask an eye roll. Perhaps I should clear out. Leave them to their unforgettable bond. 'What would you do if you were me? Hang around, find a lawyer, help him through this, or should I just get out of here?'

Becca leaned back, her gaze narrowing. 'How long have you known Gus?'

Gus. I'd never known anyone to refer to him as that until this weekend. Was that intentional? 'A few months.'

She hesitated, took another sip, then asked, 'Was it love at first sight?'

I frowned. 'There was definitely something … chemical. But, no, I thought he was rude and chauvinistic.' But not a criminal arsonist like Grayson wanted me to think, or a thug like his reputation at the school staff room implied. And definitely not a murderer.

'You're not wrong,' Becca said with a laugh.

We smiled. 'He can be a little antiquated.' I didn't want to warm to memories of him – this stranger – but I found I was. He wasn't exactly a smooth operator, but he was real, even if a little rough. 'He checks rooms before I enter, walks on the roadside of a footpath in case a random car mounts the gutter … he's like a security guard.'

She laughed. I was starting to like her, despite trying hard not to. 'His dad taught him that. He was a soldier, so was his grandad.'

Her knowing this when I didn't made the disconnect feel thick and dark and foreign. Had I imagined what we had?

'Gus is an old-fashioned country bloke at heart – but he'd also take a bullet for you. Not too many progressive modern men would. They'd say you wanted equal rights, fend for yourself.'

Did I think he'd take a bullet for me? Or was that privilege reserved for the owner of the 'B' on his forearm?

'I know who your dad is,' Becca blurted. 'Bit of a celebrity. Gus used to say he'd never vote 'cause it didn't matter which box he crossed, a politician would always win.' She laughed.

I pretended to. I knew he hated politics, but he was surprisingly community minded – there were many ways you could try and do good. Augie was just the yobbo in the tinnie saving old ladies from floodwaters, not the guy standing on a soapbox in a suit.

'So, Gus was a rebellion for you, was he? The man of mystery with a patchy past.' She used past tense. I didn't like it.

'I don't think so.' I was right the first time. I shouldn't befriend this woman. Liking your partner's exes – which I knew she was without her admitting as much – was bound to end badly. And did she have to be so direct? She'd be asking for details of our sex life next. I didn't even talk about that with Augie.

Becca was right in a way – I was privileged, raised to respect power, education, breeding. August had none of that. Perhaps that was part of his appeal. His type was as far away from Grayson and my father's crowd as was humanly possible. But I felt safe with him. I felt loved. I was entirely myself, and that was too rare to throw away over something he may or may not have done when he was dealing with more than most ever face.

Becca sat forward on the chair, her mug of wine in her hand. 'I've known him since I was born. And I know things aren't always black and white. If he and Brookes are responsible for whoever died at Brightside, it was a long time ago, and there was a good reason for it. Neither of them are talking – it's their code, call it loyalty or stubbornness – but I'm pretty sure it had something to do with the Australia Day fire in our last year of school.'

'What makes you think that?'

She sat back, he eyes locked with mine. 'Because I'm the reason it started.'

Chapter 16

AUGIE, 1989 – Brightside

We were bone dry by the time we reached the iron gates of Brightside, first Brookes, then his sister, and me. Steph lagged behind, complaining like a pre-schooler, asking if we were 'there yet' every five seconds, until we were.

'This is what I got sweaty for?' Steph moaned, stomping through the long grass to the ring of buildings. 'Isn't there, like, a pool?'

I shook my head at her. I needed a minute. I'd spent one hundred and eighty days there, and left just a few months before, but the sight of it unsteadied me. I'd known every inch of it – the basketball court, the cricket pitch, those damned horse paddocks and the thistles that had spikes as long as my dick. In my mind the place was a living, breathing monster. But in the light of day, without people pulling strings, the hum of voices, the whiff of Aeroguard and cow pads, it seemed like just another abandoned place. At least, that's what I told myself. I still didn't want to be here.

It was clear the security patrols had been cut, and the place had gone to shit. The grass was out of control, weeds as high as my waist between each cottage, dry and crackling underfoot. Brookes pulled some wire cutters from his bag, snipped a gash in the temporary fencing and slid through. The girls followed then ran ahead to explore.

Brookes did the lap around the back of the cottages, across behind the church and down to the horse paddocks and old splintery stables, and I tried to keep up with his angst-fuelled pace. He even checked the old piggery, getting more and more worked up with every minute, more fidgety, more erratic in his movements until he stopped outside the barn.

Neither of us offered to check inside. 'No one here, bro, let's not worry, hey?' There was no point. I still had nightmares of that place, one of the older kids laying into a whiskey mother sow with a chain like it was all part of the fun. That same kid doused himself in petrol later that term, lit himself up. We were told he was taken for treatment but when he came back to the cottage, rumour had it he got the cell, naked, with no water for his insolence.

Yep, it was all coming back. Even when I sprinted away from the memories of this place, they caught up. The faster I ran, the harder they hit. If I was in flight mode, Brookes was up for the fight and it was escalating fast – stomping from cottage to cottage like Mad Max, throwing bricks through windows, yelling at the clouds. 'Show yourself, you fucking coward!' he called, yet it was obvious no one was here to listen. Was he still searching for ghosts?

I waited for his tantrum to run its course, like it always did, hoping the release was somehow cathartic for him. But his anger didn't ebb. When he was close to hyperventilating, I stood behind him and grabbed him around the shoulders like a human straitjacket. 'You're alright, mate.' Thrashing. Kicking. He struggled a little more, socked me one in the nose, but I hung on until he calmed. Eventually the rage turned to tears and my oldest mate sat in the gravel, yanking out clumps of old grass, roots and all, kicking the dust. An icy shiver ran the length of my arm. Trying to tell myself that they were just buildings was drowned out by voices telling me to run.

'The water and power are cut off. There's, like, tumbleweeds in the hallways and holes in the walls. I can't imagine any of the old gang are desperate enough to hang around. We should just piss off.'

Brookes' eyes were misty, his breath ragged and fast.

I stepped closer to where he sat, patted his back with a slap. 'Let's go get some chips, huh?'

He shrugged, said he'd go find the girls. I huffed, but figured I had to follow him, and walked around the old weatherboard A-line cottages. So quaint. So homely. What a beautiful setting to turn around troubled young lives, I'd heard the politicians say on open day, the smell of scones in the oven, the cream and jam in the centre of flowery tablecloths.

I stalled at Cottage 9. My 'family' cottage. The place we were meant to be taught we were 'lovable'.

My heart was in my mouth and the taste of metal strong in my throat, but I charged towards the derelict building, unwilling to let an empty room get to me. *No one can make me feel anything.* The girls were inside, exploring, but not a minute later I heard Steph scream. Without thinking, I ran inside. It was, at once, terrifying and familiar. The kitchen ripped out, the bunks gone, the parents' quarters empty but for an old heavy wardrobe no one could fit out the door. The smell remained. The smell of boiled cabbage and disinfectant. My stomach heaved.

Steph was pressed against the wall in terror.

'What?' I asked, looking where Steph was pointing. 'A fucking spider? That's all?'

'It's just a huntsman waiting patiently to pounce on its prey,' Becca joked. She grabbed an old jar and picked up the huge crab spider from a pile of leaves that had gathered in a corner. As it jolted into the jar, Steph raced as far away from it as she could get. 'That thing was as big as my hand!' She almost sounded Australian when she said it. 'We don't have them in the States.'

The door slammed, the room darkened. The sound of the creak of the hinges set off something. Every corner unlocked a memory and triggered another, like falling dominos. First it was lame stuff – the twins blowing a tune on two recorders at once, one shoved up each nostril. The oatmeal that tasted like Clag. Then the memories dived deeper. The Friday night brawls, the initiation ceremonies. The incessant fear that at any moment you'd be called upon to do a hundred push-ups, clean the bathrooms for some made-up sin you'd committed. I slept with one eye open the whole six months. I took a breath, telling myself it was just fibro. It couldn't hurt me. But the walls bent in, the air was sucked from my lungs and my feet shuffled me back until my heels hit the wall. Heavy sinkers weighed down my veins, and a deep ache pressed heavy on my soul. I thought I'd gotten over this in the months I'd been away, but here it was, taking hold of me as fierce as ever.

Becca's voice brought me back. She handed me a water bottle, like I was some old man, but I pushed it away. Brookes sat by my side, a look of resolve on his face.

'What's wrong with you?' Steph laughed.

'Your face is what's wrong with him, bitch!' Brookes said, scowling at her.

'Calm your farm, dude,' Steph laughed and walked outside.

Becca stayed and sat by my side, which only made me feel pathetic. So, ignoring the wobble in my legs, I got up. 'Just need a sec,' I said and she nodded, went outside.

I ventured into what was left of the boys' bathroom. That's where the strip searches happened, a bunch of brothers sitting around making sure we had no contraband after our weekend visits home. I took it out and pissed all over the tiles. It was satisfying, watching the yellow river settle in the grout that they'd made us clean with a toothbrush. I walked away, left it to stink.

The late-afternoon cicadas gave way to the soft churring notes of nocturnal frogs and birdlife. We got out of there – outside was always safer – and headed over to the amenities hall with its high ceilings, large windows, less dark corners. There was even a fireplace. The main doors were wide open, the windows smashed, and everything that wasn't bolted down had been nicked or trashed. The background of the main stage, the set of so many crappy nights of bullshit concerts about God and peace and other myths, was now vandalised with painted cock and balls and random graffiti tags. The place had gone to ruin, with nothing but stained old mattresses, a bookcase of prayer books and a few broken chairs inside. The whole place smelled like possum piss.

Brookes dumped his bag on the ground, opened the canvas top flap and pulled out a wide-tipped aerosol. The can rattled as he shook it harder than necessary, approached the main fireplace and started spraying the outline of a word across the wall in his signature block, in a font size taller than him.

DEVEL.

Brookes sprayed saliva over me as his goofy laugh rose in his throat. I didn't have the heart to tell him he'd spelled it wrong. The graffiti shone red and vibrant in the dim light.

'What does that even say? Stupid loser can't even spell,' Steph said.

Brookes looked wounded, like he'd self-combust, and started to bash his hand on the side of his temple. He prided himself on his destruction of public property.

'Haven't you heard of them? They're a new reggae group,' I bullshitted, and that shut her up. 'They rock. Aren't they American?'

'Oh, yeah, that's right,' Stuck-up Steph said.

I smirked at Brookes. The whole place smelled like dead rat and rot, the carpet sodden in places from the rain leaking through the smashed skylight.

'How can grass grow inside?' Steph asked, disappointed at the standard of accommodation.

'God's will,' I joked.

'You don't believe?' Becca asked.

The fact that medieval bullshit got any airtime in schools made me shake my head, but I'd forgotten Becca was still into Jesus. 'No more than any other supernatural being – *The Hitchhiker's Guide* answers the ultimate questions of life.'

Becca tilted her head. 'Like what?'

I twisted my lip, and thought about my favourite Douglas Adams quote, the one that made total sense, more than any bible verse. 'Like how it should be enough to see that a garden is beautiful without having to believe that there are fairies at the bottom of it, too.'

Becca rolled her eyes. 'Since when did you get so philosophical?'

I'd had time to think in this place. Most of the thoughts weren't good ones.

'I'm cold,' Becca said, the cool wind in her hair.

'This will help!' Steph said, holding up a bottle of vodka and taking a slug, passing it around.

I took a huge swig. Becca shook her head.

'Time for you to do your thing, Pyro,' Brookes called.

'What – in here?' I asked, my throat still burning from the booze.

'I don't think they'll care if you stain the carpet,' Becca said, picking up an old shoe and throwing it further away with a look of disgust.

We moved some of the furniture around, chucked a stenchy mattress out of the main area we decided was the least feral. I needed a calming effect, but I wasn't letting the place burn down while we were still in it. The bathrooms had been partially demolished, and I slid a half-wrenched-out shower base into the cleared space to be the foundation of my creation.

I was keen to take an edge off the creeps I'd felt ever since we'd cut through the fencing. I couldn't help but think the brothers were watching. One of them had chased me right under the sink with a cattle prod, laughing the whole time. Snapping the legs off one of the broken chairs I could still imagine old mate Jock-itch telling stories from, I made a classic teepee-design bonfire in the middle of the centre court of the amenities hall. And it felt good.

'Fuck you!' I yelled, sipping vodka from the bottle, the heat burning my throat. With no lights, the only glow was from the bonfire, and it cast distorted patterns on the walls. For some whacked reason it made me feel closer to Mum, as if the ghost of her was in those flames, furling in the air, watching over me.

The fire roared, sucking the oxygen from the room, flicking embers onto the crusty old carpet as it came to life. Luckily most of the windows were smashed and we had enough airflow to not be smoked to death. Brookes and Steph cosied up in the corner trying to get the Orchybottle bong to work, while Becca and I focused on the fire. She sat, cross-legged on a pink beach towel, the dancing glow from the fire highlighting the curves of her neck. The dry branches crackled, but died out fast without catching the logs. Becca had found old magazines in the toilet block and started balling them up.

'It's dying. We need kindling.' She threw a book at my feet.

I froze. 'Rip a book?' They were Mum's words. A memory of her smile as she finished up work one day at the council library, filing cards in those tiny wooden drawers.

Becca smiled, holding one up. 'Is that look because you'd miss *Classic Prayers for the Modern World* or is burning books against the Library Monitor's code?' She ripped it in two.

I laughed. 'That was grade four. You remember that?'

She smiled, those green eyes flashing in the crimson light. 'I remember you before you were *Pyro*.'

I remembered *everything* about her. How she dropped care packages to the cottage after Margo shoved me here. How she understood my mum. How she was the only one who didn't judge. Before Mum died, before I came to this place, we'd fooled around every Friday club night behind the school pool's grandstand. It was quiet and dark and despite the chlorine in the air, kind of nice, overlooking the state school oval. We hadn't quite gotten back to that schedule since I got out. All that seemed like a dream now. I threw her a *Playboy* I'd found under one of the single seaters. 'That I can destroy.' That, too, had been ruined by this place.

She laughed and started ripping it up, commenting now and then about the shape of the boobs and what fruit they resembled. 'Honeydew melons.' She held up a centrefold with huge norks.

'I'm more of an orange man myself,' I said, the nips of vodka I'd had earlier kicking in.

Her cheeks went pink in a way I hadn't seen in months. 'I missed you at swim club.' Her eyes locked with mine. 'I was hoping you'd do the weekend visits, like Brookesy did.'

I shrugged. Coming home only made going back more unbearable.

We'd smoked half our weed stash and drank most of the vodka and were feeling the effects of both. We didn't even notice the waning of the batteries of Brookes' ghetto blaster, only that something sounded a little off with 1927's 'If I Could'.

Steph came over and pulled up Becca to dance with her, and I watched the two girls attempt a tipsy slow dance, the heat of vodka on my tongue, the weed dulling my senses. Was this what I needed? To make new memories of this place to erase the old? Or was I just refreshing the paint, making the picture brighter in my mind?

Brookes stepped into the light of the fire, passed me the Orchy bottle with the hose. I could barely hear the skid of brakes above the sound of the fire crackling and the stereo dying a slow death, but the arc of light across the roofline confirmed my fear.

'Shhh ... there's someone here,' I said. I could tell by the lumpy cam and a worked exhaust that it was a Holden Torana. I had names for all the ingloriously ugly models and this one I'd named Keen on account of the mustard paintjob.

The girls stopped dancing, hid behind an old mattress that covered most of the window and gawked outside, still giggling like it was a game.

'Who's got a yellow Holden?' Steph said louder than it needed to be. 'Total bogan.'

My eyes met Brookes'. There was only one, and we knew who owned it, and what that meant.

We were in deep shit.

Chapter 17

LOTTI

Otto's eyes opened wide from what I'd hoped would be his proper all-night sleep, but apparently was just a late afternoon nap. 'When's dinner?' his sleepy voice asked.

There was no way I was taking this kid out again, so I called over to the tavern and ordered some hot chips with tomato sauce via room service and they said they'd be ready in ten. When they hadn't arrived in twenty, I called back.

'It ain't the Hilton, precious. You gotta come get it, hon. It's at the bar window. Near the pokies.' Another parental fail.

I wasn't leaving Otto alone, so we snuck through the carpark and found the food window.

'Ten minutes,' the waiter said.

I smiled without warmth given it had already been twenty. Otto and I loitered nervously at an empty table out of the main hum of the place, thumb wrestling while we waited. I tuned into a conversation occupying a group of patrons near the kitchen. My ears picked up on mentions of Brightside and 'remains'. The men laughed at a theory that it was probably some old hooker. His partner said there was a homeless man living in the shanty, and he probably just drank himself to death. While their theories varied, all of them seemed intrigued as to finding the truth, as if it was the most entertaining thing to do in Eldham.

Our order was called, and as we approached the window, Otto said, 'There's that arsehole again.'

'Excuse me? Language!'

'That's what *you* called him.'

'Who?' I said, the chips bagged up for us, hot and salty.

He pointed in the way only a kid did – direct and unapologetically. Joel was inside with another man who looked just like him – another of the brothers? Otto was mesmerised, staring in wonder, which only made me more certain it was a mistake leaving the room.

'Let's go.' I grabbed the basket and pulled Otto towards the safety of the room, the long way so we wouldn't be seen. 'It's rude to stare.'

'Why? People stare at me all the time.'

'Only because you're brilliant.' I couldn't believe that man was here – but then realised – where else would he be? It was the only place in town.

As we got back and deadlocked the door, Otto asked, 'Did he know Mum? Or is he talking about a whole different Freya?'

'Sorry?'

'Mummy's grown-up name was Freya, not Mummy. That's what they called her at the church.'

'Yep, that's right, clever boy. And I bet she loved being your mum.'

He smeared sauce all over the chips. 'What's a lard-arse?'

'That's not a nice thing to say.' I tore a chip open and blew on the white flesh so it was cool enough for him, once, then again.

He was chewing and talking at the same time. 'What's it mean, but?'

'It just means you're a bit chubby. But you know what? Sometimes the nicest people are the bigger ones – because they just enjoy life and don't spend time worrying about what they look like on the outside. Don't judge an egg by its shell. It's what's on the inside that counts, so judge it by the yolk.'

'Is the yolk the runny bit you dip toast in?'

'If you cook them right it is.'

'The arsehole said Freya got skinny and turned hot. But Mummy threw up, so she didn't ever get fat. Isn't being hot, bad? Mum said I got hot when I was sick and that's why my ears broke.'

I kissed the kid on the forehead, hoping he wouldn't see the sadness in my face. 'Oh, sweetpea. That's a lot. They were probably talking about a movie star with the same name.' I tucked him under my arm and helped him eat the chips, enjoying just the two of us. I felt unsettled, the chips had burned my tongue, and I wished we'd never left the room. 'You lip-read from that far away? You're a clever pumpkin, you know that? You have superpowers.' He was satisfied with that. 'Do you always watch strangers to see what they're talking about?'

'Yep. I see you and Ms Kingston talking about Mr Kurkowski. How he's a "chest talker" – which isn't really true because I watched, and he definitely talks through his mouth.'

I tried not to laugh. As we ate, I thought for a minute. 'Out of interest, stinkbug, you know that night before Daddy left, when he got a message from his mate, then went outside the van to ring him – were you watching from your bunk?'

He was cautious.

'You're not in trouble. It just might help me work out how to help Daddy.'

'Daddy said, "what's up, mate", then after a bit he said

something like, "what do you mean they know we did it?" then he turned away.' Otto gazed up at me. 'What did they do?'

I wished I hadn't asked. 'It was probably winning the footy back in high school – he's always saying his old mates argued about the scores and who won.'

'You reckon?' Otto wasn't convinced. 'His face *did* go the way it does when he watches it on TV – kinda mad.'

'Yeah, that sounds right. You know your dad – footy is serious business,' I said, wishing I could fool myself as easily. 'To bed for reals this time.'

I thought of Becca's offer to stay at hers – was it really necessary?

After a few paranoid peeks out the hotel curtains, I figured there was no harm done and he fell asleep with a full tummy not long after.

Alone with my ruminating thoughts, I tried to decide my next move. The mirrored wardrobe door caught my reflection, and I hardly recognised myself – tired, worried, unsure. Where had all my guts gone? The gumption I'd mustered to drive across the state to find my man, not sit and wait for him to dictate how this would play out, had dissolved. All I'd done was change the venue. I was still waiting for him, still clueless about what was really going on. Perhaps I should just pack up, take this kid out of this town, and wait it out? I flopped on the other bed with a twang.

'You still awake?' I texted Jess.

'Are you still alive?' was the text response followed by her calling straight away. 'What's wrong? Are you okay? Where are you?' It came out in a torrent.

Her voice must have signalled my brain to release the floodwaters because the tears started, and I was blubbering a moment later. 'No, I'm fine, I'm …'

'You're not fucking fine. Are you at home? I can be there in an hour.'

'I'm still out west.'

'This is still about Wrench Boy? Did you find him?'

'He's in jail.'

'What? For a sec I thought you said he was in jail.' She laughed melodically.

'Well, he's being held for questioning in a tiny jail-like room, been there all night apparently. There was a fire when they were kids and then they found human remains near it and the local cops think he might have something to do with it.'

'With the fire? Or the remains?'

'Both? I don't know. Grayson said something about a man with the same name being charged with arson in the eighties so …'

'Grayson? Since when are we talking to Grayson?' She said 'we' as if we were unquestionably united on all things.

'Since I have no clue what's going on with anything and thought he'd help me.'

'Have you spoken to Wrench Boy?'

'The police officer's in some sort of bush mafia.' I filled in my best friend on the combined offerings from the two women of August's past. About his mum's house burning down, about some other fire in their teens, and the bones. I left out Becca, as if saying the name out loud would give my fears more oxygen to thrive.

Jess was silent, as though she were writing it all down, drawing lines between circles of scant data. 'That hole you found – not just a coincidence? Your phone tracker doobie placed him at the grave, now there's human bits – no wonder he's being questioned. Lotti, you're a smart girl. You don't need me to join the dots. Get out, fast. Go home.'

I huffed out a long, ragged breath. But there was sweet Otto, asleep with his cheek so mashed into the depths of the pillow that his lips formed a cupid's kiss. 'That's what the logical answer is, but my innate instinct is to see this out.' *To trust him.*

'You can do that from Brisbane – behind a locked door, with your own support network around you. Not out there, in his patch.'

'Can't I get some credit for being a good judge of character?' I knew everyone had shades of darkness, that no one was all good or evil, but the person who stroked my arm when I was worried just to let me know he was there for me, who checked my car's oil and water before I drove, could not also be a raging violent axe murderer. 'He's not a bad man, Jess.' I sounded naïve. It sounded exactly like what foolish wives of serial killers said after discovering rotting corpses under their garden shed. But it's what I felt. And this was Jess, and she got the whole spectrum of me, even the thoughts I was ashamed to say out loud.

The line was silent. 'Perhaps he isn't anymore, hon, but it sounds like he might have been. And do people change that much, in their core? I just don't want you near him if we don't know what he's capable of. Think of Dexter Morgan. Just because they're hot doesn't mean they should get away with murder.'

I huffed. 'Hasn't everyone done things they regret? We killed an old lady's cat, remember?'

'You mean when that tabby ran beneath our car, and despite maxing out your card to save the thing, it was rude enough to cark it anyway? Not exactly brutish behaviour.'

'We shoplifted in Greece!'

Jess laughed. 'You walked out with a book under your arm, too busy flirting with the cute shop boy about your blow-up pineapple.'

'I married someone I didn't love then left them the next day.'

Jess took a moment to respond, and the weight of my sin sat heavy on the line. 'Yeah, that was pretty brutish. Did you ever tell Wrench Boy that you're still technically married to the next attorney-general?'

I swallowed. 'See, that's exactly my point – I haven't been honest about the shittiest thing I've done.'

'You didn't kill anything, well, except your father's political career ...'

'Fuck. Dad's going to go ballistic if the media gets wind of it.'

'Listen to you – swearing like a sailor – he's infiltrating your psyche.'

'He's not a serial killer, Jess. He's a mechanic who's here, helping a friend, assisting the police with their enquiries.' I wasn't sure who I was trying to convince. 'He made me a shower, J-girl. A shower. He makes smiley-face pancakes, and took on his sister's child when she died.'

'His *sister's* child? *Otto's not even his kid?*' There was a distinct shrill in the last part.

I huffed. 'Yeah, that's the other thing ... it's complicated though. The father's an arse.' I wondered how much of this resistance to extricate myself from August was because of the six-year-old he lived with. Would it be different if it was just Augie I had to leave in the lurch? Men could fend for themselves, but this kid – he'd already had his share of that.

I tuned back into Jess's voice, who was still questioning why I wasn't packing and clearing out. 'But he lied to you about the kid being his – you know that for sure,' she said. 'I think that's your answer, Char – he's been selective in what he tells you to give a false impression of who he is. What's he hiding?'

'Maybe nothing? Maybe he was just taught he was second-rate and not to show his real self? You don't get it, Jess.

He was orphaned at fourteen. His house burned to the ground. His mum died.'

'Is it just me seeing the pattern here? And the common denominator is always Wrench Boy. Isn't this the guy you said refused to get involved in the firemen's calendar charity thing?'

'Exactly! He's a volunteer firefighter! He doesn't light them up – he puts them out.'

She did that silent thing again, as if she were recording every blight against his record to spit back at me later. 'One of my students was a firebug – mixed-up unit. They get off on it – the chaos, the control – it's a serious condition, and they often end up as firefighters. Google "Hero Syndrome". They love the attention.'

'Augie hates attention.'

'At least the version he shows you does. Hon, have you considered he might not be your forever guy? I mean, sounds like you haven't told him about Grayson, and does he know about your endo, how that complicates things?'

'No comment.'

'I know you're trying to find your own agency, find a life apart from your family name, but maybe your dad was right – don't date him out of spite. You've been to uni half your life, sounds like he barely passed high school.'

'Did you just say that? I am proof that going to uni is no guarantee of making sound life choices. Look, I gotta go.' I sniffed. 'This is not making me feel any better.' I held the phone to my chest, but her muffled voice still registered.

'Promise me you'll tell your father. You've put up with all the bullshit, having to grow up in the public eye, you may as well reap the benefit. They'll call the election any day – you know how paranoid he gets during the campaign, you need his help to get ahead of this.'

'I don't need his help.' My father will think I need rescuing. That I'm powerless. That I can't handle my life, which all may be true, but I didn't need him to know it. 'And he's not exactly getting ahead of his own scandal – still haven't seen anything in the news about him shagging his EA while his wife forgets more and more pieces of herself every day.'

There was a shard of sympathy for me before Jess returned to publicist mode. 'Exactly. That's why you need his help.'

'No one knows about this either, Jess.'

'Not yet.'

She didn't get it. 'Jess – did I tell you about when I first met Augie?'

'You said he was a dick.'

'It was the same energy I felt the first time I watched a student's face when a concept clicked into place. That buzz, that unquestionable feeling – as certain as any fact – that this is what it's about. He makes my brain come alive.'

I heard the eye-roll through the phone. 'Your brain? Or your lady bits?'

'Don't be crass. And don't even think about saying "use your head" or I will totally think you're slowly morphing into my father, and I'll have to defriend you. I'm hanging up because I'm really scared you will and I will have to follow through and that will totally suck, so, goodbye, loser.'

Now I could get back to the small problem of working out if my boyfriend was just a garden-variety liar, an arsonist, a murderer … or all three.

Chapter 18

AUGIE, 2009

After twenty hours breathing the stale air of Interview Room 2, Harris let me out.

I'd lost nearly a day to that stinking hole, hankering for the minute I could leave, and now that I was standing on the federation-brick entry of the old cop shop, I had no fucking clue what to do with my freedom. I was sixteen again, unsure what level of shit I'd get back home at my aunt's, whether I was better off facing her now or being a gutless wonder and hightailing it home. To my garage. To my kid. There were things that needed to be said.

The fancy Apple phone Lotti passed down to me beeped a melody of notifications as soon as I powered it up – twelve missed calls and six unread messages since the pigs confiscated it and shoved it in a drawer. Ten of them were from Lotti. She'd be worried sick. Where did I start with her, explaining all this?

The screen went blank, the battery dead, which saved me from confronting whether things with Lotti were, too.

Brookes was being held for further questioning. My truck had been impounded behind the cop shop, the contents now in police custody. Let them open it. It was still a long shot that anything in there would point to us, not yet at least. I told them we had nothing to do with any bones and, for once, my tendency of saying as little as possible seemed useful. I can't speak for my friend though. He was still in there. Talking? Not talking? Who fucking knew?

With no wheels, my only choice was to walk – or stumble, I was that sleep deprived, and there were only two places that'd welcome me in this town.

Becca was married now, with a kid and a suit for a husband who I guessed would be less than welcoming to a bloke that used to snog his wife. They lived near the bus depot three blocks over, at least, they used to. I toyed with the idea of drowning my sorrows at the pub but decided against it. I grabbed a sausage roll and a Solo from the garage, thankful the kid on the counter looked about twelve so didn't recognise me. *The pyro with the quirky mum whose god-bothering aunt kicked him out of her house.* It was strange how small towns reduced everyone to a sentence. We all had a few main adjectives that people arranged in different orders. Becca was 'Miss Eldham Bicentennial Year' raising her halfwit brother because their parents were too busy getting wasted to notice them. Freya was the nice fat girl who played guitar. Margo was every underdog's friend. Everything was either black or white with no room for the complexities of in-betweens. Perhaps that's why the city slickers thought we were simple.

I screwed up the sausage roll packet and chucked it in a wheelie bin, walked, half delirious, to the fancy house Brookes told me had been Becca's. The front yard was scattered with coloured toddler crap, a unicorn toy that had seen better days, a discarded sun hat and a shell-shaped sandbox. I was psyching myself up to knock – I hadn't seen Becca since Freya's funeral two years ago – when a car pulled into the drive and there she was, in real life. She unclipped a sleeping toddler from a childseat. The mini Becca looked so helpless, her arms slung over her mother's neck as she was carted towards the front door of a grand, renovated colonial. She'd outgrown her bogan upbringing. 'Becca?'

Her eyebrows pulled together when she saw me. She stepped over the junk in the yard and, without disturbing her kid, threaded the other behind my neck in a half hug. Her whole body ran the length of mine and I breathed her in, thinking of the treehouse under the stars and the first time I'd lay down with her in it. When she pulled out of the hug I kissed her on the forehead, a little longer than was probably wise. She pulled away to reveal one wet circle on her left boob which she covered with an open palm.

'Shit,' Becca whispered, blushing.

'That's a new trick,' I said.

'I need to feed her,' she said, looking everywhere but at me.

'Isn't she like, three? Looks like she could chew a medium-rare steak by now.'

'She's nearly two. And are you seriously qualified to give me parenting advice?'

I smiled. 'I missed you belittling me. Did you name her Charlene?'

'Piss off.' She kissed my cheek, then lingered. 'It's Ruby.' Her eyes were closed when I opened mine, and I thought she was overwhelmed from the contact, the memories, but then she exhaled and said, 'You reek. Go shower, I'll settle this one, get some of Pete's clothes for you.'

'Nah, gross, not doing that. I'll shower and double spray the armpits of these.'

'That never worked, Gus.' She smiled her two dimpled grin, and I was sixteen again. If I hadn't known this girl since kindy, if I hadn't shared baths, run naked in sprinklers, got my aunt to help when she had her first period, it would have been impossible to be myself again after so long. But it was Becca. Becca had seen the state of the house I grew up in. Seen me bawl like a baby after Mum died. Seen the worst of me. Even though our childhood friendship had morphed into something else around the time I started shaving, she was still Becca. I'd even forgiven her for choosing her brother over me.

'Where is Pete? Let me guess, away?' I was sure that bloke had a wife in every port. He didn't deserve this one.

We met back at the kitchen table a while later, her with her arms free after dealing with her leaking issue, me with my hair dripping but feeling almost human. 'Fancy taps. Couldn't get the fuckers to start.'

'They're sensors.'

'They're gold.' I gave her a look that said 'what the fuck' and we both laughed for a minute before remembering why I was there. Brookes. I knew he'd called her earlier from jail. I needed to know what he said.

'I tried to keep him out of it, Becks. But they've still got him. They held us there two days, the bastards.'

'I know. I've just come from the station.'

'What – just now?'

'Well, I went via your girlfriend's room.'

'Who?'

'How many girls do you have? Hair like a Pantene ad. Big eyes. Long legs.'

'Lotti's *here*?' Everything clenched.

She nodded. 'At the pub. She introduced herself as Charlotte – how did she go from that beautiful name to Lotti?'

'Doesn't like Charlotte. Too traditional.'

Becca shrugged. 'Who'd want to be traditional?' She threw her hands in the air, gesturing to her family home, adorned with baby photos and her husband's trophies. Her kitchen was bigger than my whole bus and looked like the cover of a home magazine, clinical and sleek and with a thousand useless appliances covering the stone bench. She assessed me, saying everything in a look like she always had, but I was distracted by the fact Lotti was here. In my patch.

'Where's Otto then?' I asked.

'With her. At the pub. She knows about him, Gus.'

I nodded. I was almost relieved. One less thing.

Becca looked down her nose at me. 'Haven't seen him since the funeral, thanks for keeping me in his life.'

The twist in my gut returned. 'Jesus – that place is swarming with Harrises.'

'I know. I told her to come stay with me. He's safer here till you can all leave in the morning.' She said it like I could just drive into the sunset with my woman and my kid and forget all this.

I relaxed. 'Thank you.' I then realised I'd have Becca and Lotti in the same room, and wasn't sure how that would play out.

'He's adorable.'

My mind spun. Otto. Here. Near Joel. 'And the spitting image of his father.'

'He was always a version of you with thicker hair and fewer scars.'

'And no fucking character. Thankfully the kid got the heart of his mother.'

She reached over and turned my wrist, exposing my forearm, inspecting it as if she'd dreamed it seventeen years before. She, who refused to take responsibility for it, not wanting the burden of thinking I'd permanently scarred myself for her. She dropped my wrist.

Becca's eyes fell away as she gave a sad smile. 'It's weird, I took Frey for granted when I knew she was just up the range, I barely rang her, but now she's gone for good I miss her face every day.' Crinkles around the eyes, a new line etched along the bridge of her nose, but her thinking face was the same as it always was. 'It's the spaces she left – as my bridesmaid, as Ruby's godmother, as my friend. I can't even walk past the pub without imagining her singing, her guitar was like an extra limb.'

'Same.' Being home had coloured the images in my head that time had yellowed. I could see Freya clearly, multitasking with a *Dolly Fiction* in one hand and a slice of bread smothered in hundreds and thousands in the other. The way she'd scream out to me 'it's oooooon' after the ads finished, watching *Roseanne* or *The Henderson Kids* in the TV room so I wouldn't miss a minute. I took Becca's hand, told myself it was all platonic, uniting in grief, but the dirty look she lobbed back said I'd gotten that wrong, and she retracted her hand. 'You were always bad at reading a room.'

'C'mon. I was a legend with the chicks. It was the rat's tail that reeled them in.' I thought I was out of practice with this banter, but I delivered it with a straight face.

'Took me three years of flirting for you to kiss me,' Becca said, a flush on those pale Irish cheeks.

I shrugged. 'Yeah, maybe I am better with engines.' I knew I shouldn't look at her, but I couldn't help it, and as soon as I did her eyes flicked to the floor. Pristine marble tiles, shiny and new. It represented a state of perfection that I just didn't think existed, at least, not for people like us.

'Lotti is lovely,' she added, squaring her jaw. 'You've got some hard yards to make up there.'

'I know,' I said and a silence settled between us. 'What do I tell her?'

'How 'bout the truth? Whose bones are they, Gus?'

I exhaled. At least she'd waited ten minutes before hitting me with it.

'I know you know so don't lie to me.'

I closed my eyes, certain this interrogation would be deadlier than the one with her cop cousin, this woman a better truth-serum. I couldn't bullshit Becca. She knew me too well.

'Please tell me those bones are some random backpacker's, not Steph's.'

I said nothing.

'You and your bro-code bullshit. What is it with you two?'

'We made a promise. It's between me and your brother. I don't break my promises.'

Now she was the one clamming up. She stood and walked to the adjacent benchtop, flicked on the kettle and opened a door in the cabinetry to reveal a huge hidden fridge. 'I can't help you if I don't know what I'm covering up.'

'For fuck's sake, your cousin just held me in a tiny jail all fucking day and night with nothing but questions. I can't take any more.'

She shook her head, almost pleased at me firing up. 'Twenty minutes and you're already angry.' She put on a tone as if she was mocking me. 'You with your plan to put a mattress in the back tray and sleep under the stars.' She shook her head as if the idea was ludicrous. 'If you ever wondered why I didn't go with you, that's why – it wasn't Brookes at all.'

I looked her straight in the eye. 'That true?' She made me wait for an answer, and in that time, I felt a tremble in my chin I'd die rather than let her see. Ten seconds, still no answer. One thing was for sure, I'd never have given her marble tiles and gold taps. 'Just tell me, are you happy, with … Pete?' The snarl was still there, hiding between the P and the E. Boring old man. He was ten years older, bald, but rich.

She jiggled tea bags in two fancy-looking cups. I reckoned tea tasted like grass clippings, but I didn't want to piss her off more, so I took one when she offered it, ignoring the touch of her hand on mine. 'He's kind to me. He provides for us. I never want for anything.'

He sounded like a father, not a husband. But who was I to judge? I turned away, scratching fingers over my three-day growth. Was that the question I came to find an answer to? I had one now. I nodded, resolved. 'Well, you always made better choices than me.'

She sipped her tea. 'Yeah, well, me staying didn't really help Brookes – he's still in trouble, never really been out of it.'

I huffed out a breath. 'I tried to help him, told Troy if they had anything on him, he wasn't fit for trial anyway 'cause of the –– what do they call it? Because of your mum being on the turps when she was up the duff?'

'Fetal Alcohol Syndrome,' Becca said, her jaw tight.

'Reckoned that he wasn't right in the head 'cause of it. And you know what they said? "Yeah, half the fucking jail's got that, and a bit of everything else, he'll fit right in."'

Becca shook her head. 'Have they DNA'd the bones yet?'

'Don't reckon so.'

Her eyes narrowed in on mine. 'You know, after that night, you know the one I mean, when Steph never came back to school, I went past the house Steph said was hers – that nice big Queenslander with the tin flamingos. I got talking to the old lady there who was pruning her roses and she said she'd lived there her whole life, never heard of a Stephanie Lawley.'

I shrugged. 'So? The brat probably lived in a dump and wanted to look rich.'

'Back when it all happened Margo was worried Steph would blab about what we did. Remember the cops were asking who the anonymous caller was who reported that Brightside was on fire? Steph always said she was an exchange student at the private school but did you ever see her in uniform? She was always just 'around' that summer, hey. She just inserted herself into our group from thin air. Always wondered why someone would come all the way from America to hang out in Eldham. Margo said Steph wasn't even in the school system. Your aunt never liked her much.'

'She was a blow-in. A bullshitter. Reckon she just moved away when people started to look too hard at who she really was.'

Becca's eyes narrowed, like they were scanning mine for the truth. 'You and your conspiracy theories. How much history could a fifteen-year-old have?'

I'd had a bit, at that age. 'Didn't Tom from the Mobil reckon Steph told him she got a part in some pilot back home, saw her board a McCafferty's heading to the big smoke?'

'Does it sound like Steph to slip off without so much as a goodbye? No fanfare, no party in her honour or chance to skite? Convenient story.'

It hurt more than it should, and heat filled my head. 'Convenient? You think I offed a girl to stop her snitching about a fucking fire? 'Cause from where I'm sitting, her vanishing that night is fucking *in*convenient.'

'Gus …' Becca's eyes were wet with tears, her baby monitor squawked, and she seemed relieved at the interruption.

'You think I actually killed your friend? You sound like your fucking cousin. Is that what you told Lotti this is all about?'

'No, why would I do that?' She shook her head. 'Does she know anything?'

I glared at her. 'What's it to you? You want to be in on my life, suddenly? You had your chance.' I exhaled a long breath. 'Thanks for the shower,' I said. 'I'll find my way out.'

She harumphed, stood up quick and slid her chair back beneath the long table. 'Gus, c'mon – I already asked Charlotte and Otto to stay. I made up the beds.'

I turned away, but she reached out to grab my arm.

'Gus?'

I kept walking. She paced towards me with the same look on her face she'd get when she'd cornered a bully belittling her brother: pissed, and determined to make it right. Her palms flat on my chest, she kissed me hard on the lips. Perhaps it was the shock of it, the unexpected, after years of wondering, but it didn't feel half as good as I'd imagined. It had all the nostalgia of childhood but meant nothing as adults, nothing in the here and now. And she wasn't Lotti. All it did was muddy my mind, clocked up yet another thing to come clean about, and I wished she'd left the past in the past. She was right about one thing – I still didn't get women. I thought I was about to get hit, not kissed.

Becca looked up and whispered, 'Just' – she swallowed hard – 'look after our boy, please?'

I first thought she meant Otto, but with her it was always about Brookes. Never about me. My nostrils flared and I wanted to say, 'When have I not?' But we wouldn't be in this predicament if that were true. I paused for one last thing. 'She's beautiful, your daughter.'

'We named her Ruby Jude.'

I nodded, wondering what Mum would have thought of Becca's kid with that putz being named after her, when she'd have wanted the father to be me. I did too, once. But I wasn't that bloke anymore.

'Wait – speaking of your mum. Did they ever find her … remains? I mean, could they somehow be …'

'For fuck's sake.' I was already fired up. 'You've moved on from me killing Stuck-up Steph, now I killed my own mother, dumped her in a ditch? You're as bad as the fucking Harrises and you can all go fuck yourselves.' I yanked free of her touch and stomped towards the front. I was back on the footpath, the buzz of insects swarming a streetlamp.

Seeing her was a mistake that only complicated things. I still had no charge in my phone, no money and no car. All I had done was confirm another woman didn't trust me.

Chapter 19

AUGIE, 2009

As I walked through the main street of Eldham, all the reasons I hadn't been back here since Freya's funeral shone brightly. The library Mum had worked at. The Meals on Wheels where she and Margo had volunteered. The footy field where Mum watched every game of mine. Even when things with Mum started to break, she still turned up and sat under her sun umbrella with her blue drink decanter every Saturday morning, handing out orange quarters between halves in tiny freezer bags.

I wasn't sure if Lotti had checked out of the pub yet to hide at Becca's, but there was only one way to find out. Becca and Brookes' uncle still ran the place. I wondered if he still ran the drug trade, too, along with everything else, and if Joel was still his debt collector.

There was no one I knew on the bar, and only a few Hens night girls dressed in pink tulle veils dancing near the juke box. They were murdering the REO Speedwagon hit, 'I'm Gonna Keep on Loving You ...' as if the song list hadn't refreshed since the eighties.

'This track sounds like your era,' said the pretty goth chick drying a glass behind the counter.

'Easy on.' I asked her if a dark-haired woman with a little boy had checked out just now and she said she hadn't seen her – that most of the rooms were full of miners and single old farts.

'I'm knocking off at ten though if it's a girl you're chasing.'

I blushed, told the woman with black lipstick that that wouldn't help me dig myself out of trouble, but that seemed to egg her on.

I weaved out the back of the pub, past the beer garden and drive-through, and there she was, Frida the boring beige Volvo with the dodgy wiring, parked at a pitiful angle across two bays. They were still here. She'd come after me. They were right in front of me.

Every thought distilled down to them.

The door was closed but I could hear Lotti cursing from the verandah, and let my ears find her. I had to laugh – she used to flinch when I swore. 'Get in there you piece of crap.' She'd done her best to shut the curtains, even had pegs on the sides to keep them in place, but I could see them through the sheer orange fabric; Otto eating salt and vinegar chips, smearing oily fingers on the bedspread, Lotti failing to close her designer suitcase, billowing at the sides. That explained the temper. That had rubbed off, too.

I used my knuckles to knock. She saw my shadow and I could see her tense through the gap in the curtain, took Otto's hand, guided him and his bag of chips into the bathroom and closed the door before returning. 'It's just me, Lotti.' Everything depended on how her face arranged in that split second, but she leaned her forehead against the door as if working out how to be, what to do. When she looked up, the curtain was in the way, so I had no clue if she was about to hug me or stab me with scissors. The security chain slid.

The first look at her in days was a fragment of her face between the chain, but it floored me. She was tired, pale, worried as hell and it was all my doing. The right words wouldn't form. I had no idea how to play this. All I knew was I had to play it right.

The door closed, the safety released, then the door opened at once and we just stood there, her eyes reaching out, telling me everything I needed to know. They were hurt, they were tired, but they weren't turning away.

I took a risk, pressed into her, my cheek rough on her ear as I wrapped my arms around her thin waist, nuzzled my cheek into her apple-scented hair. She was non-responsive for a moment, not hugging me back and I was terrified this was it, the last time I'd ever touch her. I'd fucked this up, not just for me but for Otto too. The kid was stuck with me and, if I carked it early like the rest of my lot, soon he'd be alone in a silent world, with no one and nothing but an ever-present sense that everyone leaves.

It'd taken me too fucking long to realise she was what I needed. Not loneliness. Not Becca. Charlotte Hill was worth the risk, and I'd fucked it up.

Then I felt her long elegant arms envelop me, her chin press into my collarbone and her hands reach up to the nape of my neck. Her breath shuddered, and we both released a few ugly sobs that had been building for days and I saw with a deep sense of clarity than she was my safe place. I ached to kiss her.

It'd always been about the kiss, with us. You can chat with a mate, you can have sex with a stranger, but a good kiss? That was a rarity. It's like it aligned us again, got us in sync. I was bone-tired, stressed off my nut, but it felt so good to have her lips on mine, and feel her want them there. 'You don't know how much I missed that,' I said.

Yeah, the gush of it even surprised me, but I was so far out on a limb anyway these past days, venting raw emotion was nothing. She kissed me again, and we sank into its deep, slow familiarity, filling up the tank of good feelings that had been sucked dry, until she pushed away. My eyes snapped open.

'Wait …' She backed off, stepped away, her arms crossed. 'Not before you tell me what's going on.'

I nodded. I needed to tell all – code or no code, let her in on everything I had. The choice to keep her out of this had been lost the second she drove past that sign that said "Welcome to Eldham, population 3145" and didn't turn away.

'Can we just backtrack?' She paced around as if plotting something. 'You got my message then, about being here. You know I tried to see you – at the station?' She blurted through snorts and sniffles. 'Did they just let you out?'

I nodded.

'Is it all sorted now? Can we just go home?'

'I need to wait till they've finished with my truck, but soon, maybe.' I waited for the logical flow of questions to follow but they didn't arrive, and I wondered how much Becca had told her, and how much of it was true.

'Has Otto been okay? Is he pissed at me? I need to see him.' I gestured towards the bathroom where she'd stored him for safe keeping, as if asking permission.

Lotti shrugged. 'He's your son …' She shook her head. 'Except, that's right, he isn't.' She laughed as if this was all some stupid practical joke, not her life. And then it began. She exhaled, then her eyes refilled with tears.

'I get it.' My hands were up, palms exposed. 'I have a lot to explain but, to be fair, I never said he was my actual son.' I sat on the bed, when all I wanted was to see the kid, hold his wiry little arms.

'He calls you Dad.'

'I gave him that choice when I adopted him. Margo told you about the situation with my sister, I'm guessing.'

Her face became rigid. 'And some …'

I nodded, felt it all surge up my throat, three days of guilty mistakes, wrong choices, and fear of what was to come. I'd kept it together for Brookes, but I couldn't sustain it any longer and my face crumbled without my permission, my vision misting over in a way that hadn't happened for years. I'd thought they'd dried up, after Freya.

She noticed, and I felt weak for not trying harder to keep it together. But then I just let go of it, let my feelings guide my actions, and stepped over to the bathroom, opened the door, and there he was, sitting on the closed dunny seat with his Nintendo DS.

'Daddy!' he yelled, throwing his arms around my neck as I bent down to pick him up, carried him out to the bedroom. 'Knew we'd find you!'

Lotti's stood, hands to her mouth as she watched us, conflicted, and I cried like a moron into Otto's hair, snorting like a toddler with a cold.

'Missed you, kid,' I said when his eyes met mine.

He was beaming, rattled off highlights from the last few days; a Mario Cart level completed, getting stuck in a fridge, playing fetch with Margo's dogs, eating a whole packet of chips on his own. His legs were swinging like a pendulum off the side of the ugly bedspread and his ease, his happiness, gave me the rush I needed, the sense of hope everything might just still work out.

'How'd you even get onto Margo?' I looked at Lotti and she didn't elaborate, but she clicked her tongue in that way she did when she was buying time. She was never dishonest, but she was also the kind of girlfriend who would help you look for chocolate that she knew damn well she'd already eaten. 'Quite the detectives, aren't you?' After another hug with the boy, it seemed as though I was caught up, and he returned to his game as if all was right in Otto's world. The band was back together.

My new strategy to just go with my feelings seemed to be working out, so I approached her like a cat, slow and cautious. The tip of my nose, my lips, grazed along her cheek to her hairline and I let myself breath her in.

Her hands fanned across my chest, like a brake, a way to keep me at bay. 'I can't reconcile the man I knew with all this ... Did you do what they think you did?' she asked, her eyes petrified of the answer.

I felt like a mongrel for ever getting involved with her. I should have walked away, never pursued her like I had a chance. It was a wall she couldn't get past, and I got that.

Then she looked puzzled, raised her fingers to my damp hair. 'Is it raining?'

I shook my head. 'I went to Becca's, got cleaned up.'

She pulled away. 'Becca's?' Her smile held no warmth. 'Is she the reason you're here?'

'What?' Tiredness hit me like a wall. 'Lotti – I'd been up for days, slept up a tree, spent a night at a cop shop ... I just needed a shower.'

'Oh, for a minute I thought it might be because I messaged you to say I was on my way there. Silly me. It's not like I left you a thousand messages telling you I was in town looking for you.' She shook her head.

'I didn't get those messages.'

'They why did you go to Becca's? Not because you knew I was going there.'

I got up. 'Listen, I'm really sorry to fuck up your week, but this is my life going down the toilet. You can walk away any time you like. I never asked you to come here. I never wanted you involved.'

She frowned but in a way that a three-year-old did before they stomped their foot and asked for more ice cream. This woman didn't have an aggressive molecule in her body. She couldn't even get mad when she had every right to.

She struggled to find words. 'It's not a choice. When you love someone, you are involved, August. Or Gus. Or whoever you are today.' Lotti's face fell, and she wiped tears, continued to try to join two halves of a suitcase that would never close, and my heart sank. She was leaving. This was it.

But then she went on. 'You just don't get it – I was worried sick, drove half a day to find you, petrified you were in trouble because you didn't answer my calls, and then discover you're in jail! But the second you get out, you don't call me, you go to your ex-girlfriend's to take a *shower*?' She had tears in her eyes. She'd circled back to the present, to my wet hair, as if that was the issue at hand.

I, on the other hand, had no problem displaying anger, chopping the air with my hand with each thought. 'My phone was dead. The cops had it in their filing cabinet all day. I had no car to get home to you, anyway. No money. Seriously, Charlotte. All this shit they're throwing at me, and you want me to explain that? I didn't drive all night back to this dive to sleep with her if that's what you think.'

'But you have …'

'Not today. And it was long enough ago that it doesn't even count.'

A sad smile I'd never seen shaped her face and she seemed less familiar. She took my forearm, and ran her finger over the curl of the B. 'Do you always get tattoos of women who don't count?' Her face hardened, another new look. 'I was fiercely jealous of this, figuring it was some old flame, but knowing what I know now, I'm guessing you probably got it in prison.' Lotti squared her jaw then looked away.

I closed my eyes, feeling like less of an arsehole now she was acting like one, too. Lotti had never done 'mean' before. I didn't have the energy to rebut. I didn't have a right to be angry.

She swallowed hard. 'She's beautiful.' She approached as if about to land one on my lips, but then pulled away with a scowl. 'I bet she missed kissing you, you're annoyingly good at it.' She retreated, fiddled with the broken edge of the table, a sullen look on her face. 'Did you? Just then, at her house. C'mon, all these years of wondering how she'd turn out – pretty well, if you ask me. She the one that got away, Gus?'

'Don't call me that.'

'Why not, it's your name, Gus.'

I twisted my jaw. 'Is this what you meant when you said you're a pain in the arse when you get hurt?'

She tilted her head to one side. 'Did you kiss her?'

'Not the way you're suggesting.'

She stepped closer, again. 'So, like, in a way you'd kiss Otto, or a way you'd kiss me?'

'Neither. Jesus.' My best friend is facing murder charges and she's upset about a fucking pointless kiss? 'You know how petty you sound? You know what they think I've fucking done? Why is that small detail the thing you're pissed about?'

She jumped a little, stepped away from me and it was only then I realised how angry I was. I took a breath, tried to calm down.

'Because how you feel about her changes what I am to you, and that's what matters to me. That's about *right now*. Not your past, not what Gus Nash did or didn't do before. I only care what *Augie Silverfell's* done.'

I was out of breath. I was gasping for air but couldn't fill my lungs. 'Gus Nash. August Silverfell. Cottage Nine, Bed Two. They're all me, Charlotte. And I've learned to live with that, but you don't have to. I don't want you to know that guy.'

She swallowed hard. Charlotte Hill was hell-bent on trying not to appear like a fragile woman – forever wearing boots and minimal makeup to tone down her femininity. But those curves. Those lips. Those eyelashes. She wouldn't pass as a bloke in a welder's mask and overalls. And she looked every bit as vulnerable now as I'd ever seen her. All I could think was, I did this to her. She let me in, and this is what she got back. Uncertainty and secrets. I wouldn't stay with me. Right now, I didn't even want to be around me.

Otto paused his game down the other end of the room, where he'd set up a haven of pillows, rubbed his eye. He couldn't hear but he didn't need noise to read a room. He was already better at it than me.

She pulled me into the kitchenette out of view of the kid but she kept the cold detachment. 'So, it's true – those remains – you know who they are, why they're there. It's not just a misunderstanding?' Lotti asked.

I shook my head, hoping this place wasn't bugged, that she wasn't wired. But even if she had been, I couldn't lie to her. 'No, the cops are right. I put 'em there. And they'll figure that out sooner or later.'

She inhaled sharply.

Otto stepped over to her, the side he was on clear as hell.

She squeezed his hand and folded him behind her, like a chick tucked under a mother's wing. Her eyes misted over. 'But you didn't mean to kill, right? It was an accident. You didn't want them dead.' Her hand was shaking. She was convincing herself to love me. She had to lie to do it.

'No, I wanted them dead. I just didn't want to get caught.'

Her face stiffened. Lotti ushered Otto further behind her legs, shielding my kid from me. She was scared for herself. Scared for Otto.

He looked up at Lotti. 'Miss Hill?'

'What does that even mean, Augie? Just tell me what the hell's going on.'

The words sat on my tongue, but I couldn't spit them out.

Pressed into the side of Lotti's hip, Otto's eyes locked with mine. 'Did you do something bad, Daddy? We say sorry if we make bad choices.' My kid, my life, stood there, his hand securely in hers yet his eyes fixed on me, alert and waiting for me to answer.

I'd already gotten mine. I wasn't needed here.

I approached him slowly. He didn't flinch when I reached to kiss his hair, but she stiffened. I decided not to push my luck with her - none of the versions of me had ever had much of that, and walked away.

Chapter 20

LOTTI

The motel's rusty fan oscillated with clear direction, the pipes rattled with purpose, but as per the default setting for Charlotte Hill, I was clueless, paralysed into inaction.

Seeing his tired, worried eyes framed by that substantial browline, all plans to make Augie explain his wild omissions (at best) or blatant dishonesty (at worst), loosened and dissolved. Was my brain that fickle that it had stored neural maps of Augie making me weak at the knees, and instantly interpreted his presence as safe? I'd never seen Augie cry. It was unexpectedly hurtful to witness. At first glance, I just wanted to dry his tears like he was a wobbly-chinned child with a gravelly elbow. I could hear his voice say he missed me. I could taste him on my tongue. I could smell his skin as his fingers traced my cheek, wanting them all over me.

The simplest solution was to take this beautiful man and his adorable son, get in my dusty car with my broken suitcase and leave this stinkhole motel for good. But could I trust my gut? The way the skin of my stomach shuddered a little as his hand touched my hip – but did that mean anything? It wouldn't have been the first time my senses had betrayed me.

But then he admitted he did something unspeakable, and the previous hurt I'd witnessed seemed insignificant in comparison. Going with your gut was dangerous. I finally did what Jess had been begging me to do since this whole thing started – I defaulted to my tried-and-true method of surveying the facts, and let my head take over from my heart. My monkey mind had me chasing a man across the country, but I'd spent barely a moment considering the facts of my reality. When my dad campaigned, we didn't go by instinct, we polled, we crunched the numbers and relied on facts. All I had accomplished going with my gut was absenteeism from work, a thousand k's on my odometer and a question mark over the first relationship I'd chosen entirely for myself in years.

I needed answers, but he wasn't giving them to me, hovering in my musty hotel room, slowly depositing a few scant (but harrowing) details in the air between us. I was ambivalent, flip-flopping between the emotions clamouring for my attention – reassuring me there was an acceptable explanation for how the skeleton in that scrubland wound up there, to my logical brain cautioning that no man was worth risking my mental wellbeing and physical safety, to grab the boy and run.

I was still reeling from the shock of Augie's appearance and days of worry after he vanished as swiftly as he'd appeared. Where would he go with no car? Did my wariness force him back to the green-eyed redhead and that snog of indeterminate nature?

The moment Augie said he killed someone, I wanted him gone.

The moment he left, I wanted him back.

The decision I had to make felt pivotal.

If I went with Jess's suggestion, and shared my predicament with my pragmatic father (who until recently, held the reins of my life by his wallet), he'd say to gather evidence and listen to my analytical brain. My heart and my head were clearly at odds and my terminal ambiguity was counting on a resolution so I could avoid another relationship failure. I'd let my father spend a hundred grand on a reception that was only a tad shorter than the marriage. To be fair, my current perspective on that pivotal, atrociously bad-mannered decision (based on pure instinct on my part) was that it turned out to be the right one – it was the decisions made during the five years before it (with my head) that were questionable.

From the day Grayson Wright (back when he fact-checked my father's speeches as a law grad) shimmied up to me with his neon-white grin and his voting sign, he had remained the logical choice of life partner. Rich, handsome (unlikely to have ever spent the night being questioned about human remains) and most likely to change the nation's view that politicians were unmemorable, balding, middle-aged blokes. He had the charm of McDreamy from *Grey's Anatomy* and the shoulders of Thor, which made him a born candidate. But despite social pressure to comply, I never really warmed to either character (or the way Grayson's tongue-heavy kissing technique came across as a little reptilian). In short, he just didn't make my brain come alive.

Otto paced around the room after his dad abandoned us again, leaving a scrape mark as he trailed a one-armed Spiderman figurine along the wall. After picking it out of the lost property box at the station, the policewoman let him keep it. Was that only this morning? 'It's been a pretty crap day, kiddo, but I'm glad you're still here with me.'

He shrugged. 'Dad told me to look after you.'

A lump formed in my throat, and I wasn't sure who it was getting all bothered for.

Otto made adjustments to the haven he'd built with all the pillows in the corner, his little face peering out like ET in the closet. Randomness was the best thing about little kids. Why did I hate randomness in life? Was it the stats major in me, wanting predictability, aiming for certainty without too many confounds throwing out my data?

I felt entirely clueless on how to handle this.

It was past Mum's bedtime, but I needed her. I needed her arms around me, the smell of talc – fresh and clean, her skin, now mottling and thin but soft and familiar as old sheets. Mum was lucid when I'd called her from the diner, and I clung to the hope she was still orientated to the here and now. Mothering worked better in person, but the phone would have to do.

'Mum?'

'Charlotte, love?' Her recognising my voice was a strong start, and even hearing hers grounded me. I realised how late it was, but she was spritely for the hour, rattling on with tales about Watson's jowls blowing up after swallowing a bee, and the aqua aerobics instructor being easy on the eye, which sounded within the realms of possibility. It was calming just to have a benign conversation. She grew silent and I worried she'd slipped and fallen into the abyss, but then Mum said, 'You're quiet. This is about a boy, isn't it?'

Then it came out, all bluster and snot. My whole life, Mum had been my safe place, the recipient of my unbridled truths, and the person I trusted more than anyone. 'So … now I have no clue if he's the man I thought I knew, what will happen to Otto if he does get arrested …'

It was rambling drivel, but she distilled my dilemma like a research question as the brilliant economist she was. Before dementia, she built her life creating statistical models to predict future trends. What was August's likely trajectory?

'You don't know whether to trust your head or your heart. But who said you had to pick one? Your father raised you to believe sound decisions can only be arrived at after extricating the emotion – but you, my daughter, have always shot from the hip. You know what you must do – you used to do it for all his campaigns unconsciously – sure, establish the facts, but you must view them through the lens of your gut instinct.'

Her wisdom, her brevity and relevance to my predicament amazed me, and tears welled at capturing a moment with the mum I grew up with. But then she said, 'It's your senior year, Charlotte, you need to focus on study, not boys! Plenty of time for that at university!' And the conversation swerved to a decade before, pulled the sense of connection from under me, and left me feeling more alone than ever. 'Are you still leaning towards Political Science or sticking with Statistics? Can I not persuade you to economics?'

I did find comfort in numbers, how they could help put an obvious choice into a hard decision. Mathematics has certainty – it has answers that are absolute, and makes risks quantifiable. But I didn't want my life to be about avoiding risk. 'I want to teach,' I said, and wished I'd had the same clarity when I was as young as she thought I was.

'I can see you doing that. You know what Lincoln said,' Mum went on, 'no man stands so tall as when he stoops to help a child.'

The lump in my throat ballooned a little. As we said goodnight, I reassured myself that her advice still held water, regardless of what age she thought I was by the end of the conversation. I sniffed, shook the emotion from my mind and huddled into the nest of pillows Otto was loafing on. I put my arm around the kid, who still had the superhero figurine in his lap. I considered Spiderman's deadpan expression despite his missing arm and maimed hand. 'Margo's dog wrecked it,' he said, touching the twisted plastic fingers that looked different, as if he could rub it better. They weren't shiny and smooth like the other parts.

'He's still a superhero,' I said.

Otto's dark-chocolate eyes looked up with hope, and he pressed into my side a bit more, and the sweetness of it hurt a little.

In the classroom, I told the kids what we'd do, went through the task, then reiterated what we'd covered that day. When I did that now, recapping the last two days in my mind, it all started to hit home. I thought about how unsettled it felt yesterday afternoon, with Margo filling in the blanks of Augie. Becca's insights into the man I thought I knew. How heightened I felt seeing Augie again, how needed I felt now, with this kid leaning under my arm on a dusty dog-poo-brown bedspread. I could walk away from a – let's be honest – still unfurling relationship if it wasn't what it promised to be, but how did Otto fit in to that? Would I revert to just being Miss Hill, his classroom teacher? What would happen if Augie was charged, or sentenced? What then? Foster care? And how would I pick myself up again, after trusting my instincts and them failing me?

Just when I'd lost all hope of Augie being a decent man of character and was ready to pack it in, the man kissed me like that, admitted what he did with no excuses, and took responsibility for it – whatever 'it' was. Then he just left – and it was up to me. Didn't he know I'm useless with choices? And without facts, the choice was more like a guess. Mum was right, I needed facts, and then I could see how I felt about said facts. With Otto's small frame still pressed against my side, I knew I needed to act. This little boy was counting on me to sort this out.

I was a teacher. I worked out 'who did what', and who was fibbing about it, for a living. I could solve this puzzle. If there was even a chance Augie was some well-disguised cold-blooded killer like Dexter Morgan, chopping people up by night, I couldn't let him anywhere near this little boy.

Adrenalin charged my tired limbs. I grabbed our last few belongings, clipped Otto into his booster seat, shoved my half-open suitcase in the back and left the room key in the early-checkout box. Calling Becca felt too weird, but she was expecting me. I couldn't risk hearing August's voice in the background – forcing me to imagine the two of them cosying up, reconnecting – distract me from the bigger picture, so I messaged her to decline her offer to stay.

'B', as she would now be referred to in my mind with a slight sneer, texted back at once to rebut that it wasn't safe for Otto, that Joel was hearing rumours around town. But how was *her* place safer? I wasn't letting the whim of others steer my life. I switched off my phone.

A cottage-like B&B twenty k's out of town had a room vacant and once we arrived, I carried a sleepy Otto into our room, curling him slowly onto the twin bed. There were frills on the patchwork quilts and lavender stems by the bed. It was basic, but homely and clean and there was no chance of anyone knowing we were there. I just needed to think.

I could have sought answers from Becca or Margo, but I needed facts, not opinions, and while the internet was full of falsehoods, at least it might provide an unbiased framework to piece this all together. House fires, dead bodies, secret fathers. All I knew for sure was that I had to hide, add to my dataset of facts, and figure it out before I let this precious boy near any of them. I started investigating with the help of the ancient-looking computer station in the hallway, sitting on a sticky vinyl seat with the door of my room never out of view. Where did I start? Anything was possible. What was it going to be, Augie?

Who did you kill, Gus Nash? Who did you kill, and why?

Chapter 21

AUGIE, 1989 – Brightside

The Torana spun, leaving a skid mark on the once-paved roundabout outside Brightside's amenities block, and ended with a burnout that smelled of smoked rubber.

'Whose car is it?' Steph asked. 'Some hoon?'

Brookes and I said in unison, 'Joel Fucking Harris.'

'What's he doing here?' Steph asked, her voice full of interest.

'Drug run?' Becca joked.

I knew that loser would dob if he'd seen us, tell the town that we'd broken in, lit a fire. I didn't need Margo getting more evidence that she was right about me. That I was trouble she didn't need. Maybe he hadn't seen us? The bonfire was down the back of the hall, and Cottage 2 would block the glow of the flames. You could probably smell smoke, but he might put it down to an incinerator or burn-off.

Seconds later the Torana was back doing another lap, another burnout. The sedan idled, then the driver killed the engine right out front.

Becca, Steph, Brookes and I snuck down past the cottages, hid behind the rusty tank so we could see him in the glow of the headlights, but he couldn't see us in the darkness.

A car door opened, and fragments of AC/DC littered the

main court. Joel, the oldest and worst of the Harris brothers, went and pissed on a tree but didn't seem to notice us or the smoke. He checked his watch, looked around for bit, saw the hole we'd cut in the temporary fencing.

'Joel's a wanker,' Becca said, sobering up. 'He'll snitch.'

'We should bolt,' I said. 'He won't dob, but he'll hold it over us forever. You girls could double on our bikes. I'll go back, chuck something over the fire.' I waited, watched our visitor sticky-beak around the cottages, then disappear near the lake. 'What's he doing?' I asked.

'No idea,' Becca said as a cigarette was lit down near the water – a tiny tip of red flashing in the black. 'I don't think he saw us. Let's just deal with the fire and go.' We returned inside to the fire, but I'd lost the calm feeling that had washed over me when I lit it. I was back to hating every atom of this place.

'What's your problem with him?' Steph asked turning to perve out the window again. Joel was in Year 12, had his licence, and shaved for real. But everything else about him was bad.

'He'll see you, get down, Steph,' Becca said.

But Steph ignored her. Becca hid behind me, her hand warm on my arm.

'We haven't even done anything,' Steph said. 'And I've got the munchies and need a lift to the shops.' She pushed her boobs up to the neckline for better exposure.

'I am pretty hungry,' Brookes said from across the smoky hall, flinging the flap off his hessian bag. 'If it wasn't for Snak Pack, a kid'd starve.' He held up a twin pack of chocolate custard and offered the other around as if there was no problem here.

'Guys, we gotta go – we'll be in deep shit for this,' I said. Me and fire didn't exactly have a responsible history. Me and Joel didn't either.

Bec grabbed her bag, was halfway out the door then stopped. 'We can't leave the fire burning.'

Looking for something to douse the flames, I tried the taps in the laundry room and the spout dribbled drops of rusty water into the sink before a splutter of dry air burped out. I thought there might be a fire blanket under the sink, or something to smother it, but there was nothing but a gas fire extinguisher, and it was way too big to stomp out.

'I could bucket some from the lake?' Brookes said, which would have worked if we'd had a bucket. And an hour.

'It's a dive anyway. Who cares if we wreck it more?' Steph said, parading around, poking her head outside to see where Joel had skulked off to. 'You guys are total dorks. I'm seeing what Joel's plans are and breezing this place.'

Becca grabbed Steph's arm. 'Don't get with him, Steph – he's a total dick.'

She shrugged. 'Kinda sexy if you ask me. Looks like Johnny Depp from *21 Jump Street*.' She shoved her Walkman into her bag and sashayed out. The American screamed at the sight of a harmless huntsman but ran towards a Harris.

Becca scowled at me like Steph was my problem. I scowled back, like she wasn't. 'We should stick together,' was my lame attempt at looking like I gave a shit.

Steph rolled her eyes. 'If my dad has his way, he'll ship me back home pretty soon to make him rich off my screen career. This could be my last night of freedom.' She dipped a shoulder. 'Don't wait up.'

For the next while, Steph was MIA and Brookes was drinking and smoking himself into oblivion on a piss-ridden mattress. Becca and I relaxed into talk. Talk about Freya eating her feelings since Mum had died, about Becca's mum drinking more, about how badly she wanted to leave this town.

'She looked so sad the day she realised I knew all the places she stashed her alcohol, as if she was clinging to the idea I had no clue she was ever a drunk. Feels like I'll replay Mum's life living my own if I stick around. But I don't know, maybe it's in the genes – maybe I'll marry an arsehole too, inherit the caravan, drink myself to sleep every night.'

Not if I marry you first. I thought it, even opened my mouth, but didn't have the guts to say it.

Becca kept talking, but I was distracted by her face. I missed it being next to mine and talking about stuff other than New Kids On The Block and *Baywatch*, but my mind was cloudy from the booze, my eyes watery from the smoke.

A thump.

The bong fell from Brookes' hand on its way down and he was soon slumped to the side with his head resting on a backpack that was hard and lumpy from the arsenal of spray cans in it. I got up and righted the Orchy bottle out of the way of his arm.

Becca came over, crouched next to her brother and placed a towel under his head, brushed his fringe out of his eyes. She looked up at me. 'It's kinda stuffy in here. Reckon we can leave him and take a walk?' she asked. She stretched out her hand for me to help her up.

'Leave him?' I asked. 'He's been in a weird mood…' This place could do your head in fast.

'He's mellowed now. He's fine.'

'Okay … as long as your cousin's gone.'

'I'm sure he and Steph have probably driven up to the lookout by now to make out.'

Outside, Joel's car was gone, and I breathed easy.

I kept her hand in mine as I led her through the rubble of broken bunks, faded chip packets, old bottles and abandoned chairs.

We wandered towards the water's edge, looking up at the pinpricks of light scattered through the sky between the rustling trees. You could hear the slosh of the waterhole – a dam by day, but it almost passed as a lake in the moonlight. We followed the shoreline for ages, talking about plans and school and music, until we got close to where I wanted to be, then I gestured to head into the bushland.

'Where are you taking me?' she said, slightly puffed from the walk. 'Not the clubhouse of secrets.'

I laughed. 'Is that what he calls it?'

'Are you sure it's not far? It's kind of freaky out here in the dark.'

I took her hand. I paced a hundred steps from the tree with the fork trunk, and there it was. The foot-hole carvings up the trunk were fresh, but still subtle enough to go unnoticed unless you were looking for them. The rope was secured high, and the branch we needed to hook it down was still where we'd left it. Becca swung her bag up to me, then I threw down the rope. She was surprisingly agile, using her lean thighs to hold the rope and caterpillar herself up to the platform in the sky.

Clearing a space to sit, I flicked fallen branches off the edges and spread the Spiderman sleeping bag Brookes and I had nicked from the donations box at the church on the slatted floor. 'Quality furnishings, as you can see.' I had a quiver in my voice that hadn't been there before and I hoped she put it down to my voice breaking and not the nerves I felt. We hadn't done this in months. Since the old version of me. I was supposed to want this, but something felt wrong.

She went shy. 'I thought you were avoiding me, till you asked me to the dam.'

'Nah,' I said. There wasn't much more I could say on the matter. I felt like I was still getting used to normal life again.

Life post-Mum. Life post-Brightside. But I was sure the new version was better with Becca in it.

A canopy of stars beyond the branches glittered like fairy lights. We lay like lizards, gazing at the trees trembling in the night breeze. Becca jumped when an eerie call echoed through the sky. She sat up, ready to fight. 'What was that?'

I deepened my voice to mimic David Attenborough's. 'And if you listen closely, you can hear the throaty coughs and growls of a brushtail possum.'

We talked and kissed, and everything escalated the way it usually did before I flinched, which was just as surprising to me as it was to her. I was supposed to want this. What was wrong with me?

'Sorry,' she said, but she looked so mortified I felt I should be the one apologising. Her eyes fell away, and she gazed out at the clouds racing past us. 'At first I thought maybe you liked boys now.'

'Gross.' My face scrunched in disgust. 'I mean, each to their own, but Jesus, no thanks.'

'But then Brookes has been like a meerkat, on edge, since he came home. And you're … different.'

I said nothing. I had no answer to that.

'I've heard the rumours. I know something bad happened.'

'Rumours?' So much time and money went into appearances at Brightside, I was shocked anything remotely like the truth left its walls. I'd never actually considered people knew and just didn't act. Somehow that was way worse.

'Abuse. Rape. Violence, you name it. They hurt you, didn't they, Gus? That's why my uncle got the land so cheap, they wanted an excuse to shut it down. I can see you've changed. You know there are people that will listen.'

'That's not it. They never got to me. Nothing like that. That's the truth.' I had no reason to feel as violated as I did. They hadn't even tried. It was the way they humiliated me that took its toll. But how could I even explain what they did, what it took from me – it didn't even have a name.

'There's no shame in it, Gus.'

'You don't need to tell me it's not my fault. I know I've done nothin' wrong.' And what good would telling the world about it do, anyway? The place was shut. They were all run out of town. It was over. My brain got stuck on one word: shame. I heard the word in church often enough, but I wasn't even sure what shame meant. 'Shame – is that, like, guilt?'

'Guilt's not as bad 'cause it's just about something you did, not who you are, and you can try to make it right again.' She grew quiet. 'Shame's a whole other beast. It just makes you feel bad about who you are.'

I looked up at the stars and thought that had to be the evilest thing of all, cutting in on another person's basic right to accept themselves. Was that how her parents made her feel? Heat crawled up my neck.

'We should go back.' I frowned, stretched out my shoulders and got up, petrified she'd drill me for more details I wasn't going to give. 'Brookes has probably slept it off by now, probably freaking out, wondering where we are.'

She nodded, a little surprised. I got it. We hadn't done more than pash and I was pulling the plug already. The two of us walked back through the bush, and I felt lonelier than I had in a while, and had no idea why. I had no clue about anything I felt anymore.

The air was thick with smoke, thicker than before, but there was still a low, glorious glow coming from the window of the hall where we'd left Brookes, so I presumed the fire was still under control.

The Torana. It was parked down near the barn now, the headlights blazing.

'Tosser's still here,' I said, shaking my head.

'But he drove off,' Becca said, as I pulled her behind a tree out of view.

'I think he just did laps and parked further away, like he was waiting for someone,' I said. The beams from the headlights showed up a frenzy of insects and two figures standing near the barn. The barn door. It was open. My stomach flipped.

'That must be Steph, then?' Becca's teeth flashed white in the darkness.

It was hard to see in the dark when they stepped outside the arc of the headlights, but there were definitely two figures a hundred metres away – a giant that I presumed was Harris, and a normal sized person which must have been Steph. Heated words were exchanged but they were so muffled I didn't recognise either. The couple embraced before one of them moved closer to the light, the tall bloke's face visible for a moment.

'Wait – yep, that's Joel,' Becca said, both of us still crouching, sticks sharp in our knees. I guess we'd known that already.

'But are you sure that's Steph with him?' I asked.

'I dunno. Who else could it be? No one else is here but us.'

To me, it seemed like a married couple's tiff, not a girl flirting with a new conquest. Then the two seemed to waltz for a moment, I heard laughter, an empty bottle of something was thrown across the courtyard. The man facing away from us must have unfastened his belt, his jeans crumpling to his ankles before the couple stumbled out of the light as if wanting privacy. In the shadows, the other person crouched to their knees and began doing the sort of thing Steph had no doubt had in mind.

Becca blushed. 'I guess Steph found her pretty boy.'

I couldn't watch, and we both looked away, but after a bit I could hear them stumble inside the barn to continue what they'd started. In the silent beats of the music blaring from the car stereo, we could just make out the sound of moaning.

I had no time for Stuck-up Steph, but I didn't like any girl getting messed up with that bastard. It would only end up either broadcast in detail at the school lunch table the next day, or worse. 'Maybe I should …' I got up, ready to take pleasure in punching his lights out again.

'Wait.' Becca frowned, concerned. 'Listen.'

I'd never done it but knew enough to know the noise when I heard it. I didn't hear any cries for help. Only good sounds. We both laughed nervously as the tempo sped up, a moan of desire rang out, then silence.

'Steph'll have something to write home about this week,' Becca said, blushing.

We sat in awkward silence for longer than I cared to, thoughts of what we didn't do at the treehouse swirling in my head.

Then we heard trampling noises through the trees, the rustle of bushes and I winced as a torchlight shone in my eyes from the other side of the bank. 'There you are.' Steph squashed between us. 'I thought you'd left me with the drunk moron. What are we looking at?'

Becca and I stared at each other. 'How'd you get back so fast?' I asked.

'What do you mean? I've been wandering around for half a goddamned hour looking for you bozos. Where'd you get to?'

'That wasn't you in the barn with Joel?' Becca asked.

'He's still here? Oh, frick. I got mud all over my shoes looking for him before I saw his car was gone.'

'He's here – he just parked it down there,' I said, the Torana's headlights still blazing into the barn doors.

Becca met my gaze. 'Wait, what?' She looked at Steph. 'If you weren't with Joel, who was he doing God-knows-what with in the barn?'

Chapter 22

AUGIE, 1989

'Who was doing what in the barn?' Steph asked, the three of us peering over to piece together the clues.

A tall, broad figure with dark wavy hair stumbled out of the barn and into the beam of yellow headlights shining through the bush.

'Okay, so that's definitely Joel …' Becca said. 'I can tell by the way he flicks his fringe.'

He approached where we'd stashed our bikes on arriving after our swim that afternoon. Mine was the only BMX in town with a layback seat post and yellow chain. He'd know I was here. 'Shit. He's seen them,' I whispered.

Joel left whoever he was fooling around with in the barn, lowered himself into his car, slammed the door, and sped off with a burnout for good measure.

'Thank fuck for that,' I said, when there was nothing left of him and that Torana but dust, but I knew this was far from over. He'd use that snippet of intel, threaten me with it, make me cop the blame for something, I was sure of it. I would be forever linked to this night as a potential witness for whatever had happened in that barn, and Joel knew it as well as I did.

'My shoes are totally ruined from this dive! I am so sick of this place!' Steph said ahead of us.

'Let's just get our bags and get outta this shithole,' I said, walking the gravel road to the amenities block.

Becca frowned. 'Wait, don't you want to know who that was in the barn? And why did he just leave her alone in the dark?'

I looked down my nose at Becca. 'Did you think he was the type to stick around, pick out curtains?'

Becca narrowed her eyes. 'Shut up.'

'Only other person here is Brookes,' Steph said, wiggling her eyebrows and dropping her jaw.

Becca's face pinched. 'You reckon Joel and my brother…'

Steph shrugged, as if she was worldly enough to understand these things better than us stupid hick kids. 'Maybe Brookes'd rather beat off to Han Solo than Princess Leia, if you get my drift? I don't blame him …'

No answer seemed like the right one, but then I couldn't help myself. 'Even if that were true, he hates the Harrises.'

'And der, they're cousins!' Becca added. 'Is the mystery person still in there?'

'I doubt it. Dark and stinky in there. She probably snuck out while we were distracted with Steph.'

Steph's eyes widened. 'Why don't we just look for ourselves?'

'Is it any of our beeswax who he shags?' I said. But secretly I did want to know. The more ammunition I can use against a Harris, the better.

As we contemplated what was going on, booms erupted like the last night of the Eldham show.

Bang! Bang! Bang!

'Is that fireworks?' Steph asked. 'Back home in the States—'

'Can you shut the hell up? What is that?' I got up.

'The fire?' Becca asked.

'It was contained, should be coals by now,' I said, but wasn't convinced enough not to start running across the complex towards the hall. Towards Brookes. As we approached, another explosion not ten metres from me ripped off a roof panel just where we'd been inside, sparks and flames swirling into the night sky.

'Brookes!' Becca called, her voice ragged as she raced towards the hall entry.

'Wait. I'll go in. You two stay out here. Maybe run down the service road – there's a phone booth by the freeway, call triple 0, okay?'

Eyes wide, Steph nodded.

Becca shook her head. 'I can't leave! He might be in there!' Becca yelled over the growl of flames.

'I'll go get help!' Steph said, a little panicked, and I'd never liked her more. She gathered her things, then hugged Becca longer than necessary before hurrying down the street to where I'd pointed.

'Wait!' Becca said as I raced towards the hall, tongues of red flames licking the rims of the windows and doors, smoke billowing from the exits. She grabbed the stiff-dry towel I'd left hanging near our stashed bikes, wadded it up. 'Here, breathe through this.'

I nodded, took a deep breath, covered my mouth with the towel, and charged in. Smoke so dense I couldn't see my feet, but I knew I had to move fast. The hole in the roof had injected an influx of fresh air into blaze, and it was howling in thanks. The remaining rafters were alight, fumes filled the spaces the air should be, and I coughed my way to where I'd last seen Brookes, stoned in the corner.

'Brookes!' I yelled. I could barely hear over the roaring flames. This was all wrong. I thought back to what I'd been taught, experimenting with fires in bathtubs. More than anything, I'd learned to respect fire. I'd made sure the only accelerant – the bottle of booze – was nowhere near the fire when we left. Unless the explosion was deliberate, this should never have happened.

I couldn't see, had to move by feel, clawing my fingers in front of me in the smoke. 'Brookes!' Another bang – it was an aerosol. I remembered Brookes'd had a few of them in his knapsack. The knapsack he had been sleeping on. 'Jesus, Brookes!'

I reached a wall, and then tripped over something soft and long. 'Bro!' I dragged him out by an arm, either unconscious or dead, I wasn't sure. 'Brookesy!' I said again but my throat was burning from the smoke. I dragged him out the back steps, just as another of his spray cans ignited inside.

Out in the night air, I could see how quickly things had got worse. The flames had travelled along the carpet of dry grass, engulfed the next building, and were lacing across its farthest beam towards the barn.

Becca grabbed Brookes' legs and helped me pull him free of the flames as I coughed into the towel. 'His shirt!' Becca screamed. There were flames smouldering across the fabric covering his right shoulder.

'Roll him!' I shouted. Smothering them, we rolled his skinny frame on his side. I couldn't lose Brookes to the same thing that stole my mum. Was this the fire's way of taking revenge on me, telling me not to mess with it?

Becca was just leaning over to give mouth-to-mouth when he came to life, pulling himself up on his good elbow, coughing up spit and ash.

'Lucky. I really didn't want to see you kissing your sister,' I said, and they both smiled. I acted cool but my insides were mush. I sat back and watched the whole place light up like Christmas, the splintery old wood ripe for the taking.

You win, fire.

After spluttering and chundering up whatever alcohol he hadn't already absorbed, Brookes started making sense. 'What the hell happened?' he asked, touching the tender burn on his shoulder in agony.

'Your spray paints mate – the aerosols musta got too close to the fire and blew up.'

'Oh, man. My broad tips – no way!' he said, forgetting the physical pain. Then he looked up at me and cried.

'You moron – you nearly died, you dick, who cares about your stuff.'

'Man, you don't know how hard they are to come by, dude.'

'Yeah, neither are doofuses like you.'

His eyes widened, making him look half his age. 'Shit. Where's Steph?' Brookes tried to rise up on his unsteady feet.

'Woah, woah, she's fine, mate,' I said, gesturing for him to chill. 'She's gone to call for help.'

He relaxed and sat once more, brushing grass off his knees like it mattered. I couldn't hear his sobs over the crackle and hiss, but the ugly tears were hard to avoid. He bawled like a baby. I wasn't sure if it was still about the spray cans.

Becca and I shared a look. A look that said *we nearly lost him*. Cause of death: stupidity. Mine, not his.

I craned my neck up towards the main entry, and away from the fire a bit I could hear the scrape of gravel on the road. What happened next? Cops. Investigations. Blame. I started that blaze. It was lapping at the stumps of the last cottage, threatening the whole complex. Derelict or not, someone would have questions.

'Is that them?' Becca asked, looking towards the gates.

'There's no siren,' I said. Selfishly, I was relieved. I needed to get out of there.

But then I saw it. Margo's sunshine-yellow XD Falcon with the purple flower stickers pulled into the drive. I could hear the dodgy muffler even over the fire. Margo hurried from the car.

'Oh, my Lord!' She ran to me, arms wide open. 'I was on my way home and saw the smoke. Something told me to head towards it.' She enveloped me in her arms then surveyed the fire surrounding us, overwhelmed, aghast. There was no water, no extinguisher except for one I'd seen under the sink for a gas fire. Part of me didn't even want to snuff the flames eating the joint away. I wanted it to burn. I wanted to witness its power, its beauty. I wanted this place obliterated.

'Is anyone inside?' Margo asked, her arm around Becca.

I shook my head, sat back and watched, waited for her next question – did you do this? But it never came. Perhaps she didn't need to ask.

Whatever happened, at least they couldn't send me back here. The roof of the main hall fell, tumbling in slow motion with a rumbling roar, letting a blast of oxygen coax the flames. The pergola struts had burned through, and the barn roof – mostly dry old timber and whatever was left of the hay – would only take minutes to ignite. I could have stamped out the flames, slowed its course, but the anticipated pleasure of seeing that barn crumble to ash fixed my feet to the gravel. Fire was the ultimate god. It controlled whatever it wanted, and I was mesmerised.

'Gus!'

Becca was guiding a coughing Brookes into the back seat and beckoned me to join them, but I was mesmerised watching the dancing blaze. I was addicted to this buzz. This feeling was as good as it got for me. It was the only time I felt anything.

'Gus! We have to get out of here! You can't be seen near this thing. Bring your bag, anything you came with.'

That pulled me out of my trance. 'Our bikes.'

'Get them later!' Brookes said, his voice stripped.

'They'll know we were here.'

'Chuck 'em in the back,' Brookes said, still coughing, bracing his shoulder. He'd struggle to ride anywhere.

'The wagon's full of donations for the church,' Margo said. She was big on confession and forgiveness so I figured she'd want us to stay and face the music. But she seemed just as keen to get us all home as I was to leave.

'You guys go, I'll deal with the bikes,' I said, grabbing my bag and heading towards where we'd stashed them that afternoon.

'I'm fine. I'll ride mine with you.' Brookes struggled to pull himself out of the back seat of Margo's car then followed.

'What about Steph?' Becca said. 'She went for help.'

'As long as you're sure she's not in *there*, we can look out for her on the way home,' Margo said, getting in the driver's seat. 'Boys – clear out fast, okay? I'll call the fire brigade as soon as we hit town to make sure they're on their way. See you at home.' She blew us a kiss, Becca waved from the back as they drove off.

Brookes and I untangled handlebars from tendrils of shrubbery. This hiss and crackle of flames fed my adrenalin. I could barely hear Brookes muttering on.

'Man, it's really going off. That barn'll be cactus soon,' he said between coughs, almost as excited by it as I was.

Carbon soot had blackened the small barn windows, and short puffs of smoke shot from the gaps around the eaves and anywhere there was ventilation feeding the fire within. As I held my handlebars and watched, the smoke was behaving uncharacteristically – shooting out, then instead of continuing to rise, it was sucked back in. The barn was breathing, the fire devouring more of it with each exhalation.

It was spectacular.

I wanted to stay, watch, learn, but I knew we had to run.

'Sure you can ride?' I asked, thinking of that leathery burn on his shoulder. I remember the worst burn I had I couldn't feel. Aunty Margo said that meant it was bad, that I'd killed my nerves.

I heard him mumble again. A deep, low moan.

'Hey?'

'I didn't say nothin'.' Brookes said.

Another moan. 'Then who the hell did?'

'It's just the fire. Let's just get outa here, man!' Brookes said.

I waited for a roar of the fire across the foyer to die down. I knew the dense smoke could distort sound, the particles were so thick. But there it was again, a muted cry. It was coming from the barn, kind of like before but this noise was more pain than pleasure. I'd forgotten that mystery with all the drama.

'Shit, someone's still in there.' The roof was teetering on the brink of collapse. The sliding door, the one they'd latched to keep us where they wanted, herded, trapped like stock, was shut. I knew firsthand that if anyone was in there, there was no escape.

'Jesus, that's hot. Stand back,' I said.

'We gotta go, man. Cops will catch up to us. There's no one here.' Brookes said, agitated, hurrying me.

'Nah, Joel was with someone. Prob'ly some backpacker.'

'Mate, just leave it.' There was a hitch in his voice, the same one he always got right before he cried.

I scoffed. 'We can't just leave.' I pulled at the beam to slide it open, then stood back.

Like a storm cloud, murky black smoke filled the top half of airspace. A support beam had collapsed into a bale of hay which was dissolving into blackened threads before our eyes. The entire room was filled with smoke except for a foot of air above the floor, which was freakishly clear. A sleeping bag. A stash of clothes, a pile of books, booze and a bong. The moan again. A tall figure stumbled towards us, gasping for breath.

Brookes stepped back, coughing madly.

I knew him by the shape of his shoulders, the slight limp in his gait before he tumbled to the floor with a pathetic wheeze. He'd been in the barn the whole time.

Brother John.

Chapter 23

AUGIE, 1989 – Brightside

'Is he *dead*?' Brookes recoiled at the lump on the dirt outside the barn.

'I don't think dead people moan, dude.'

'Won't he snitch on us, if he knows we were here?' Brookes asked, doing a quick step with his feet the way he did when he couldn't contain the energy firing through him.

'Dude, we can't leave him like this. They'll blame us for all of it.'

We took one arm each and dragged Brother John clear of the building, laid him flat on the yellowing grass.

The sight of Jock-itch, so helpless, made him seem like someone else. Not the man you'd stand straight for just to have one less thing he could discipline out of you. The dim moonlight revealed nasty fresh burns all over his arms, blotted with dirt and ash, blackened fabric melting into flesh like plastic in a microwave. One side of his face was disfigured, red and charred and pulsing with heat. It was like something from the AO-rated films that my mum banned me from watching.

I leaned on his chest, the smell of him – that mix of Blue Stratos cologne and bourbon – made me want to puke more than the smell of burning flesh. He wasn't breathing.

'On *Cop Shop* they check for a pulse,' Brookes said.

'You do it. I'm not touching him,' I said. 'He's like, half flesh.'

He used his thumb to touch Brother John's wrist.

'Not your thumb – it's got a pulse and it can get mixed up.'

'Huh?' He screwed up his nose. Jock-itch's skin was bubbling, red and black down his arm.

'Use the fingers you use to give the forks,' I said.

That he understood, placing his index and middle finger on Jock-itch's blackened neck. He shook his head, then looked away. 'Nothing.'

'Man – are you sure? He was moaning a minute ago. So, like the smoke got him the second we opened the door?'

'I don't bloody know.' Brookes put his ear near his nose. 'Nup. He's toast.'

'Maybe he's just passed out drunk. He stinks of booze.'

Brookes whispered, 'You reckon Joel gave him a blowy?'

Maybe that was what we saw. The man was standing so I'd thought Steph was on her knees. But if it had been two men? 'It was dark…. All I know is someone was getting one.'

'Like, on purpose?'

'I guess his supply of boys ran out,' I said, and felt disgust rise in me and shook the body at our feet. When that didn't rouse him, I shook the bastard again. 'Wake, you motherfucking arsehole!' I kicked him. No response. I kicked him again, so hard his body shook a little, but he didn't wake, or moan. No signs of life.

What other connection could there be between Jock-itch and Joel? The Harris family were always donating money to the school, I knew that because their logo was on the bottom of the Brightside newsletters. Always big-noting their charity work – giving back to the community that supported them.

Joel used to turn up to take the piss out of us now and then, pretend he was 'volunteering' with the horses.

Sirens. 'Jesus, we gotta get outta here,' I said, panicked. 'There's nothing we can do for him, and the ambos will take care of him if he even survives.'

'Nah, he's clearly fucking fried. Look at them burns. His legs. His face. He's fucking dead, Gus! We fucking killed the cunt!' Brookes was wailing now, sobbing in fear. 'You're the pyro, they're gonna say ya burned the fucker to death, then them pricks will find his charred arse in the ash and it will be on us! C'mon, help!' He started dragging the disfigured body through the dirt like a sack of pig feed, sticks pressing into Brother John's burnt flesh, leaf debris gathering at his shoulders. 'We've gotta get rid of it,' Brookes cried, his voice strained and desperate.

Sirens drew nearer.

'Bloody hell!' Was I really taking advice from a kid who still couldn't tie his shoes? But he was right. We had no choice. 'Grab your bike, and we'll take an arm each,' I said, grabbing the hose from the side of the barn.

'What's the hose for?' Brookes asked. 'You gonna hang him?'

Sirens, louder, closer.

'Just get him outta sight.'

We dragged the body between us as quickly as we could in the dark. The pattern of it gave me chills. Drag, rest. Drag, rest. The feel of his hand, warm in mine as we yanked his arms through the dark. The smell of him, like pork crackling Mum had left in the oven too long. Wasn't this what I wanted? What I promised the bastard I'd do to him? I'd told him to sleep with one eye open, that one day I'd come for him.

He was dead. I'd have thought I'd feel relief – the bastard who took more from me than I realised, who made me doubt my worth, was dead, but as we towered over him, his limbs floppy, reliant on us to control his path, he was just a helpless old man, and we were dragging him through the dirt like a rotten stump.

I froze.

If I hadn't lit that fire inside a fucking building, if Brookes hadn't fallen asleep next to a stash of aerosols, he'd be alive.

We did this. We were going down for this.

The realisation charged my mind with adrenalin. The bastard wasn't taking anything else from me. 'Find a big-arse boulder, the heaviest one you can find, and tie it to his chest with the hose,' I said. 'Otherwise, he's gonna float when it rains.'

'What you gonna do? Chuck him in the dam?'

'Not the dam.' I hesitated to say it out loud, and stopped in my tracks. If I couldn't even say it, could I really go through with it? I pointed to the useless fence that surrounded one of the old, disbanded mine shafts up the hill, timber boards securing the top of the vertical opening. 'Down that thing. We'll just have to be careful sliding him in – don't want it all to cave in.'

Brookes frowned as if the finality of what we were doing had just hit him. I feared he was going to flake out on me, but he nodded and began searching for a rock.

Another bang went off back at the school, but it was several hundred metres away. The old splintery wood of the barn would have become a pile of ash in minutes. Perhaps a can of CRC or Aeroguard in the barn? They'd have become missiles by now. I just hoped no one else had gotten hurt. I'd learned to read smoke. The white smoke of an early-stage blaze that was mostly steam. Thicker, blacker smoke of hotter fires with heavy fuels. Then there was the brown cloud like the one obscuring the cottage near the barn which told me untreated wood was burning. I could read fire better than people.

We stood at the edge of the old mine, shoulder to shoulder, and looked at each other, his lanky limbs and my solid frame.

'We never speak of this, right? Not to anyone. Not even in our sleep,' I said.

Brookes nodded.

I grabbed smaller rocks, threw them into the mine shaft to make sure it still held depth, not filled in with rubble or blown up by explosives before the owner abandoned it.

'He's got no one, so no one is gonna report him missing, are they?' I said.

By way of answer, Brookes got one shoulder, I got the other, and together, we pushed. I still remember the sound of Jock-itch hitting rock bottom, more of a soft slow thud than a distinct crash.

'Are we meant to say a few words?' I asked.

'Fuck you, arsehole!' Brookes spat. I hated the man, to be sure, but somehow, I couldn't muster the same anger. All I felt was shame. Isn't that what Becca called the hollowness that ate you from the inside?

'C'mon, Margo'll be having a hissy fit since we're not back, and the town'll be coming out to watch soon,' I said. Fires were even more spectator-worthy than car crashes around here. Nothing much happened in our town, so anyone with a ride would be sneaking out to watch Brightside burn, probably with rugs and snacks so they could settle in.

Before we'd even left the clearing, the sirens grew impossibly loud. Then they were silent. The cops would arrive at Brightside next, come in hordes, scour the scene for clues as to why it happened. I would have loved to have seen the joint turn to ash, but couldn't risk it.

We spoke all the way home like this was just another night. Not a night we burned down a school and dumped a body in a mine. But we were shell-shocked, in denial any of it was real.

I swallowed hard. Brookes looked like he was about to blubber, rubbed his eye with the heel of his hand to stifle the tears. We'd got into shit before, but not like this.

I knew it wouldn't be the end of it. We hadn't even made it home before another complication reared its ugly head. I just wanted it all to stop.

Brookes lived on the outskirts of town in the Lake View Caravan Park, and Joel Harris had been doing laps of the main street near the entry to it, waiting, stalking — as if he hadn't had enough action for the night. We'd avoided taking the main drag home, using the side entry to the park, down near the dunnies, but he still hunted us down, veered up behind us in his mustard-yellow Torana down the back streets of the cabins no one ever rented out — they were abandoned but for a bunch of possums in the roof.

He got out of his car, sloped over to us. That's when it hit me. Joel hadn't cased us like prey to give us lip about the fire. He'd come to make sure we didn't spill about him blowing off Jock-itch in the barn. I realised we had the upper hand here. It was a small town. We lit a fire. He did it with a dude. His shame was bigger than ours. For once, we had something over him.

Joel was wearing Michael Jackson fingerless gloves even though it was thirty degrees, but I didn't have the energy to mention it. 'J-boy,' I said, trying to pretend I was just accompanying my friend home after an average summer night. Nothing to see here.

'If it isn't the stars of the moment,' Joel called. 'Smell the fire from here.'

I wanted to point out that fire doesn't smell. It's what burns that smelled, and this one had the sweet undertone of paper like marshmallows burning. 'Having a nice ride, fellas? Oh, is that a burn on your shoulder there, Shit-for-brains? Better get home to Mummy – sure she has some alcohol to clean it up for you ...'

Brookes went to punch his face in, but I stretched out my arm to stop him. Our roles had been established in kindergarten when he'd stolen the pet turtle from the fish tank and lost it in the playground. He knew to leave the talking to me. I knew Joel had seen our bikes near the barn. There was no point pretending we weren't there.

'Only way you'd know where we've been is if you'd been there, too. Exactly what were you up to at Brightside, Joel? Didn't drop a cigarette butt by chance?'

His smile dropped. I expected bravado, but there was something I'd never seen etched on his face – fear. My feet balanced the pedals of my BMX for a quick exit, my fingers gripping the handlebars. 'Tell me, Joel – I always took you for a heartbreaker, bit of a stud, but what was that you were having for dinner tonight?' I rode closer so I could see his face. 'Tacos, or hotdogs?'

Brookes laughed his goofy, infectious laugh. 'Good one! Tacos look like them fannies! Ha!'

We weren't big on bullying, but when it was the worst of the Harris brothers in the firing line, I saw the appeal. The guy was a senior, captain of the footy team. He'd screwed half the girls in town, but he was shitting himself. I was surprised there wasn't a pile of it by his feet. It was confirmation enough. He wasn't a victim of Brother John. He was a foot taller than that slight, middle-aged man and twice as strong. He was into it. It was part of who he was, Joel was just too cowardly to admit it. I couldn't care less where his dick had been – each to their own – but there was nothing I hated more than cowards who pretended to be someone they weren't.

'You don't know nothin',' Joel said, spitting in the gutter, working out his next move.

'If I don't know *nothin'*' I mimicked him, 'doesn't that mean I know *something*?' Brookes went along with it despite looking confused by the logic. 'Because I was right next to that barn when you were inside, doing your thing.' I circled Joel and his stupid car, then stopped again next to Brookes in a show of solidarity.

It was starting to make sense. Brother John had had a habit of sneaking off to the barn, back when we were in his charge, the place smelling like weed, the red-eyed morning runs. It was obvious, now I was out of there. The Harrises controlled all the coke and weed in Eldham and the towns either side of the dam. Joel must be their delivery boy. 'Don't want word to get out that you give out free blowies with your blow – or was that you who went first?'

'You bogans don't know shit,' Joel yelled, grabbing me by the shoulders of my sweat-soaked shirt.

'Tell you what, Weed on Wheels, let's just pretend none of us were anywhere near that dive, okay?'

'You better keep your fucking white-trash mouths shut.' He stared a moment longer, then pushed me away and drove off. His breath smelled like alcohol, and I wondered if he had already started relying on the same strategy Brother John had used to cope with life. Mum loved the Beatles, and along with *Hey Jude*, *All You Need Is Love* was forever on repeat at our house. She said everybody deserves to find a love strong enough to survive life. I figured some people never quite found that. But did Brother John choosing the church over love excuse his life of cruelty? Did Joel's complicated life earn him any sympathy from me? No, not a bit.

After Brookes went home, I felt the adrenalin charge my limbs, the smoke draw me back, and I returned to the scene of the crime.

I waited down by the lake so I could hear it, smell it, but was out of view. Yelling echoed through the bush, the hustle of noble, community-minded volunteers doing the right thing, fixing the wrongs the local losers created. I imagined them finding the hydrant, securing the water supply to the fire engine's pump, cordoning off a perimeter. Doing their best to appear as if the humans were in control.

Just like they did when I watched my mother burn.

Chapter 24

LOTTI

Local librarian Judith Nash died in a house fire in 1988, along with an estimated two hundred books. At least, that's what my research (downloaded from the PC at the B&B) told me. A firefighter informed the *Courier Mail* that the Nash family home burned for days, necessitating closing the street, and the investigation into the cause of the fire was 'ongoing' at the time. He went on to say the mother of two, known as a tireless community volunteer, was alone, her children, August (twelve) and Freya (ten), fortuitously at a Blue Light disco when a passing motorist called in the blaze. 'With all the synthetics and new materials in houses these days, what used to be a leeway of about seventeen minutes to get out has reduced to around three. She really didn't have a chance.' While investigators had not yet found the 44-year-old woman's remains, as the site was too unstable to enter, she was assumed deceased. The article had a photo of their street, days later – the house nothing but a depressing pile of soot and charred rubble. Nothing recognisable remained but for a swing set in a barren yard, blanketed in ash.

Explanations blossomed in my tired mind. Was Jude not even home at the time, murdered, and dumped in the bush – and the fire only a distraction from the real crime? But what possible motive would someone have to kill a middle-aged mother? The estranged father? A jealous boyfriend? My memories spooled back to Margo mentioning August had a hard time with his mum leading up to her death. But that was a long way from wanting to kill her.

Or maybe the bones had nothing to do with the Nash family? It seemed more than a coincidence that unidentified human remains were found near that awful, abandoned school. Was it a suicide cover-up? Many of the boys were orphans or vulnerable in some way that could lead to that end – but when trying to search for anything about Brightside, there was suspiciously little evidence it ever existed. Was that by design? Or was it just that there wasn't much information to mine from the pre-digital eighties without delving into archives? No online school yearbooks, no Facebook or Twitter. It all took place in a bygone era that required patience.

In the eighties, everything was on film, developed for $9.99 at the pharmacy and returned in a week. People saw friends in real life, spoke over the fence instead of via text, and didn't feel entitled to tell strangers online how to live their lives. It also meant things were far less transparent than they are today when more and more people had cameras in their pockets and a world wide web to share their thoughts.

Margo's photo album had been full of little Augie. Strange, at the time I thought I saw a resemblance with Otto. But Otto's father was not in that album, any more than he was present in his life. I didn't know Joel Harris, but what I did know, I didn't like. He was a roo-shooting, ute-driving, alternative-rock fan who was also an intolerant arsehole, and that understanding wasn't something you could find online.

I thought of the notes dripping with sentimentality next to the pictures of Augie and Freya. For her to have all those pictures and keepsakes, their aunt obviously had a big hand in raising them, even before the house fire in 1988. Whatever this was about, I was sure it stemmed from some sort of family or emotional conflict, and Margo had a front-row seat.

My mind reached back to the 'do not touch' box in Augie's bus that I'd opened seeking evidence of child neglect. What I'd found was a rather benign collection of old toys. But they had to have been significant for Augie to keep.

I didn't want to talk to 'B', but I needed answers. I turned on my phone and called, and she answered on the second ring.

'Is Otto okay?' she asked in a groggy voice. It was close to midnight.

'Sorry it's late, yes, we're fine. Becca, I just had a question …'

The phone went dead, and I thought I'd lost her, but then she spoke in an almost whisper. 'He told you, didn't he? About me kissing him. I'm sorry, I feel like such a cow. I'm not about to steal him, really. It was just – you know, he was such a big part of my life and—'

'He's so good at it?' The words tumbled out. Friendly, forgiving words.

I could hear her smile, her breath exhale, and wondered what I was thinking, bonding with this woman.

'It was about the past, not the future. Augie is a cliff dive, and I need a cosy fire. I know Gus talks Pete down and, yes, my husband might be unremarkable at most things but he's my cup of cocoa. After a lifetime of cold nights, I need that.'

'I get it …' I had to change the subject before this got worse. 'Actually, I just had a question about the house fire in '88. Can you remember if anything was salvaged?'

'Salvaged? Um, I mean, no not really. There were a couple of his grandfather's war medals, a bit of jewellery that didn't melt. Gus's bike was at the disco with him - he had that for years after, and his mum's dictionary, which was in his school locker.'

'Do you remember any toys, photos?'

Becca was quiet. 'Not that I recall. There were just a few things like a mixed tape I'd borrowed so it was at my place, that sort of thing. Look, I know what you're getting at – I've heard the town gossip for decades, blaming Gus. We were all at the disco the whole time. I even have photos – I got a new Kodak camera that week for my birthday and went a bit mad taking pics.'

'You don't think he could have, at least, been there, grabbed a few sentimental things as it burned?'

'What? If he was there, and he wasn't, he would have saved his mother, not photos of her.'

Her words had a bitter edge to them, but I asked the next question anyway. 'Margo said Jude and Augie fought in the weeks before she died.'

'I guess. He was a teenager. That's par for the course. He didn't want to murder her if that's what you're getting at.' Her voice changed as if she was finally awake. 'I don't think the Gus I knew has changed that much, and if you'd known him for more than five minutes, you'd know that's unthinkable. He was a normal kid, not a psychopath.'

'I'm not suggesting that. I'm just trying to work out what the police are on about.' I was that close to confiding in Becca. Telling her that Augie basically admitted wanting to kill whoever was dumped in that bushland long ago. I just wanted to find out who it was, and why he wanted them dead. 'It's just, some things don't add up – Augie has old eighties things like cricket cards, letters and photos at his place. Now I know some might be Freya's that he inherited, or keepsakes for Otto. But wouldn't they be gone, too?'

'Maybe he found similar stuff at a garage sale, maybe they were in the tree house, I don't know. But I had to pick up the pieces from those two when their mum died, and there is no way Gus was responsible for his mother's death.'

'Okay, I know you're right, but based on what? I haven't known him all my life like you, but right now he *is* my life, Becca – him and Otto. I just can't sleep until I find out how bad things might have gotten. I need to know.'

Becca huffed. 'Lotti – what's the worst thing you've ever done?'

I exhaled, rubbed my eyes. 'I don't know … there're a few contenders.'

'Think about it and think about if you've shared that part of yourself with him.' Becca yawned and seemed frustrated at me. 'Is it really a betrayal if you haven't, especially if that part has nothing to do with who you are now?'

'This isn't just a childish mistake, we're all guilty of them. It's – it's who he is, I mean, what sort of person is capable of …'

'I get it. I do. I found a whole heap of receipts for women's lingerie, clothes, shoes, the works on our bank statements just after we had Ruby that I certainly hadn't bought. I was hysterical – convinced my husband was a cross dresser, couldn't eat until I knew.'

'And was he?'

'He'd bought me a whole new wardrobe to return to work after maternity leave. I know, not the same, but I understand how hard it is to breathe if you have any inkling the person you sleep beside at night might just be someone else entirely.'

'Can I ask what you think the real reason is that August doesn't have contact with Margo? You don't think she knows, or suspected, or accused him of whatever this is?'

Becca was silent for a sec. I thought the call cut out, but then she spoke. 'I don't think Margo would ever believe he had, even if she suspected. That's not how she works. She's a devout Catholic, can be rather old fashioned, but she's fiercely loyal and would do anything for us kids. Gus and Frey, they were like hers after Jude died. She was gutted when Gus took Otto and never looked back. He said it was about her sending him to Brightside, which was rough from what I hear, so he saw her as not having his back, said she taught him to look at people's feet when they speak, not their mouths. But that was so long ago. It was a slow burn, him being estranged from her, but it definitely peaked with their blow-up at Freya's funeral.'

'Blow-up. About what?'

'Gus lost it when Freya died. He'd never grieved his mum well, and then he had to do it all over again. He wanted someone to pay for taking away his family. He was convinced Otto's dad was to blame for Freya's death. Margo told him he was a small hateful man, and that he had to stop blaming others. I don't know Gus well now, Lotti, but I knew him then. Anger was the only thing he knew what to do with.'

That part hadn't changed. He'd never shown anger directed towards me or Otto – he was tender and kind – but towards others who crossed him, definitely. 'That's what scares me.'

'Joel's the only guy he's hated, and he's alive and well so that doesn't fit, and those bones – I watch enough *Homicide* to know that even in the humidity we get here they're at least a decade old. Probably two. So likely to link to that fire somehow.'

'And Freya died here, in Eldham?'

'Toowoomba. She studied music at USQ, had made a life for herself. That's why it's even weirder that Gus thinks Joel ran her down – the truckie stopped, rang the ambulance, witnesses saw it – Joel was off fruit picking then anyway, wasn't anywhere near her, and certainly not driving a Mack truck. Anyway, it's been a long day …' Worry was etched in her voice.

'Is Brookes still at the station?'

'He hasn't called, but probably thinks I'm asleep. As if. He's forgotten what it's like to have a two-year-old. But, Lotti – thanks for understanding – I was in the wrong with the snog earlier ... don't be angry with him, not for that.'

'I'll let you sleep.' I hung up but feared neither of us would be getting much of that.

A headline in the *Toowoomba Chronicle* from 15 October 2007 urged locals to exercise caution on the range, with the town's road toll climbing to a record high, and gave a passing mention to the fatality near the USQ campus the night of 14 October 2007. Otto would have been about to turn four. Was he at the accident? Is that why he's obsessed with death? Another crash of grief pummelled me, like the aftermath of an insult. August expected me to care for this kid like my own without even knowing who he was, what he'd survived.

My brain pinged. There was a girl's name Becca mentioned at Margo's when they were hypothesising whose body might have been dumped in the bush, and from the depths of my mind I pulled it out and my fingers started typing 'Stephanie Lawley'. I scrolled through the pages of results from the search. If she was of similar age to Becca, she'd be in her early thirties now, and pretty, from what I gathered. I put my political research skills to use and honed in on a blonde theatre actress in Sydney by the same name, who claimed to draw on a troubled past in outback Australia to inform her performances.

I left the internet nook and turned to the B&B owner, half asleep in the common room behind me with biscuit crumbs on her chin, and asked if there was a printer I could use.

The older woman shuffled over, a limp in her left leg and said, 'Printer ink costs more than your rent, hon.' She pulled down her glasses and peered at the monitor. 'Why would you want a picture of that stuck-up little tramp? She was a right old cow, if I remember – thought she was better than everyone else.'

I pointed to the monitor. 'You know this person?'

'The younger version. She used to steal clothes from the op shop I volunteered at over in Eaton's Flats. I'd recognise those cheekbones under an inch of makeup. Yeah, I knows her, alright,' the owner said, locking up the front door for the night and zipping closed the venetian blinds. 'Got into acting, I hear – always was good at bullshitting.'

'So, this is a girl who lived around here a long time ago, and she's still alive and well, living the dream in Sydney?'

'Far as I know.'

At least she wasn't the body in the bush. I felt relief.

'Some people say she was wanted for shoplifting all over the state, left town before the cops caught her again. Saw her in *New Idea* – dating that arrogant tennis player. Still got tickets on herself, by the smug look on her nasty little face. Why do you care?'

'I have no clue. Probably got it wrong.' My head spinning, I returned to my room, slipped into the twin bed next to Otto's, and slept.

I thought I hadn't caught a moment of unconsciousness all night, but woke with the thin, warm spaghetti arms of a six-year-old around me in a solid choke hold. I had thought this period of intense decision-making, which I gathered was the crux of adulting, would make me better at it. But it turned out the more decisions you made, the more chance you had of making wrong ones. Perhaps remaining indecisive wasn't such a flawed plan?

Otto woke and asked for *Cars* and Coco Pops before he'd had his first wee. When that was done, he moved on to repeating, 'Can we visit Margo's dogs again?' My heart sank. Was that even safe? What if his real dad was casing her place, ready to pounce just to be a dick about things? I had my suspicions Margo knew more than she let on, but I was confident I could take on the old bird if I needed to.

Even though I had no idea where we'd sleep that night, we checked out of the B&B and were at Margo's house by the empty lake, half an hour later. The front door opened before we knocked, and Otto ran into her dressing gown arms before I'd even grabbed his water bottle from the seat. Otto had a piece of bacon in his hand and was trying to keep it away from the dogs when I approached Augie's aunt in the kitchen. She'd put that big square frypan to use, by the looks. It was now chock-a-block with eggs, bacon and mushroom.

'How you doing, pet?' she asked, passing me a plate stacked high with breakfast. It smelled amazing.

'Confused. Exhausted. Hurt. Scared,' I said.

'So pretty much par for the course,' Margo said in the voice I recalled from last night, distinctive in its rough edges, but now it had a melody in it too.

'What course are we on, again?'

She laughed. 'Life.' It was too early to be drunk, but something had shifted in her mood.

'You always cook all that for yourself?' I asked.

She looked confused for a moment, as if she wasn't sure herself why she was cooking.

'Bev from the B&B said you'd driven back this way.'

I rolled my eyes.

'And Gus will be hungry.'

My breath caught. 'He's here?'

'He's sleeping it off – bone-tired.'

Nerves crept in and I wasn't sure why. I wasn't sure how I felt yet.

She smiled. I ate. It helped. With Otto setting out an obstacle course for the dogs outside, I centred my knife and fork across my breakfast plate. She picked her teeth, took off her dressing gown and started clearing dishes.

I generally avoided confrontation, but hated living in limbo. I was desperate to find answers before letting that man any closer to me or the little boy I had no right to love like my own but had started to, anyway. When the last of my tea had warmed my soul, I broached the reason I'd come. I hadn't intended to rush my interrogation but now I knew Augie was here I had to act fast, before he woke.

I asked Margo directly about the photo album she'd dug out to show me when we met. Something didn't add up. 'Margo – that album – is it yours, or was it your sister's?'

Margo didn't answer, and I waited. She seemed tiny in her thin, cotton nightdress, a triangle of creped skin exposed at the top, hair limp instead of the scrunch-curl style from the day before. Her face appeared more weathered than yesterday, as if a night contemplating the past had sucked the life out of her. 'Sit down,' she said formally, gesturing to the sitting room, 'and I'll tell you what you need to know about Judith Nash.'

A shadow in my peripheral vision. I turned, expecting Otto had smelled food and returned upstairs.

Augie was standing, rigid, in the hall, still rubbing his eyes in sleepy haze. 'Why are you talking about her?'

The room charged. I had no idea how to be with him, but no part of me felt scared. It was only what I could describe as feeling alive.

Awkward silence ensued, and I felt responsible for it.

'This is my fault, Augie, I was asking about the photo album …'

'Photo album?' Augie asked in a quiet, unsure voice.

'The one wrapped in a pillowcase on the top shelf of that cupboard.' I gestured to the place Margo had taken it from last night.

His eyes met mine directly, then he made his way gingerly to the linen cupboard, grabbed the old mango box, and placed it on the kitchen bench. The photo album was still wrapped in an apricot, flower-patterned pillowcase. 'What the fuck is this?' He placed it on the table, fully awake, his anger recharged along with his attitude.

'Gus,' Margo cried. 'You need to hear this too.'

'That pillowcase. I remember it from Mum's bed as a kid.'

Wrapped inside was the family album. An album full of photos I am guessing he hadn't seen since the house fire twenty years earlier. My heart skipped a beat.

'That's impossible,' August said. 'It burned. It burned with everything else.'

Margo settled into the cracked recliner. Her voice was clear and calm when she said, 'Let me tell you both how my sister died …'

Chapter 25

MARGO, 1988

The widely held opinion, at least among the Eldham community, was that Judith Nash died of carelessness. That the house fire started when she was reading in bed in her nightgown and left a candle burning 'unattended', like a child left home alone. That part made me laugh because Judith could have had a gaggle of swans in that sprawling chamferboard house and you'd never find them. But a candle was the culprit, allegedly. At least, that's what the mongrels settled on after months of blaming faulty Christmas lights, or the electric blanket she turned on in the morning to treat her arthritis. They gossiped for months after the fire, when neighbours mingled in their Sunday best over Flo Bjelke-Petersen's pumpkin scones, blaming everything on the heat because that was easier than admitting the real problems in this town. We even had tyre-kickers join the congregation simply to hear the rumours firsthand at the after-mass gathering.

My sister Jude was gossip-worthy even in death, despite every effort to make her unremarkable. But the truth was, Judith died in a hot-pink leotard. It was me in my nightgown, not that anyone saw – God, I would have been the talk of the town.

See, Judith Nash, and the two beautiful kids (even if they were born out of wedlock) could never be unremarkable. Out of the four of us Nash children, Jude was our parents' favourite. She was always prettier, kinder, skinnier and, as it turned out, more fertile. Despite my lifelong jealousy, she was hard not to love, even at the end.

I had no idea how unconventional things had become until I caught her having a conversation with her microwave. I'd spoken to my GP, who thought it was either drugs or schizophrenia, but neither of those explanations fit with my Jude. She was a normal, good girl who'd never taken more than an aspirin.

She'd always been precise, which is why she loved the Dewey Decimal System. Her sheets had hospital corners. She got a special mention at Girl Guides for the perfection of her cleaning skills, was the first to be awarded the home-maker badge. Her underwear was folded neatly, organised in colour, a hair tie couldn't touch another if it was a different colour. Our mother said her neat-freak ways would make her an excellent wife one day. And they did, for a while. But she hadn't been the same, the months leading up to the fire. Gus even said something about her getting angry at objects before that. I was no doctor but knew she'd lost the plot.

It was when the kids' father left that her mental health went on the blink. The first year she was depressed, chronically nostalgic for the time they spent together – even though I reckon he did her a favour by leaving as they were never happy. But she was obsessed with the idea of saving every worthless item from their time together, as if the memories they conjured up were her only source of joy. In her early forties her habit of 'collecting' had generalised to any useless crap, justifying keeping it cluttered in the house in case she needed it in future. As it turned out, a future was the one thing she didn't have.

It formed a wedge between us, my interfering with her affair with 'things', which peaked the weekend she had to go to a course and I'd hired a skip, made a dent culling her clutter. It took a month for her to speak to me again – accusing me of being more concerned about appearances than about her. So I stopped interfering. I decided to just love her the way she was. That was probably why it was me she called the day she died. I'm still not sure if that was a blessing or a curse, but I'd give anything for another moment with her, so I guess it was a good thing.

I was cooking up the dogs' lamb and rice when I was startled by the wall phone, grabbed it on the third ring, and held it between my shoulder and cheek as I kept stirring, distracted by trying to avoid the wooden spoon scraping the burnt bits off the bottom. I didn't hear the strangeness in her voice to begin with.

'Tell them it wasn't really me, you see?' her voice was staccato.

'Sorry, what? The line's breaking up, bloody Telecom.'

'It was the *disease*.'

I stopped stirring and listened. 'What disease? You mean your collecting? I know, hon, I know you can't help it. It's an illness, yes.' I sat down on the orange padded seat of the telephone table, thinking it was just a bout of melancholy. God knows, I'd had a few of those myself.

'Maggie – you know last weekend when you watched the kids …' Jude said. The phone went silent, and I thought we'd lost connection, but then her voice came again, slow and breathless. That's when panic took over. 'I told you it was a day spa. I really went to town to see Bruce Hendrick. Call him. He's on Wickham Terrace.'

'What's this about, Jude? You want me to call this bloke?' I asked, wondering if I should get a pen – my memory was so shot, and it sounded so important.

'He'll explain me, to you. Say you will, Maggie. Say his name.'

'Bruce Hendrick? Who on earth? But, darl, who is he?' Her exercise tape was blaring in the background. I could barely hear her.

Jude's voice quickened in panic, then slowed like a toy with a flat battery. 'And look after them. You're all they've got now, Mags. Tag team assemble, you're it.'

It was a game we played on the farm. It's the promise I'd made when she'd collapsed in awe of the prospect of raising two kids after the bozo left. *You're not alone. We're a tag team, remember?*

'Look after them, won't you?'

'You're frightening me, woman. What's going on, Jude? Jude?'

The alarming beeps of the engaged tone. She'd hung up.

Leaving the house open, the stove on, I nearly did my back out rushing into the car and sped the twenty-minute drive out to her place in my frilly nightdress. I hadn't been inside her place for a while. Every time I'd drop her home after Tuesday bake sessions, she'd forbidden me from crossing her threshold. 'Let me guess, the place is a mess?' I'd joke. It didn't seem funny anymore. *How had I let this happen?*

Gus had told me his mum left a key beneath the purple flowerpot near the fuse box, in case they ever locked themselves out. I found it, but when the door didn't open, I thought it must be an old one. Then I realised it was the right key. The door wouldn't budge because the entry was chock-a-block. I pressed my shoulder into it, sliding the boxes out of the way enough to allow my scrawny shoulders through a thin gap.

The state of the house fed the panic rising in me. The clutter had multiplied, shrinking the hallway to a thin gap you had to pass through sideways. It felt like a dungeon. There was no trace of the room I'd cleared all those months ago. No light could filter through the many windows — most were obscured by boxes, those that weren't were covered by tin foil or cardboard to ensure outsiders couldn't see in, inform an impression of who she was.

I screamed, 'Jude! It's me! Where are you?' I followed the sound of the tv, up the hall cluttered by another table stacked with newspapers and a tarnished candelabra she'd brought home from the church jumble sale. How did the kids live in this tiny space?

She was sitting on a weird angle on the lounge-room floor with one leg stretched out like she was doing the splits, a white off-the-shoulder sloppy jo with a hot-pink leotard beneath and a strange look on her face. But she was there, alive, still breathing, with a dark throw rug over her waist, and a graze on her elbow.

'Oh, good Lord, what happened!' I knocked over a stand of ornaments in my rush to squeeze through to where she was crouched. She was smiling sweetly and reminded me of her younger self, my little sister, curled in her sheets, a pink-and-white bedside table away from me. 'Jude?' I tried to calm the rising panic, told myself she was fine, she was smiling at me, just feeling silly about all this kerfuffle. 'Oh goodness me, I didn't think we were at the age where "having a fall" was a hobby,' I joked.

Her elbow was badly grazed, but she just needed someone to help her up, clean the wound. The telephone table had fallen with her, the teledex scattered, the Telecom White Pages skewiff on the floorboards.

'C'mon, let's get you cleaned up, huh? The kids will be back from that dance soon, can't let them see you all spread-eagled,' I said. She didn't budge.

The high energy of Jane Fonda's workout VHS was blaring in the background. *And three, four, five and six ... go for the burn! Sweat!* She could barely swing a cat in this room, but she managed aerobics with Jane.

'Were you trying the splits and fell? Silly old thing.'

Jude's face was as pale as her enormous white triangular earrings, but she was smiling. 'Remember when Gus fell from the tyre swing out front and ran with a bone poking out his arm and asked you for a Band-Aid. And you just smiled, Maggie, and told him you'd fix it right up.'

I laughed at the memory. 'Yes, yes, let me fix you all up, too, come on, you old biddy.' I pulled the throw rug away from her lap and shrieked. Her lower limb had been swallowed by a mouth of ragged splinters. She looked like an injured, one-legged seagull. 'Oh, Mother Mary, what have you done!' I cried, panicked, trying to ebb the flow of the blood dribbling from her leg whenever she moved.

By the grace of God she'd been in arm's reach of the phone when the floor gave way, the slight mew of the engaged signal chiming, the forest-green handset laying off the hook at her side with the curly cord twisted around the furniture.

'Um, ah, a tourniquet, we need something to stem the bleeding!' I looked around but it was wall-to-wall books. 'Where's the bloody ambulance then? How long did they say?'

She shook her head. 'No ambulance.'

My hands shook so much I couldn't even grab the spiral cord to yank towards me. She didn't have long. Gus had mentioned a few months back that the toilet leaked, that the floorboards were spongy. The leak must have rotted the subfloor joists, given way to the sheer weight of the wall-to-wall clutter stored above it. Jude's thigh had been ripped open by the exposed splintery floorboards, a jagged pattern of white flesh laced with blood, gaping open.

'No ambulance,' she said again. 'I can't let them see …'

I tried to feign calm. 'Okay, I'll just put this back on the hook then.'

I nodded, still reaching for the phone, which she tugged with whatever strength she had left, yanking the socket from the wall. I yelped in the realisation this was real. 'Jude, no!' I cried, trying to reconnect the phone, but the wires sprang from the wall, cut for good.

'The neighbours, then…' I screamed, distraught. But Betty and Roger were away and there were no other houses for a ten-minute drive – besides, I wasn't leaving her for a second. I ripped a panel off my nightgown, then, hands shaking, praying, crying tears into her wound, my sister sat compliantly as I edged it beneath her thigh, looped it through again and tied it off. It was only then that I saw the extent of her injury, the blood, seeping into the wood like stain, so much blood. Blood loss not sustainable with life.

Jude's eyes met mine and I sat there, a rip in my nightie, a gaping hole in her leg. Tears streaked her lovely face. 'Lucky, I had my old leg warmers on, or I'd have stained my new yellow ones.'

I thought she was delirious – that she hadn't realised the seriousness of her wound but then I saw the look of acceptance, of relief in her eyes. It was like her illness – she knew what was happening to her wasn't good, she just felt powerless to change it.

'Lucky,' I said, my hand covering my trembling chin, falling in a heap beside my sister and taking her hand. The aerobics video marched on. 'And who better to share the occasion than Jane!'

My sister moved so slightly, and a stream of blood pulsed from her gnarled inner thigh even with the torniquet, and I knew all was lost. We were twenty minutes out of town. It was too late for an ambulance even if we had a working phone.

Jude's long, elegant arms started to tremble. Her face drained of whatever colour had been left and her eyes darkened like a horror movie. 'Tell my babies I love them.'

Her calm had rubbed off. There was nothing I could do. 'They know, honey, but I will,' I said, reaching out to direct her face to mine, to see her properly one last time. 'Jude?'

She stilled, and I knew, just like all the other Nashes before her, she was gone.

Perhaps she had been gone already. My sister hadn't been herself. Not for months. And I prioritised loving her over keeping her safe, and I was no longer sure I'd chosen well. I sat there with her in my arms, crying in that airless room soaked in my sister's blood, revising old memories tainted with the knowledge of how her story ended – a beautiful soul whose world shrunk till it was so small even I couldn't fit inside.

All I could do was make sure she was known for more than how her life ended.

Her wishes were clear. She had fought hard to live this way, but it had still poisoned her with shame. No one else should see it. Others would storm in, pick over her habit, and take that to be the truth of her. But my sister was more than this. She was the woman who showed a brave face even though she was crumbling inside. She was a mother, a daughter, a sister, a friend. A Beatles and ABBA fan. A brilliant singer. A Jane Fonda-obsessed librarian with a kind heart and beautiful soul.

I searched what spaces I could within the house, collecting items the kids would miss – Gus's cricket cards and Donkey Kong with the broken screen, Freya's Peaches N Cream Barbie, the family photo album with the waterfall on the cover. A four-bedroom house and all there was of any sentimental value fit into a grey plastic shopping bag. I returned to the hallway, kissed Jude on the forehead, gave one last glance at my sister surrounded by all the things she loved. Things I said would kill her one day.

The candelabra was grotesquely ornate, with an unstable base and rust spots. It was out of place and ridiculous in the tiny, jumbled hall. But she loved the potential it offered, the glory it once had. Was that the real disease? Optimism? Seeing value in even the most worthless trash?

The unstable hallway flooring creaked as I approached it, unsteadying the boxed matches which fell from the stack of newspapers beside it. By the grace of God, it *had* to be a sign, confirming this was the plan that was best for everyone. For Freya. For Gus. For Judith Nash, and the story she would become tomorrow. I slid out a match, lit one wick, then the next, let it catch the wax, melt a translucent puddle at the tip.

The shopping bag of special things was looped under my hand as I paused in the hall. All it took to save my sister from humiliation was one finger, extended at a precise angle to slightly graze the long stem of the wobbly candelabra. The three wicks trembled as the stems tipped towards a mountain of dusty newspapers, which, without hesitation, burst into flames.

Chapter 26

AUGIE, 2009

Margo's face hollowed, and she looked old to me, for the first time. Or maybe this was the first time I'd seen my aunt for who she was. Margo Nash, arsonist.

Smoke. The smell of the stuff lingered, long after the flames were doused. It was still in the air, stinging my eyes, catching my throat.

'The whole town thought I started that fire. They called me "Pyro" for years. Used to call me a mummy burner, when it was you – you started it on fucking purpose!' That inner fire, that anger, it burst from me, unchecked, despite the cries of a sixty-seven-year-old pensioner begging me to stop.

'Please forgive me, Gus. You know I did it out of love. She was gone, there was no bringing her back, all I could do was save her self-respect, her reputation and yours. I'm so sorry I lied but it wouldn't have brought her back.'

'All our stuff. Not to mention the insurance never paying out, leaving us with nothing but land worth less than the mortgage. Why didn't you just call an ambulance?'

'She didn't want that. She told me.'

I lurched back. 'She probably had no blood flow to the head – why did you listen? Fuck me, I've heard enough.' I charged past

Lotti into the kitchen, bashing a chair out of my way, feeling the heat surge in my cheeks. I was getting my kid and getting out of this place.

'Wait – there's more, Gus. More I'm sorry for, that I need to get out.'

I shook my head, turned back and let out a cry that sounded more like a laugh. 'What's that, Margs?'

'The reason you went to Brightside.'

'You gave up, made me a ward of the state. I know that one already.'

She shook her head, sheepishly. 'Not all of it.'

I approached her, my eyes narrowing in. Lotti was standing off to the side, uncomfortable as I'd ever seen her, but she was still there. That was something. And part of me didn't care what she was about to hear. All the versions of me formed part of who I had become. She had to see all of me if we had any chance.

'The police, you see,' Margo said. 'After you got caught with that last fire, on the farm, I could have vouched for you, taken you in formally instead of sending you to Brightside.'

'You've got to be fucking kidding me.' Heat brushed my neck.

Her voice went all high-pitched and hysterical, the way it did when me and the foster kids would get in a brawl she couldn't control. 'You were off the rails, Gus. I'd tried everything, but I wasn't enough for you. I refused to vouch for you, yes, and that's what got you sent there, but I did it for your own good.'

'My *own good*?' My eyes dropped to the floor, smiling but without warmth. 'You sound like them, Margo.'

'I know. And I'm sorrier for that than anything I've ever done, you have to believe me. I didn't know. I suspected, with Brookes, after you both came home. I never would have sent you there if I'd had any inkling. I'd never have recommended John for the job. He was a good man, a man of God, or so I thought. Why do you think I've been helping Becca look out for Brookes ever since? And trying to look out for you? It was all because of me.'

I let out a long breath. 'They never really got to me, Margo, if that's what you're all twisted up about. Your conscience is clear.'

She looked relieved, but it didn't last.

'But you're right about Brookes. He used to take it for the both of us. Cigarette burns. Couldn't sit down for a week, more than once.'

'Oh, Gus …' Her face fell, her hands shook but I didn't care. 'Wait, Gus, please … I can't lose you again, not now that we're talking.'

I couldn't be there another minute, couldn't look at that woman who'd been behind the worst two things in my life. I tuned back into my surrounds – Otto outside, Lotti standing in dismay by the door. I had no idea where we stood, if she'd side with Margo, or me, or if she'd bolt out of town as fast as she could. Who'd want to get involved in any of this?

'I've had enough of this shit,' I said, grabbing my stuff to leave just as the back door clicked open and footsteps approached.

'Daddy!'

My face crumbled, seeing the kid, holding him close to me. After a pathetically long hug, Lotti dealt with the boy, guided him to her car and waited in the driver's seat. Without meeting Margo's eyes, I followed, sat beside Lotti and we drove in silence. It could have been twenty minutes before my heart stopped racing.

Lotti kept glancing at me, reaching out for my hand. 'Want me to stop? Talk?'

'Nope. I want to get as far away from this fucking town as I can. I want to go home.' This place was no longer it.

I spent the next few hours replacing stories in my head, slotting in the new facts, while Lotti drove on, not saying another word unless I did.

We saw a sign for a petrol station and Lotti looked at me, her face scrunched up. 'I'm going to pee my pants if we don't stop soon, and Margo's eggs wore off about two hours ago,' she said. 'Is it okay if we stop for a bit? You might need some fresh air.'

I nodded. How did I get so lucky to have this woman in my life?

She filled up, grabbed three sausage rolls, a bag of chips for the little tyke and a few drinks, and later pulled up at a deserted playground across the tiny highway town that had an old swing and slippery dip rusting beneath a gum tree. She put down a tartan picnic blanket, like this was any ordinary day in the park.

We ate in silence, watching the trees move in the breeze as Otto raced around the grass. 'I'm so sorry, Aug,' Lotti said, her chin trembling with the emotion of it.

I still hadn't processed what Margo had told us about my mother's death, but I owed it to Lotti to try. 'Yeah, well, I don't actually know why I'm so pissed. She's right. She was dead either way, wasn't she?'

'I don't mean about that.'

She looked at me. 'When Margo told me Otto wasn't yours, I wasn't sure where the lies ended. I was scared you weren't the person I thought you were. Then when you said you knew whose body that was in the bush, and that you wanted them dead, I just had to question everything – even ask myself if you may have been involved with the fire that … the fire Margo lit.'

It hurt, but I didn't blame her. I wrote the plot. I'd told her I was a killer. She had just furnished the scene. 'I was there, too, you know, watching my house burn at the end. I was wired to smell smoke, could taste it all the way from the PCYC twenty minutes away – I'd always worried she'd get stuck in that shithole. I rode home when they were all doing the time warp. It was a complete furnace by the time I got there. I stood behind the police tape, helpless, knowing for sure she'd have been in there doing her aerobics, then having her frozen meal in front of *The Bill* like she did every week. That there was nothing I could do. I just had to watch. It was the worst moment of my life up to that point.'

She gasped. 'Brightside?'

'Now she tells me she put the worst of them there too. Bloody beautiful symmetry, hey? Stupid part is, I still love the old cow.'

We were on the rug watching Otto try to swing himself but getting the footwork all wrong. But he persevered. He was a trooper, that kid, and I was determined to not let any of this change that.

'The staff hurt you?' she asked, disbelieving.

I stretched my legs out, thinking it would make me more comfortable. 'Yeah, well, like I said, they never touched me, not the way you think. I was spared the worst.' I swallowed hard.

She reached over and squeezed my hand. 'I know that's what you told your aunt …'

My throat tightened. I turned away, leaned back on my wrists.

'You don't have to tell me, not now, not ever if you don't want to. But I suspected …'

We both knew what she meant. My issues. The thing we never spoke of. Every inch of me recoiled from the idea of saying it out loud, even now, twenty years later. What sort of man was I, blubbering like a wuss?

But the planets aligned and, without warning, it all came out. 'I've never told anyone. I could never find any reason to bring it up, so I just shoved it down. The shame. The embarrassment. I figured I'd just lodge it down deep and hoped it'd never show its ugly face again. Sure, it made me look like a fuck-up with women, but I'd just move on when it did.'

Lotti's eyes closed, and she stroked my arm. 'I never thought that. You're actually pretty confident in that department, as long as you're calling the shots.'

'The sex? It's pretty good, though – right?' Surely, I was on the money about that. There was no faking some things.

'Yeah ...' She smiled. But then her big blue eyes scrunched closed as if the rest was hard to push out. 'I mean ... physically.'

I leaned back. 'Physically?' I grunted. 'But not ... what?'

Lotti's eyes fell, she stretched her shoulders out, leaned back on the blanket, then after a bit, her eyes met mine. 'But, emotionally ...' She tilted her face to one side, trying hard to wipe the tear streaks from her face on her shirt without me seeing her hurt.

I twisted my jaw, bit my lip, and looked anywhere else but at her. I guess that avoidance was exactly the sort of shit she was talking about. I huffed out a breath, nodded to myself, and looked at her, staring at me trustingly, sticking by me through this shitshow. Looking like an angel.

The gates of time opened, and I had to purge it all.

'The level-five arsehole was a prick we called Jock-itch – on account of us lads filling his dacks with itching powder once and making him bolt from the shower block in agony. One of the highlights of my life.' I paused. 'One of the lowlights was when I was nearly fifteen and he caught me getting busy with a *Playboy* in my bunk …' I didn't elaborate but her expression told me she understood. 'He locked me in the barn.' Her smile fell. 'He told me if I wanted to behave like a primitive animal, he'd rub the stiff out of me the same way he did for the horses.'

She didn't shy away, or recoil. She just sat up, listened, waited, and I relived it in my mind like it was yesterday, not twenty years. Trauma. It was like smoke, I realised. It sunk deep into the fibres of you, and even when the bulk of it blew away with the breeze, a faint whiff of it remained.

'He chased me round the barn, poking me with the cattle prod, telling me chastity meant no sex with others, no sex with the self, nothing until marriage.' I kept blubbering, then laughed. 'What is wrong with me? Jesus, you'd think I'd be over this – it's been twenty fucking years!'

'Don't say that. Some things aren't healed by time.'

'He didn't even … not like some. I have no right to cry over this.'

'Just because others hurt more doesn't mean your pain is any less real.' Her concern turned to anger. 'This happened where you met with Brookes the other night?'

I nodded. I was nowhere near the place now, but every inch of it was burned in my mind. The thistles. The horseshit. The smell of baked beans and scraped plates. 'The barn door had a long wooden plank that slid into place to keep the horses in at night. He got the other brothers to secure it shut when he had someone in there to "discipline" and whistled when he was done. And the best part was, when he had me cornered he'd pull the waistband of my shorts out at the back, shove his hand right round to the front of my balls, squeeze them hard and yank his fingers up the arse crack. It always took a second for the burn to set in.' I felt weak. I hadn't been raped, nothing game-changing like that. It was just sadistic pranks designed to humiliate. And it worked a charm. It still did, half a lifetime on.

Her face twisted in torment, tears tracked her cheeks and I regretted putting her through this. 'The burn?'

'Horse liniment. He'd wipe it all over his hands before he swiped my nuts.' The smell of piss-ridden hay. The slow build, waiting until it became excruciating. It was like I was fourteen again with nowhere to run. The long shadow, I'd never outrun it. Never outgrown it.

She swallowed, crossed her arms. 'That heat-rub stuff?' Now she was shocked. 'That's just ... so evil.' She blinked tears away.

'It burned for days. I can still feel it, even now.' I wiped my own tears from my cheeks that I hadn't realised were coming, silent and insidious. 'It's what I thought about every time anyone ...'

'Oh, God, Aug,' she said. 'I'm so sorry if I ever made you remember ...'

'No, it's not even like that, not anymore. It's ingrained in me, a natural reaction like sneezing in a dust cloud. But then at other times, something like the smell of manure at the EKKA can send me back to that moment.' He'd made sure his humiliation branded me for life. 'I can't change it. It's part of me.'

'Well, that's horseshit.'

'I tried. For years, I tried.'

'Maybe *we* can.' She crawled over the blanket and kissed me, and the force of it made me believe her. I watched Otto, chasing an ibis around the grass, laughing as he mimicked the funny way it ran. I wanted to sit in that moment, but I couldn't. I needed to get the rest of it out. But then she spoke, and I didn't have to.

'It was him they found in the ditch.' She didn't ask, she just said it.

Nodding, I was back there, seeing it all. 'It wasn't our fault. Not really.' I walked her through the night of the fire, how we lit it but never expected it to burn half the place down, let alone spread across to the other buildings. I told her how the prick must have gotten smoked to death. I told her how Brookes was stoned, didn't realise his bag of aerosols was inches away from the fire until they blew, that he had barely escaped. That we heard the bastard moaning in the barn, tried to revive him but he was dead, so we hid him down the mine, figuring if they stung us for the fire, they wouldn't blame us for his death, too.

She wasn't shocked, she didn't recoil. I'd admitted killing the man I hated most, and her eyes didn't waver from mine. 'You sleep-talk, you know. I've been piecing stuff together. The word devil came up a lot – I thought it was just some garden-variety Catholic guilt.'

'Sleep-talk? Bullshit. I barely sleep.'

'That was another clue. Your mind, it never rests, like you can't let your guard down. But you know what? Just because you associate touch with pain, doesn't mean you always will. He's gone. You're talking about it. That's a good start.'

'Hopefully Brookesy isn't. We said we'd take it to the grave.'

'Speaking of graves – the trench you dug in that school. What was that about?'

'It's from a time capsule from the Bicentennial. We dug it up. That's why they've got my truck. There was a letter inside. I was taking it home to bust the capsule open when they found us at the school.'

'You were, what, fifteen when you wrote it?'

'I also thought it wouldn't get dug up for fifty years. I figured I'd be dead by then at the rate my lot carks it.'

'What was in it that you wanted to hide so bad?'

'A letter. A letter to Brother John, telling him to sleep with one eye open as, one way or another, I was going to kill the motherfucker. But in the end, I wasn't even man enough to set out to kill him, he just died by accident.'

'Or karma.' Lotti had edged closer and closer as I'd spilled my guts, and was close enough now to hold my face in her palms, plant kisses across my forehead, soft and light and innocent, and it felt like a hot bath on sore muscles. 'You know,' she whispered, crawling onto my lap, legs curling around my back, 'the stats on weight gain in preterm babies suggest that human touch can be very healing.' She was kissing my ear now, and she was right, it was like a balm.

Lotti's mobile started pulsing and chirping as if it were trying to edge itself off the blanket onto the grass. Becca's name flashed on the screen. Lotti looked at it, then at me.

'Better get it,' I said.

Lotti pressed the green circle and turned on the speaker. We huddled close to it, two bodies, one blanket.

'Lotti?' Becca's voice was stripped. 'Where're Gus and Otto?'

'They're with me, he can hear you,' Lotti said into the phone. 'What's wrong?'

'The bones – they're Brother John's. Matched him with dental records.'

Lotti frowned and asked, 'Did they find the letters? Are they looking for August?'

'If it's the death threat in the capsule you mean, they know about it, but what they've got on Brookes is worse. There was an old Kodak photo packet.'

'Photos?' I said, confused. 'Anything incriminating would have burned.'

'They got them from the tin in the treehouse.'

'They were just lame-arsed fun pics,' I said.

'The photos were, but the negatives…'

'Negatives?' I said. 'From twenty years ago?'

'That's the thing – the envelope had a dozen random pics, but negatives for twenty-six, and they were all of the same scene – Brookes and Brother John … Let's just say they are strong grounds for motive.' Becca's emotion turned to resolve. 'They've charged Brookes with murder.'

Chapter 27

LOTTI

August was driving faster than I was comfortable, straight back to Eldham.

'Do you want me to drive?' I asked.

'No, I just need to get there,' August said, accelerating harder.

I rolled my eyes. It was clear August's red beast had been poked and he was on a mission to help Brookes. I just wasn't exactly sure how we could. I was secretly thankful I had the statistically safest car on the road, even if it was covered in a blanket of dust.

I was about to call Margo to see whether the cops had gone there first, when my father rang. I ignored it but he rang straight back so I answered with a cringe. 'Dad, I'm kind of in the middle of something, can I call you back?' I said.

'Where are you? On your way home?' he demanded.

'Dad – if this is about your publicity shoot, I won't be there. I'm sorry. I'm kind of dealing with a cluster-fuck here,' I said, as August drove us closer to the epicentre of it.

'When did you become a mud-mouth?' he asked.

I ignored it. 'Wouldn't it be fine with just Mum? She loves getting her makeup done.'

'Your mum's not well today.'

'Oh, shit.'

'You're still at Eldham? Grayson said you called in a favour – your bloke. Is it his family involved in that mine mess, Charlotte?'

The phone was still on speaker and August's face changed. There was no point covering anything from my father. He had researchers and police on staff. He was still joined at the hip with my ex, politically and personally. I went to turn off the phone speaker, but Augie put his hand on mine and shook his head, signed that he wanted to hear it all.

I braced myself. 'His friend has been charged,' I told Dad.

'Christ, Char – you've got to steer clear of that lot, you hear me? He's beneath you.'

'Dad – stop.' My throat tightened. 'I'm not a child. I can make my own decisions.'

'This is why I told you not to get involved with bloody country hicks – none of this would have happened if you'd stayed in Canberra. You know you're the best number cruncher we've had in the office. It's not too late to come back.'

'I hated being an analyst. I love teaching.'

'I've got a lot of respect for the teaching profession, but little kids, Charlotte? You could be lecturing on finance at a university if you'd listened to me and finished your degree, not blowing noses.'

I rolled my eyes at my father's words. For some reason they didn't have the power they once did.

August glared at me, a snarl stretching across his mouth as if I couldn't let my father get away with that.

'Let's not even mention your personal life ...' Dad's commanding voice went on and I panicked, fumbled for the phone. 'I don't want to say I told you so, honey, but things have gone from bad to worse since you abandoned a fine young man a day into your marriage. At least have the decency to give him a divorce.'

August glared at me, veering into the trees before righting Frida the beige Volvo back into our lane. I muted my end of the phone while Dad rattled on. After all the revelations of the day, me having married before didn't really seem important.

The look on August's face said he didn't agree. 'You're fucking *married*?'

'I have a lot to explain. But to be fair,' I said, mimicking August's words, 'I never actually told you I *wasn't* married.'

His brow furrowed but he was too distracted by his own lies to be concerned with mine. Dad continued, clarifying my involvement with the 'body in the bush', if I'd made any statements, who he had to contact to get this cleaned up.

'And I can assume you are no longer in a relationship with this man. You know what this will do to our family, to the campaign. Where are you staying? I'll send a car for you.'

August had met Dad a few times but had never heard this version of him. He'd met the charming parliamentarian who could convert his constituents to any agenda he wished. I could only imagine the spin with this scandal: *Charlotte Hill, only daughter of Alexander Hill was seen at an Eldham court hearing today where her partner, August Nash, was co-accused of murdering his childhood teacher.*

'I'm not leaving, Dad,' I butted in when my father paused for breath. 'I'm nearly thirty, old enough to make my own decisions, even if that means I'll make some bad ones.'

'Selfish, that's what it is, Charlotte, always thinking of yourself! Just like your mother. Never thinking of what's best for the Hill family.'

At that moment I wondered if Mum had been faking dementia just to have a good reason not to speak to this man. 'Dad, I'm going to hang up. You'll be fine. Take the photos in that big wing chair with you in the centre.' That way they'd be true to life.

'I'm not going to hear about this in the papers, am I?'

'If you're that worried, Dad, why don't you send us one of your lawyers? They seem to get you out of all the other messes.' My voice was strong, my back a little straighter in the seat, a little taller. I felt bolder than I had since I was fifteen.

August grabbed the phone, said, 'Scratch that, mate. Us hicks don't need your fucking help.' Ended the call and threw the phone in the foot well.

I shut my eyes, a little shocked. August had always toed the line with my dad, stroking his ego the way he liked to keep him on side. He'd told me after meeting him at Easter that he was country, not stupid, and he might have to ask him permission to marry me one day, so he may as well try to get on with him.

'That mean you don't plan on asking him for my hand any time soon?' I asked. I checked the back seat to make sure Otto wasn't reading my lips from my side profile, but he was asleep.

'I changed my mind on that. It's your fucking hand. Why would I ask him for it?'

I pulled his face to mine and kissed his lips hard and fast, and my head flipped like a spin cycle. It took everything I had to pull away from him so we wouldn't crash. My brain buzzed, aligned with my heart. His forearm rested on the length of the driver side window, exposing his damn tattoo and my mood shifted. 'Becca told me she was to blame, for the …'

His eyes left the road and clicked with mine. 'I want you, Lotti. I can see that even clearer now.'

I rested my head on his shoulder as he drove. 'What are you gonna do, Augie?' *Especially without a lawyer or the money to pay for it.* 'If you're wondering, I told my dad to use my trust fund to pay for the wedding I didn't want, so despite this fancy car, I'm kind of broke. And, well, defence lawyers aren't fucking cheap.'

'Listen to you, mud-mouth.' He smiled. 'I've got savings.'

'Really?'

'What, you thought I was a penniless hillbilly? I've bought up three Mobils down the east coast that rake in a few grand a week, supplements the pitiful loss I'm making on the garage.'

The envelope. *Silverfell Holdings.* I laughed out loud. 'You are full of secrets.'

'But that doesn't matter anyway. I don't want a stinking suit making my case for me. I'm gonna confess.'

It sounded admirable and idiotic in equal measures, and I only had three and a half hours left of driving this desolate highway to change his mind.

'It's the only way, Charlotte. I don't want everyone stressed out, a court case. Me and Brookes just have to say it like it is, take what's owing and be done with it. There's no point us both going down for it. I know it's me they're looking for. Brookes could barely write his name back then.'

I couldn't believe we were having this conversation so calmly. My level of heightened emotion had just been set to a new baseline. This was just another day. 'It could mean years in jail. You don't deserve that.' And then I remembered the little human in the back seat, the bead bracelet on my wrist that he made me. 'What about Otto? Is that what you meant when you said to look after him for a "bit"?'

His jaw twisted. 'It's not like I haven't thought of him with all this. I stayed quiet and defended myself for twenty hours straight in that bloody station, telling myself it was justified so I could be free to raise him, because that'd be fair. But he's too good a kid to have a liar as a dad, and there's only so long before you are forced to answer the big questions.' The way he looked at me said he wasn't just talking about the charges.

'They were right – the town. Calling me Pyro. That's what I was, after the fire that took Mum. I mean, Margo just said it was ADHD, attention-seeking, whatever, but once I grew up, I knew it was about the emotional rush, a way of coping with the boredom of growing up in a shit town, of all the Brightside baggage. Freya had some issues with eating disorders and, the way she explained it, the purging relieved a build-up of tension. Seeing things being destroyed slowly kind of released something in me. Burning was my bulimia.'

Jess was right about one thing. Pyromania was a complex beast. 'Have you always been fascinated by it?'

'Didn't start till we lost everything to it. Then I'd spend all my pocket money on lighter fluid and matches, started burning shit in the bathtub, graduated to bonfires. I didn't want to hurt anyone, I didn't want to burn the whole town or seek revenge, I just liked to light fires.'

'You were a volunteer firefighter …' I said.

'Yeah, I know. Margo forced me to see a shrink for a while when I was eighteen – which is rich coming from the woman who burned my house down.' He shook his head, incredulous. 'Some of it was useful – told me to find constructive ways to feed my obsession. I took a welding course to scratch the itch. But some of it was batshit crazy. Freud reckoned flames were phallic symbols that represented a desire to control nature or some horseshit.'

I thought about it. 'Maybe you just wanted to gain control over your environment.'

'Yeah, well, after today, after Margo's lies, I reckon fires are more predictable than people. You can switch 'em on and off, make 'em bigger. You know what you're gonna get with flames.'

I wasn't so sure. Even with all the new facts, I felt I knew exactly what I'd get with Augie. Making that decision, once the haze had gone, wasn't hard.

Yellow grass, dry creek beds. The scorched landscape flew by the windows at warp speed as August sped down the bitumen, Otto sleeping in the back, catching up on his couple of late nights.

A few hundred k's later, we'd worked out a strategy. I'd take Otto to Margo's and August would go to the station and explain his truth. Maybe then the heat would be off Brookes.

As we approached town, the concept seemed terrifying.

My voice was patchy, unsure. 'So just tell the whole truth?' I said as if the concept was barbaric. 'Do you even know what that is? I mean, the way you explained it to me, you still don't know why Joel happened to be in that barn or how Brother John got locked in there.'

'The barn self-locked when you slid the beam across,' Augie said. 'We always shoved a boot in it to make sure it didn't lock us in when we didn't want it to.'

'Was he depressed – could he have locked himself in?'

'Nah, musta been Joel. You couldn't lock yourself in as you secure the beam from the outside, but it was clear he was sleeping rough, down on his luck.' Augie's face pinched. 'Joel was there. He brought him drugs every Friday after pension day. Figured he just wanted to make sure Jock-itch didn't come out when we were watching, expose his little secret meeting.'

I thought more on that. 'It was the eighties. Joel doesn't strike me as a forward-thinking guy. If he was fooling around with an older, God-fearing man, and saw your bikes after the fact, wouldn't he be more likely to want to sneak the man out so you didn't find him there – not lock him in?'

Augie frowned. 'Anything is possible with that prick.'

'Ana's Song' came on the radio. Daniel Johns singing 'open fire' made me smile. I guessed it was a little early to start making fire jokes.

August's face had softened from the tension it showed when he was discussing the barn. 'My sister loved this song.'

'Silverchair, right?' I asked. 'Isn't it about anorexia?' A pulse of fear. I blurted out the thought that popped in my head before thinking of the consequences. 'Joel was wearing their tour shirt.'

'Huh?' August said, confused. 'You met him?'

'Wait …' I thought of the T-shirt I'd read repeatedly while waiting behind Joel at the bottle shop the other day. I searched my phone for the tour dates and gasped. 'Um, when did your sister lose weight?'

'What kind of question is that?'

'I was just thinking about something Otto said – he lip-read Joel at the pub.'

He thumped the steering wheel and the car swerved a little before he corrected it. 'Why the fuck did you let Otto anywhere near Joel?'

'I didn't leave him near Joel … well, not that time … Otto told me Joel said something awful about Freya dying thin. How did Joel know she was thin if he hadn't seen her for years? Then the tour T-shirt I saw when he was getting served ahead of me got me thinking. Probably a coincidence, but … the group toured Toowoomba in October 2007. Isn't that when Freya's accident happened?'

The first clue to the unravelling was when August didn't stop at the cop shop as planned. He kept driving through town at high speed. 'Gotya!' he said, doing a wheelie at the corner so fast Otto cackled in excitement in the back seat. Augie stopped behind a dusty white ute. And there was the man himself in the driver's seat, Otto's father. August revved the engine like the hoon I always suspected lurked beneath his calm exterior. I don't think the Volvo did it justice. 'Pull over, prick!' Augie called.

'Just the man I'm looking for!' Joel called in return, doing an equally philistine burnout and stopping his ute up a side street near an abandoned lot. What were once a butcher, a hairdresser, a gift shop, were all boarded up.

'What are you doing, Augie?' He ignored me, snapping his belt release and hurling himself out of the car.

Those hands, those hands that I'd only seen offer gentleness, grabbed a muscle-bound man inches taller than him and shoved him against the wall with a sickening thump.

'Rumour has it you've got somethin' of mine,' Joel said.

I feared I knew what that meant, but August had tunnel vision and ploughed on with his agenda. 'I knew you were involved, you piece of shit! Talking about my sister at the pub – you dobbed yourself in.' He grabbed Joel again, who was yet to react. 'T-Bar – Silverchair. You were fucking there! What did you do to her!' August kept pushing him hard, but the guy was a cockroach and stood tall.

Otto was sound asleep. I was about to just drive off, leave them to it, keep the boy safe, but then Augie clocked a right hook in the face and my whole body flinched. I couldn't leave him alone with that giant. I opened the windows, took the keys and locked the car with Otto still in it. This went against my instincts, but I had no choice.

'August!' I yelled. 'Stop, Augie.' I ran over and stepped between them, pulling his arms off the giant man. 'Is it worth getting done for assault?'

'Nah, technically this part, it's battery.' His voice was low, unrecognisable in the way it intimidated. He punched Joel once and again. In the course of me trying to intervene, Augie's arm almost hit me in the movement and the shock of it reigned in his anger. He looked at me, then over at my car. Otto had woken, his face squashed against the back window, his hands on either side, watching his every move. It was enough of an audience to make Augie think. He exhaled, backed away, slumped into the gutter, cradling his right hand with the palm of his left. 'Motherfucker, that hurts.'

'We're not made of rubber anymore, mate, hey?' Joel said, with a smile I wanted to wipe off his face with my boots. The carpark outside the old mall was as empty as the shops, and the heat from the sun was harsh on our skin as the men wiped blood from their lips and took a break from their thuggery. Joel must have been pushing forty. Too old for this childishness.

'I'm not your mate, prick,' Augie said to Joel. 'Admit you were there. I knew it, always fucking knew it.'

'I swear, mate, I was flirting with her – that's all. The concert was on that night at the campus I'd overheard Becca say your sister went to, and I thought I'd catch up. And what do you fucking know, she'd lost the lard-arse.'

August got up and I thought he was going to start hitting again, but then I saw his face, the emotion in it, hearing about the one family member who hadn't let him down, about missing links to how she left this world. Even if it was spoken by his nemesis, it was clear he wanted to hear it.

'I had a crack, mate – can't blame me, she was smokin' hot with that sweet little arse. I just called out, said I'd buy her a drink. I swear I didn't even touch her. I don't know why the bitch ran, it was like she was scared.'

'But you saw her get hit.' In the way he said it, it was clear that August was a different man to the one before he lost her.

Joel slumped onto the edge of the gutter, nodded for a long while. 'Yeah, man, I saw it. Brutal, that, but at least it was quick, hey? But while we're on your sis – where's her fucking kid?'

'What did you say?' August said.

'Yeah! I fucking know! Reckon I have a right to – being its dad'n all?' Joel arced up, pushing August back. 'As if I wouldn't find out – you coming back, all the whispers about why your sister left town. Bazza saw her at some market in Dalby like a year after she moved away with a kid strapped to her and we both know I was the only one slapping your sister's fat arse back then.'

August answered with his fists again, hooking punches when he could, before Joel pushed Augie to the ground and straddled him. 'Where is he?' Joel spat. 'I already went by your old lady – gave her a bit of a stir. Not there. Not at Becca's. Man, you musta been pissed when she told you who the baby daddy was.'

August flipped him off, rolled on top, Joel threw him off and they were a tumble of arms and legs, their clothes, their hair gathering sticks and gravel as they rolled along the hot bitumen before separating again, exhausted.

The teacher tone came out. 'Can you guys just stop? That's enough. Both of you!'

The two men were puffing, crouched beneath a nearby tree, stretching their backs and touching their split lips like old men.

'How old are you, Joel? Pushing forty? A little old for high-school punch-ups, aren't we?'

Joel's eyes met mine, then looked over to my car, adjusted to the back seat and his eyes narrowed back on me. 'Wait, you're the chick from the drive-through,' Joel said, nodding to himself. 'The hottie – with the ...' Joel scraped his jaw with his forefinger and thumb. His jaw dropped. 'That *retard*? But he's your kid, ain't he?' His face dropped. 'He can't be mine.'

August was at him again, punched Joel on the cheekbone so hard I flinched. Every punch before paled in comparison. 'What did you fucking call him?'

I though the giant man had passed out as he lay limp in a bed of dried leaves, but then he shook his head, pressed his cheek and swore. 'Motherfucker.'

'How'd you even manage to father a kid?' August said to him, cradling his swollen red fist in his palm. 'Thought you didn't even like women.'

Joel's cheeks flushed. 'You asking me out, Gus? I'm flattered.' He stretched out his back as he sat with his legs in front under the tree. 'All about the coin, mate. I'm a businessman, told you that back then. I provided a service. So what if I blew him off with his ounce every week? Only problem was you bloody saw it. It's kinda like fucking a big girl, hey? A lot of fun 'til your mates find out. The night of the fire was when I said I'd had enough of wrinkly cock, and he wasn't too happy. And that's all there is to say on that.'

'You locked him in!' August said. 'You're just as culpable as me.'

'Locked who in where?'

'The barn. So we didn't see who you were meeting.'

Joel's face was transparent for once, and was shocked. 'That's what this is about? Nah, no way, you're not pinning that on me – you musta fucking done that. Old man liked to get off to help him sleep.' Joel shook his head. 'I fucking swear it.'

August scraped the stubble on his face with his hand, and walked towards me, depleted. 'Yeah, whatever mate.'

Joel stilled, hesitated. 'So, the boy. Why didn't she tell me?'

'Why do you reckon, fuck nugget?'

'I'm the fuck nugget but you're a model citizen? My family runs this town, business is booming, you're nothing but a white-trash pyro.'

'Booming? Look at this town! The pub's monopolised everything – it's the corner store, the takeaway, the only place to get a feed. Your father drove the rents up of every other owner-operator in town, drove 'em out to line his pockets. I wouldn't want any kid near you lot.'

Joel got up, spat on the ground. 'What's even wrong with him?' He looked over at the car, parked in the shade, Otto now out of his car seat and climbing around the car like a monkey, probably looking for snacks. 'He slow or somethin'?'

'Nothing's wrong with him except for shit-for-brains like you. And nothing will be wrong with him if you stay the hell away.' August shirtfronted him once more. 'You hear me, Harris? Or are you gonna admit you boned a big girl?'

But Joel held up his palm, started laughing. 'Mate, no way that little freak's my kid. Your lard-arse sister coulda been doing half the town for all I know, little whore.' He laughed but there was no humour in it, and he stumbled back to his car, imitating some sort of animal sounds. 'He's a reject, man, you can keep the son of a bitch!'

Chapter 28

AUGIE, 2009

She looked even smaller in cuffs.

That was the image that unsettled me most, seeing them frogmarch a tiny old lady from one room to another. Despite burning down my house, I'd have been dead without her in my life. And now she was restrained like some lowlife, threat to society by the men in blue.

'What's going on?' I was ready to face up to my mistakes, and there's my elderly aunt, handcuffed.

The fit cop with the short hair was still here. Did she ever leave? She was a cow to me last time, but something had softened her expression and I wondered what she'd been told. She approached me, asked me to calm down and she'd explain.

'Why is she even here?' That's when it hit me – Margo's confession about how Mum died, about lighting that fire to bury Mum's sins. Surely she hadn't told the cops what she told me – she'd be charged with arson, interfering with a corpse, giving false and misleading information, and that was just the start. The fact that it was twenty years ago didn't seem to matter to them. And what would it achieve? My mother was dead anyway. Freya and I still became orphans even if Margo lied about how.

Fit cop gestured to Margo in the side room and spoke. 'It's about the Brightside bones.'

Then I was even more confused. 'No, that's why I'm here. I wanna change my statement,' I said. It felt good.

'Yeah, nah, it's done, Gus,' the policewoman said. 'Margo came in a couple of hours ago, she's been arrested and charged.'

I huffed. 'With what?'

'Murder. Although I think her lawyer's trying to get her to retract her statement, beat it down to manslaughter.'

'She hasn't killed anybody.'

'Yeah, she did, says it right here. Old mate from the church.' She picked up a clipboard from the desk. 'Jonathan Jones.' Jock-itch, Brother John, John the Divine, the disciple Jesus loved. All the evilness he exuded – how could his real name be so benign, so inconspicuous.

'This is bullshit!' I said. 'Let me see her.' I called down the hall, so she'd know I was there, that this was not going to happen. A ferocious heat expanded in my chest.

'Shhh. Keep your voice down.' The officer grabbed her ring of keys, a look of sympathy on her face. 'The DS's on a shit break so you'll have at least ten minutes, more like twenty. Come out when you hear the flush.'

That mental image of a Harris on the crapper made me cringe as much as the idea of Margo behind bars. 'It's not bugged or anything, is it?' I asked.

Fit cop laughed. 'We've uncuffed your aunt and put her in the family room – since she came here voluntarily. She's not exactly a troublemaker.' I followed her down the hall to a room with a *Toy Story* poster stuck to the wall and plastic furniture. I sat on a tiny purple chair across from the woman who raised me, now in prison-issued cotton overalls, council stamped, as if anyone would want to pinch them. I checked the room for a matching camera to the one I counted the blinks on over the course of my night of hell in the interview room adjacent. There was none. I felt for bugs under the table, too, and all I found was a wad of chewing gum.

Her face crumbled when she saw me. I think it was from relief, but I was exhausted from trying to figure out women. 'What are you doing, Aunty M?' The words came out as sobs, which I wasn't expecting.

'I'm Aunty again, am I?' She smiled. 'I'm doing what I promised, what I shoulda done years ago – protecting you. We were a tag team, your mum and me. When I couldn't have kids, she said I could share the ones she'd prepared earlier, and we laughed so much.' Margo cackled in an almost manic way. She couldn't be enjoying this, but it seemed like she was.

I shook my head. 'I lit that fucking fire. The prick died. I dragged that body up the bush and dumped it in the mine to rot. You were nowhere near it.' I still felt stupid saying it out loud in a cop shop, whispered it conspiratorially as if this was all a ruse and Harris was outside with a recording device. 'You came and helped us get out safe and drove off. I'm not letting you do time for me. It's not a speeding ticket. It's fucking murder!'

'Maybe not that man's death, maybe not directly, but don't I have blood on my hands? Isn't it my fault, standing by while your mum got so sick? I put her there, in that crowded room that couldn't take the weight of her problem. I didn't see the signs with you either – I put you there, in that place that promised to make you a better man, but only filled you with shame. I helped hire that awful man – I gave the church a reference, said how great he worked with kids! I didn't have a clue. None of this would have happened if I'd kept you with me and Freya. This is my penance, Gus. Let me do this.'

'This is wrong. How could those stupid cops even think you did this? What horseshit did you come up with?'

'I'm not just a silly old woman. When Becca called about Brookes being charged, I got the rundown, made sure I got my facts straight. That I was returning from my counter meal at the pub and saw the flames, drove in and took all you kids to safety, but before I left, I saw the man guilty of abusing my boys – my Gussy and Brookes – and Lord knows how many others. That you hadn't been right since returning from Brightside, and I'd pieced it all together, that I felt responsible for John being put in a position of trust, that the church wouldn't listen, and I decided to take matters into my own hands. The rumours were rife by then, Gus. Everybody knew. I hatched a plan based on the facts – that it was me who knew the barn only had one exit, which locked from the outside because you boys told me that's how they cornered you. It was me who slid that door closed, slotting the beam into place before it burned to the ground.'

But I didn't tell you. Lotti was the first and the last. 'That makes no sense. Even if that was true, how'd his bones turn up way up in the bush? Did all five foot of you drag him on your own to the mine?'

'Yeah, I couldn't think of anything for that bit. The lawyer said the dozers might have disturbed the soil and to let him deal with that.'

'Lawyer?'

'Some pretty boy in a suit turned up – really white teeth – said he'd do it for, what's the word? I don't want to say the wrong one. I know it upsets you. Just like your mother.'

'Pro bono.'

'Yeah, he said his name was … a colour. Mr Black?'

'Was it Grayson?'

'Yes! That's it! Grayson! Smells like citrus. He's a Rhodes scholar, you know! Some fancy politician from the TV.'

I shook my head. Lotti's fucking husband, Grayson. 'Tosser.'

'Language, Gus. I never understood how you use such disrespectful cuss words despite your respect for the English language.'

'I do respect it. It's just that they don't have a word in the dictionary that encapsulates my feelings towards the guy Lotti married as well as "Tosser" does.'

'Lotti married that fella? Oh, my, lucky girl.' She frowned. 'She's not still …'

'It only lasted a day. Apparently. But that's another story.'

'Well, he said to say' – she looked as though she was remembering a line – 'I just smoked him to death and left. I was home with my kids then – you and Freya, making you cocoa – remember? That part was even true!' She took my hand, pleased with herself.

'What makes you think I'll let you do this – not walk back there and repeat everything you just said?'

'You have Otto to look after. I'm sixty-seven. I've lived my life. It will make me happy to know I gave you this shot at being happy – you and Lotti and Otto. She's good people, Gus. I told you at your mother's funeral I had your back, but I didn't, did I? I don't want you to think that I put you there, discarded you at Brightside like it was a too-hard tray. You're good people, too, August Nash. Good to the core. I never gave up on you, Gussy, but I didn't have your back like I promised. Let me make it up to you.'

I was blubbering then. 'I can't. I can't let you rot in jail – you could have twenty good years left.'

Her head tilted, her jaw softened. 'I'm sick, Gus.'

'What?' Margo was a five-foot dynamo. She'd never had a day off. She was indestructible.

'That's the other thing you didn't let me finish telling you, about what your mum told me, on the phone when she rang me the day she died. She said to contact some bloke she met in Brisbane that she'd been seeing, that he'd explain things. So after she died, I did.'

'Hey?' That didn't sound right. Mum never took off her wedding ring after Dad left. Never had a date. 'A boyfriend?'

'A neurologist. Just before her fall she'd been told she was sick, too.'

'What sort of sick?'

'She'd complained about having cotton wool in her head, getting forgetful, awful mood swings, depression – I told her I was getting clumsy and dopey in my old age as well, it was just menopause. Remember she used to do those funny dances when she was stressed? I just put it down to another one of her quirks. Anyway, things must have gotten worse – the doctor told me he'd diagnosed her those few days she went to Brisbane suddenly, remember? That she had 40 CAG, which means she found out she was a carrier.'

'A carrier of what?' I asked.

'Now, don't panic, it won't kill you, directly. Not to say it isn't cruel, but it's lifelong. The worst thing – half of all descendants inherit the gene.'

My voice was impatient, stripped. 'What gene, Margo?' Bad fucking luck, that's what it felt like.

'Huntington's.'

I glared at her. 'You're saying Mum had Huntington's disease?'

'I'm saying your mum and I both. I thought it was menopause, too, when I got symptoms – God – back in my forties. Then after your mum told me, after she fell through those boards, I thought if the chance of getting the gene was fifty-fifty and your mum got it, then I was the lucky half, you know? It wasn't until I was done with all that hormone business in my fifties and started twitching that I got tested.'

'Jesus, Margo – why didn't you tell us? Mum didn't know until the end, but you did! You let Freya have kids.' Realisation dawned and I raked my fingers through my hair. 'Shit – did Frey have it?' A lump formed in my throat. 'Does Otto?'

'No, oh no. He's not even a carrier – there's no need to worry about him. I felt awful, not telling Freya, but I got him tested behind her back when I babysat him when he was one.'

I started crying, the relief of it overwhelming. 'But you've known since Mum died twenty-two years ago. You let my sister have a kid without knowing the risk.'

'She was already pregnant and there was no way I was giving her another reason to get rid of that child, carrier or not. You know my view on that.'

I exhaled a long breath. 'But you're sure he's fine?'

She nodded. 'But you, Gus – it's a possibility. You need to decide if you want to know.' Her chin trembled, and she took my hand.

I pulled away, paced the room. 'The family bullshit, it never ends! You didn't think I had a right to know I could be fucking dying?'

'That's why I've been calling you lately. You finally got a phone!'

'What, the last few months? What about the twenty fucking years before that?'

'I didn't think you'd want to know – you're so full of life, I thought it would just worry you. I couldn't find you even if I'd wanted to tell you, till the last month. I'm at end-stage now, figured the window was closing to tell you.'

'You didn't just lie to me when you found out about this, you've lied to me every day, every day you didn't tell the truth.'

'Forgive me, August. I honestly thought you'd live a better life not knowing. I was too unwell to travel all that way to tell you in person, so I've been calling, hoping you'd finally talk to me. I wanted to spend time with you before I go, but—'

'Before you *go*? But you seem fine! You look fine, you made Lotti breakfast!'

She laughed that cackle I missed. 'Hah! You didn't see me try to cook it in the dishwasher first.'

The idea of it reminded me of Mum. Mum was sick, but not the way we thought. My eyes narrowed in disbelief, retracing other signs that she was not dying. 'You read Otto a story.'

'By heart. I haven't been able to comprehend words for months. My brain, it's packing up, Gus.'

I huffed, the guilt coursing through me. 'I can't believe this. I let you deal with this, alone.' I took her hand again. She was just like Mum, never complaining, never putting herself first.

'Oh, don't worry about me, I'm a tough old bird. I've been fine, for the most part. The medication masks a lot of the movement problems, the moods, but my quality of life's gone to ruin this year, Gus.' She grew quiet, thoughtful, then looked at me. There was a lot said in that look. 'I don't know myself. It's like I'm slowly being robbed of all the parts that made me who I was, like the colours of me are fading away. I was always so colourful, don't you think?

'You still are, Margs.'

She nodded, proud of the fact. 'I'm just finding it harder and harder to find reasons to keep living, and it's only a matter of time before I get pneumonia or take a fall.'

'You're sixty-seven!'

'The average life expectancy for HD patients is sixty-three, Gus. Some only live ten years from diagnosis. I've lived for twenty. Your mother wanted you all to know it was the illness that made her like she was – her OCD traits, even hoarding has been linked to stages of the disease. Please don't blame her for it. It wasn't her fault, how she behaved. She knew things weren't right and made sure I contacted the doctor that could warn us about her condition before she died. She loved you.'

I sat beside her on the tiny plastic chair, took her hand and kissed it, and cried like a baby.

'You see, love? This makes sense, hey?' She smiled. 'You were kids. You didn't mean for him to die – even though I wouldn't have blamed you if you did. Doing this for you – it's the one thing that will bring me joy.'

The door unlocked. The police officer gestured for me to piss off. 'He's washing his hands, mate, get going.'

'Go live, Gussy. Live for all of us.'

They'd released Brookes after Margo took the fall for the bones, but I decided to keep the family inheritance situation to myself for the meantime. Lotti seemed disturbed at first but became less so when I said Margo was sick and wouldn't live long in any case. I didn't mention the diagnosis. There was no need to worry her with another drama. I'd had my quota for the week.

The cops said they'd finished with my truck. It was parked in by a paddy wagon and an RBT van at the corner of the police compound covered in bird shit and leaves. 'There she is. Oh, and you've got a visitor,' Fit Cop said, and there was

Brookes, waiting under a tree in the cop shop car compound like a stolen vehicle.

He stubbed out his cigarette. I'd like to say he looked shaken by the whole getting arrested experience, but he'd bounced back like a shock absorber, kind of invigorated by all the drama now that it had come to an end, for him at least. We'd both been charged with destruction of public property for digging up the time capsule. 'The charge won't impact you having access to your girls?' I asked him.

'Put it on the list, hey, mate?' Brookes smiled. 'Do we get to pick up roadkill in those orange jumpsuits again?'

'Can't wait.' Lotti's father would love that. I'd be sure to tip off the *Eldham News* to get some footage of it, give them the finger while I'm at it like the country hick I was. 'I got the gist from Becca that there were photos,' I said, testing the waters with what, if anything, he wanted to share. 'But the brothers didn't get that good at covering up stuff by being stupid.'

'I found them in the barn, months before the fire, took 'em, and burned 'em, but I didn't get that the strips could make copies, you know? Not back then. Figured it out later and reckoned they might get me out of trouble one day. Had them on me when the cops got us. They were, like, a guarantee policy?'

'Insurance?'

'Yeah. That's what I meant. You always knew what I meant. Always had to fucking point it out, too, you bastard.' He kicked a stone towards a parked car.

'I'm sorry I didn't do more to stop it.' It was all I could think to say.

He sniffed, shook it off, and I didn't force it. I knew how deep it was buried, but I was no longer sure it should be.

'Hey, Lotti found some info on Stuck-up Steph. Get this, she was born in Newcastle, some street kid, and was a serial shoplifter. That's why she did the Harold Holt when we got her to call triple 0, I reckon. She's some actress now.'

'For reals?' His goofy grin, it could light up the darkest night.

'Hey, mate, you said you'd chucked your bag in the lake that night. But I'd always thought it woulda burned – your spray cans, remember?'

Brookes looked like he'd gotten caught farting in church. Scratched his head. 'I dunno, mate, yeah, musta got it wrong.' Brookes was easier to read than a UBD. Something was up.

I tried another approach. 'Turned out Jock-itch was camping out at Hotel California before the fire, like Steph reckoned, got his stash every Friday night from the runners. Joel paid for that Torana with the money he got running drugs, giving blowies with his cut of the weed.' I guess in a small town in the eighties it wouldn't have been easy for him. They were still arresting gay people in the street after Mardi Gras not long before. Nothing but shame and pub brawls. But it wasn't the eighties anymore. Maybe we had achieved something in the twenty years since Expo 88 showed the world. Maybe we hadn't.

'I've gotta get home, feed Margo's dogs,' Brookes said.

I nodded. I wasn't sure how long it would be before I saw him again, when the next SOS would appear on my screen. I hoped we were done with them. That we could save ourselves. 'Wait, bro. One last thing that's getting to me – Joel swears he didn't lock Brother in like we reckoned.'

Brookes stalled, went to speak then hesitated. Finally he said, 'You know what? I reckon it was that village idiot. Reckon the pricks that ran Brightside thought he was too stupid to matter. Reckon they thought no one would notice that he couldn't sit down for a week without tearing up. That he hated the prick, kicked the brick out that he'd wedged in to keep the door ajar, locked him in and sacrificed his favourite aerosols in the fire to make sure the motherfucker burned. Same idiot prob'ly went back to the fire and stoned himself out some more to try to die with the place, too. But some bloody hero came and dragged him to safety.'

I closed my eyes, pieced in the new parts of the puzzle, saw the full picture and it all fit.

'What, when me and your sister left you by the fire? But you were out of it.'

He nodded. 'For a bit.'

'How'd ya know Johns was even there?'

'Didn't. Went to find you guys, finally got the balls to check the barn...brought it all back.'

I huffed out a breath, went to resort to my faithful friend – anger. 'Christ, Brookesy. What happened to SOS? Wasn't that the whole point of our system? That I was there for you?'

'And I knew ya woulda been. That's why I didn't tell you. I didn't want ya saving me. It was too hard to keep living.'

My throat tightened with the thought of it. He had broken down after we got him out of the burning hall – I thought he was pissed about his spray cans getting fried. 'But you're still here, mate, twenty years on.' I'd always wondered what the difference was between the ones that jumped and the ones that didn't. I thought it was having each other, knowing in your gut that at least one person's life would be worse off if you left. That, like Mum said, you had a love strong enough to survive life.

'Yeah, that was the crazy thing – when you and Becca pulled me out, I was so surprised to find that I was glad about it. I wanted to die five minutes before, no question, but somehow seeing your ugly mug through the smoke was the best thing I'd ever seen.'

It wasn't knowing someone else cared if you lived or died, it was that you had someone in your corner worth living for. I was just trying to process that, form a response, when the screen door at the back of the station banged shut and the lady cop came outside to the yard. She gestured that she'd move the van out of the way so I could get my vehicle out.

'Hey, Jude,' I whispered quietly to my truck. I smiled and pulled up the leather tray cover. The time capsule, now busted open, a scar from a serrated grinder blade through the middle of the metal case, was still there, the contents strewn around the back of the tray. 'What do I do with this?' I asked the officer as she backed out a paddy wagon.

She spoke out the driver's side window. 'Ah, that – yeah, we got the evidence we need. Too bleeding heavy to move without a few blokes, so it's all yours. The historical society had a gander too – got a few notable bits out for their records but the rest is mostly rubbish. Dump it. Keep it. Whatever you like.' She drove the truck out of our path.

I covered the tray and Brookes and I drove the Ford out of the fenced yard. I dropped him back at Margo's thinking he could manage the dogs, maybe even see about Otto keeping one of the mutts. I got out and we were both standing at the back of my truck, looking at our past scattered around like litter, like we had just a few days before, over at the place that started it all. But my world had tilted since then.

'Want to take a look at this shit before we dump it?' I said, sorting through the piles with caution. It all smelled like mouldy shoes and anything usable had been pilfered. There was a calculator, as if we wouldn't have them in the future.

'Wouldn't it be funny, man, if it still had BOOBS typed on the screen, huh?' Brookes laughed.

I laughed with the stupid fool.

There was a photo of me at fifteen, bareback on a poddy-calf, a second before I landed on my arse in the ring. I'd been an orphan like that calf for twenty years, but never felt like one 'cause of Margo. That too, was changing. I didn't even want that rodeo memory, as good as it was. It was too close to the ones I wanted to forget. I was done being a cowboy.

We'd checked out of Hotel California long ago, but it seemed we'd only just begun leaving it behind. The smell, it clung like smoke.

What was left was only of value to the person who put it there. A gum-wrapper collection. A jar of rocks with sayings on it. There were a few copies of the *Brightside Calling*, some newsletter the charlatans printed out with lots of propaganda to reassure the community we weren't just the dumping ground for local troubled kids. Stories about chapel renovations, happy snaps from a family day, pictures of us on the old BMX tracks, quotes from kids saying how tops the cottage house parents were. It was all lies. It was all edited, curated, a con, all of it.

I wanted to burn it all, and the shame and guilt that came with it. These lies, they just created an idea of something that either wasn't true or shouldn't matter anyway.

Finally, I understood why Margo did it.

Chapter 29

LOTTI

The heat from my coffee warmed my hand, the broadsheets of *The Australian* sprawled wide over a few packing crates in the morning sun. The creek behind the bus was flowing fast, a long brown snake meandering through the green field. Grayson's headshot, the one that made him look like a preppy wanker, was on the third page of the paper along with a story outlining his career highlights. He'd been sworn in as the attorney-general that week. I wondered if his government would have the gumption to unravel truth and give a voice to the kids like Brookes, like Augie, like a million others.

'I can't believe you were married to that putz,' August scoffed.

'Only for a day,' I said. I didn't mention we dated for years before that twenty-four hours. Or the fact that I'd asked Grayson to gather evidence against him.

'He looks like a bank teller.'

I laughed. 'What have you got against bank tellers?'

'Nothing, except they look like this knob.' He rustled through the storage flap on the van. I mean, bus. 'I hope you didn't want to keep this for your husband.' He'd found an old biro and started drawing a cock and balls on Grayson's forehead, along with a moustache that rivalled Hitler's.

'That's not right. He'd never have given preferentials to the Nazi Party.'

'See, I don't even know what that means.'

'That's one of my favourite things about you.' I smiled. My eyes fixed on the new part of the landscape, my sweet old VW Beetle squatting in the shade, curves beautiful in the morning sun. It wasn't duck-egg blue (well, some panels were, but some were missing entirely) but her bones were good, according to the mechanic who'd been scouting the wreckers for months for her, unbeknownst to me. Greta was a rusty pile, and I wasn't giving up Frida until she ran, but her potential – it made my brain come alive.

Margo had asked to borrow Otto before we left Eldham, assured us her health was up to it, that Becca was going to be on hand if she had an episode, and that she wanted to spend the last few weeks before her sentencing trial with her only grandchild. I had a sneaking suspicion that he'd return with at least one dog, but I think we were all okay with that.

August finished his eggs and stretched out his shoulders, revealing an inch of skin above his boxers. It had been a while since we'd done anything but hug. I grazed the tattoo on his forearm with my finger before he ended the silence by asking, 'Want me to get a proper tattooist to make it an L?'

I liked that he even asked. That he had enough compassion to know it was weird for me, now having met her. She was part of his before. I was part of his after, and I knew which end I'd rather be in.

'How about an O?' I said. 'I get you didn't want to talk about what that man did. But the rest of your childhood… why didn't you just share all that Eldham stuff before you were forced to? Did you think I'd judge you for it? Not love you? Because I'm still here.'

He screwed his eyes closed, leaned forward in his folding chair. 'It wasn't that. I'd made peace with what I did. I'd just had so many screwed-up false starts with other people. I saw you as like an engine rebuild – a big, red, reset button. I didn't want it all hanging over me.'

I wasn't sure I believed him, but the idea felt good. He was more than the missteps he made in the past. He was all of his next choices, too, and those he would make tomorrow.

He went to say something, put down his coffee cup, but his lips sealed closed again.

'Spit it out,' I said.

'What?'

'Whatever you were about to say.'

'It's just ironic,' Augie said. 'You driving across the country to find out my secrets, but the whole time you had your own. I was technically sleeping with the attorney-general's wife.'

'Not anymore – he sent me the papers. Seemingly didn't want to be linked with a woman associated with an ex-felon raised by a convicted murderer. I think he only helped Margo out so that I would be nice to him and not contest the annulment.'

'Such a soft-cock,' August said. 'But he was okay with the fact it would free you up to marry a killer?'

My throat tightened a little. He saw me tense, and assumed it was the marriage part of that sentence, but it wasn't. Soldiers, policemen, doctors killed people all the time in complex situations and that didn't make them all bad. 'Just because you killed someone doesn't make you a killer.'

'That's the bit you questioned?' His eyes narrowed.

'Was the marriage bit about you wanting a babysitter for your non-kid again?' I asked.

'Never was.'

I was on a roll, ticking off the wad of worries in my mind. 'Is it because you think you're a carrier?'

He flinched.

'Becca told me – I'm sorry.' We'd sort of become friends. It was annoying.

'Fucking Becca.' He exhaled, and we looked at each other for a long time without saying anything. 'If you ever say yes, you have to assume I'll outlive you at ninety-three.'

I slowed down my barrage of questions. The thought of losing him to a disease scared me more than I imagined, even if it wasn't for twenty years or so. 'Are you going to get tested?'

'Nope.'

I nodded. 'Can I ask why?'

'Because you don't want kids, so the gene'll end with me either way, so what will be will be.'

I wanted to say, what if we did, but he'd had enough bombshells this week, and I didn't know how I felt about a fifty per cent chance of a child of mine inheriting a disease that slowly robbed you of yourself. And that was even if I managed the miracle of pregnancy with the state of my uterus. That would have to be another day's dilemma, and the choice didn't scare me as long as I had all the facts. 'It's more than that though … how would knowing or not knowing affect your life, now?'

'Because I don't want to live every day categorising every bit of fatigue, wondering if forgetting my PIN or having a muscle twitch was a symptom, waiting for the bomb to go off. Nope. If it's gonna rob me of who I am, it can wait until it turns up, and not a minute before. I'm not ready for it to have me yet.'

'What if you don't have it and it wouldn't control your decisions at all?' I wanted to believe he didn't. I wanted him around forever. Well, vital and strong.

'It won't control me. Nothing does. I've got no one to blame for my choices but me, and I stand by every one of them.'

That decisiveness had rubbed off on me, and it felt powerful to have the reins of my own life in my hands. I understood he wanted to keep his. I leaned over his folding chair and kissed him, his coffee breath mingling with mine. I was in awe of his confidence, knowing what he'd endured, knowing how hard it would have been for him to separate the things that happened to him from who he was. To not let the shame others tried to place on him seep into his soul. August and Otto – they'd buffered the rocks life had pelted at them, so the dents didn't change who they were. They'd known they were good, even if the things that happened weren't, and I was grateful for that. Some weren't so lucky.

'You know the other thing you asked me to think about when you ran into the night.'

He shook his head at my dramatics. 'Well, I used to do the rock, paper, scissors thing as a kid because I sucked at making choices …'

'Don't tell me you're staying with me 'cause of a lame-arsed kids' game.'

I took August's hand in mine and pulled him inside the van. As I kissed him, a warm glow spread its tentacles up my spine, through my limbs, making me feel alive. 'I decided you are my paper, my rock, my scissors.'

'That's like, the best soggiest thing I've ever heard.'

I sat him on the bed tucked in the corner behind the mini kitchen and mini table. Two tiny windows cast squares of sunshine on his sheets. I now understood that he lived with so few material items because his mum lived and died with a suffocating amount. 'Did you ever understand, with your mum, why she felt the need to keep so much? Is that part of Huntington's?'

He was perched on the edge of his tiny bed, his palms down on either side of him as he leaned back. He thought before answering. We'd both been doing nothing but thinking and talking for days, but we still had unshared nuances of many years to fill in. 'Maybe. Either way, it was the hand she was dealt. I think she was so scared of losing the things that mattered, she clung to everything else to fill the void. Shame it never worked.'

I straddled him, my crotch nestled, warm against his. I took it slow, kissing a line from his lips to his neck, and down the circles of soft hair on his pecs. He'd always been okay with that. We'd spent many nights marking the map of his body with the territories that were off limits, and those that were fair game. I knew he had cigarette burns he didn't speak of. My hands had never been to the southern states, but it was time to expand my horizons. We'd kissed longer than we'd ever kissed without me wanting more, and I could tell he was already suspicious about my intent. I ran my hand across his butt cheeks and felt his surprise.

'What are you … ?' he whispered.

I tried on my most sultry tone. 'Is this okay?'

He huffed. 'This is what I was worried about – you treating me like a whack job. Plenty had it worse than me.'

'We're all bent in different ways. Some of us snap, some of us flex.' I nibbled his ear, breathed into his hair, and felt him groan. 'We're all broken, but they say that's how the light gets in.'

His brow furrowed like all this psychobabble was unnecessary, which was very August, and I was glad he was still the man I knew. 'I don't need fridge-magnet quotes. I don't want you to treat me differently.'

'You say that like it's a bad thing.' I kissed him long and hard to stop him arguing. 'It was always about me, before. I don't want that.'

He shook his head, looked away.

'For you, touch equals pain, and I get that now, but maybe we can try to turn that around, make it about something else …'

He pretended this was a dumb idea, twisting his jaw with attitude. But I could see something settle in his expression: hope.

'Maybe, even … love.' Now I was the one with the stupid face.

His eyebrows rose. 'Love, huh?' He was trying not to show it, but he seemed okay with that.

'I have no expectations. I'm not saying this will be easy or quick but I'm not going anywhere. One of my girlfriends was assaulted, ended up with PTSD. It's common and it's real.'

He scoffed. 'That's for Vietnam vets. That's not me. I haven't survived a war.'

I pulled my shirt over my head, slipping it behind his neck and using it to draw his face closer. 'Yeah' – I kissed his nose – 'you have, of sorts.'

He slipped off my bra, sliding the straps over my shoulders in the familiar way he always did. 'Can we stop with the talking now?'

'Can I show you something, then, without words?'

Ignoring me, Augie kissed a row down my neck to my breastbone, groaning with the feel of it. I gingerly inched my hands around to his front, but he blocked them, knitted my fingers together with his.

'These warm hands of mine have magical, healing properties …'

'Thought you said no words?'

I slowly slipped my hand from his and began stroking the fine hairs circling his belly button, then lower. 'Can I? Will you let me? Just for a sec.'

He looked up and his eyes locked with mine before he was lost to me again. Tears pooled in those impossibly dark eyes.

I stifled a sob, guided his chin back so his eyes were level with mine. 'Just look at me, don't think of anything else.' My breath was hot on his cheek, my breasts firm on his chest as I nibbled his earlobe. 'Please?'

He gave a small nod as I reached between his legs, the contact so light it was almost a breeze. His breath caught.

'And again?' I asked, and met his eyes.

As he held my gaze, I talked him through each stroke, two seconds this time.

He grew impatient, nuzzled into my neck, forced his hand to dig beneath the lace of my knickers.

I guided his hand to my stomach and shook my head. 'My hands, loving you …'

He took my palm with his hand, kissed the centre, as I touched him again with the other. 'Longer?' I asked and ran a finger across his perineum, around the bend of his scrotum and up the shaft. 'My hands, erasing your pain …'

He was hard in my hand. His eyes locked with mine and he said, 'Do that again.'

Acknowledgements

It's hard to fathom I've written five of these things. I remember being scared that my first publishing offer was some kind of unfunny joke, as it didn't seem possible that my first crack at a manuscript, written in the sleep-hazed days post-partum would be published internationally. And yet ten years on I'm still here, doing what I love. I'm so grateful to you, the readers, for that.

I feel nothing but a warm fuzzy glow for the whole crew at Pantera Press, especially Kate Cuthbert for herding my thoughts into line. Thanks also to editor Lauren Finger for dusting the cobwebs from my prose and finding meaning amongst the mess, and to Lucia Nguyen for her proofread.

Thank you to my husband Jamie, and three boys Finn, Nate and Josh for finding their own lost socks and scavenging food in the wild while I was hidden away, spending time with my imaginary friends.

Among other things, this story explores resilience. And for that reason, it's dedicated to the memory of the most unstoppable man I know. Even cancer had to have three swings before it won. My dad died at aged 80, 38 days after a fall and subsequent brain tumour diagnosis. It's hard to fathom a world without him in it, but his passing has taught me that grief is the price we pay for love.

One of my personal missions is to craft a differently abled character in every story, and this time 'round, that goal was aided by Rita Rowland and Sandra McLaren who gifted me their insight regarding teaching and living with a deaf child. I never intend to speak on behalf of those with disability but I am passionate about ensuring fiction reflects reality in all its fabulous diversity.

This story is a work of fiction, but unfortunately institutionalised child abuse is all too real. One boys school, from which aspects of this story were drawn, resulted in over 350 claims of abuse in one Queensland site alone which a judge later described as a 'Gulag right in our midst'. While confronting, I hope dragging these issues out of the shadows reminds survivors they are not alone, and may provide a voice to those silenced.

If themes in this story prompted concerns for you, help is available 24hrs at Lifeline (13 11 14) or further information on the National Redress Scheme can be found by calling 1800 737 377.

About the author

Kylie Kaden has an honours degree in psychology, was a columnist at *My Child Magazine*, and now works in the disability sector.

She knew writing was in her blood from a young age when she snuck onto her brother's Commodore 64 to invent stories as a child. Raised in Queensland, she spent holidays camping with her family on the Sunshine Coast.

With a surfer-lawyer for a husband and three spirited sons, Kylie can typically be found venting the day's thoughts on her laptop, sometimes in the laundry so she can't be found.

Kylie is the author of *Losing Kate* (2014), *Missing You* (2015), *The Day the Lies Began* (2019) and *One of Us* (2022). *After the Smoke Clears* is her fifth novel.